A Duke by Default

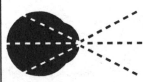

This Large Print Book carries the
Seal of Approval of N.A.V.H.

RELUCTANT ROYALS

A DUKE BY DEFAULT

ALYSSA COLE

THORNDIKE PRESS
A part of Gale, a Cengage Company

Farmington Hills, Mich • San Francisco • New York • Waterville, Maine
Meriden, Conn • Mason, Ohio • Chicago

Copyright © 2018 by Alyssa Cole.
Emojis throughout © browndogstudios/Shutterstock, Inc.
Thorndike Press, a part of Gale, a Cengage Company.

Thorndike Press® Large Print African-American.
The text of this Large Print edition is unabridged.
Other aspects of the book may vary from the original edition.
Set in 16 pt. Plantin.

LIBRARY OF CONGRESS CIP DATA ON FILE.
CATALOGUING IN PUBLICATION FOR THIS BOOK
IS AVAILABLE FROM THE LIBRARY OF CONGRESS

ISBN-13: 978-1-4328-5405-8 (hardcover)

Published in 2018 by arrangement with Avon Books, an imprint of HarperCollins Publishers

Printed in Mexico
1 2 3 4 5 6 7 22 21 20 19 18

For all of you, really,
but mostly for Bree. ♥

CHAPTER 1

Project: New Portia was off to a fantastic start.

The Portia Hobbs of old had been no stranger to waiting for cabs at the asscrack of dawn, bleary-eyed and disheveled, but she'd generally been hungover and making a hasty exit from her fuckboy of the night's bed.

New Portia was stone-cold sober, as she had been for months, and halfway around the world from her usual New York City stomping grounds. It was cold and rainy outside of Edinburgh's Waverley Station, her new boss had almost certainly forgotten to pick her up, as planned, and — yup, there was a dude peeing less than five feet away from her.

I could've stayed in New York for this, Portia thought irritably.

She pulled her rain-frizzed hair back out of her face, slipping the hair tie on her wrist over the mass of tight rust-gold curls to secure them, and then smiled and snapped an obligatory selfie to capture her arrival in Scotland.

She'd appreciated the beautiful ticketing room of the recently restored station after stepping off of the red-eye train from London — her master's in art history and string of museum internships *hadn't* just been a way of putting off responsibility, despite what her family thought. But outside of the ticketing room and at this early hour, Waverley was just a creepy, unfamiliar train station like any other. It was nestled in a valley, and the silhouettes of medieval structures and Edinburgh's natural terrain loomed up around her, adding to the doom and gloom. The city *felt* old, like it emanated a sense of history impossible to find in even in the oldest parts of Manhattan.

She shifted the straps of the Birkin travel bag that were digging into her shoulder and glanced irritably at her phone, switching from the camera to the Super-Lift app. A car driven by someone named Kevyn was supposedly a minute away, but she'd watched the car circle Edinburgh station and the countdown clock reset four times in the last ten minutes, so she didn't get her hopes up. Her boss standing her up had already set a bad tone for the three months of apprenticeship that awaited her.

Of course, it isn't going to work out. There's this little thing called "a pattern," and this is how yours always plays out.

Portia hummed under her breath, as if that could drown out the annoying voice inside of her head, the one that reminded her that fucking up was the one thing she could do consistently and well.

It wasn't her fault that her boss had stood her up. Maybe he had overslept, or something catastrophic had occurred, like the armory had burned down or he'd spontaneously combusted?

Or maybe it was *her* fault. What if she'd gotten the date wrong, or misunderstood something, or forgot to submit an important form? Had she even *really* been chosen for this apprenticeship? She might show up and be turned away at the door. She would have to return home and everyone would look at her with pity because Portia had made a fool of herself again.

Portia sucked in a deep breath and tried to pull the brakes on her rapidly escalating catastrophic thoughts. She was imagining trouble where there probably was none and besides, New Portia didn't make those kinds of mistakes. Well, not as much as Old Portia had, at least. Her calendar was checked faithfully, most mornings, and her to-do list had alarms set and reminders for her reminders to keep her on track. She'd made sure she had everything about her arrival in Scotland planned out perfectly, but that didn't stop the anxiety tightening in her chest like a fist.

"Hey, Oracle. Call Bodotria Armory, please." The peculiar buzzing ring tone that had taunted her since she'd set foot in Scotland sounded through her earpiece.

She hadn't found much info on her new boss when she'd performed her obligatory internet dirt search: a low-resolution picture on the armory's atrocious website in which he was dressed like a cosplayer at a medieval fantasy con. A video of him in some type of armor that covered his face, showing the proper technique for wielding a broadsword.

"Hello. You've reached the voice mailbox of Tavish McKenzie, master-at-arms and proprietor of Bodotria Armory. Please leave a message."

The voice was Scottish. Like, *really* fucking Scottish — deep, with a strong burr that would have had Old Portia frantically clicking on the "Yes, I would like to subscribe to your sexy accented newsletter" button. New Portia pulled the hand brake on that cart before she started barreling toward the Bad Ydeas Towne section of the renaissance fair.

Men were not a part of Project: New Portia, most especially not Tavish McKenzie, who was her boss and who also seemed to have forgotten her existence before she'd even arrived. She was done with fuckboys, and fuckbosses for that matter, no matter how sexy their accents were.

She sighed and busied herself with posting her selfie to her InstaPhoto account while she waited for Kevyn.

Yes, that is a man peeing in the background. #GoodMorningEdinburgh #WTF #IThinkIveMadeATerribleMistake

She deleted the last hashtag before posting the pic. Negativity was too Old Portia. New Portia was resilient, could roll with the punches, and wasn't thinking about running into the station and away from this frustrating setback.

Her phone vibrated, and she was sure it would be her boss, gravelly-voiced and apologizing for running late, but it was a new message in the *International Friend Emporium* group of her message app.

Ledi: What the hell is up with that

11

picture? Where are you? Are you okay?

Portia: Um, I *just* posted. How did you see it so quickly?

Ledi: I turned on notifications for you so I wouldn't miss any updates from your adventure.

Portia: Awww, you lurve me. I'm fine. I'm still at the train station. My boss never showed so I'm waiting on a SuperLift.

Ledi: Well, that's one way to make a first impression. 😔 Do you have the pepper spray I bought you? It's not technically pepper spray, since it's illegal there, but it's apparently the same formula as bear spray so you should be safe from criminals and Ursidae.

Portia: <photo of pepper spray clutched in hand> Come at me, bears.

Ledi: 😂😂

Portia: I'm tired and annoyed. 🙁

Ledi: I'm annoyed on your behalf.

Portia: ☺

Nya: I'm up, too. Sorry your boss is a jerk. Could this be a test? Like a mission in an RPG? Maybe you get bonus apprentice points for navigating your way to the armory.

Portia: I sure as shit hope this isn't a test. My boss already failed. What are you both doing up so late?

Ledi: Same thing I do every night: studying viruses and trying to stop them from taking over the world.

Nya: Playing a dating sim to make up for the real date I had earlier. Rognath the Vampire Lord is much better at courtship than Luke, who started the night by calling me Sexual Chocolate and went downhill from there.

Portia: Oof. Ew, Luke. Yay, Rognath? Good old, dependable Rognath.

Nya: Rognath is a gentleman and all, but ☺

Ledi: You've already become a cynical

13

New Yorker, cous! One day, your Rognath will come.

Nya: I guess. If a prince can track you
down and trick you into falling for
him, I can find my brooding, misunderstood vampire lover.

Portia chuckled. Nya was relatively new to
their friend group, but Ledi had been
Portia's friend since they'd met in an un-
dergrad club for people into both science
and the arts. Ledi had stuck with Portia
through thick and thin — a hell of a lot of
thin over the last couple of years. Almost
losing her best friend was what had sparked
Project: New Portia.

The project had three main pillars: getting
organized, being a better friend and family
member, and not using booze and men as
an escape from reality. Instead, she was using an apprenticeship in a foreign country
to escape, which was clearly much healthier.

*"Three months in Scotland? Making swords?
This sounds like a great opportunity! Can you
tell me a bit more about what you hope to get
out of it? Moving to another country is exciting, but also a huge change. You've talked
about the urge to run away before . . ."*

Change was exactly what Portia wanted,

and even her therapist Dr. Lewis's annoying but necessary questions hadn't deterred her. If anything, they'd made her even more resolved to go.

She'd had this romantic idea of summer in Scotland, running through the moors with the Highland winds whispering her life's purpose in her ears. Instead, she was alone at the station, forgotten. This was more like stepping into a smelly bog and realizing there was no easy way to extricate herself.

A horn honked, and when she glanced up, a small blue car that managed to be boxy and egg-shaped at the same time had pulled up. A man with spiked brown hair stuck his head out the window.

"Portia?"

The license plate matched what was shown on the app, though the Vauxhall was slightly more dented than the one in the image on her phone.

"Hi. Kevyn?" She watched his eyes light up.

"An American!" His tone was one of slightly disgusted squee, like when a New Yorker spotted a rat carrying a slice of pizza to its subterranean lair, or a pigeon taking a bath in an oily puddle.

He hopped out and began loading her luggage into the trunk; it was a tight fit considering the car's toylike size.

Portia: My car is here. You two make sure to get some rest. I'm going to try calling the armory again.

Nya: Okay! Be safe! I hope the rest of your day goes better!

Ledi: Let me know when you get there. If you don't, Thabiso will call the Thesoloian embassy there and have them send out SWAT. Is there SWAT in Scotland? SCWAT? You know what I mean. ♡

Ledi was still somewhat new to this royalty business, but would clearly use what pull she had to protect Portia if necessary. That knowledge eased the tension in Portia's neck a bit. Someone had her back, even if only through an invisible link between their mutual phones.

Kevyn moved around to open one of the car's two doors and pulled the passenger seat forward so she could slide into the backseat. She didn't like the idea of being trapped in the back of a random car, but it couldn't be worse than loitering around the station.

"In you go, my lady," he said jovially and Portia forced a smile as she climbed in.

"First time here?" he asked. "Work or pleasure?"

How is he so chipper? she thought crankily, then remembered it was his job to engage with the strangers getting into his car. Maybe he'd also had a shitty night, but he wasn't going to take it out on her, was he? It wasn't his fault she was in a bad mood. Besides, if she knew anything it was how to feign polite conversation. Faux niceties had been ingrained in her through years of deportment lessons and dealing with her parents' rich family friends.

"Thank you. Yes, it's my first time," she said. She'd traveled extensively, but somehow never made it to Scotland. "I'm here for work."

"Welcome to Edinburgh," Kevyn said, hopping into the front seat. "You're gonna love summer here. As long as you enjoy rain, that is. And darkness. And drink."

So her hair was going to be jacked up, she was going to be depressed, and one of the two things she was trying to avoid most was going to be a constant temptation? Awesome.

She closed her eyes and inhaled, allowing herself a moment to settle as the car carried her toward her destination. She was in *Scotland*. She was starting a new adventure. She should be excited and ready for anything, not focusing on the negative. This was not the vibe she wanted to put out into the universe.

I am the heroine of my own story. I choose my own path . . .

Portia's phone chimed and she jumped up in her seat, disoriented and unsure of where she was. She'd nodded off for a second. She glanced out the car window; they were on a residential street now, with rows of squat brick houses.

A message from her twin sister, Reggie, slid into view on her phone screen.

Hey. Did you arrive? Thanks for finding that information about that . . . thing.

It'd been weird when Reggie asked Portia to find one of her online friends who had disappeared, it'd been weirder when Portia had discovered the friend was a guy, and it was peak weird that Reggie was now referring to it as "that thing," but Portia wouldn't pry.

I did. And no prob! You know I love playing internet detective.

She saw the three dots that indicated
Reggie was typing and wondered if she'd
get an explanation, but apparently none was
forthcoming.

Do you want to do posts for GirlsWith
Glasses/Adventure while you're there? I
understand if you won't have the time, with
all your swordmaking and whatnot, but I'd
love it if you could. Readers were super
into the first post about the call for an apprentice and when I said you'd been
chosen. Plus people like the Wonder
Twins aspect of us making content together. I like it too, tbh. Later, loser. ✌

Portia smiled. She and Reggie were still in
the process of rebuilding their relationship,
mostly via chatting about Reggie's popular
site, GirlsWithGlasses. It was Reggie who
had forwarded Portia the link about the apprenticeship after one of her followers had
sent it in for the weekly Cool Opportunities
posting. Another key aspect of Project: New
Portia — stop putting up roadblocks in her
relationship with her sister.

I can def write posts. I'm on it! Portia

19

replied, then decided to try to call her boss again.

"Hey, Oracle. Call Bodotria Armory, please."

"What's that, lass?" Kevyn asked.

"Just talking to my phone," she responded brightly, her gaze automatically heading to the left of the car before readjusting and flicking to the right, where it landed on the back of his head. The phone kept ringing and she was sure that *this time* someone would answer, but then she heard the familiar click as she was transferred to voice mail.

"You say 'please' to your phone? I didn't expect an American to be so polite."

"I just want to be spared when our AI overlords take power."

Kevyn laughed. "Did you get a hold of anyone at the armory? Not sure anyone is about now. The area is by the docks and pretty deserted this early."

Portia shoved a hand into the Birkin and rearranged the mess so that her pepper spray sat atop all the other crap she'd stuffed into the giant bag.

"I'm texting with my boss now," Portia lied. Kevyn didn't need to know that she was in a strange country for the first time *and* that the only people who should have been expecting her likely wouldn't notice she was missing.

"Tav knows how to send an sms? He's finally getting it together now that he'll have you for an apprentice, eh?" Kevyn caught her eye in the rearview mirror and Portia stiffened, though he was grinning. This had gone from friendly to stalkative way too quickly for her liking.

She was too tired and frustrated to be polite. "Am I going to have to mace you?"

He barked out a laugh and smacked the wheel. "Aye! Definitely American! Don't stress," he said. "I take lessons at the armory, and everyone's been on about the American apprentice arriving this week. Cheryl said she'd stalked her InstaPhoto account and the woman was beautiful and glamorous, and seeing as how you're going to the armory and you're . . ."

Portia didn't think psychopaths had the ability to blush as bright red as Kevyn was up in the driver's seat, so she relaxed her hold on the pepper spray. Besides, anyone who would call her glamorous after the hours she'd spent in transit deserved the benefit of the doubt.

Her anxiety about her apprenticeship eased, but then ratcheted up a notch. People were discussing her and excited for her arrival?

Are they in for a disappointment.

"So people *are* expecting me. Mr. McKenzie forgot to pick me up at the station and I was starting to wonder if I hadn't imagined this whole apprenticeship thing."

"Oh, yeah. Tav is . . ." Kevyn paused, and in the rearview she could see his brow crease. "Tav is a right bawbag at times. But a bawbag who grows on you, I suppose."

Portia pulled up her web browser and searched "bawbag scottish slang."

The term bawbag is a Scots word for "scrotum," which is also slang for an annoying or irritating person.

She'd had only brief contact with the man who would soon be teaching her the ins and outs of Scottish swordmaking, so she couldn't agree or disagree with that. They'd spoken briefly on the phone, once, and he'd kept the conversation to a minimum — at the end of the call she'd realized that he'd barely spoken at all. Her other correspondence had been with someone named Jamie McKenzie, who seemed cool or, at the very least, more interested in a two-sided conversation.

"Leaving me stranded at the station is

pretty bawbagish, so I have to agree," she said.

"Aye, this is going to be grand," Kevyn said, then the car slowed and stopped just in front of what looked like a wooden telephone box, but blue and on steroids. Portia was fairly certain Reggie had dressed up as one of those things for Halloween the year before, with the words *police box* around the top; it was from a TV show she loved.

"Here we are, Bodotria Armory," Kevyn said, hopping out.

Portia fought her way out of the backseat, struggling with the front seat that refused to push forward as Kevyn busied himself pulling her bags from the trunk — *boot* — of the car.

In the picture on the website, the building had looked charming, but in the early morning darkness with mist rolling in from the nearby bay and creeping over the cobblestone streets, it had a distinctly menacing air. It was Georgian neoclassical, if she was guessing correctly, three stories of perfect symmetry and imposing bulk. The gray sandstone was dark and grimy with age and moss grew in fissures between the stones. The windows were all dark, except for a circular Palladian window at the very top floor.

"There better not be any wives locked in the attic," Portia muttered.

"Maestro Tav is single. No worries there," Kevyn said cheerfully as he handed off her rolling suitcase. "I'll wait for ye to get in, lass."

"Thanks," she said. Now that she was here, the entire plan seemed ridiculous.

1. Go to Scotland.
2. Make swords.
3. . . . ?
4. Prosper?

Her parents' objections replayed in her head.

I could really use a shot or two, for fortitude.

No. A shot wouldn't do anything but lower her inhibitions. She didn't need to be fearless, or reckless. She was great at trying new things; it was the finishing that was the problem. *Starting* was her damn forte, something she had never failed at, and there was no reason to think she would this time. She inhaled deeply for fortitude and began walking toward the front door when a loud cry broke through the fog.

"Oh, stop it, you fucking tosser!" It was a woman, and she was mad or scared or both.

"I said cut it out!"

Shit.

Portia's suitcase clattered to the cobblestone and she looked around wildly, gaze landing on the giant blue box.

Police! Yes!

She ran to it and pulled at the door with all her might, but it was locked tight.

"Oh, those were decommissioned ages ago," Kevyn said calmly, as if there weren't a crime in progress. She'd heard the Scots were a levelheaded people, but this was a bit much.

The sound of renewed struggle reached her through the fog.

Portia didn't think. She jammed her hand into her purse, rummaged around, and then took off toward the sound.

"Och. Wait!" Kevyn called out, but she was already around the side of the building and stepping through the fog into what seemed to be a courtyard. She heard a grunt and the sound of scuffling shoes, then saw movement in the fog. The courtyard was illuminated by a few dim lamps, and she could make out a woman with a crown of pink hair trying to fend off an attacker. He was large, broad-shouldered, and looked like he could bench-press both Portia and the woman at the same time.

The woman kicked out.

"Let go!" she growled.

The man laughed, deep and menacing. "Make me." Portia was paralyzed by panic for a moment, but she had taken self-defense courses. She had played this out in her head many times before, what to do if she saw someone being attacked, but she'd never had to act on those imagined combat scenes until now.

She took a deep breath, ran up — holy *shit* this guy was huge — and rammed into him with her shoulder, bouncing back a few feet from the force of the impact. The blow didn't seem to faze him, but it got his attention. He turned toward her and had the nerve to look affronted.

His skin was tanned, surprising for all the talk of cloudy days and pasty British men she'd heard. His eyes were a distracting shade of hazel green beneath a fringe of salt-and-pepper hair, shorn on the sides and longer at the top. His face was that of a man too young to be going gray, though rough-hewn, with stubble darkening his jaw.

Portia blinked, and then she saw a flash of metal in his hand and his attractiveness became the last thing on her mind.

He had a knife.

Portia focused on those gorgeous green

eyes, lifted her hand, and sprayed like he was a cockroach that had invaded the sanctity of her morning shower.

"What the bloody hell!" There was the clatter of metal hitting the ground and then the man dropped to his knees, the heels of his palms pressed to his eyes. He muttered a string of words Portia didn't understand, but she was pretty sure that they were invective against her.

"She told you to let her go," Portia said, feeling a strange light-headedness that was probably an adrenaline rush chased by pride — she'd just arrived Scotland and had already stopped a crime in progress. She was mentally composing the text message to her parents, some variation of *See? I can be useful,* when she felt a burning that had nothing to do with victory.

"Ow, ow, OW!" She dropped the spray and brought her hands to her eyes, too.

"Did you stand downwind?" the attacker asked. For a moment she thought he'd started crying, but the sound was in fact low laughter. He was laughing. At her. "You did. Oh, you bloody tosser."

"Tav, are you okay?"

Through her tears, Portia could make out the woman she thought she'd saved run to her attacker and help him up. Her attacker named Tav.

Wait.

"Be a love and go get some milk, Cheryl," he said, pulling himself to his feet.

"Did you just mace Maestro Tav?" Kevyn had arrived on the scene. Perfect. "Tav, did she? Oh, this is bloody brilliant."

"Aye, she did. And herself," Tav added. Tavish McKenzie. Her new boss.

She pressed her palms more firmly into her eyes, waiting for Cheryl to bring the milk or for the cobblestones to part beneath her feet, allowing the earth to swallow her. She'd just arrived in Scotland and had managed to assault the man who would be her boss for the next three months — and herself in the process.

Project: New Portia was off to a fantastic start.

CHAPTER 2

Tav sighed and removed the cold compress from his eyes, then leaned forward, his office chair creaking under his bulk as it followed his motion. On the other side of his desk, Portia sat with her eyes squeezed closed. He didn't think she was suffering from the side effects of her attempt at superheroism, judging from the way her eyes occasionally fluttered open to peek at him, then slammed shut. Her whole face was scrunched, like she was caught in a rictus of embarrassment.

He would have pitied her if she hadn't tried to burn his eyes out without so much as a "Good day."

"I have . . . questions, but first let me explain something to you," he said.

She peeked at him and tried to force a smile. It was more of a grimace, but that didn't stop the realization that the apprentice Jamie had picked out for him was lovely, scrunched face, red eyes, and all. A bloody fool, to be sure, but lovely.

Her curly hair was a dark auburn, high-lighted here and there with strands of wheat and honey. Her skin was golden brown, and a spray of freckles dusted her high cheek-bones. She looked posh as fuck, too. Her shirt and trousers were obviously tailored, perfectly accentuating her curves, and her luggage was on the high end of high end.

Tav imagined that her being wealthy and beautiful was likely related to her lack of common fucking sense. Problem was, com-mon sense was in high demand at a place where one small mistake could result in slic-ing, stabbing, or burning yourself or others.

He exhaled deeply against his frustration. "If you are going to carry a weapon, and mace *is* a weapon despite that hot pink container you carry yours in, make sure you know how to use the bloody thing."

She nodded.

"Had you ever even given it a test run before? Out in a park or something?"

She shook her head miserably. "I know you're supposed to, but it seemed . . . dangerous?"

"Right. Next. You arrive at an establish-ment that's home to a historical European martial arts training center, see two people

30

fighting with weapons, and it doesn't even occur to you that they might be sparring?" he asked. "Did you think we were having some kind of medieval turf war?"

Her eyes fluttered open again, her long damp lashes framing deep brown orbs. Jesus, why hadn't Jamie chosen some tosser from down the pub with a face like a hairy ass?

Enough. You're too old for this shite. It's not like you've never seen a pretty face before.

"I didn't see her weapon," Portia said quietly, as if she hadn't hurled herself at an armed man twice her size half an hour ago. "And I didn't know about the European martial arts — or that it even existed, to be honest? It's not on your website."

If Tav didn't know she was apologizing, he might have thought that was judgment in her tone.

"I heard someone in danger and I just rushed in without thinking," she continued. "I tend to do that."

"Save strangers?" he asked. "What are you, a vigilante?"

"No. Rush in without thinking. Or thinking I've thought, but . . ." She looked down at her hands and frowned. "Never mind."

"We were practicing for an exhibition," Tav explained, feeling a bit like an ogre as

31

she sat hunched in her seat. "We do them from time to time to attract new customers and showcase the products. We also take part in competitions. Cheryl, my sister-in-law, can get a little feisty when she's losing. You've got to be careful from here on out, though. You could have been seriously injured running at me like that."

That was what got to Tav apart from the pain and the interruption to his day — he could have accidentally killed her if he'd been more poorly trained. Christ, what a way to start the day.

"I'm sorry," Portia said again, her voice low and husky with fatigue. That full, dusky pink lower lip trembled a bit and her teeth pressed into it to still it. "This wasn't quite how I envisioned the apprenticeship kicking off, but . . ."

She lowered her head so that she was glancing up at him through her lashes, with her pouty lips slightly parted, and something dropped in Tav's chest like a hammer striking an anvil. She had Tav's full attention, that was certain. And that was a problem.

Her gaze suddenly sharpened, pinning him. ". . . if you'd picked me up at the station like you were supposed to, I wouldn't have accidentally sprayed you."

Tav snorted back a disbelieving laugh.

"You cheeky . . ."

He rummaged about through the books and bolts of steel on his desk, snatching up a piece of crinkled sandpaper and the ivory grip of the medieval dagger he'd been working on the evening before. He began sanding the blade slowly, deliberately, the comforting scrape of it distracting him from the fact that he'd apparently lost any and all cool he'd accumulated in his thirty-eight years of life.

He let her sit there in silence as he worked; in battle, sometimes it paid to wait before an attack, to let your opponent grow more unnerved as they anticipated your next move. He also didn't know how to respond.

"So, you're saying this is my fault then?" he managed, which was shite. He *had* forgotten to pick her up, but Jamie had forgotten to remind him to remember. Tav's phone battery had died and he hadn't bothered to charge it and . . . well, and then he'd started sparring with Cheryl, leaving Portia alone at the train station at a dodgy hour of the morning.

Portia took a deep breath and her long, delicate fingers flexed in her lap before she threaded them together. She was sitting all prim and proper, like she was a schoolteacher explaining why picking bogies in class was distasteful. "I'm merely pointing out that this could have been avoided. Leaving a guest waiting is impolite, even if it's an employee."

"You're right, but I don't think forgetfulness merits this," he replied. He pointed toward his face with the hand holding the sandpaper. "I have to go teach the weans in a bit. I stink of turnt milk and I'm probably gonna give them nightmares, fuck's sake."

"Weans?" Her brows rose.

"We run a program for weans in the neighborhood." Her head tilted, augmenting the confusion expressed by those dainty brows. "Wee ones. *Children.*" Recognition sparked in her eyes and he continued. "We run programs for neighborhood kids of varying ages. Gives 'em something to do besides hang around the park and get into trouble."

And with the new police presence in the neighborhood, thanks to the influx of people they thought worthy of protecting, there was plenty of trouble to be found.

"This isn't on your website, either," she said.

"Because I'm not asking for a bloody medal for it," he snapped. He *had* in fact received a medal for it, from a community group, but that was none of her concern.

"Letting people know it exists would be effective in extending the reach of the program, though," she said. Her hand reached toward her purse, where her phone stuck out of a pocket, then she seemed to think better of it and returned her attention to him.

Tav wouldn't admit that he already had more weans enrolled than he could handle. He couldn't afford assistants other than Jamie and Cheryl, when they had time from their own busy schedules. The food he handed out, as well as clothes, school supplies, and other expenses that cropped up, were already stretching his meager bank account thin. All shite that was none of her concern. He'd figure it out. On his own.

He fixed her with a stern look. "You're changing the subject."

"Right. About the incident . . ." she said gingerly.

"The attack, more like," he cut in.

She sighed. "Is there anything in the employee manual that covers this?"

Tav didn't return the hopeful smile she laid on him — he wouldn't be charmed. Not by someone who was going to be underfoot for the next three months. He was going to have to work in close quarters with her every day.

The back of his neck went warm.

"We don't have an employee manual. I *am* the employee manual," he replied brusquely, annoyed at his reaction to her. She was too young for him — he had at least a decade of age and an infinite amount of raw cynicism on this woman. And more importantly, she was off-limits. He refused to be *that* boss, using his employee roster as a dating pool. Given that his only other two employees were his brother and his sister-in-law, it would be particularly egregious.

And business ethics aside — Tav was done with relationships. He wasn't the type to convince himself he didn't believe in labels or just wasn't a relationship guy or whatever knobs were telling themselves these days. He'd married young; he'd been a silly kid fresh out of uni and so besotted with his wife, Greer, that he hadn't realized divorce was a thing that could exist in the perfect world they'd envisioned with each other.

He'd tried. He'd failed. He didn't want to feel that awful, impotent guilt as his hopes and dreams for the future circled the drain ever again, and there was only one surefire way to avoid it.

"Oh. I just assumed —"

"Jamie is the one who set up this apprenticeship, lass. I had nothing to do with it," he continued, ignoring the way her expression caved a bit at that. His younger brother had said it would be a clever way of bringing attention to the business and for Tav to finally get the help he needed, and Tav had gone along with it. He'd never been able to say no to Jamie, but then again, Jamie had never been one to ask unreasonable things of him. Until now. Expecting Tav to put up with Portia for three months was entirely unreasonable.

"He's the one who contacted the newspapers to promote it, went through the applications that came in, and selected yours. I'd say it's because you had a pretty face, but now I'm wondering if maybe he wasn't just trying to find a way to aggravate me to death."

Her tentative smile dropped then, and her brows raised in a way that was both delicate and dangerous. "I have an MFA from NYU and a master's in art history from Columbia."

"That's n—"

She cut him off with an impatient swipe of her hand.

"I've interned at the Museum of Ancient Arts, the Museum of New York City, and several prestigious art galleries. I'm also quite confident I have the technological skills that you so clearly lack, judging from your crappy website and general lack of a web presence. I mean, honestly — Papyrus for the site's header?"

"What?" Tav had no clue what she was on about.

She leaned forward a bit, holding his gaze. "Exactly. Perhaps Jamie didn't make this clear, so I will. I'm the pretty face that's gonna save your business for the low, low price of room, board, and a meager honorarium."

Tav dropped the sandpaper and knife on the desk and stared at her, his hurt pride edging out his professionalism. "You can keep your American saviorism shite, lass. Bodotria Armory is doing just fine, so you can roll up that 'mission accomplished' banner and haul it over to someone who needs it."

He gestured toward the door with his chin.

That wasn't exactly true. Orders had dropped to the lowest they'd been in the armory's ten-year history with no explanation. The rejuvenation of the neighborhood had been a boon, but it also meant higher taxes and the council breathing down his neck about the historical status of the building and the million repairs that needed to be done to get it up to code. His gaze tracked to where he had gestured, landing on the huge crack in the wall beside the door.

Tav hadn't asked for the property and all the worries it brought — his knob of an absentee father had put it in trust for him, like some kind of shitty "sorry for denying your existence and hiding mine" eighteenth birthday surprise — but Tav had eventually turned it into the headquarters for his passion. He was bleeding money, stalled in sales, and worried he would lose his business, but he'd be damned if he revealed any of that. Tavish took care of people, and he'd take care of this.

"Mr. McKenzie, do you know what my nickname is?" she asked. There was that brow raise again. "And if you say bawbag or some other weird Scottish insult, I'll be forced to mace you again."

Tav suppressed a laugh at that. He gave her as stern an appraisal as he could muster, his gaze lingering on her nose for some reason. It was a cute nose, which made no fucking sense to him. A nose was a nose, but hers was the kind of nose you could imagine dropping a kiss onto, if you were into sappy shite like that.

She's annoying, remember? You're not that *boss,* remember?

"Freckles," he responded drily. "Freckles McGee."

Portia smirked, and he hadn't thought smirks could be beguiling, but fucking hell if hers wasn't.

Christ, take a cold shower, McKenzie.

"Cute, but it's Search Engine Brown. Friend is going on a date with a strange guy? I can have all the info on him, from his middle school to his favorite T-shirt, in under an hour. Museum can't track down info on a rare piece? I'm on it. Going to work for a new employer and need to know what the deal is with them? Guess who can dig up that info for you?"

She tilted her head to the side and gave him a know-it-all grin that conveyed a very explicit message: she saw right through him. He should have known that from the moment she'd looked him in the face all wide-eyed innocence and then maced the fuck out of him. There was no point in playing coy.

"What did you find out?" He thought he did a good job of sounding unconcerned.

"Everything available in the public record," she said. "People always underestimate the public record. Lots of interesting stuff there."

"So you want to add blackmail to the as-

40

sault charges then, eh Freckles?"

"I want to do lots of things. I want to learn how to make swords, and I want to know the how and why behind every decision that goes into a blade. I want to rebuild your entire web presence, from social media to the website, and I want to get Bodotria Armory positioned as the premiere manufacturer of Scottish swords, knives, and various other weaponry. Basically? I want to do what I was brought here to do, which is to be your apprentice. Whether you allow me to do all, a fraction of, or none of that in the next three months is up to you."

Tav allowed his chuckle to escape this time. She'd gone from doe in the headlights to brash businesswoman in no time flat. It shouldn't have surprised him. Jamie was no fool, goofy as he was, and he had selected Portia. That and she'd shown uncommon bravery when she'd thought Cheryl was in trouble.

She held his gaze, but then her shoulders drooped and the fight left her eyes. Tav's gaze dropped to her hands, which were clasped tightly in her lap.

"Look, I know we got off on the wrong foot, but don't fire me," she said quietly. "I . . . really need this right now. You don't even have to pay me the honorarium. I'll make my time here worth your while. I promise."

Suddenly, she wasn't an annoying apprentice or a savvy shit talker. She was a woman in freefall searching for something solid to hold on to. Tav knew that feeling well; he'd spent his whole damn life looking for a foothold, a sense of stability, and he was going to lose the one he'd found if he didn't try something different. Portia Hobbs was most definitely something different.

He hadn't planned on firing her, and he wished he'd made that clear earlier because the pleading look in her eyes gutted him. He felt an illogical need to soothe her, and despite all the swords and armor, chivalry was most certainly *not* his thing.

He scrubbed a hand over his stubble.

"Aye. Jamie will be back this evening to teach a class and he can talk over all the administrative shite with ye. Enough with this puppy dog face." He waved a hand dismissively in the air between them. "I prefer the 'I'm about to burn your fucking eyeballs out, ye creepy bastard' look you gave me earlier."

He schooled his expression into a scowl and reached his hand across the desk, holding it in front of her. "Welcome to Bodotria Armory."

She let out a sigh of relief and took his hand, giving it a good, firm, professional handshake. Tav touched women all the damn time during training and demonstrations without feeling a thing, but the feel of Portia's slim fingers curling against his sent something bright and electric zipping through his veins.

Bloody hell, *it's going to be a long few months.*

He noticed her gaze had slipped past his face, over his shoulder to where the framed photos lined his bookshelf next to souvenirs from trips to his parents' respective homelands; a Moai statue from Chile and a small Jamaican flag. There was a photo of him and Jamie and their parents, a spectrum of browns with Tav's face the only pale one. Portia was a smart woman — she'd figure it out.

He released her hand. "Come on, I'll show you to your room."

He'd doled out cash he didn't have for a new mattress, bedding, and towels for her, and Cheryl had decorated the room for him. He wasn't sure the New York skyline duvet cover and matching lamp from Tesco would be to Portia's taste, but she'd deal with it.

He maneuvered around her giant suitcase

and rolling bag. He couldn't imagine how much the set had cost. "What've you got in there, an elephant?"

"No, I've got several folding chairs for men who act like fitting your entire life into two bags is some kind of diva move."

It seemed she'd tucked vulnerable Portia away again. Good. He didn't need her giving him calf eyes when he was in the mood for veal.

He hefted the larger bag and headed into the hallway, stowing his complaints, and the only sound behind him was the wheels of her rolling suitcase on the thin runner that covered the old hardwood floor. His office and room were on the topmost floor, and he tried to manage some sense of dignity and grace as he lugged her bag down the stairs to the next landing.

"This is a beautiful building," she said, as they walked down the corridor toward the guest room. Her room. In Tav's home.

Fucking hell.

"It looks imposing on the outside, but up here feels homey," she said. Homey was a nice way of saying "run down," he figured. He could tell she was trying to be friendly, but his eyes still burned and the bloody bag was heavier than he'd anticipated; he refused to give in and roll it.

"How old is this place? The exterior looks Georgian but I'm guessing it's been renovated more recently than the seventeen hundreds."

"It's old," he said.

Beads of sweat were breaking out on his hairline and her room was still a few meters away. Dammit. How had she carried this on a train? He imagined men had fallen over themselves to help her with the luggage. After all, Kevyn was the one who had dragged it up to his office unnecessarily.

"When did you move in?" she asked.

"Almost twenty years ago," he said. "Let out the extra rooms to my uni friends for a few years, and then I got married and moved and rented out all the rooms. When we separated and I started the business, I moved back in and stopped renting."

And he regretted it every time he saw a moving truck carrying away one of the neighborhood's residents and replacing them with people escaping the even higher rent of the tonier Edinburgh neighborhoods. He knew time stood still for no man, and he couldn't run a boarding house, but sometimes he felt like an alien on the streets he'd walked since he was a wean.

"Twenty years?" The sound of her luggage wheels grew louder and then she was beside him, peering up into his face with her bloodshot eyes. "How old are you?"

"Thirty-eight." Just a few more steps to her room.

"Whoa. That's . . ."

He shot her an annoyed look.

"Not old at all!"

She was near thirty herself, according to what Jamie had told him, but Tav had never felt older — huffing as he carried a suitcase with a bright young thing chirping up at him.

"Wait, so you bought this place when you were eighteen?"

They reached the door and he dropped the suitcase in front of it with a thud and took a controlled breath through his nose. He opened the door and ushered her in ahead of him, mostly so he could have a second to wipe the sheen of sweat that had gathered on his forehead.

"One of the benefits of having a rich shite for a biological father. They leave you their extra properties. Was probably a write-off for the codger."

Tav wouldn't know. He'd never met his bio dad and had never sought him out either — he'd never cared to meet the type of man who'd impregnate a refugee who'd lost

46

everything, then abandon her and their child.

He glanced at Portia and took in her look of discomfort, then realized he was scowling hard.

"Sorry. I shouldn't have pried," she said. "It's just a fantastic building. My entire place in New York is about the size of this room, has walls as thin as tissue paper, and would sell for as much as the GDP of a small nation."

Tav kept himself from commenting on the last bit, by the skin of his teeth. She was a spoiled, rich American, but he didn't want to see those puppy dog eyes again.

"Pry away, it's fine. It worked out for me. Mum married when I was young, so I got a life with a great dad and property from a shite one."

"Sounds like a pretty good deal." She flopped down on the bed and sighed, snuggling into the duvet. "I'm sorry, all the traveling is catching up to me."

He looked at her sprawled out on the bed with her eyes fluttering shut, with that damn nose, and that damn mouth, and those damned freckles. He liked looking at her, and he hated that he liked it. He didn't want to.

A passing fancy was one thing, but this

jittery awareness of her felt both new and devastatingly familiar.

Nope. Not dirtying my soles on that road again. The destination is always disappointment.

Her eyes flew open and she gazed up at him, one hand pressing into the bed as if testing it. "Do you have a mattress topper or something? This mattress is kinda . . ."

"Oh, for fuck's sake."

Tav turned and walked out of the room, closing the door soundly behind him.

He was going to kill Jamie.

CHAPTER 3

"Now thrust like you're trying to disembowel me. Come on! I'm the English marauder come to storm your castle, and those weak-ass jabs aren't going to stop me!"

Sweat poured down Portia's neck. The gray silk blouse she'd chosen to wear was soaked through beneath her breasts and down her back; she was sure she looked like a Rorschach test in which one could find the image of a woman who was going to need an Epsom bath soon. At least her jeans were proving they'd been worth the money for the stretchtech/ denim blend. Her heels were lined up on the bleachers because she was good in heels, but not *that* good.

She hadn't expected to do anything but observe the class; Jamie and his wife Cheryl had been out all day, so they hadn't been able to go over the parameters of the internship earlier. She'd avoided Tavish as best she could by walking around the neighborhood and checking out coffee shops, trying not to replay her disastrous first morning in Scotland on a humiliating mental loop, then fallen asleep in her room for a few hours. She was dressed more "casual chic" than "CrossFit" when she'd walked into the gymnasium located just off of the courtyard, she'd realized that when Jamie said "come check out my class before we chat" he'd actually meant "come meet my sadistic drill sergeant alter ego."

Jamie — tall, dark-skinned, with short, glossy curls that made her want to ask what product he used — had pulled her into a welcoming hug, then turned and lined her up with the group of students waiting for the evening's class to start. She'd thought herself reasonably in shape, but the Defending the Castle boot camp was kicking her ass.

They'd lifted kettle bells in a "pour boiling oil on the bastards scaling the wall" maneuver, then did wall sits in an exercise called "battering ram resistance" just before entering the hand-to-hand combat training. The gray-haired older woman beside Portia was leaning forward and faux-parrying with all her might, but her shirt was dry and her face serene.

"Jab! Jab!" Jamie commanded, his curls

bouncing as he cheerfully stabbed imaginary attackers while jogging in place.

Portia's thighs burned and her arms were getting heavier and heavier, but even so . . . it was kind of fun. She'd tried barre, and yoga, and Pilates, but pretending to ward off attackers fulfilled some primal urge that had apparently been lying dormant within her.

Or maybe this one showed up after you stopped indulging your other primal urges.

Giving up sex had been surprisingly easy. She'd replaced happy hours and hookups with quiet nights with friends and courses on social engineering, marketing, and tech. Then Reggie had sent her the apprenticeship application and Portia had become infatuated with the idea — she'd even uploaded the application days ahead of the deadline instead of at the very last minute, like she usually did. When she'd received the email saying she'd been selected, she'd looked forward to it, thinking she already had her physical longings under wraps. Her vow of celibacy hadn't been a problem until she was sitting across from Tavish McKenzie.

She'd realized several things at once in his office: (1) She'd been wrong to scoff at the silver fox phenomenon, because Tavish's salt-and-pepper hair was like the perfect seasoning on a slab of delicious Angus steak. (2) Her diet had definitely been lacking in protein. (3) She had committed to sexual veganism, there was no way in hell she was going to mess up Project: New Portia by sleeping with her boss of all people.

"Don't you want to protect your castle?" Jamie shouted, doubling the tempo of the imaginary dagger thrusting where he led from the front of the class. "Don't you, mates?"

A few scattered grunts and roars were his response.

"Fuck off away from me castle!" the woman beside Portia yelled as she kept time with Jamie. Her jabs were vicious but precise, belied by her pleasant smile.

Portia's castle needed defending. There was some invisible pull between people, woo-woo as it seemed, and years of nightlife adventures had honed her ability to find that connection and see where it led — specifically, whether it was to a bedroom. Or a couch. Or kitchen table. It was a skill that had been invaluable in the late-night campaigns waged in bars across New York City, as she pillaged her way through the singles scene.

Tav had been gruff, combative even, when

they'd spoken in his office, but she'd felt the pull so hard that it'd nearly jerked her up onto his desk. This was a game of tug-of-war that she wouldn't lose, though. She couldn't. She was in Scotland to learn and grow, to see who she really was, not to fall back into the same patterns she was trying to break.

"What do you get out of these encounters, Portia?"

Portia wheezed and jabbed as she jogged in place. She had no regrets about her sex life; some hookups had been pleasurable, some had been boring, but none of them had amounted to much in the grand scheme of things. She'd drank her fears away, and fucked them away, but the thing about distractions was they didn't make the real issues go away. It took work to do that, and not the kind of work she wanted to put in with Tavish McKenzie.

She jabbed with her left hand and then her right, her body finding the rhythm even though she'd thought she was ready to drop a minute before.

This was about more than whether or not to give in to fleeting pleasure. It was about proving that she didn't *need* a drink, didn't *need* a hookup — that she could be good enough without any of the "oh honey, no"

53

accessories of her past. She was fine, or on her way to fine, and she didn't need any damned sexy-annoying Scotsmen getting in the way of that.

"Protect your castle at all costs," Jamie shouted encouragingly. "Don't give up! You can do it!"

"This is *my* castle!" Portia shouted as she stabbed out with her imaginary dagger. "The drawbridge is up and you can't come in!"

"That's it, Portia! Now you've got it!" Jamie called out with a bright smile, then lifted a hand up to his brow as if shading his eyes while searching the horizon. "Look! The invaders are running off, the mangy cowards! We've won!"

A cheer rang out from the group, and Portia joined them. A sense of victory fueled by endorphins was a powerful feeling, even if the invaders weren't real. She felt like maybe she could conquer anything, even her own hopeless tangle of flaws. A sudden, embarrassing wash of tears warmed her eyes.

She blinked hard.

"Okay, let's wind it down now." Jamie dropped down into a stretch and the students followed suit.

After the class had ended, the students

54

grabbed their bags and began to mill around Jamie. A shock of bright pink hair that Portia recognized as Cheryl barreled through the crowd toward him, standing on her tiptoes and pulling him down into a kiss when she finally reached him. Portia could see both of their smiles and wondered at that. Being so happy to see each other that even the serious mouthwork they were putting on display couldn't stop them from grinning like fools.

She looked away, pulling out her phone and snapping a sweaty selfie.

First evening of internship! Just finished defending my castle with @JamieMac007 at a @BodotriaArmory boot camp. So much fun! #DefendingYourCastle

She uploaded it to the various social media feeds that catalogued her daily activities. She was planning on asking Jamie to let her take over Bodotria's social media accounts, which hadn't been updated for months. The pic would be something she could share later to start beefing up their internet presence.

"You're the apprentice, then? The American?" The woman who had been working out beside her was now dabbing her face

55

with a towel and looking at Portia appraisingly.

"I am. My name is Portia. It's a pleasure to meet you." She held out her hand, her finishing school lessons kicking in.

"I'm Mary," the woman said. "I run the bookshop down the street, Bodotria Books. Not a very imaginative name, I know."

Portia shrugged lightly. "Hey, it serves its purpose. I know where to go if I need books in Bodotria."

Mary responded with a friendly smile. "Right. I'm sure I'll be seeing a lot of you since Tavish always has book orders coming in."

"Really?" Portia asked, and then realized that was rude, and also that she already had her answer. His office had been jammed with books, though she'd been too concerned with losing her apprenticeship and having to return home with yet another failure stamped on her forehead to pay much attention. That and his eyes, hazel green and arresting, bracketed by crow's feet. His mouth wasn't half bad either — wide, just this side of plump. And his hands . . .

What the hell?

Portia cut off her fantasy rundown of Tav's attributes. He wasn't a newly acquired

56

statue at a museum that had to be measured and catalogued. He was her boss. He was a jerk. He was off-limits. *Fin.*

"Oh yes, that boy has always been mad for books, the older the better. I just tracked down a quite rare one he's been searching for, *Techniques of the Consummate Swordsman.*" Mary looked proud, as if she'd found a Rembrandt work on the back of a posterboard. "Dates from the mid seventeenth century. Just waiting for it to come in now."

"I'm sure he'll be pleased," Portia said politely, although she doubted much pleased Tavish besides glaring at people while brandishing a sharp object.

"He also pays for the books for the children's book club each month," Mary said. "He's a good man, lass. Keep that in mind because sometimes it takes a bit of digging to see that. Good men can be stubborn asses, too." She nudged Portia with an elbow. "And as far as asses go, he certainly has a fine one."

Oh. Ohhhhhhhhh.

Mary was trying to play matchmaker. Portia didn't know how to say "No way in hell" politely, so she just smiled.

"Ah, you've noticed, too! Good taste, you." Another conspiratorial nudge. "Well, you're always welcome to come by the shop, and you should let me know if you need anything. We have the latest releases for adults and children, the classics, and rare books."

Portia had been struck by inspiration for a project while walking the halls of the building earlier. The armory was old and beautiful and probably had an interesting history, like any structure that had lasted so long.

"Actually, if you have any books on the history of the neighborhood, I have some plans for the website they might be helpful with," Portia said. She left out the fact that the plans hadn't been approved yet, but she was sure Jamie would be supportive of them. He'd seemed really interested in her ideas. That had been one of the reasons she'd been so excited for the apprenticeship — and so put out when she came face-to-face with the surly brick wall that would be her real boss. "I've found some stuff about the docks and local guilds, but I was thinking more architectural history."

Mary looked off to the side, as if going through her mental shop inventory, then nodded. "I have a book or two that might interest you, if you want to come 'round. You should also check the library — they have deeds and newspapers and the like on microfiche."

"Is it available online?" Portia asked.

"The library is two blocks away, love," Mary said gently. "Getting out to see the neighborhood wouldn't hurt for a new-comer, now would it?"

Portia appreciated the woman's subtle shade too much to be bothered by it.

"Okay, I'm off." Mary gave Portia's arm a quick squeeze, then leaned in to whisper, "I know you Americans do things differently, but may I suggest some trousers with more breathability for the next class? Denim causes thrush, dear."

Portia made another note to self to look up *thrush,* but nodded her appreciation and waved as Mary strode away. The crowd around Jamie and Cheryl was breaking up, so she headed over to them. She felt a little awkward, and sweaty, but they both seemed nice and Jamie had told her to come find him when the boot camp was over.

"Hey," Jamie said over Cheryl's shoulder. "How did you like it?"

"I loved it! It's such a great concept. I feel like I can crush my enemies and take over the world," Portia said.

Jamie grinned. "Brilliant! That's exactly how I want people to feel. I sometimes wonder if I lay it on a bit too thick, so I'm glad to hear that."

Cheryl turned, eyes going wide when she saw Portia.

"My champion!" She ditched Jamie and ran toward Portia, her ponytail trailing behind her like a streamer. She didn't lay a giant kiss on Portia, but she did pull her into a hug, which she quickly released her from.

"Oh sorry. I just didn't get to thank you this morning, or introduce myself. I was too busy fetching the milk and compresses." She was trying to joke about it, but Portia still cringed at the reminder of her grand entrance that morning. "I'm Cheryl Hu. Partner of Jamie. Tolerator of Tavish." She beamed up at Portia with a smile so welcoming it made Portia's throat go rough.

"There's nothing to thank me for, no worries," Portia said with a shrug.

"Nothing to thank you for? You thought I was being attacked and you ran in like bloody Eowyn ready to take out the Nazgul, and all. It was grand!"

Portia didn't know what Cheryl was referring to, but being on the receiving end of the closest human incarnation of 😊 Portia had ever seen made her cheeks go warm.

"It was silly," she said shifting uncomfortably. "I should have realized what was going on instead of just rushing in and ruining your practice. And hurting your boss."

Classic Portia. Think first, regret later. She twisted her mouth at the memory of how proud she had felt for that one moment before humiliating reality had set it.

Cheryl placed an arm on her shoulder. "Ach, no. Don't feel too guilty about the mix-up. Tav deserved it, even if he wasn't really attacking me. Comeuppance for being such a wanker all the time. You're fine."

"Well, glad I could do my part in wanker comeuppance delivery," Portia said, trying to sound normal even though Cheryl's compliments made her want to stick her head in the ground.

"Is that so?" a deep voice asked, cutting into the conversation.

Portia sighed. Of course, Tavish would sneak up behind her in time to overhear that. She turned to face him, propping her hands on her hips because they suddenly felt large and ungainly and she didn't know what to do with them.

He'd obviously just come from his workshop, judging from the dirt smudges all over his clothes and exposed skin — the unshowered tradesman look really, *really* worked for him. He was like a rustic wooden table that grew more attractive from weathering, if tables could be sexy. 13 out of 10, would hit that — if she was hitting anything, which she wasn't.

"Yes, that's so," she retorted.

What? What kind of weak comeback was that?

He was holding her heels, their straps slid over two of his thick fingers, and Portia had no idea why the sight of it prompted a pulse of want in her.

"I suppose this is your heroine pose, for when you're out impulsively saving strangers," he said, his dark brows arching upward. "Freckles McGee, vigilante at large."

His tone was dry, but his gaze slid over her body like a pour of molten metal. She was already sweating, and looks like that didn't help. Neither did the fact that the sleeves of his Henley shirt were pushed up to the elbow, revealing his veined wrists and forearms.

She reached out and snagged her heels from him, suppressing the shiver that went through her as their fingers brushed. "Yes. I've been busy keeping Edinburgh's streets safe from the likes of the villainous . . . Knife Man."

Tavish blinked several times. "Knife Man?"

"You had a knife this morning," she said

stubbornly. "You are a man. Knife Man."

Jamie and Cheryl burst out laughing beside her. Tavish rolled his eyes and wiped his hands against his jeans and she noticed that Thigh Man would have also been a good name for him.

"Jamie, are we going to talk details of my schedule now?" she asked, turning away from Tavish. "Do I get to make a sword soon?"

Jamie looked sheepish. "We're gonna start off slow, I think. Data entry is almost as fun as swordmaking, right?"

He elbowed Cheryl.

"Totally as good," Cheryl said cheerily, but shook her head and gave a thumbs-down as soon as Jamie looked away from her.

"It'll be a wee bit before you're allowed to work with sharp objects," Tavish cut in, drawing her attention back to him, though it hadn't wandered far. "Especially since I'm the one who has to train you for that. Let's see if you can go a week without doing me bodily harm and then I'll consider it."

She had messed up, badly, but she wasn't down with being infantilized for the next three months because of it.

"A keyboard is a dangerous thing in the right hands, too, you know," Portia said.

"I agree. Jamie for instance, used a keyboard to place the apprenticeship advert, and look what that got me." He gestured in her general direction.

Portia faltered; Tav's verbal jab had hit a soft spot, one that had been hidden under a sea of distractions for years and had only just begun to harden. She had no witty comeback for someone telling her they didn't want her around. It reinforced what that ugly voice in the back of her head whispered at the most inopportune moments: *no one would care if you left and never came back.*

"You really are a wanker," Cheryl said with a tsk, moving closer to Portia. She rested her hand on Portia's back, not even pulling it away when it landed on a damp sweaty spot.

Jamie came to stand at her other side. "He's always been like this, you know. I'm pretty sure my first words were 'Mum, Tav is a right wanker, aye?' And her reply was, 'Yes, son. *Su hermano* is the one true wanker, the wanker to rule them all.'"

Cheryl giggled and Tav rolled his eyes. "Why are you bringing Mum into this? And why are you both surrounding her like I'm the threat? Might I remind you that *I* was the one attacked today?"

64

"Do you fancy some dinner, Portia?" Cheryl asked, ignoring Tavish. "I have some Char Siu pork in the slow cooker."

She kissed her fingertips and threw her hand up to the sky, the universal expression of "this is going to be fucking delicious."

"Cheryl runs the little restaurant out front, Doctor Hu's," Jamie said. "Trust me, you want this dinner."

Portia had planned to pick up something from the chip shop, aptly named Chip Shop, that she'd spotted down the street, and eat it in her room. Companionship and home-cooked food were unexpected surprises, and pork was clearly the only protein she should be thinking of to satisfy her cravings.

Cheryl bit her lip and fidgeted a bit. "I just thought it would be nice to welcome you properly. I understand if you have other plans, though, or you don't want to."

Portia had thought of her apprenticeship from so many different angles, but she hadn't factored in new friendships. Not really. Actual humans had kind of been hazy peripheral players in her journey, but now Cheryl and Jamie were standing there looking at her expectantly and she realized she'd made a huge miscalculation.

"Dinner would be lovely. Thank you,

Cheryl."

"Yes, yes, it would be," Tavish said in a mockingly formal voice. "Assuming my place hasn't been usurped?"

"Of course not," Cheryl said, patting his shoulder reassuringly. "Even wankers need delicious slow-cooked meat."

"I'll be there after this lesson, then," he said, then walked toward the center of the gym. Portia looked away from him and noticed several kids sitting on the bleachers, fencing masks atop their heads.

"All right, young squires. Are you ready for your lessons?" Tav asked in a booming voice.

"Yes, Master Tav!" the kids replied obediently, but many were bouncing in their seats.

"People entrust him with their children?" Portia remembered he'd mentioned a program for kids but seeing it in action was different.

"Aye, Tav has a knack with the wee ones," Jamie said. He held up his hand beside his waist. "You must be ye high or smaller to enter the 'gentle Tav' ride. We're all out of luck."

Portia turned back to see the kids were lined up in a row, all holding multicolored lengths of Styrofoam attached to basic wooden hilts out before them. Tav stood watching with his arms crossed over his chest and eyes narrowed, but he was smiling.

"We didn't have much to do, growing up around here, and we got in trouble from time to time. Tav likes trying to keep the kids out of trouble, and all that. Has classes for teens, too."

"Do you want to wash up before dinner?" Cheryl asked. She plucked at her own ponytail. "I've got to deep condition before dinner."

Portia nodded and followed them out. She heard the children break out into peals of laughter behind her, but didn't look back. She didn't need anything that could remind her that Tav was a friendly human being — her imagination was already having a field day without that fuel.

"You sure you don't want a beer? Or a digestif? We have Tia Maria." Cheryl stood before a cabinet stocked with glass bottles of all shapes and sizes while Jamie hopped up from where they sat around the battered wooden table and jogged to the wailing electric teakettle.

"I'm sure," Portia said, trying not to be weird about it. Cheryl was better than most hosts in that she didn't keep pressing until

Portia was forced to make up some reason why she wouldn't have a drink since "I don't want one" apparently wasn't good enough.

The kitchen in the armory was large and comfortable in a way that her own at home wasn't. It had obviously been used well over the years, though it was clean. Portia usually ate out or ordered takeout so hers, done in shades of white and gray, hadn't been used much. Her parents' kitchen was always sparkling clean, bright and modern, even though her mom cooked often. The armory's kitchen was rustic, but not like something you'd see on a home renovation show. The walls were painted a cheery orange and dark wood cabinets lined the walls and floor. It had two fridges, one normal-sized model and one huge industrial steel one, and along one wall was a professional kitchen prep station that served as the home base for Cheryl's small food stand.

"Tea?" Jamie asked, placing the electric kettle down in the middle of the table. She nodded and accepted the mug he poured for her taking a moment to absorb her surroundings. Her first night in a strange country, after a miserable morning, and she was sharing a delicious meal and talking about how to slay, literally.

"So then I told the kids that they had it all wrong," Tavish said, pushing his chair back and standing. "They had to grip the hilt like this, plunge up like *this,* through the opening in the side of the armor, and then twist, like so. That ensures they'll hit the most vital organs. Theoretically."

He made some strange jabbing motion that was a swing of his arms followed by a thrust of his hips, and Portia forgot how to swallow, barking out a cough as her swallow of tea tried to go down the wrong pipe.

Jamie and Cheryl laughed as he demonstrated the technique, but Tavish was serious. She could tell by the way his gaze settled on each of them as he spoke, as if willing them to understand why this particular fact was important. She'd sported that same look while escorting her parents around exhibits at the museums and galleries where she'd interned, where they'd respond with tight smiles and "Isn't that nice?"

She tried to think of what she wished her parents would have asked all those times she'd shared something she cared about with them. What Ledi and Nya asked when she was going on and on about her latest interest.

"How did you get into all of this stuff?

The swords and the European martial arts?" she asked, her voice gravelly from fatigue.

He glared at her for a second, either because he thought she was poking fun at him or because he just didn't like her, then dropped into his seat. "I dunno."

She rolled her eyes. "Yes, you do."

"I like swords," he said, peeling at the label on his beer bottle.

"I like architectural history," Portia pushed. "That doesn't explain why I could take you on a tour of this place and point out the tics from each era it was remodeled in. What is your origin story, Knife Man?"

He looked at her for a long time. "Fuck's sake, you Americans and the Dr. Phil shite." He took a sip of his beer then sighed in annoyance. "There was a fencing lesson put on by the European martial arts club, the first week of uni. Something for the first years to do other than get pissed and vomit fried pizza. And it was grand! Holding a sword, feeling the weight of the metal in your hand and the shock of a blow up your arm, and knowing that only your skill determined whether you won or lost. I was hooked after that."

She could imagine him young and bright-eyed, with dark hair and a devilish smile. "Because you won?"

"No, because I lost so badly." He plucked at the beer label and chuckled gruffly. "I became obsessed with getting good enough to win a competition. I'd always loved reading about knights and medieval history, actually. I started studying old treatises and history books in the university library, collecting information about swordsmanship and swordmaking. I went down a rabbit hole and never quite made my way out, even when the real world came a calling."

Portia realized that they were both leaning across the table, gazes locked on each other. Tav's eyes were dark with passion, and even though it wasn't for her, the fact that he felt so deeply about *anything* made her stomach do some kind of pirouette.

She leaned back in her seat and cleared her throat. "Interesting."

"Whoa, bruv, I didn't know all that," Jamie said. "I thought it was because you just liked brawling. That's some real Harry Potter, aye? Did your first sword choose you, like the wand?"

"Again with the Harry Potter shite," Tavish grumbled, but a smile played at his lips. His full, kissable lips. Portia took a sip of tea and reminded herself that whatever this feeling was would pass. She didn't do crushes. Usually she saw what she wanted and went for it, aided by a drink or two or five. As much as she hated to admit it, she wasn't quite sure how to deal with attraction in a world where both drinking and fucking were off the table. This was her first big test, and Portia had always been the twin that did horribly at tests.

"King Arthur would be more accurate," Portia pointed out, dragging her thoughts back to the conversation. "The Sword in the Stone. Excalibur."

"Aye," Tavish said. He glanced at her. "Though in the original Welsh legend the sword was called *Caledfwich*. It was known as *Calisvol* in Middle Cornish, and eventually Latinized to *Caliburnus* by —"

"Okay, we get it, bruv," Jamie said. He gave a long-suffering sigh.

Portia was not having the same reaction at all. Her boss acted like a gruff, annoying jerk, but dammit there was something about a man who could casually mention Middle Cornish at dinner conversation without sounding pretentious that Portia found irresistible. It didn't matter — she would resist.

"What do you think Tav's patronus would be?" Cheryl asked, grabbing Jamie by the forearm and hopping in her seat.

Jamie sighed. "We've already discussed

this, love. A honey badger."

"Oh, that's riiiight. He's such a Huf-flepuff."

"A Hufflegruff more like," Jamie said, hand at his chin as if he were giving the matter real thought.

"All right, all right," Tavish said, standing again. He feigned annoyance but ran his hand gently over Jamie's curls as he passed by him, as if his brother were a boy instead of a man almost as large as Tav. The small act made Portia's chest go tight. It was a protective, possessive movement. She remembered stroking Reggie's hair in the ICU, partially to give comfort to her sister and partially to assure herself that her sister was still there.

She didn't know much about Harry Potter shite, as Tav had called it, but Jamie's patronus would probably be a grumpy Scotsman with a sword.

Tav's gaze turned to her. "If you find any peas under your mattress tonight you'll have to deal with it yourself. I've got a busy day tomorrow, and no time for your nonsense, Princess Freckles."

He downed the last of his beer, tossed the bottle in the recycling bin, and stalked out.

Cheryl and Jamie shot each other looks, but Portia didn't mind his rudeness. It was a reminder that she wasn't there to make friends, as the saying went, or at least not with him. The only role Tav would play in Project: New Portia was showing her how to make a blade and, possibly, how to use it. That was dangerous enough.

CHAPTER 4

The cold breeze off of the firth buffeted against Tav's track suit as his trainers pummeled the concrete along the waterfront. Icy droplets of misty late spring rain slapped his face and hands, as if reprimanding him for his recent behavior.

He pushed himself at his slow and steady pace, hoping the sea air and the exertion would clear his head. The past few days hadn't gone as expected, and he needed to discharge the nervous energy zipping through him.

Maybe then he'd be able to do his damned job.

He'd understood that taking on an apprentice would be an intrusion. Jamie had talked of "publicity" and "free marketing," and those had both sounded like good things. And Tav had even grown somewhat excited about the idea — he genuinely enjoyed teaching, and it felt like he was leveling up in his craft. He was skilled enough to produce another swordmaker, which was a career milestone. He also wasn't enough of an ass to forget that *he* had once been an apprentice, that this was the best way for his trade to be passed down. You couldn't learn what it takes to be a master swordsmith by watching a blasted video alone. It required time at the side of a skilled professional, which was his problem. He hadn't been feeling professional at all when it came to Portia.

How the fuck am I supposed to pull this off?

They'd received thousands of applications. There had been Highland boys, a cluster of girls from Mexico, a man from a small village in Kenya — applicants from all around the globe. Why had Jamie chosen her of all people? There had to have been more qualified applicants, or someone who needed the opportunity more. Or at the very least, someone that didn't make him feel like a lad about to stain his britches at the sight of her.

Bloody hell.

He'd been unable to get the sight of her lunging and parrying out of his head since he'd watched her participate in Jamie's class. She should've looked foolish, carrying on in her fancy jeans and blouse — he'd

76

expected her to give up after the first exercise. But she'd stuck to it, chest heaving, curls in disarray, skin flushed from exertion. Her expression had been so determined that Tav hadn't even paid much attention to her poor form. Portia wasn't afraid of a little hard work, despite her whole put-together posh vibe.

He pushed himself a bit harder as he ran. Tav wasn't a playboy, but he wasn't a monk either. He'd married young, tried to make it work, and failing that, stuck to what he knew best: weaponry and fighting. He had a good time with women he met at the pub, or the occasional longer-term acquaintance, but he preferred it when the only call he had to answer was the singing of metal against metal.

A woman had once told him he was like the weapons he made: cold, sharp, and designed to repel those who got too close. Tav had gotten a laugh out of that, but any blade lost its edge over time, and no metal was invulnerable if you heated it enough.

Tav lifted his knees a bit higher as he ran, upping the intensity as he passed a dog walker wrangling four large, wet dogs who were none too happy to be outdoors. One leapt after him, sniffing, and Tav grimaced at the visual, since that was how he felt when Portia was in his proximity.

His reaction to his apprentice didn't make sense. He'd gone years without this . . . whatever it was that made him feel like a grumpy beast skulking around his castle. At meals, it was a battle to keep from glancing at her across the table. And she was smart, too. Interesting. It seemed like anything he, Jamie, or Cheryl brought up she could either discuss or was excited to learn more about. There had been an excitement in her gaze when he'd spoken about Excalibur, a hunger to know more where Tav was usually met with boredom. If Tav had been intent on diving into disaster, he wouldn't have hurried out of the kitchen. He didn't know how he'd face that hunger — not for him, but for his knowledge — when he had to train her, and survive it with his wits intact.

What is it about her? Tav couldn't pinpoint it, and that's what worried him.

He'd once believed in love and all that tripe — he'd thought what he felt for his ex-wife, Greer, would never fade. He'd thought their connection was something that would grow deeper with time, like the roots of a strong oak that delved deep into the earth. Instead it had been uprooted, and not even by a strong gale. Love had just kind of eroded out from under them while they weren't looking, and their marriage had come crashing down with the slightest nudge.

Greer had moved on and seemed happy with her life. Tav had his family and his work and his students; that was all the fulfillment he needed, and it didn't require giving his heart to someone and waiting for the other shoe to drop right onto that vital organ.

But this thing with Portia bothered him. She made him nervous, had him sprung like an old coil that had been rusted down for ages and didn't know how to restrain itself when it got a spritz of lubrication.

Tav turned the corner, onto his street. He could see the armory in the distance and began pushing himself harder, a last sprint to round off the jog. He'd feel it tomorrow — his old knees would make sure of that — but he needed the burn of muscles and lungs to crowd out the other, deeper burn.

This is madness.

Why were thoughts about a woman he barely knew crowding out matters of more importance? He should be worrying about crumbling walls, the leak in Jamie and Cheryl's bathroom, the council tax, and the inspection that would point out every repair needed in the place. The local renaissance faire was in two weeks, and he still hadn't even put an advert in the paper or nailed down a final lineup of students to spar during the exhibitions. Instead, he'd been figuring out *why* he liked someone when in the end it didn't matter. Basic decency said Portia was off-limits, and his own rules of engagement said likewise.

He pushed himself hard, past the people milling about in front of Doctor Hu's with umbrellas, up the stairs and into the armory's alcove, where he found Portia standing with three older women.

"Oh, so there aren't any tours then?" one of them asked, sounding put out. It was something that happened every other week or so.

Portia glanced at him, brows lifting as she took in his panting rain-soaked state, and then turned her attention back to the women. "No, but I do think it's a wonderful idea. It's something we're thinking about setting up. Do you want to sign up for the mailing list?"

Tav wasn't about to turn his home into a tourist trap for strangers, but he gave Portia the benefit of the doubt and assumed that she was just trying to get them to bugger off. Adding them to the mailing list was a good touch, he had to give her that.

The women left, giving Tav a wide berth, and then Portia turned her smile onto him. "Hi."

"Herm." Tav wasn't sure what that sound was even supposed to be, but it was the closest he could come to a greeting. Portia was wearing a T-shirt made of some kind of expensive fabric that managed to be loose and clinging at once. The deep vee exposed her freckled décolletage. Tav wanted to run right back out into the cold rain — Christ, he was the worst kind of creeper.

Greer had once come home agitated and near tears, weeping with anger and shame as she'd told him how her supervisor had leered at her as she'd tried to explain something to him. Tav had thought he wasn't the kind of man that would let his base desires make a woman uncomfortable. He didn't want to *become* that kind of man just because someone he was attracted to now worked with him. Worse, *for* him.

"Thanks for taking care of them," he said, his gaze now on her simple black flats.

"No problem," she said. "Though that wouldn't be a bad idea. I was actually going to ask you if —"

"No," Tav cut her off, meeting her gaze. "No tours."

Tours would mean strangers crawling

around where he worked and steps away from where he lived. It would mean that every crack in the wall, every flake of old paint, every repair that had to be put off until he could afford it would suddenly be given priority.

"You're not even going to hear me out?" she asked.

"Nope. Setting up tours of the armory is about a million and one on the list of things that need to be done around here."

"Well, what exactly are you doing? I've been trying to set up a meeting to figure that out but you keep putting me off."

"I'm busy, lass. Don't have time for messing about. We'll talk next week."

"Next week. Meaning two weeks since my arrival. Okay."

She was annoyed, but it was the disappointment in her tone that grated at him. He faltered.

"Hasn't Jamie given you work to do?"

"Jamie? Your brother, who is not a swordsmith? Yes, he has."

Tav nodded and turned to head toward the stairs. "Well, that's this week sorted then. I'll have something for you next week."

With that he glanced somewhere in the area of that damned nose of hers, nodded, and took off up the stairs. He heard Jamie's voice coming from the kitchen and made a beeline for it. His brother was hunched over a pad of paper that lay on the counter, the cordless landline held to his ear with his shoulder, writing something down.

"I said he's busy, mate. You asking to talk to him again doesn't change that. Do you want to leave the message or no?" He scribbled something down. "Aye. He'll ring back when he can."

He dropped the phone onto its cradle with annoyance.

"What's the script?" Tav asked, trying not to show the panic that surged through him. Had it been a call about the taxes? About the work that needed to be done on the building, or collections inquiring about his maxed-out credit card? He thought those would all go to his decrepit cell phone, but sometimes bill collectors got pushy . . .

Jamie straightened and when he spoke his voice took on a pompous air. " 'I'm calling once again on behalf of Mr. Douglas, with a new, increased offer on the property.' "

Tav slumped a bit in relief.

"They're offering more? Fuck's sake, what part of no don't they understand?" Tav scrubbed a hand through his wet hair.

"You know these rich knobs. They can't take no for an answer." Jamie's face was taut with annoyance, and he looked so much like their mother that Tav couldn't help but chuckle.

"Well, no is the only answer they're gonna get, aye?" Tav said. "I'd sell the armory to a stranger for a pound if it meant this Mr. Douglas wouldn't get his hands on it."

There was an awkward silence and when he glanced over, Jamie was staring at him.

"Are you really thinking of selling?"

Tav could imagine the thoughts running through his brother's head. What would happen to the classes Jamie was working so hard to build up? And Cheryl's food stand, that was just beginning to take off? Where would they live, and how would they rebuild? They were the same questions that had been plaguing Tav over the last few months. The property was his, but so many others depended on him. Cheryl. Jamie. The neighborhood kids and his students.

"Ach, no! It was just a hypothetical," he said cheerfully. He realized too late that he wore cheerful like an ill-fitting jacket, and changed the subject. "Speaking of rich annoying people, I have a question for you. Why her?"

"Who?" Jamie said, his gaze sliding to the counter. He turned to the little pile of greens, carrots, and bananas sitting on a cutting board and began loading them into the blender.

"Is there another *her* who's moved in recently?" Tav asked. "I've asked before and you keep dodging the question."

"Oh. Portia. She had the most thorough application," he said. "Most people said 'Swords are cool!' or 'I've always wanted to go to Edinburgh' or 'Looks like fun!' Or there was some sad story about why they deserved it; it was hard to reject those. She was the only one who sent a clear reason for why she was interested, what she hoped to learn from it, and also what skills she thought we could learn from her. It was impressive, mate. Also, I just had a . . . vibe, I guess. She was the best fit."

"A vibe. What the hell, Jamie?"

Jamie shrugged and Tav knew that was the only answer he'd get.

"You have all the non-*vibe* info anywhere?" Tav asked.

"*You* have this info. In your email. Along with all the other emails you've been ignoring. Seriously, bruv, it's been days since she arrived, months since she was selected, and you're just now really digging into this?"

Well, yes. Tav had been hoping that maybe the problem would sort itself out. But Portia wasn't a problem. She was a person in his

85

employ and she deserved the minimum respect of him knowing what she was about, even if she did get under his skin like splintered steel.

"I guess I'll give it a look," Tav said, which was met with a mock gasp from Jamie.

"Tavish McKenzie, agreeing to check his email with no threat of mutilation. That's *something.*"

"Jamie," Tav growled.

"Next time Mum and Da' ask me why you haven't returned their emails, as if they're just down the street and not all the way in Santiago, maybe I'll tell them to send it Subject: Portia Hobbs, yeah?" Jamie pressed on with a waggle of his brows.

"Oh, shut up and make me a smoothie," Tav said.

"Shutting. Up." That didn't stop Jamie from grinning as the whir of the blender filled the kitchen.

Brothers were really the worst.

CHAPTER 5

"What do you mean there's no Wi-Fi?"

Portia gripped the cup of watery, luke-warm coffee she'd served herself and looked around Mary's snug little bookshop, with its pastry nook and comfy seating. The walls were lined with shelves so stuffed with books that they seemed to be art installa-tions, and old, warm-bulbed lamps hung from the ceiling. Portia had thought it would be the perfect spot to relax and get some work done on her second GirlsWith-Glasses travel post and her brainstorming for the armory's website, but apparently not.

"Well," Mary said, pausing in bagging the books she'd dug up for Portia, "I believe in old-fashioned connection, not internet con-nection. Everyone having their faces glued to their phones all the time is unhealthy. If people want to read, this is a bookstore, love."

She said it in a pleasant tone that implied

that she would cut anyone who tried to argue otherwise. This was backed up by the large box cutter on the counter in front of her.

"Right," Portia said, taking the handles of the plastic bag with her purchases in it. She could use her phone as a mobile hot spot, but she didn't have an unlimited data plan and, honestly, what kind of shop didn't have Wi-Fi? She wasn't going to butt in, though. After all, this was New Portia, who didn't stick her nose in other people's business all the time and worried about fixing her own flaws. But . . .

The bookshop was beautiful — it had the shabby chic atmosphere that trendy boutiques all over Brooklyn tried to replicate, but with the warm, cozy feeling that came with real aged wood and worn-in furniture. She knew Bodotria had a healthy number of young freelancers and artists, people who worked from home who would probably jump at the chance to work elsewhere. It seemed criminal not to mention a possible source of revenue.

Her motivations weren't entirely altruistic, though. She needed a place where she could get away from the armory, and whatever weird tension there was between her and Tavish.

"Besides," Mary continued, hefting a box from the pile of deliveries beside the counter and placing it in front of her, "I don't want a bunch of people sitting around cluttering up the place."

Portia looked around the shop, empty on a Saturday afternoon, then sighed.

"I don't mean to be nosy —"

"Then don't be," Mary sang cheerily, stabbing her blade into the tape on the box.

Portia sighed. "Okay, I do mean to be. I was looking for a place to work on my own away from the armory."

Mary paused and looked at Portia. "Is Tavish giving you any trouble?"

"No! Not at all." That was part of the problem. Tavish had barely talked to her over the last week. He was always either locked away in his workshop or in his office or giving lessons in the gym — he was, it seemed, any place Portia was not.

When he was in her vicinity, he directed most of his conversation to Jamie and Cheryl, or to the floor. After a few rebuffs, Portia had stopped trying to engage him. She shouldn't have cared, but it hurt her feelings to be boxed out like that, especially when she had already seen that he was capable of making pleasant conversation.

She'd imagined herself showing up in

Scotland, winning everyone over with her mysterious New Portia ways. Instead, she'd immediately proven herself a liability and annoyance to Tavish and would be treated as such for the remainder of her apprenticeship. He hadn't even chosen her for the job — that shouldn't have stung either, but he clearly wasn't thrilled with Jamie's decision.

It didn't matter, though. She'd only be there for a few months, and then she'd . . . do what? She didn't know exactly. A speedbump loomed beyond a curve in the road for New Portia — what she was *really* going to do with her life — but she'd figure it out.

She focused on Mary again. "I just like having a space away from where I live to work. A lot of younger people do."

"Is that your way of telling me I'm old and out of touch?" Mary asked archly.

Portia took stock of the situation; Mary was about as prickly as Tavish when it came to taking advice about her business it seemed, and honestly, Portia was in Scotland to make swords, supposedly, not to help reluctant strangers. She should apologize and just go about her business.

She dropped her elbows onto the counter and leaned toward Mary.

"Age has nothing to do with it, actually. The new coffee shop down the street is run by a man older than you, and it has Wi-Fi. And really good, strong coffee. It's also packed right now."

Mary drew herself up and looked down her nose at Portia for a long moment. Portia was not unaware that the woman was holding a sharp object.

"I see," Mary said. She retracted the box cutter and lifted her chin. "Sorry for being so touchy. There've been people sniffing about lately, telling me my business can't survive here and that I should just sell to them as I'm getting on in years."

How the neighborhood was being gentrified was something she'd heard Tavish, Jamie, and Cheryl discussing over dinner. She'd listened awkwardly, wondering if they knew about her parents' real estate ventures or how much property she owned in neighborhoods that had once been like Bodotria: emerging, as realtors liked to call them. She'd thought herself conscientious, someone who gave back and participated in her community, but she hadn't really questioned what exactly the hoods were emerging from and who was left behind when they did. Her parents made sure there was low-income housing in their rentals and that they minimized displacement, but was it enough? Could anything be?

"Are you looking to sell? Or is someone trying to force you into it?" Portia asked.

"The latter, I suppose. There's one thing you should know about me, though, Portia love," Mary replied.

Portia was scared to ask, given the borderline frightening grin that Mary was sporting. "Um, what's that?"

"I'm a spiteful old thing. I've been here since this neighborhood was called the Armpit of Edinburgh, when yuppies came through to gawk at the poor, pick up drugs, and for the thrill of maybe seeing a rumble.

"I don't like asking for help, but if you're offering advice other than 'sell to the highest bidder' . . ." Mary heaved a sigh. "If perhaps I *did* decide to allow wastrels to come in and bleed my internet dry, how would I go about doing that?"

Portia's quick stop at the bookshop had turned into an hour helping Mary look up affordable internet plans and better wholesale coffee, which then led to a discussion of ways she could bring in more customers. Portia had left Mary to call the owner of the wine shop down the street in order to arrange a book/wine pairing event, and was headed back to the armory when her phone rang.

The fact that she was receiving an actual call, and not an email, text, or video message from someone with a puppy filter over their face, meant it could only be one of two people.

She glanced at the incoming call flashing on the screen, and a familiar mix of happiness and aversion assailed her as she swiped to accept the call.

"Hi, Dad," she said, putting the phone up to her ear. "You're up early."

"Hey, pumpkin." Dennis Hobbs was a businessman who had succeeded in a sector that tried, and often succeeded, at keeping men like him out. He could be cold, arrogant, and ruthless — he wouldn't have survived otherwise. But his Dad tone was warm and loving, and almost lured Portia into lowering her defenses. Almost. "Your mother and I just wanted to check in and see how your little trip was going."

Little trip. There it was.

"My *apprenticeship* is going great. Scotland is beautiful." She hadn't seen much of it outside of the armory, but she was sure it was. "I've already launched a few projects to increase revenue for the business, and I'm working closely with my boss to come up with an entirely new marketing program."

Okay, so none of those projects had been approved yet, and "working closely" meant "working in the same general latitude/longitude point on a map since he's avoiding me," but whatever. She'd had way more intense internships, and a stubborn man wasn't some newfangled invention. She'd get through to him eventually, or Jamie, who actually seemed interested in her plans, would.

Her dad made a familiar sound, something like a chuckle mixed with an indulgent sigh. "As long as you're having fun. But you know, we have Regina's investment analyst position here waiting for you. We have a temp doing it now, since your sister's media empire is really taking off and she's decided to do that full time."

Little trip. Media empire. Portia and Reggie's relationship with their parents could be summed up in four words, it seemed. Reggie had always been the twin that got things done. Portia hadn't been able to unless she was interested in them, or after putting them off for a few days, or weeks, or months.

"We're going to need someone serious to take on the position, and we think it should be you," her father said.

Pleased surprise tentatively fluttered in

her chest. She didn't want the job, but the fact that her parents were going to trust her to handle it had to mean something, didn't it? This was their business after all. Maybe Project: New Portia had already begun to pay dividends.

"I know you don't have a serious bone in your body, but your mother and I think this could be good for you," her father continued, carelessly crushing that happiness with the weight of his words. "Really get you into a routine, you know? We just want to see you settled down."

She was well aware. They'd made it abundantly clear before she left.

"It's only three months, I suppose, but really, when are you going to get serious about your life? When we were your age, we were already married, parents, and starting our second business."

"Your mother's right, Portia. We've indulged you for years but . . . you're almost thirty. Enough with the grad school, and the internships, and the 'experience.' You need to make some decisions about what you're going to do with your life. Just look at how well Regina's doing, and you don't even have her . . . . issues."

She closed her eyes for a second, the disappointment rearing up over her and making her feel small and silly in its shadow. They were right. What was she even doing in Scotland? Project: New Portia was about getting on track for her future, but what future could come from this? It wasn't like Tavish thought her any more capable than her parents did.

A familiar, clawing shame raked its nails down her back and over her shoulders, leaving tension in its wake.

"Portia?" Her father sounded concerned. Of course he was. He'd been saddled with a ridiculous daughter who thought a sword-making apprenticeship was a step in the *right* direction.

"Yeah. Of course. I'll think about the position and let you know soon."

"I suppose swords might be more lucrative than real estate." Her father's voice was jokey, but there was that edge of tension that reminded her how many times she'd told her parents she'd *think about* something in the past. For her, thinking about things often meant putting it off until she forgot what she'd even been asked to do.

"Dad, can you send some more info about the job? I'll do some research. I . . . yeah, it sounds like something I could see myself doing." She usually reserved her research for things that actually interested her, but she could do this for her parents.

"Of course, pumpkin." The pleasure in his voice made her throat go rough. She didn't want the job — she knew that — but would it be so bad? She could make her family happy. She'd get to see them more, and maybe they would actually be proud of her instead of feigning interest in whatever she was dabbling in at the moment.

That was nice in theory, but then she imagined the reality: going into the office every day and having her parents ask her to do important things while totally expecting her to screw them up. Walking on eggshells to make sure her ideas weren't too outside the box, too silly, and throwing her own dreams, hazy as they were, out in order to please her parents. That hypothetical future — constantly being held up to what her parents thought she should be capable of, but also never being able to forget her own past mistakes — made her body tense and her stomach start to ache. Disappointing her family from a distance was bad enough. Did they really want her doing it on a daily basis?

"Great. I'll keep an eye out for the email," she said. "I have to go work, Dad. Love you!"

She disconnected the call, feeling suddenly exhausted even though she'd already acclimated to the New York City/Edinburgh time difference. Echoes of previous conversations with her parents bounced around in her head.

"Maybe we shouldn't have let her have access to the trust until she was thirty," her mother had said before she boarded her flight to Scotland. *"Just look at everything Regina has done, and Portia is still flitting around like a butterfly."*

One of the downfalls of the whole "gestating in the same womb" thing, apart from the matching outfits throughout childhood, was that her parents had always seen Reggie as a handy measuring stick instead of a completely different human with different strengths. Reggie had always been the smart twin, the levelheaded twin, the one who could impress with her immense knowledge and humor and common sense. And then she'd gotten sick, and after that it had been even more pronounced. Portia's B's and C's had been nice, but Reggie had maintained her A average *despite.* Portia's latest internship was interesting, but had she seen that Reggie had made another thirty under thirty list, *despite?*

She knew the truth that lay beneath the *despite,* though no one had ever really said it aloud. She'd overheard her mother on the phone, voice gravelly with exhaustion as she sat in the hospital waiting room. *"What if we lose her? Regina was the one with so much potential. No, that didn't come out right . . ."* Portia had thought the same thing. She'd thought it as Reggie lay in the pediatric ICU, hooked up to tube and machines, while Portia with her perfect health began to fuck up even more. She'd thought it when Reggie was graduating magna cum laude and she was a year behind after switching colleges twice. She'd been running from that thought for years, a trail of mistakes in her wake. She could hardly blame them for it.

Her phone vibrated. Reggie had messaged, as if summoned by Portia's angst.

Reggie: Hey, I just read through the first post you sent. It's great! People are going to love it! ☺

Portia braced herself — her sister was kind, but not bubbly, and the exclamations/ smiley face combo meant she was softening a blow. Had she hated the piece? She'd wanted to make Reggie proud . . .

Reggie: And

Reggie: I appreciate you trying to appeal to the geeks on the site

Reggie: Buuut

Portia: Oh no. What did I do wrong?

Reggie: What? You didn't do anything WRONG. Geez.

Reggie: Just

Reggie: The character Banshee is Irish, not Scottish. I'm going to stick in a reference to Moira MacTaggert and mention that you felt like you were being banished to Muir island.

Portia: Have no idea where that is but sounds good.

Reggie: And a tardigrade is a microanimal. A TARDIS is the time and space travel machine from Doctor Who (Doctor, not Dr.–that's his name, not his title), though the food at Cheryl's "Doctor Hu's" stand looks amazing. I might commission an additional piece on this for the Foodie section . . .

Portia: 😌 Thanks for catching those errors and saving me from being ripped apart in the comments, lol.

Reggie: No prob. You know I'm always here to 'Well, actually' you on these matters.

Portia: . . .

Reggie: Well, on any matter, I guess.

Portia: lol

Reggie: Speaking of, one of our contributors started a video channel. I just shared the latest video and thought of your whole "New Portia" thing. Maybe it would be helpful? Talk to ya later!

Portia clicked on the link that popped up, which led to a video entitled *Hot Mess Helper.*

She'd been feeling a little better after the brief text chat, but damn, Reggie could be blunt sometimes. She hit play because, why not? What was one more reminder of her perpetual fuckupitude?

A wide-eyed Latinx woman with brown

skin and perfect contouring stared out from the screen with a look of exaggerated horror. "Heyyyyyyyyy, it's Caridad, or as you'll come to know me, your personal hot mess helper."

Portia rolled her eyes and moved her thumb to hit the pause button, but then Caridad grinned and shook her head. "Don't get offended! I'm one of you! Let's see what we have in common." She held up her hands, hitting her right index finger against the fingers of the left as she began her list. "Always missing deadlines? Fuck yeah. Is 'Impulsive' your middle name? Yup! Do you constantly forget to pay your bills, even though the money is just chillin' in your bank account? Come on, you know you could have paid that shit three months ago. Can you play guitar, paint a still life in watercolor AND oil, and bake a seventeen-layer cake, but can't remember to move your laundry to the dryer?"

Caridad paused for emphasis and Portia simply stared, shook. She felt personally attacked. The cake she had baked had only been ten layers, but still . . .

"Maybe you're a lazy, selfish, fucked-up hot mess. Or maybe . . ." Caridad looked around conspiratorially, then tapped her finger against her forehead. ". . . it's just how your brain is wired. And maybe there's nothing wrong with that. Maybe there's nothing wrong with *you*."

Portia paused the video again, tears stinging at her eyes as she tucked her phone into her bag. She'd watch the rest later. This was all too close to home and too much to take in at once. It was nice to think this might be true, that Portia was just wired differently, but she had years of evidence and a string of eyewitnesses who would testify to the contrary. She had just never tried hard enough — everyone knew that. And now she was trying, legit trying, and things still weren't going to plan.

Portia worked her bottom lip with her teeth, the press of enamel just a touch below painful. The description of her mistakes had been so accurate, though. Maybe the explanation was, too?

She was so deep in thought that she would have passed the armory by if she hadn't bumped into Cheryl, who was dragging one of the bistro tables they stored in the courtyard toward her sidewalk shop.

The blue wooden police box Portia had seen upon first arrival served as Cheryl's restaurant. She'd retrofitted it with a small kitchen setup, though she used the kitchen in the armory for large-scale prep and storage. She had a rotating menu of *Doctor Who*–themed Chinese entrees and made brisk business with locals and tourists alike.

Portia jogged up to help Cheryl with the table.

"Ta, Portia," Cheryl said cheerfully, fishing a few sauce bottles from her deep apron pocket and placing them on the table once it was settled. "How's your weekend? Did you explore the neighborhood?"

"The weekend's good," Portia said, pushing the conversation with her father and the snippet of video she had just watched out of her mind. "I haven't really explored yet. I just came from visiting with Mary and stayed longer than I thought, and now I have to work."

Cheryl frowned.

"But I've been to the supermarket and the Chip Shop. I'm planning to go to New Town and do some shopping soon, too."

Cheryl glanced at Portia. "I wish you'd take some time to see the sights, and all. You've been fiddling with the database since you got here! It's that American work ethic, I guess."

"Yeah," Portia said a bit sheepishly. She had spent the first two days designing beautiful, mentally ergonomic spreadsheets for the database . . . and then the last three slowly transferring the data, which was her own personal hell. She would have been done, but there was always something to look up for the website, or a sword design schematic she wondered about, or a neighborhood history question . . .

"To be honest, I didn't think there'd be much for an apprentice to do, but you're finding all kinds of stuff without even touching a scrap of metal!" Cheryl said this with bright-eyed enthusiasm, but then winced when she realized she'd touched a sore spot. "I'm sure Tavish will start teaching you soon. He's just been busy."

"How was your morning?" Portia asked. She didn't want to talk about Tavish's crystal-clear avoidance of her.

Cheryl windmilled one of her arms. "I'm a little sore from the broadsword practice this morning, but I think we're ready for the exhibition. What about you? Do you need to borrow a dress? A corset?"

Portia had no idea what Cheryl was talking about. "Exhibition?"

The front door to the building opened then, and Kevyn walked out, hair mussed and sweaty as he demonstrated some sort of swinging sword move to Tavish, who followed him. Tavish was also sweaty, but for some reason he wore the sheen of sweat like a fine suit.

Cheryl waved her hands dramatically to get their attention. "Tav! You didn't tell your apprentice about the exhibition?"

Portia could already feel the embarrassment gathering in the air, ready to rain down on her.

Tav turned, and his gaze flicked from Cheryl to Portia. His aggravation with her very presence was etched into the scowl lines that deepened on each side of his lush mouth as he looked at her. "Aye, I told her. Told her that's what you and I were practicing for a week ago."

He had mentioned an exhibition during that first meeting, but he hadn't elaborated and Portia had been too busy imagining her humiliating return home.

"Well, did you invite her?" Cheryl asked archly.

Tav chuckled ruefully. "Why would I do that? So she could barrel into the middle of a match and attack someone again?"

Kevyn laughed, too, shaking his head as he took a seat at one of the tables. "Because she bloody works here?"

The tension that had started to release its grip on her back and shoulders readjusted and dug its claws in even deeper. Getting talked down to by your father over the phone was one thing, but being humiliated by your boss in front of people you barely knew was quite another.

"And because I run your social media and need to promote special events, like a public exhibition," she added, trying to hide the hurt in her voice. She was a grown ass woman, and even when she didn't feel like one she still had to keep up appearances. "And because I could help out."

Tav sighed and rolled his neck. "I don't have time to manage the exhibition matches, answer questions, handle sales, *and* watch over you."

She didn't think he was trying to be mean, but it was like he instinctively knew she was the kind of woman always teetering on the edge of disaster. As if he could tell that fucking up came naturally to her. *"I know you don't have a serious bone in your body, but . . ."*

Tav glanced at her and his expression changed. Softened just a little bit. "What're you looking at me like that for? I simply don't have time to mess about."

"Tavish," Cheryl said, her voice low with warning. "You're being a wanker."

"No. He's right," Portia cut in before he could respond. She wasn't sure how she managed to keep the waver out of her voice, but she could be proud of at least one thing. It was likely smoothed over by the flash of anger that currently had her in its thrall. "If Tavish is incapable of explaining basic things to his apprentice, it's probably best that I don't go."

"Wait a minute —"

"I mean, it's not like I've streamlined the databases and reorganized the shipping process to save money over the past week because I'm apparently too silly to bother teaching swordmaking to. It's not like I upended my life to move to a strange country, expressly to learn a new skill, only to be told I'm not capable of handling something that a child running a lemonade stand is entrusted with. So yeah, maybe it's best I don't go to the exhibition. Wouldn't want to inconvenience anyone."

Her eyes were glossy with unprofessional tears and she wanted more than anything to disappear, or perhaps get carried away by a passing flock of birds. She felt ridiculous. She *was* ridiculous. She'd traveled thousands of miles just to be reminded that at the end of the day, Portia Hobbs wasn't the kind of person you counted on — a lesson she'd learned well enough in the US of A.

Cheryl and Kevyn were silent — the *oh shit this is awkward do we stick around or make ourselves scarce* kind of silent. Tavish sighed and dropped into the seat beside Kevyn.

She was ready to go inside and pack her bags. If she stayed, he might see her cry, and she'd been humiliated enough for one day. She had a job waiting for her in New York after all, not that she would embarrass herself any less at that one.

"Come here, Freckles." He looked up at her. "Please."

She walked over stiffly and sat down across from him, not meeting his gaze.

"The problem is . . . ."

She braced herself. She should stop him. She knew her own faults better than anyone and didn't need to hear them listed out.

". . . that I'm a bit of an arse. Grumpy. Stubborn. Recalcitrant — I'm sure you've got a thesaurus on your electronic hingmie."

"What?" Portia asked. She had been so ready to be told about her faults that she had no response to Tav listing off his own.

He folded his hands together and spoke to her like he was taking her concerns seriously, something she hadn't been expecting at all. "I'm used to working with my family, and my family is used to said arseyness."

Cheryl had gone inside the food stand to continue setting up for lunch, but she made a sound of annoyance at that. "That's no excuse! You're supposed to treat your family with kindness, you muppet."

Tav shot her a look, then turned his attention back to Portia. His expression was . . . contrite?

"I'm not suddenly going to be puking rainbows and hearts, but you're right. I haven't been a good boss. I pushed everything off onto Jamie and then left you to figure out the rest. If my master had done that during my apprenticeship, none of us would be here right now because I wouldn't have become a swordmaker."

"Are you apologizing?" Kevyn asked incredulously. He turned to Portia. "Did you hit him in the head when you maced him the other day, love?"

"I'm not *apologizing*. I'm saying that my behavior has been shit and I'll try to do better." His gaze was on Portia and even though he was frowning, she could see the slightest hint of vulnerability.

Fuck. No! Unfortunately, it seemed that "gruff but vulnerable" was a trait she could really appreciate in a man. She ignored the way her breath caught and reminded herself that *gruff* was a synonym for "acts like an asshole because other people enable him."

"That sounds like an apology," she said,

then worked her bottom lip with her teeth. New Portia didn't do enabling. "But if you're really trying to be a better boss you can give me a real one."

She felt the sudden, ingrained shame of having asked for something she wanted, but fought against it and waited.

Tav cleared his throat and inhaled deeply. "I'm sorry that I treated you like one of these knuckleheads instead of like a delicate flower," he replied, eyes narrowed. "How's that work?"

"Works great if it means I'm getting the delicate flower treatment from now on," she shot back, and was shocked to see a ruddy pink begin to spread over both of his cheeks.

Shit. Gruff but vulnerable Tavish was bad enough, but flustered and blushing Tavish landed a direct hit on all her attraction buttons, pushing down on them with the pressure of a sonic boom. She sucked in a breath.

Actually, both are your boss and both are off-limits.

Tavish slapped his hands on the table and stood. "Right then. I've got work to do. Kev, you can tell her about the exhibition."

With that he was up and swaggering back into the armory, moving quickly for such a big man.

111

"Ha!" Kevyn looked at Portia with wide eyes. "I just witnessed a miracle. The taming of Tavish."

"I don't do taming," Portia said nonchalantly. "That requires time and effort that I could be putting into myself."

"Are you both hungry? I have some tasty ribs on the menu today!" Cheryl called out.

Kevyn raised his brows. "Do you want to grab a bite while I tell you about the exhibition?"

Portia had writing and research to do, and should really finish those damn spreadsheets, but work could wait.

"Sure," she said, then turned to Cheryl. "Can I have some dumplings with the ribs?"

Cheryl carried over their plates and joined them at the table, ready to spring from her seat if any customers approached.

"So. What are your feelings about renaissance faires? I know they're dorky and everything but —"

Portia held up a hand to cut her off.

"Cheryl, I think there's been some misunderstanding," Portia said. "I'm not a geek, but I *am* a dork. There's a ren faire every year at this park near where my friend Ledi lived in Manhattan, and I used to drag her along with me."

Cheryl clapped with glee and Portia bit

into the delicious lunch she'd been served. She could worry about Tavish and his weird behavior later. She had somehow come out of their conversation the victor, and she was going to celebrate.

CHAPTER 6

Tavish had been grinding in his workshop for hours and the restless energy hadn't left him. Two weeks of body-intensive labor, really putting his back into production and sparring, plus a newfound interest in jogging, and he still hadn't gotten the sudden, simmering need that had coincided with Portia's arrival out of his system.

He turned on the power grinder and began the first passes of the *sgian-dubh* blade over the whirring, textured surface, smoothing away the imperfections in the metal. Someone had placed a somewhat substantial order for the small traditional daggers, and he was trying to get them out as quickly as possible, before the customer could change their mind. With his recent business luck, he couldn't risk delay or sending out anything but perfect products.

He tried to clear his mind of everything else but the work before him. He braced himself against the shock that ran up the tang, gripped tightly in his hand, and reverberated through his body. Beveling the edge of the blade to make it sharp required slightly less concentration than other parts of the process. It required focus, like everything he did, but years of experience meant that stray thoughts of his business woes, or of his apprentice, wouldn't result in the loss of hours of work.

Portia. Something about her clung to him like the fine steel mist thrown off by the grinder that was a pain in the arse to wash away. He was interested in her, and that talk of treating her like a delicate flower hadn't helped. He wasn't one to keep floral arrangements about the house, but he knew that you nourished flowers and in return you got to inhale their fragrance and run your fingertips over their soft petals. He didn't need to think about either of those things when it came to his apprentice.

He growled, twisting his wrist to turn the blade back and forth. He didn't mind getting dull with age, but was he really all hot and bothered about a snooty American? Pish. It was infatuation, like when he saw a well-made sword with an ornate hilt and brilliant artwork etched into the blade. Beautiful, but not essential.

Essential or not, he had to train her. That's what she was here for. For the last two weeks he'd had her working on updating databases and shipping and anything that would keep her behind a desk and out of his sight. He'd admitted to being a bad boss, but the only thing he'd done to change it was growling slightly less when in her presence. Even that had him worried. Growls served as a warning to keep potentially dangerous creatures at bay. If he stopped, she might figure out that he was bloody terrified.

He turned off the grinder and examined the blade, running his thumb along the bevel. Still a little rough, but he needed to take a break. He placed the knife onto a soft towel on his worktable and was in the process of removing his protective ear coverings when a sudden, animal awareness went through him.

He turned, still holding the ear coverings over his head, and there she was.

Dammit.

She leaned against the doorway of his workshop, quite comfortably, as if she'd been there for some time. She held a folder or something to her chest, but Tav fixated on the way her lips were parted and her eyes were fixed on him.

Her gaze skittered to the ground, but in the second during which they'd locked eyes, Tav had felt *it* like a solid thing knocking into him. *Desire.* He wasn't a fucking mind reader, but he was old enough to know when someone was giving him the eye. Portia had been thinking something decidedly naughty. About him.

Fuck's sake.

"Need something?" he asked, sounding more aggrieved than he'd meant to.

She stepped forward, expression polite and professional. Good. Between their age difference and the fact that she was working for him, Tav had no interest in knowing what exactly had been going through her mind a moment ago. He wasn't trying to become some kind of midlife crisis cliché.

"I was talking to Jamie about the website and he said that my initial plans look good, but nothing could be changed without your approval."

Website?

"The site is fine as it is," he said, glad she'd landed on the topic most like being dunked in ice-cold water for him.

"Actually, it's not. It's really not."

"It lists our name, phone number, and address, and it has pictures of the products and their prices. What else does it need?"

She opened her folder and pulled out a slim, sleek tablet.

"I should have known you'd have that hingmie with you," he muttered as she approached. She always seemed to have her nose stuck in her phone or tablet, and her tapping away at a keyboard was generally what alerted him to her presence around the building, allowing him to avoid her.

She leaned back against the table next to him, leaving a bit of space between them. That didn't stop the scent of whatever perfume she was wearing from drifting over to him. Delicate. Floral.

Tav sighed.

"So. Here is your site," she said, pulling it up.

He glanced over to placate her, but what he saw drew a grunt of perplexed disgust from him.

"Why do the pictures look stretched like?" he asked, taking the proffered tablet from her. It looked like someone had copied the photos on Silly Putty then pulled.

"Because you're not optimized for mobile. You also have a weird pop-up that blocks the site and is really hard to close out unless you're on a desktop or have a large screen." She took her tablet back, as if she didn't quite trust him not to drop the thing.

118

"The majority of hits to the site these days are coming from mobile devices, in case you were wondering."

"The pop-up is for people to sign up to be notified about sales," he explained. That's what the designer had told him when Jamie had forced him to commission a site upgrade. He couldn't remember the last time he'd actually had a sale or even looked at the email addresses that had been compiled. "Can't people just look at it on their laptop?"

"I guess they could. But when I navigate to a site that I can't access because of a pop-up like that, I keep it moving and find a store that cares enough not to annoy me. Customers are fickle. You shouldn't make them work to see what you're selling."

Tav couldn't argue with that. "Okay, so you want me to . . . optimize for mobile, then? Because of the hits?"

"Well, no. I want to make a completely new site." She swiped her fingertip over the screen and now he was looking at a different site. It had his business's name on it but bore no relation to the monstrosity she'd just clicked away from. It looked clean and modern, but with a background like a faded medieval tapestry to give it an aged look. Simple but engaging. He didn't know tech, but he knew what good, solid design looked like.

"This is just a mock-up," she explained as she scrolled. "But there'll be a separate page for the armory, with detailed lists of products — I'll talk more about that later. One page for the European martial arts lessons. Another for Jamie's workout classes. A history page, with information about the armory building itself, and the history of Scottish swordmaking. And there'll also be a gallery with photos and videos, like of Jamie giving a quick workout lesson that people can do at home, and you in action with that thing."

She inclined her head toward the grinder. Tav abruptly pushed off of the table to face her. "Why do I need to be recorded?"

Her brows raised again. He had the oddest compulsion to smooth his fingertip over one dark arch as it scrunched in annoyance.

"You don't have to do anything but what you were doing just now, except I'll be recording a couple of minutes of it."

"And throwing it up on the internet for everyone to gawk at. I don't see the point of it," he said, shaking his head. "Jamie's lessons I understand, I suppose — people can get a taste of the boot camp and see how fun it is. But I'm certainly not inviting strangers here to grind with me."

Portia licked her lips, then pressed them together.

"Actually, I was invited here to grind with you, as you put it," she said. More brow scrunching — he was fairly certain she was capable of carrying a conversation with just her eyebrows. "But since you're too worried that I'm going to cut you, in the meantime I'm trying to set you up with a website that will attract potential buyers. And if what I just watched is any indication, video of a large, attractive man using a power tool to hone a sharp object is going to induce a significant portion of the population to at the very least click, and some portion of those who click to buy."

Tav's throat went dry. She was giving him that look again and, worse, he didn't think it was on purpose. Her gaze passed over his body and her chest rose and fell as she took a deep breath.

"How long were you watching me before?" he asked. His voice came out low — much too close to a groan for his liking.

"A few minutes." Her voice had gone quiet, too. "At first, I didn't want to bother you, but then I was peeping because you still haven't let me do any work in here and I wanted to see what I was missing out on. I thought there'd be more banging." Her eyes went wide and she glanced away. "With hammers. On a forge."

Tav blinked against the image of Portia bent over his forge, that look of determination he'd glimpsed at the boot camp on her face. He had to hope that she'd be so bad at swordmaking that he'd get to kick her out of the workshop.

She grinned suddenly — this time she knew what she was doing, he could tell. The heat in her eyes was replaced by a friendly glimmer. A challenge. "Come on. People will watch the video. They'll tell their friends to watch the videos. And then they'll buy the fruits of your labor."

Tav took a step closer to her, and that step was so natural that he realized he'd been holding himself away from her the entire time. He leaned in a bit, caught a hint of that scent that seemed so out of place in his workshop. "Are you saying you want me to use my sexy body to hawk my wares, Freckles?"

She held his gaze for a moment, then her head moved an inch closer to his . . . as she burst into laughter. Her forehead grazed his shoulder, and when she lifted it away, there were tears of mirth in her eyes and a smudge of metallic filings on her forehead. "Can you say that again? Please?"

Tavish crossed his arms over his chest, mostly to resist the urge to wipe the smudge away.

"Muh sexay buhdy," she said, squaring her shoulders up in what he supposed was an imitation of him, then broke character as laughter took her again. "I'm sorry, that's really adorable."

He would have kicked her out if he wasn't enjoying her uninhibited joy so much. And she had called him adorable. Not a descriptor he'd had tossed his way in recent years.

"My sexy body," he repeated, laying the burr on thick, and was rewarded with Portia's renewed laughter. He turned and started cleaning his workspace so she wouldn't see the broad smile on his face.

"I'm sorry. You can make fun of my accent too if you want," she said.

"Oh, I don't need your permission, *dude,*" he replied, knowing he sounded more Valley Girl than New Yorker. "Did you need anything else?"

She shifted from one foot to the other. "You're cool with me relaunching the site, then?"

"Do what you want, Freckles. I don't know much about tech shite, but what you've made looks good, professional, and like it took a lot of work. Thank you."

She stared at him and he shifted uncomfortably. He could be an arse, but was praise from him that off-putting?

"Thank you?" she said.

"Aye."

"Oh! Your ludditeness reminds me. I stopped by Mary's shop again and she had a book for you." She pulled a small velvet sack from her shoulder bag and handed it to him.

"Mary's catering to the hipster crowd now, is she?" he asked, running his hand over the bag.

"Oh, the bag's mine," Portia said. "I mean, she is trying to bring in some new business, actually. That's what I was talking to her about. But she said it was a rare book that you'd been searching for a while, so I thought maybe it should be handled with care."

Tavish rubbed his thumb over the book, feeling the velvety fabric covering it bristle beneath his fingertips. He could make Portia out to be a pain in the arse all he wanted, but she was a pain who had tried to do right by him so far. The least he could do was try to be cordial and act like a grown man in control of his libido.

He grabbed a tissue, reached out, and

roughly swiped away the smudge from her forehead. Not exactly treating her like a delicate flower, but he didn't want to know what her skin felt like beneath his fingertips. If he knew that, he'd have to find out more. He'd always found it hard to let go of anything his curiosity snagged on, and he was certain Portia wouldn't be the exception to that rule.

"What —"

He turned the tissue, showing her the metal filings, and she drew the heel of her hand over where he'd swiped, looking at him with those wide eyes again.

"Thanks. For the book. And the website, and all," he said gruffly.

She gave him a quick nod, turned on her heels, and then stopped, looking back over her shoulder. "Thanks for trusting me to do this."

Then she was gone.

CHAPTER 7

[International Friend Emporium group chat]

Ledi: Portia. What is this video? I just woke up, my brain isn't ready for all of this.

Nya: *fans self* I never thought I would enjoy watching a man use a power tool, but perhaps access to the Home and Garden channel here in the States has warped my brain.

Portia: that's my boss guys

Portia: THAT'S MY BOSS

Portia: ☹

Nya: Wait, this is the jerk you've been going on about for three weeks? Girrrrrrrrl. You said he was attractive, but you've been holding out.

Ledi: Um. I love Thabiso very much, but your boss could get it. Hold my crown. *limbers up*

Portia: What have I done to deserve this speedbump on the road to Project: New Portia?

Ledi: . . .

Ledi: Do you want the annotated list or the summary? I have to finish this thesis but I can find the time.

Portia: ☹

Ledi: ☻

Nya: Is everything else going okay, besides your boss being fine af?

Ledi: Nya, where are you picking up this lingo? You need to stop hanging out on Tumblr.

Nya: I can't win. You made fun of me

when I said a man steams my head-
wrap. ☹

Ledi: LOLOL

Portia: LMFAO

Ledi told them about the latest Thesoloian
intrigue, something involving goat poop
recycling, and her studies. Nya recounted
her latest dates and the newest dating
simulator game she'd found — *Byronic
Rogues from Mars.* Portia gave them an
update on the armory's website and shared
a bit about her deep dive into researching
the building that housed the armory and
the martial arts school. She was digging
much deeper than she had to, but this was
the kind of thing that excited her — random
useless minutiae. People had assumed that
her constant schooling was a way of avoiding reality — she couldn't blame them, since
her perennial studies had been paired with
drinking and partying — but she mostly just
really loved learning.

When their conversation petered out, she
switched over from the messenger app to
her social media; the little red notification
bubble had a number in the hundreds and
was ticking up as she watched.

Whoa.

She tapped into the notifications tab and began scrolling through the dozens of responses and shares.

@girlswithglasses @dideyedothat OMG, you maced him? Girl, how do you even still have a job??

@girlswithglasses @dideyedothat LM-FAO Macing your boss on your first day? #internshipgoals

@girlswithglasses @dideyedothat This was hilarious! I can't wait for the next update! (And I wouldn't trust you with any swords either, beloved.)

@girlswithglasses @dideyedothat You need to get on that haggis. Just trust me on this.

@girlswithglasses @dideyedothat Ooo, is that your boss's back in that selfie? 👀 I would spray him all right, but not with mace. #sorrynotsorry

Portia's first post for GirlsWithGlasses's adventure section had finally gone up and it was a huge success if her notifications were any indication.

She scrolled through the reaction GIFs, messages of encouragement, and people

129

playfully dragging her after reading her account of her first days of her internship. She was still mortified, but turning the experience into something useful eased her embarrassment.

She switched over to the armory's account and noted that their follower count had gone up by five hundred and it was still early in the day in the US.

Impressive, Reggie. Her sister's site really was doing well, since that five hundred was likely a fraction of the people who'd read the post.

She scrolled through GIFs and chose an animated one of a large man struggling in vain to pull a sword from a stone. Hello new followers! Hope you enjoyed our apprentice's post on @GirlsWithGlasses. Stick around, we have lots of exciting stuff coming your way soon! she typed out, then hit send.

Portia put the phone down and returned to the more mundane task before her — packing knives for shipping — but her mind was still on social media. She wasn't exactly surprised that people were into her story. It had been funny. But she had underestimated just how *many* people would be into it. She'd sent the video of Tavish she'd finally gotten him to agree to with her second post. If her friends' reactions in their group chat, and the people already ENHANCE-ing her selfie to try to get a glimpse at Tavish's were any indication, it would do even better. She needed to put the finishing touches on the armory's site before that post went up.

"Do you have a telekinetic power that allows you to pack the boxes while standing there and staring into space?" Tavish made his way across the office and dropped a box of finished knives onto the table in front of her.

She'd grown slightly used to the Jerk Lite version of Tavish, so she didn't even flinch.

"Do you think it wise to annoy me before handing over a box of knives?" She smiled sweetly at him.

He huffed. "If you're as good with a knife as you were with that spray, you'll end up stabbing yourself, too, lass."

Portia rolled her eyes at him. "Never gonna let me live that down, are you?"

"Nah." His mouth quirked up the tiniest bit, as if his smile were struggling to lift the weight of his Portia-induced frown lines but couldn't shoulder the impossible task.

"I wasn't staring into space, anyway. I was working," she said, pushing her curls back behind one ear. "I was trying to think of a new marketing strategy."

"What strategy is that?" he asked, his

brows knitting together. "The do chat on MySpace strategy?"

Portia gasped and bought her hand to her chest, feeling an actual jolt of shock at the anachronism. "MySpace? Really?"

He just stared at her.

She picked up her phone to open a social media app that wasn't from the Mesozoic era. "Look. I wrote a blog post on my sister's site — unlike me, she has her shit together, and her site is extremely popular. So all these people reblogged it and shared it on social media, then the armory got all these new followers, and . . ."

Portia trailed off, as she was too busy watching Tavish wave his hands around his head like he was being attacked by a swarm of bees.

"I told Jamie and I've told you — I don't know about this internet shite. I don't *care* about this internet shite."

"Tavish, I know your line of work might confuse you, but this is the twenty-first century. You're . . . well, you're not young, but even my grandmother has been using the internet since I was a child. Internet access has been classified as a human right. Enough with the acting like it's some newfangled concept you can just avoid. It's a business tool."

"I can find the information I need for my research in books. Made of paper," he countered. "I check my email when I have to. I don't need to spend hours killing brain cells with pictures of people's lunch or videos of wee kitties playing with a ball of yarn."

"Oh my god," she said. "You hate kitten videos, too? You *are* a monster. And FYI, baby donkeys are the cute animal of choice right now."

"Noted," he said. "Thanks for that lesson, but maybe you could get back to packing? In the real world, people have paid real money for these products and they're expecting them."

He seemed aggravated and not just at her. Portia plucked a knife from the box, grabbed one of the leather pouches it was to be packaged in, and slid it inside. "Speaking of that . . ." Talking about money was so gauche, but she had to. "I know I mentioned my internet searches of Bodotria Armory before I took the apprenticeship, but I looked at finances yesterday. Sales are down. A lot."

His mouth twisted. "I suppose Jamie let you look at that?"

She nodded, trying to hide her annoyance. "Yes. He showed me the online bookkeeping system."

Tavish ran a hand through his hair, the strands shifting from black to grayer, and back again. "You know, when I was an apprentice, I did what I was told and didn't go sticking my nose into my master's business."

Portia could have really told him about himself, and his use of the word *master*, but chose to take the honey route over the vinegar. "When I spoke to Jamie about this apprenticeship, we agreed that I would help where I could. For me to do that, I need to know what we're working with. What happened a year ago to cause such a sudden drop in sales?"

"Fuck if I know. Everything was going fine, and then it wasn't." If he had some big secret he was hiding, he had a great poker face. He seemed exasperated, not defensive. "Several of the largest buyers — castles and historical sites around the country that we'd done years of business with — just up and severed ties. I got stonewalled when I tried to find out why."

He crossed his arms over his chest and glowered.

"You weren't able to sweet talk anyone into buying again? Hard to imagine," she said.

x

134

He stalked the few steps that separated them and the smell of leather and steel and almond soap enveloped her. "Has it occurred to you that I know how to interact with people in a cordial and pleasant manner?" he growled.

"Not once." That wasn't exactly true — she'd seen him be gentle with Jamie, and Cheryl, and his students. He was gruff to be sure, but he only seemed to tap into his special reserve of assholeishness whenever she was around, even though she was trying her damnedest to help him. "I have to ask, do you even enjoy your work anymore? Do you *want* to survive this slump? Because you aren't acting like it."

"Look, princess —"

"Actually, my best friend is the princess. She's one of the hardest working people I know, so if you're using that as a derogatory term think again. *I'm* in a fairly high tax bracket, but nowhere near royalty."

His gruff expression scrunched into one of confusion. "Are you serious?"

"Yes, although I guess tax brackets in the US would be different than they are here."

"No, about the princess — fuck's sake, never mind. Look, Miss High Tax Bracket, I know how to run a business. I've done pretty damn well at it. I don't need some

135

stranger waltzing in here and acting like I'm incompetent."

Portia pressed her lips together to prevent the first thing that came to mind from slipping out. This was why she'd only dealt with men in blocks of time that could be measured by hours and were capped with "have a nice life." Any longer than that and you had to put up with tantrums like this.

"Let's rewind to when you first stepped into this room." She moved her index fingers rapidly around one another in a circular motion, then pointed one at Tavish. "The only person acting like *anyone* is incompetent is you. I'm asking you about sales because I need to know if there's a specific situation that needs to be addressed in our marketing. You say there isn't, so there isn't, but you can't get annoyed every time I ask for information. Pretending a problem doesn't exist doesn't make it magically go away. Lord knows I've tried it."

He was just looking at her again, in that way that he probably looked at a defective sword before throwing it into a scrap heap, then ran his hand through his hair with a frustrated growl. "I'm just not used to this. I really didn't expect you to be so . . . ."

"Competent? Irreplaceable?" Portia didn't think she was any of those things, but fake it till you make it was a key component of shaping the new her.

"... meddlesome," Tavish finished.

"And I didn't think you would be so . . ." Portia's gaze darted to his face, and the silver hair at his temples, and his salt-and-pepper scruff, and that full mouth, and suddenly everything she had been trying to ignore about him stuck an arm out and clotheslined her as she tried to run from her attraction to him.

Oh no. Way to fucking go, Portia.

Tav was staring at her, waiting for her to finish her sentence.

"... tall," she finished, unable to think of another descriptor that wouldn't reveal her for the loser she was.

Tav quirked a brow. "Tall. Right."

Redirect! Redirect!

"You still haven't let me know what I'll be doing at the exhibition this weekend. I made graphics and I've been promoting it on social media and getting a great response. I think I'd be really good at doing sales, despite your supposed ability to be cordial."

She liked interacting with people, especially if she got to talk about things she was interested in. She'd been researching way more than necessary for the website, and this would be a way to use her knowledge.

"Look, lass, these events are to bring in new people to the lessons and to buy our product. I need staff that really knows what they're talking about, who can communicate with both a complete amateur and someone who's been studying for years." His expression lit up, like he'd thought of something really clever, and he snapped his fingers. "It's like that pop-up ad you wanted to get rid of on the site, yeah? Let's say I put you to work at the Bodotria Armory stall. Someone comes up and asks for a *sgian-dubh* or some kind of armor. If you have to run and grab me or Jamie or Kevyn, then they might just walk off and buy from someone who knows what they're on about. Or they might buy, and then spread the word that we're not the real deal. Customers are fickle."

He gave her a self-satisfied grin, as if he'd just explained her uselessness to her with her own words, and they could now move on from this.

He was underestimating her.

Portia let him pat himself on the back for a moment and then walked over to the table where several weapons lay waiting for shipping. She picked up a short squat blade with an ornate black hilt, ran her fingertip along the dull edge, then pointed it at Tavish.

Tav held up his hands, mild alarm lifting his brows. "Hey now, I know you have a violent streak, but —"

"*Skean dhu,* a short single-edged blade, name derived from the Gaelic *Sgian-dubh,* meaning *hidden,* as the blade was something that could be kept on the body after other weapons were deposited at the door of a dwelling, per Highland tradition. Usually worn tucked into the stocking in Highland dress. Not to be confused with . . ." She put the blade down and sifted through the knives, picking up a similar blade. ". . . the *mattucashlass,* which is a double-edged blade worn under the armpits and used in hand-to-hand combat."

"Portia —"

She didn't look at him, simply dropped the knife down and picked up a knife with a longer blade and a slimmer hilt, this one in bronze. "Those knives are earlier versions of this baby, the Scottish dagger known as a dirk. It's a long thrusting dagger descended from the medieval ballock dagger, but became an integral part of Scottish weaponry."

She turned to him, batting her lashes even though she would rather have chucked the dagger in his general direction. "As for clothing, do you mean an actual suit of armor? Functional or decorative? Or more like a brigandine, a padded vest, traditionally canvas or leather, lined with steel plates? We can talk mortuary swords, claymores, broadswords, the compound Sinclair —"

"All *right,* Freckles." He held his hands up, probably to shut her up but she liked to think of it as a sign of defeat.

"I can do this all day," she said. "I told you, I've studied lots of things, and what I don't know I look up instead of just assuming. You should try it sometime."

Now that she was done and Tav was just staring at her, embarrassment started to creep up her neck. The man was an expert in swordmaking and a literal master. And she'd just thrown her 101 knowledge at him and expected what exactly?

Tav was still looking at her, then he . . . smiled. Really smiled. She could see his teeth and everything. Dammit, she'd thought she'd won that battle for a second, but if she'd known it would pull this reaction from him she would have let him go on thinking her silly.

Tavish McKenzie sporting a glower was sexy. Tav with those full lips curved up and crow's feet framing his eyes because he was grinning so hard? Her stomach lurched like she was on a crappy carnival ride and she

140

realized with horror that despite not doing crushes, despite definitely not doing bosses, she liked Tavish. For real. She hadn't had a butterflies-in-her-stomach crush smack into her full force like this since senior year of high school when she'd wanted Hector Washington to ask her to the prom SO BADLY. He'd asked Reggie instead. She'd gotten over that short-lived infatuation quickly and she'd get over this one even faster.

"Okay. You win," he said. Light, casual, as if he'd always been capable of talking to her like this. "You can work the table. If you can do that at the table, I'm sure we'll have no problem with sales."

Relief flowed through her and she let out the breath she had been holding. If she wasn't mistaken, the stats were New Portia 2–Thigh Man 0 in whatever weird Hot Jerk Challenge they had going on. 3–0 if she counted the macing.

It was strangely arousing to know that despite his stubbornness, Tav was able to concede his mistakes. She might have to retract his addition to *Fuckboy Monthly,* the fake periodical she and Ledi had started, which was now mostly filled by Nya's online dating encounters since Ledi was monogamous and Portia was celibate-ish.

No "ish," bish. Celibate. Focusing on self. Not getting ideas about your boss.

"Erm . . ." Tav shoved his hands into his pockets. His muscles flexed beneath his snug-fitting T-shirt as he lifted his shoulders in an awkward motion, so Portia fixed her gaze on his left nostril. Nostrils were safe. "What are you doing this afternoon?" he asked.

Could he be . . . ? No. No way was he asking her on a date. Her body went tense because she wasn't entirely opposed to the idea, despite her mental pep talk.

"I've got the after-school lesson with the weans if you'd like another apprentice duty. Bit more fun than packing boxes. You should come help if you aren't afraid of breaking a nail or somesuch."

"Oh." Portia's annoyance pushed any appreciation of his attractiveness, and the mingled relief and disappointment that he was still talking strictly business, to the background of her mind. "If you're going to rely on sexist clichés, at least get some fresh material. And if I *do* break a nail off, it'll be someplace extremely unpleasant for you."

He chuckled and stepped around her as he headed for the door. "The class starts at five."

CHAPTER 8

"Hey, welcome to part two of so you think you're a hot mess. Don't forget to hit that subscribe button below because if you're anything like me? You won't remember to do it at the end of the video. You might not even make it to the end of the video if something else distracts you. So hit subscribe and then we can talk about the elephant in the room: ADHD!"

Caridad sprayed two cans of confetti foam at the screen and Portia hit pause and stared out at Tavish and his students.

ADHD?

She'd never really considered it. She'd always been told that she was flighty, flakey, lazy, scattered, impulsive . . . but she was also curious, and super engaged when something interested her. Still, the negative always outweighed the positive, and she'd always figured that she was just . . . *a fuck-up.*

Something in her loosened with relief as the possible diagnosis repeated itself in a loop in her brain. *ADHD! ADHD! ADHD!* She had a word to use for her behavioral patterns. There were other people who felt the same way she did, maybe.

Still . . . it was strange thinking of herself as having a medical diagnosis for her behaviors. For years, her parents had subtly guilted her for not doing more with her life when she "didn't have Regina's issues." Reggie had been kicking ass since she'd left the ICU and went into a physical therapy program; she'd certainly never seen herself as having any "issues" that could stop her from achieving her dreams, and neither had Portia. But their parents' expectations had become a wedge that Portia had used to push herself away from everyone, even her sister. Things were different now, but what if someone had paid attention earlier? Or what if her parents had just accepted her instead of constantly comparing her?

She decided to stop getting ahead of herself. She still had to take the online ADHD assessment linked under the video before she started getting all emotional about it. It would be nice to have at least some explanation, but maybe she'd take the test and the results would read "Nah, you just suck at adulting."

"All right, we're gonna take a short break," Tavish bellowed from the floor of the gym, drawing her attention to him. She was relieved for the distraction. Her impulse was to take the test immediately, but she was technically on the job. Instead she snapped a quick pic of Tavish standing before the kids, all with their backs to her but clearly enthralled, and posted it across the armory's social media feeds.

Sir Tavish and his rapt audience. Portia had to admit, he had a way with the youths. The kids, ranging from ages six to ten, were a handful, but they were all seemingly enamored with her boss, making her feel better about her less than professional thoughts earlier. He apparently had some sort of appeal that shone through his grumpy demeanor.

She'd participated in the class a bit: handing out Styrofoam swords and making sure shoes were tied and the kids were lined up as Tavish talked to the parents dropping them off. She'd also dodged invasive questions about whether she was Maestro Tav's girlfriend. Children were nosy as hell, honestly, but she'd made sure they knew she was just an apprentice.

Mostly, she'd hovered on the bleachers

beside the pile of lunch bags Cheryl had dropped off for the kids to take home with them. Cheryl had explained that she packed enough for two meals now after the students had talked about sharing the meal with their families. The classes were offered for free to kids who lived in nearby council housing, and apparently not having enough to eat wasn't a rarity.

Tav taught one class for kids per week, and two for teens, and those were free, too, though he could have easily charged an arm and a leg to the neighborhood's newer occupants. He offered food, provided equipment, and maybe most valuable of all, he gave up his time . . . it had to add up. She thought about how pigheaded he was about the business, and how much pressure it must have added to have the well-being of Bodotria's youth at stake in addition to his livelihood. Not to mention Jamie's. And Cheryl's.

It didn't excuse his behavior, but no one had ever trusted her enough to depend on her before — though she realized with a start that these people were all depending on her, too, now. She was the apprentice and the armory was in trouble. If she didn't help turn things around, Tavish wouldn't be the only one that suffered.

Maybe it was above her pay grade, and maybe he hadn't asked for the help, but he sure as hell needed it. She'd give it to him, not because of Project: New Portia or to impress him, but because for the first time maybe ever she felt she was the perfect person for the job.

A pale girl with frizzy red hair smiled as she bopped a boy in high-water pants and glasses too big for his face on the head with her foam sword. A tan-skinned, dark-haired boy who Tavish had already disciplined twice ran up to the girl and snatched her sword away.

"Syed, stop it!" the girl shouted. She was on the younger end of the class's age range, and her face was screwing up into a wail when Tavish intervened.

"Syed, I'm not going to tell you again," he said in a firm but gentle voice that Portia perhaps enjoyed a bit too much. "You have to pay attention, and do what I tell you to do. And you should be nice to your friends. Apologize to Lacey."

"This is bollocks," Syed said, dropping the foam swords and staring at Tavish in challenge. "I don't have to apologize to anyone. And I want a real sword."

Portia expected Tavish to growl at the boy but instead he simply raised his brows and seemed to mull it over. "I could give you a real sword, I suppose, but why should I when you can't use a foam one properly?" he asked, scratching his head. The other children tittered. Portia crossed her arms in annoyance; Tavish's rationale was familiar.

Good to know he treats me the same as a misbehaving eight-year-old.

"Come on, Syed," Lacey said. "You're wasting our time. Let's just have fun, yeah?"

The boy sucked in a breath and his shoulders hunched. Portia wasn't that familiar with kids, but she'd witnessed enough subway and supermarket meltdowns to divine that this situation was on the verge of spinning out of control.

"Oy! Let me show you all something," Tavish said suddenly, tapping the boy on the shoulder and then walking toward an area covered with thick rubber mats. His voice was still firm, but a bit more playful, conspiratorial. "Come here, Syed."

The boy approached slowly, eyes wide and body braced as if he were about to be punished, but Tavish placed a gentle hand on his shoulder, demonstrating to both Syed and the other students that all was well. Syed glanced up anxiously, but relaxed a bit.

"Sometimes in battle, a knight would drop

his sword. He'd get into trouble and have to get out of it without the help of his trusty weapon. Now, I'm going to grab you and show you how to get out of those kinds of scrapes. Is that okay with you, Syed? It's okay if you don't want to."

"It's okay," Syed said, the anger and petulance gone from his voice. "I want to learn!"

Tavish spent the next five minutes grabbing the boy by the arms in ways that made Portia worry he might accidentally hurt him, but by the end Syed could slip out of the holds easily and with confidence. The boy's eyes were bright and he smiled victoriously, his earlier agitation gone.

"Did everyone see how we did that?" Tav asked. His hand rested on Syed's head and Syed glanced up at him with adoration in his eyes. "The thing is, you have to think a few steps ahead. You can be afraid, but you can't let your panic or your anger rule you. You have to be in control, yeah? Let's all try it now."

"Lacey, come let me show you," Syed said, holding his hand out to her. "It's fun!"

Parents began filtering in to pick up their children, apparently unfazed by the sight of them wrestling with their huge instructor. There were squeals of laughter from the kids as each of them managed to escape, and then Tav packed them off to their parents with a reminder not to use what they'd learned outside the classroom. Portia handed each child a bagged meal as they passed by, smiling at their shy *thank-you*s and *ta*s.

There was one bag left, and she turned to see Tav kneeling next to Syed, who was talking quietly with his gaze on the floor. Tav clapped a hand on the boy's shoulder and spoke to him for a few minutes, and Syed nodded along before running to Portia, grabbing his meal, and heading for a woman wearing a purple hijab who waited by the door.

"*Ya mama,* say thank you to the woman, eh?" she said. Definitely his mom.

"Thank you!" Syed called over his shoulder.

The woman waved goodbye as Syed handed her the food and excitedly grabbed at her arms, eager to show her what he'd learned.

"You handled that well," Portia said to Tavish, beginning to gather up the play swords that had been abandoned on the floor. "I guess you are capable of being nice to others."

Tav scrubbed a palm over his jaw and

grunted. She expected a riposte, but his brows were drawn and he was still staring out the door Syed had just passed through.

"What's wrong?" she asked. She immediately regretted her instinctive question; he'd probably tell her to mind her business. Surprisingly, he met her gaze, his eyes bracketed with worry lines.

"Eh, Syed says some lads have been teasing him and other weans at school. Weans who don't 'look' Scottish. Telling 'em that they're gonna get sent back to where they came from, and they saw it on telly so it must be true."

Portia had spent K-12 as one of the few students of color at her prep school, so she wasn't shocked that students could be so cruel. Syed had seemed to lash out at his friends for no reason, but of course there'd been a reason. She knew from experience that when you tried to bottle your feelings up inside, you inevitably sprang leaks in places that seemed entirely unrelated.

"He's been acting out the last couple of weeks. Now that I think about it, that's when the immigration debates made it onto the front pages again, with knobs in suits saying we need to block our borders and 'preserve our heritage.' Fucking hell." Tav ran a hand through his thick hair, leaving his palm splayed atop his head. "You know, you think this shite is done with, and then you see weans spouting the same rubbish you heard when you were one."

His gaze flashed to hers in preemptive challenge and his hand dropped to his side. "Mum is Chilean. And her husband, my real dad if not biological, is Jamaican. Kids thought it was funny to taunt about going back where you came from when I was growing up, too. Except they usually thought I'd taunt along with them."

This was a champagne problem compared to other forms of bigotry, but she had her own uncorked bottles courtesy of her wealth and lighter complexion. She wasn't going to downplay the fact that it had been really shitty and confusing for him, despite the fact that he was privileged in other ways.

"Racists suck, and I imagine being expected to hate on your family sucks too," she said.

Tav shook his head.

"I'm fine. People assume the *A* in Tavish A. McKenzie stands for Alistair or some shite and not Arredondo, and that the McKenzie comes from some venerable Scottish clan and not a Jamaican slave owner." He shook his head. "But Mum always told me how welcoming people were to her when she arrived. How there was a sense of solidarity with those who had suffered elsewhere and had to leave everything they knew behind, not a desire to keep them out." He blew out a frustrated breath. "People have always been wankers, but I never thought she was wrong. I look at Syed and wonder if she is now, though. He shouldn't have to feel unwelcome in his own country."

For the first time she met him, he seemed more than irritable — he was furious.

She adjusted her armful of foam. "He shouldn't, but he has you to talk to. And to show him sweet wrestling moves."

Tav made a grunt of acknowledgment.

"Aye. I wish I could do more. Half the weans are worried their parents will be kicked out of their homes after benefits are cut, the other half that they'll be kicked out of the country with all this talk of borders and nationality and refugees. It's not right."

Portia's instinct was to raise a hand to his face to soothe him. Instead, she took two steps back. That wasn't how this worked. It wasn't how it worked at all. She was at her job, and just because Tav looked handsome while brooding over the well-being of children didn't change the fact that he was her boss.

"I'm sure having this program helps," she offered instead. "You're doing *something.*"

"It's not enough. And with the way sales are going . . ." He shook his head and she imagined she knew what he felt — the sick, impotent knowledge that some things were beyond your control. She would've suggested they get a pint, which had been her usual remedy for that malady, but that was her old game plan.

"What's your favorite type of sword?" she asked, continuing to gather the foam ones scattered on the ground.

"Medieval claymore," he said without hesitation. "A nice heavy, long two-hander."

Portia fumbled the swords she'd collected and shot him a look, but she realized that he wasn't trying to be funny — she was the only one whose mind had taken a running leap into innuendo land.

"Why?" she asked. "What do you like about it? How does it handle compared to, say, a broadsword?"

Tav picked up the last length of foam from the floor and poked her in the arm with it. "Are you trying to distract me from the woes of the world, Freckles?"

She grinned at him. "Is it working?"

"You don't have to ask questions to distract me."

She would've taken it as an insult if she hadn't seen the way his five-o'clock shadow shifted as a slow smile creased his cheeks. The tension was still there around his eyes, but his hazel gaze was like warm maple syrup, and it poured awareness over her.

They were alone in the gymnasium, and he was joking with her in *that* way. This was something she was familiar with — heat cloaked behind humor. Tavish probably didn't realize it, but he was offering something, something she only had to reach out and take hold of to change things between them.

Damn, she wanted to, and she felt that want low in her belly and in her breasts and everywhere lust could make itself known in her body. She even felt a strange stirring behind her rib cage, and that was what snapped her into action.

She yanked the length of foam, trying to gather it along with the rest and put some space between them, but he held on to his end without releasing it. He was studying her.

"What?" she asked, dropping her gaze to his hand wrapped around the bright purple foam.

"Did you kill a man or something? Are you on the run from the law?" he asked.

She snorted. "What kind of questions are those?"

"I'm trying to figure out what brought you of all people to here of all places. And I notice you didn't answer."

"I'm not on the run and I haven't killed a man. Yet." She paused and looked up at the ceiling as if searching her memory. "Wait, are we talking in spirit or body? I've committed several spiritual homicides according to my friend."

"Your friend the princess?" She looked up at him again to find him smirking.

"Yes. Ledi isn't one to mince words."

"Spiritual mankiller. I believe it," he said, and then released his end of the foam noodle. She stumbled back, catching herself, and he grabbed his duffel bag and headed for the exit. "Good thing we Scots are made of hardy stuff. Can you sweep and mop and lock up afterward?"

With that he was gone.

Portia pulled out her phone and took a selfie of herself holding the armful of foam noodles, which was quite an accomplishment, and spent the next few moments choosing between filters on InstaPhoto instead of trying to figure out what exactly had just happened between them.

CHAPTER 9

The afternoon of the Ren Faire was a good one, with barely any clouds in the sky and the weather butting up against warm. Clusters of flowers and trees bursting with green dotted the park, and the attendees, many of whom were decked out in medieval costumes, were having a grand time taking part in activities like archery, basket weaving, and pottery making.

Tav made a circuit of the festival, where he'd stopped to chat with the various vendors who had set up stalls in the park to hawk their wares — there was mead and ale, homemade toiletries, leather goods, and pottery aplenty. Ahead of him, a person in a full suit of armor who was probably regretting their costume walked stiffly with their companion, who wore a red and yellow striped blanket over their shoulders and sported a horse head mask.

The faire had been growing in popularity

over the years; more businesses had begun to showcase their goods and their skills, and more and more cosplayers, or whatever Cheryl called them, had started to take part, gallivanting about as knights, fair maidens, and serfs. He found the costumes amusing, if often ahistorical, but there was nothing funny about one in particular.

Tav saw the moment both the armor's visor and the horse mask's muzzle turned toward Bodotria's booth, and he followed them as they made their way over.

He placed his hand on the hilt of the basket-hilted sword that was sheathed at his side and stopped a little way off from the booth to observe the crowd of onlookers that had gathered round. He felt a bit of pride — none of the other stalls had generated such interest, and there had been people all around every time he'd checked in on Portia. She didn't need babysitting, as he'd blurted out like a knob. The real problem was as he had suspected; he liked watching her work.

"And even though this could kill a man, it was commonly used for coring apples, chopping vegetables, and other mundane aspects of modern life." Portia smiled at the crowd while holding out the *dubh* blade, explaining how they were crafted in medieval times compared to now. Several hands shot up to ask questions when she paused for a breath.

She knew what she was about, that was certain, but he had the sneaking suspicion that her costume was also a draw.

The dress should have been plain. It was a drab puce thing, long-sleeved and with a hem that brushed the ground, hiding her too-posh-to-muck-about-in shoes. But then there was that brown leather corset. Tavish enjoyed a corset-clad woman as much as the next person, but he'd not known the true wonders of the accessory until Portia had stepped into the kitchen that morning, the leather straps pulled tight, pushing her breasts up and together and drawing all of his attention. The low, square-cut neckline of the dress's loose-fitting top didn't help.

"Cheryl actually tied this too tightly and she already left," she'd said sheepishly, turning and looking back over her shoulder. "Can you loosen this for me?"

And that was how Tav had come to know that Portia had a mole on her left shoulder. He also knew the satiny softness of her skin against his fingertips, that she ran rather warm, and how it felt to brush an errant curl away from her neck and see her shiver from his touch. He didn't need to know any of that. Fucking corsets. The devil's garment.

He tried not to think about loosening the leather straps, about the tense heat that had seemed to cocoon the both of them. He'd had extremely unprofessional thoughts about the sturdy wooden table and how much weight it could support as his fingers had fumbled thickly with the corset strings, but he'd managed to retie them and send her off with a casual "There we are now." He still felt jittery and irritable, though; not at her, but at himself and the Fates for throwing her into his path. Years and years without wanting more from a woman and of course the first one he absolutely shouldn't be interested in had him "ready to risk it all," as Jamie would say. Tavish already had enough risk in his life.

"She's doing well," Cheryl commented as she sidled up beside him. Cheryl's outfit matched his own — a black leather brigandine with the armory's name embroidered across the chest over a black fencing jacket with protective plates along the arms. Black fencing pants, calf protectors, and a black fencing mask pushed up atop her pink hair. "Our table has had the biggest crowd all day! Jamie's Defending the Castle demo had a huge turnout, and most people said they'd loved the promotions Portia posted online and decided to come check it out."

"Is that so?" Their table did look much nicer than usual, with little bundles of hay artfully arranged in wooden crates holding the products. A few books from Mary's shop — Arthurian legends, *The Three Musketeers, The Lady in the Lake,* and something called *My So-Called Sword in the Stone* — were tucked attractively amongst the products, too.

"Aye. She's handed out loads of flyers for Jamie's lessons and coupons for the restaurant, too. And Jamie just had to run back home to get another box of dirks because we sold out. She's even selling to the snooty mums pushing those bloody giant prams. Telling them to use them for table centerpieces and InstaPhoto shoots and what not." She sounded both appalled and proud.

Jamie had been on him to reach out to the new clientele moving into the neighborhood, but Tav hadn't been able to figure out a way to do it without his resentment nearly choking him. He supposed it was easier for Portia . . . she was talking to them from their level. One that was several rungs higher than Tav's.

He grunted. "It's a beautiful spring day. People are in a good mood and want to

spend their pounds. Plus, she's a novelty —
an American."

At least a quarter of the questions he'd
heard her receive throughout the day were
some variety of "Why are you working at a
Scottish armory?" which, fair enough, Tav
asked himself the same thing.

"Or she's just good at this," Cheryl said
testily. "Seriously Tav, what's your problem?
I know you're . . . well, *you,* but you're being way too hard on her."

"I'm hard on everyone," he said flatly,
remembering the way Portia had shivered
as his fingertips grazed her nape, and how
he'd been tempted to see how she'd react if
he replaced his fingertips with his lips. But
she hadn't asked him to, and his mouth
belonged nowhere near her smooth warm
skin, even if she had.

*Like you would have denied her, you bloody
liar.*

"Not like this, you aren't." Cheryl grabbed
the hilt of his sword and jerked, and he
pulled his gaze away from Portia to glare
down at her. She knew as well as anyone
that you never messed about with another
person's sword.

Cheryl wasn't cowed; it seemed his glower
wasn't effective anymore. It had been
blunted by Portia's presence, just like his

willpower and common sense.

"Let me get something through that thick skull of yours. Whatever is going on down here" — she tilted her head toward his groin — "shouldn't affect what's going on up-stairs. If you fancy a shag and it's making you grumpy, figure that out." Tav was ready to die from embarrassment, but Cheryl continued. "She didn't come here to put up with your shite, though, and, in case you haven't noticed, she's more sensitive than us who are used to you."

Tav frowned. It really was that simple: he, an adult, had been almost incapable of civil-ity with his apprentice because he fancied her. He'd used the excuse of her wealth, and her family business, but it was no bet-ter than pulling pigtails at recess.

No better? It's a thousand times worse, you git.

Still, he wasn't in complete agreement with Cheryl. "Sensitive? Portia's more than capable of defending herself. Let us not forget how she introduced herself to me."

"Tavish, you dunderhead. Of course she's capable of defending herself. Most sensitive people are. Because they *have to be.* Jamie wouldn't hurt a fly and you know what's happened with him."

Jamie had gotten into a few bad situations

over the years, defending himself and others from wankers on the street. During the last one, he'd ended up in cuffs despite having called the police himself — they'd told him he fit the description of someone wanted for burgling. Tav had exploded with anger when he'd shown up on the scene, but Jamie had sat silently on the curb, staring into the distance as the new neighbors walked by, sure he was a hardened criminal.

Tav knew his brother was soft as chantilly beneath his muscled exterior, but people often assumed he had a higher tolerance for ribbing or that nothing bothered him because he rarely complained when it did.

Hm.

Tav grunted and then plucked Cheryl's hand off his hilt.

"Careful with the inlaid ivory," he said, pretending to buff the hilt with his sleeve.

"Show-off."

"And I'll be careful with erm, other things."

Cheryl smiled smugly at him.

"Hey, you two!" Mary walked up to them. She was dressed in a Bodotria Books T-shirt and black trousers, but she had metal epaulets from a suit of armor strapped to her shoulders and biceps and carried a streaming banner that read *Gettest thou to the bookshoppe: Bodotria Books.*

Tav plucked at the banner. "Nice advertising."

"Ta. It was your apprentice's idea though, so I should be thanking you. She's a good one."

Come to think of it, Tav had noticed the bookshop was looking a bit different. The coffee was certainly better, and it seemed to be busier when he'd walked by this weekend. And hadn't Portia asked him if she could borrow some of his armor?

"She's a good one indeed," Cheryl said pointedly, then elbowed Tav. She always got a bit feisty on exhibition days. "I have to go kick Kevyn's arse for the crowd now. Don't forget to come over and fight the bloke from Skymead Armory afterward. Maybe it'll help you work off that foul mood."

Sisters-in-law weren't so bad, Tav supposed.

"Aye, I've got to return to my stall," Mary said. "I was just doing a round, trying to entice people to check out my wares since I don't have anyone so interesting as you do to lure them in. Later, Tavish!"

Tav made his way around the crowd, feeling the lure that Mary had spoken of as Portia came into his line of sight again. He stepped beside her quietly as she fielded a

165

question about whether fencing or long-sword was better for beginners.

"Ah, here we have the chivalrous Sir Tavish, who can tell you more about Bodotria's lessons." Portia's eyes glinted up at him, and her smile was a thing to behold.

She's enjoying herself.

How many times had he seen that smile fade away after she deflected one of his barbs? Tav's chest suddenly felt tight, as if his brigandine had shrunk a size.

He remembered that last awful year of marriage with Greer, where neither of them could say the right thing to one another, and every time he'd tried to she'd replied with something caustic or biting, or worse, with indifference.

"Oh, another sword? Wow, looks sharp. I'm off to the office then, as one of us has to be responsible."

It was a terrible feeling, and though he'd had some more than pleasant interactions with Portia, she'd had to be on the defensive since day one — well, after her initial attack, that is, though even that had been in the service of defending another. It was a stressful way to live, and he knew it.

"Thank you for doing such a fantastic job holding down the fort while I was away performing my knightly duties, Maid Freckles," he said grandly, bowing to her before turning to the crowd. "Maid Freckles is American, but she has a vast knowledge of Scottish arms and history. We're very lucky to have her sharing her talents with us for a few months."

He glanced at her and wished he hadn't because the shocked pleasure on her face showed him just how much of a knob he'd been for the past few weeks.

"My pleasure, Sir Tavish," she replied politely with a deep curtsy that nearly interrupted the blood flow to his brain. The rare late spring sunlight highlighted her collarbones and décolletage — her freckles were not restricted to the spray across her nose and cheekbones.

"Is this the result of the apprentice search?" someone in the crowd asked. Tav's eyes jerked from Portia's collarbones to a lean, bearded man holding an expensive camera.

"Aye," he answered carefully.

"Grand!" The man smiled. "I'm from the *Bodotria Eagle*, the paper that first covered your search for an apprentice."

"Oh, that's how I found out about it!" Portia beamed at the reporter, and Tav watched the man's expression brighten. "My twin sister runs a website, GirlsWith-

Glasses dot com — that's GirlsWithGlasses dot com, easy to remember, right? She posted a link to the article in your paper and sent it to me to apply, and here I am."

"Really?" Tav and the man asked at the same time.

"Yes." Portia kept her gaze on Tav. "You never asked me how I found you, so I never said anything. I told Jamie though, and Cheryl, since she's a fan of the site."

"And you have a twin? And here I was thinking one of you was more than enough trouble." Tav was joking, but some of the light faded from Portia's eyes and her smile sagged a bit.

"Oh, she's nothing like me. Reggie is the good twin."

She chuckled, but after having seen what Portia looked like when she was actually having fun, he could tell that she was faking it. He thought about how vulnerable she had been, sitting across from him and telling him she needed this apprenticeship, and how his careless words had hit her much harder than he'd intended over the weeks. He had to stop being so careless, dammit.

"Portia —"

"Do you mind if I snap a photo of you two?" the reporter butted in. "Our readers just loved that story and I know they'll be thrilled to have a follow-up."

"Oh, of course!" Portia was suddenly bright again, though it still seemed a bit forced. She wrapped one arm around Tav's waist and brandished a dagger with the other.

He didn't move. "Erm."

She looked up at him, her dark brown eyes serious and her brows raised as if she were waiting on something from him. Tav stared.

"Pull out your sword," she commanded and Tav was certain it was the sexiest thing a woman had ever uttered to him. He did as he was told, carefully, and held it out in front of him as if warding off attackers. She leaned up on her tiptoes, arms holding him more tightly for balance and somehow unaware that her breasts were pressing into his side.

"Turn it so people can see the craftsmanship," she whispered into his ear. "This is a marketing opportunity. Show that ornate hilt!"

Portia dropped back onto the soles of her boots. Her arm around his waist pulled him closer and he draped his one free arm over her shoulder for lack of anything better to do with it. He tried to smile, but he was sure it was more of a grimace. She was so close, and so soft, and there was that lovely scent of hers again. Plus, she was holding a deadly weapon and her stance wasn't half bad.

Fuuuuuck, this was a miserable pleasure — learning the feel of her curves pressed against him. Now that his body knew, it wouldn't soon forget.

The photographer snapped away while grinning from ear to ear, then lowered his camera. "Perfect. Thanks!"

He walked away, already reviewing the images on the digital viewing screen, and Portia released Tav and moved away without a word, tending to the customers as he stood, suddenly too warm in his fighting gear. A few customer's swarmed around, asking about Tav's sword and purchasing items and signing up for lessons.

Eventually Kevyn and Cheryl jogged up to the booth.

"Oy! Time for your match with Master Bob!"

Portia whirled around. "Are you going to fight?"

Tav shouldn't have felt a surge of cockiness at the interest in her expression, but he did. It wasn't as if he was battling for honor or anything — it was an exhibition. Still . . . He rested his hand on the hilt of his sword in what he knew was a dramatic pose. She'd called him Sir Tavish and he was playing the part. That was it. "Aye, lass."

Portia glanced at the products on the table and frowned a bit. "Break a leg!"

"If you want to go watch, I can take over for a bit," Kevyn offered.

Cheryl slipped an arm through Portia's. "Yes, come watch! Let's see if Master Bob can get Tav on his knees as quickly as you did!"

Tav shot Cheryl a look, but he was the only one aware her words had more than one meaning.

They made their way to the small clearing where the martial arts exhibition was taking place. A crowd had gathered, and Bob was already in the middle, waving his ridiculous sword around. The older man was a bit of a show-off for Tavish's tastes, but he was good at what he did and at playing up the theatrical side of their profession.

"McKenzie!" Bob bellowed, pointing his sword in Tav's direction as he caught sight of him. "Keeping an opponent waiting is an insult, laddie."

"OMG, I need to get video of this."

Tav glanced over to find Portia tugging her cell phone out from between her breasts.

"You keep things in there?" he asked in a choked voice, trying not to look *there* in

171

front of the crowd. He was so taken aback that he couldn't even be annoyed about her wanting to record him.

"Yes." She was busy navigating to her camera app. "Most women's clothing doesn't have pockets. Titty pockets are a functional adaptation."

"Ooo, titty pockets," Cheryl said, ruminating on the descriptor. "I call it my cheb shelf, but I like that, too."

Master Bob made a sound of impatience. "Are you going to gawk at your lady friend or come to fight, McKenzie? Or are you scared of being paggered?"

There was a rumble in the crowd as everyone registered the playful insult.

"Get him, Master Tav!" a familiar voice called out. Tav looked over to find Syed and some of the students from his lessons cheering him on.

Portia looked up at him, her eyes bright and the record light on her phone blinking, and he almost forgot he wasn't a knight. He was just a regular bloke who liked making shiny, pointy objects. A bloke who hated being videoed. But maybe he could put on a show for Portia and the weans just this once.

Tav lowered his mask down and stepped into the circle. He slowly pulled his sword out, whipped it back and forth for effect, then pointed it at his opponent.

"Do your worst, Robert."

The crowd burst out into raucous applause, happy for the show, and Tav remembered that first time he'd watched an exhibition — how it had changed his life. How it had infused him with a sense of joy, as had his own apprenticeship, when he'd finally decided what he wanted to do with his life.

Portia had been right — he hadn't been enjoying his work lately. With all the worries about money and the building, he was well on his way to being as dissatisfied with swordmaking and teaching as he had been with his office job. But this? This reminded him of everything he loved about the armory, and how fun his line of work could be.

Bob rushed toward him with a roar and Tav launched himself forward too, kicking up dirt behind him as their swords met with a resounding clang.

"I'll go easy on you laddie," Bob whispered as he pressed forward with all his weight against his sword. "Don't want to embarrass you in front of your woman."

Tav chuckled. He knew Bob was really asking for him to take it easy, but he wouldn't be rude enough to point that out.

"Thanks, mate. I owe you one," Tav said,

then pushed Bob back and spun away, twirling the sword above his head in a move that would have left him exposed in a real battle but would impress the hell out of Portia.

This was a marketing opportunity after all — even if the line between selling his product to the crowd and himself to Portia had been hopelessly blurred.

It didn't matter. After this fight, the exhibition would be over and the illusion would fade. But, like infatuation, it was glorious while it lasted.

CHAPTER 10

Portia wasn't fond of coding, but tweaking the website's template herself had been worth it. It had taken way longer than hiring someone, given all the web searches she'd had to do to supplement her knowledge of coding, but it had been free and was something she could use in the future. There'd been an uptick in business since the exhibition and her GirlsWithGlasses post, but she'd carved out time using the to-do list journal she'd started after bingeing on *Hot Mess Helper* videos. Caridad called it the "Brain Basura" list, though the technique was anything but garbage. Every morning, Portia took five minutes to "empty the trash" rattling around in her head and "sort" it into "bins" in varying levels of priority: SMELLY BROCCOLI — DISPOSE OF NOW; PRETTY GROSS — CHUCK IT ASAP; STARTING TO SMELL WEIRD; and *SNIFF* EH. She also jotted down random thoughts but only reviewed them later in the day when her "check the trash" alarm chimed.

The system had helped keep her on track of multiple projects better than anything else she'd tried. She was a little proud of herself, and maybe she wasn't just getting a big head. Something had shifted in the way Tavish treated her since the exhibition. It was almost like . . . he respected her? And not even grudgingly.

A vibration on the table beside her slowly broke through her focus, and she grabbed the phone while still skimming the HTML code pane.

"Hello?"

"Hi, honey."

Portia's stomach executed an elevator free fall at the subtle Southern twang on the other end of the line, an unfortunate automatic reaction that piled shame on top of her anxiety. She should have been happy to hear this voice, and yet . . .

"Hey, Mom. How are you?"

"You know how it is — well, I guess you wouldn't — busy with work. So busy! Just had a meeting with some investors and now I'm heading over to Brownsville to check out a site that's for sale. I managed to scoop everyone on this, so I'm hoping to have it wrapped up before anyone tries to edge us out."

Her mom could be vicious when it came to work, which was a boon in their profession. Reggie's innate competitiveness had helped her thrive in the family business before pursuing her own dreams, but Portia hated this kind of work, where one mistake or second-guessing yourself could lose the company serious money.

"I'm pretty busy, too, actually." Portia was embarrassed by the wheedling defensiveness that surged into her tone. It reminded her of when her parents had come home from parent-teacher night comparing Reggie's honor roll to Portia's uneven performance, and she'd point out that she'd gotten an A+ in art. "I'm totally redoing the website for the armory. Trying to get it done as quickly as possible because my marketing plan has really been paying off and —"

"That's nice. Your father talked to you about the position we want to fill, correct?"

A wave of sadness washed through her, leaving anger when it receded. She wished her mother could even pretend to be interested in what she was working on. Feigned interest was a form of politeness Catharine Hobbs excelled at, but she seemed to reserve that talent for other people. Portia

177

would love to know what it felt like to be on the receiving end of that empty cordiality.

"Dad told me you're looking to fill the position with someone who will stick around for a while." Portia picked up a pen and started doodling beside the sketches of the various layouts for the website on the pad next to her laptop, then dropped it in frustration. She was a grown woman, even if talking to her mom made her feel like a moody teen.

Her mother sighed. "Well?"

The pressure in that one word was enough to give Portia the bends. One moment she'd been happily immersed in a project she cared about and now she'd been hooked by her mother's supposed concern and dragged kicking back to the surface of reality.

"I told Dad I would think about it," she replied.

"If I recall, you didn't have to think too long about accepting this silly apprenticeship." Her mother's voice was coated in disappointment, like poison on the end of a barb that would stay in Portia's system long after the chastisement was forgotten. "Good to know you care more about some random Scottish people than your own family."

That tone had always been enough to make Portia burst into tears, and she swallowed against them now. "It's not like that, Mom."

She imagined telling her mother about the ADHD tests she'd taken online, all with the same results, but she wouldn't have been able to stand it if her mother casually dismissed her discovery.

"Oh, I know," her mother said. "It's never like that. You do what you want, skip from one thing to another, but being a Jill of all trades, and master of none, can only get you so far. You need a marketable skill and you can't even take the one we're handing you?"

Portia closed the laptop, hoping the last changes had saved but not really caring. The site was just another thing she'd mess up eventually, wasn't it?

"I have to go," she said. "I have a meeting."

"Oh, there's the woe-is-me voice. I'm not *trying* to be the bad guy, Portia. I just want you to get your life —"

"Talk to you later, Mom."

Portia sat for a moment after laying her phone down before shaking her head side to side, as if she could knock loose the unhelpful thought patterns her mother had kick-started in her brain.

Jill of all trades and master of none. Jill of

all trades and master of none.

It would be one thing if she could dismiss the words outright, but her mother wasn't totally wrong . . . still, that didn't mean that taking a job with her parents was right either.

She tried to remember what Dr. Lewis had told her.

"Just because your parents don't appreciate what you do doesn't mean it holds less value. You're trying to be true to yourself, and not to hurt anyone in the process. What more can you ask of yourself?"

Portia wasn't sure, but she wished she knew. There had to be something that would please both her and her parents, didn't there?

She didn't feel like working on the site anymore, so she gently cracked open the book about guild halls of the seventeenth century Mary had given her. Beating herself up wasn't useful; research was. She'd seen Dudgeon House listed as one of the earlier names for the building the armory was in, and searched it out in the index.

"Dudgeon House was home to the Mariner's Guild for one hundred years, after which it was bought by a private owner and converted into Firth Hospital," she read. She went back to the index, and found the entry for Firth Hospital.

She skimmed again, reading through the various public works done by the hospital. "The hospital was purchased by the Duchess of Richmond and Lennox, who opened a home for the destitute."

That was the end of the entry, but she at least had a name. She pulled up the web browser on her tablet and set to work searching for the rest of the history of the building. Two long, frustrating hours later, all of her normal internet sources, and about a thousand possible avenues, had come to dead ends. This wasn't even super important to the site, but not being able to find what she wanted bothered her.

She entered her notes into the document she was compiling in her note-taking app, then stood and stretched to work out the tightness in her back and shoulders. There was a bit of burn from the Defending the Castle class the night before, but she was getting the hang of that. It was a good release for the excess energy that had plagued her since the exhibition a week ago.

Portia had seen Tav's moves in his classes with the kids, but that had been different than seeing him take on a man his size and with matching skills. It hadn't been a *real* fight, but the way Tav had moved and the skill he'd displayed had been legit. The man could swing a sword, which Portia hadn't ever thought would be her kink. And the way he'd pulled back his mask and smiled victoriously at her when he'd won . . . like it had been for her.

No.

Portia distracted herself like any modern woman — she picked up her phone and toggled through her social media sites. The photos from the Ren Faire on the armory's InstaPhoto were getting some good engagement, but the video of Tav's fight that she'd linked to her latest GirlsWithGlasses post had taken on a life of its own. Some of the readers had even started a hashtag — #swordbae — sharing it with GIFs of his fight, which she was sure Tav would just *love.* Oh well.

She copied a link to a post with the hashtag and pasted it into her International Friend Emporium chat.

Portia: Tavish is a meme. He's going to kill me. 😣

Nya: Maybe he won't find out since he doesn't use the internet. That could work to your advantage!

Portia: Finally, his stubborness will be an asset, lol

Portia went back to scrolling the hashtag. #swordbae's admirers had apparently found her earlier blog posts about the apprenticeship (OMG, THIS IS JUST SO), descended upon the armory's InstaPhoto feed (whoa, #swordbae is talented af), and shared older social media pics (look at how beautiful this building is! I can't even!!) and the photo the *Bodotria Eagle* had shared of them (Is #swordbae wifed? ☹). #swordbae posts gushed over Tav's accent, his muscles, his talent, and the way he looked at the camera at the end of the clip — only Portia knew he had actually been looking at *her.*

Her body went warm again, and she decided it was time for a break. And for food, because she'd been so absorbed in her work that she'd forgotten to eat. Again.

She ventured out of her room in search of a late lunch. The now-familiar halls of the building were quiet; there was no whir of Tav's grinder. Maybe he was out making deliveries.

Maybe you shouldn't be conjecturing about his location because it doesn't matter what he's doing.

"Hey! There you are!" Cheryl said, looking up from her stir fry as Portia approached. It was nice to have someone be so unreservedly glad to see her, and washed away some of the bad taste left behind by her mom's call. The ribs she'd become a fan of would do the rest.

"Hey! Can I get the Dalek Delight again?"

"Oh, sorry, we're all out. He just got the last of it." Cheryl pointed her wooden spoon over to the other side of the stand, where Tav sat at one of the tables, shoveling away the ribs that would have been Portia's in a just world.

"Of course he did," Portia muttered. "I'll have the Skyfish-ball skewers and a side of Galli-fried rice. If someone didn't eat all of that, too." She shot a glare at Tav, who was happily biting into a delicious-looking rib.

"Sure thing. I'll bring it over to Tav's table when it's ready."

She'd hit Doctor Hu's during a lull and Tav was the only other customer, and apparently Cheryl wasn't aware of the fact that even though Tav was less of a jerk, he and Portia had never really been alone for non-work-related reasons. He generally made himself scarce in the shared areas unless Cheryl or Jamie were around.

There was also the actual problem: she

had a kernel of a crush on the man. She needed to grind that kernel into meal, but in the meantime she would just act like everything was fine. Old Portia had been great at that, and New Portia could be, too. Not everything from her old life needed to go in the trash. She donned her blasé employee expression and walked over to him, wishing she had fewer manners so she could just ignore him and sit alone with her phone as she ate, like a normal millennial.

"Mind if I join you?"

"Yes." He took another bite of food without looking up.

Well, someone was living her dream of a manners-free life. She wasn't in the mood for his jabs — her mom's call had wiped away the successes of the previous weeks, leaving her feeling vulnerable.

She turned to walk away, but something wrapped around her wrist, holding her in place. Tav's thumb and forefinger. He was strong as fuck, his grip enough to hold her though she knew he was exerting the barest effort. If he *really* tried to hold her down . . .

A shiver went through her and settled in her belly, warm like good whiskey and just as bad for her. Somewhere deep inside of her, the kernel sprouted one bright green leaf.

Dammit.

She looked down at him and there was heat in his gaze, a heat that probably matched the sensation that inched up her neck and over her skin. His eyes dropped to her chest and she tugged her hand away, crossing her arms over her traitorous nipples. Damned soft-cup bras.

"I was joking, Nip— Freckles," he said, his voice rough. Color flooded his face, and he cleared his throat. "Sit down already."

She slunk into the seat across from him, too embarrassed to meet his gaze. He seemed to be suddenly awkward too, though, which made things slightly better.

"How are the ribs?" she asked. "I'd been dreaming about those ribs since yesterday and you got the last of them."

He raised a brow, examining the sauce-slathered meat. "They're even more delicious than usual, now that you mention it. Mmmm."

She really could have gone her whole life without hearing Tavish make that noise. It was low and obscene and her body was totally down with both of those things. She crossed her legs. "It's bad enough I have to sit here and watch you eat them, you don't have to tease."

His gaze went from his food to her eyes. It

was warm and mischievous and she desperately wished standoffish jerk Tav would reappear because *goddamn.* "Here's the thing with teasing. It might seem like torture now, sitting there wanting what you can't have, but when you finally get it? It'll be the best you've ever had. The best ribs, that is."

Portia watched him take a bite, shocked into silence by how easily he'd managed to undo all of her resolve with his words. It had been better when he snapped and grouched at her because this . . . this was not sustainable. Project: New Portia had only three rules and she was about ready to jump across the table and straddle her boss, breaking one of those foundational pillars and bringing everything crashing down onto her head, like she always did.

"I'll be fine with my own meal," she said. She realized her hands were gripping the table and dropped them into her lap.

Tav lifted one shoulder and both brows, not really a shrug, but an acknowledgment.

"Well. How's the research for the website going?" he asked.

Portia waited a beat for him to say something rude, but that was it. It was a real question? Not a trap? She was used to having to force information onto him — and well, most people. She relaxed in her seat a little bit.

"It's going okay. I found some leads on the background of Dudgeon House," she said.

He raised his eyebrows. "Dudgeon House?"

"That's the original name of this building. You know, the one you've owned for twenty years?" She gestured to the armory looming up beside them.

"Is it now? Huh. That's good to know." He popped a fried shrimp into his mouth.

Something wasn't computing.

"How do you know about all these obscure medieval accords and treaties, but nothing about the place where you've lived for so long?"

"Because I've been too busy trying to keep the place up, start a business, and run what's basically become a community center to give a shite what it was called a hundred years ago." He shrugged. "Part of the reason I didn't sell it off is I wanted to show people that a poor kid from Bodotria could do just as well as anyone else if given the chance. And I've done okay."

Portia wasn't a therapist, but if she were she might ask him if perhaps he had projected his anger at his biological father onto the building.

"You've never considered selling it?" She'd seen the estimated market value for the building online. Tav would be able to buy a more modern building better suited to his purposes and have *plenty* left over. The building had already been worth a lot but its value had shot up exponentially compared to everything else in the neighborhood. She wasn't keen on joining her parents' business, but she did have basic real estate sense.

"Of course, I have. I'd be daft not to. Look around," he said, pointing down the cobblestone street with a sauce-stained finger. "But if I sell, that's one more building that gets converted into a place where they turn up their nose at the people who've lived here all their lives. I want to change the neighborhood for the better in a way that doesn't involve good people getting pushed out of their homes and stores."

Portia made a vague noise of agreement.

"And it's the same rich fuck buying everything up and turning it into what he thinks the other rich fucks who move in will want. Selling would be a last gasp effort."

She chewed the inside of her cheek, gnawing at the discomfort caused by Tav's words. She was, after all, a rich fuck. Her parents' investment group focused on real estate.

Her income came from rent from buildings they'd bought for her in neighborhoods that had undergone rapid property value increases. Skyrocketing rents were what allowed her to do things like be a perpetual student and drop everything to be a swordmaker's apprentice.

"That sounds . . . not great," she said.

"Verra not great," he replied drily.

Portia didn't know what to say then. Banter usually flowed pretty easily between them, but now her family's wealth felt like a dirty secret. And there was this kernel of a crush, like a pea under her mattress. Her brain bounced like a roulette ball, trying to settle on a topic, but the wheel kept spinning as she stared at Tav, feeling increasingly foolish.

"Did you know that a tardigrade is a microanimal not a police box?" she asked.

His brow creased in confusion. "What's that now?"

"Never mind," she said, shaking her head. "Just ignore that."

This was why crushes were ridiculous. They sapped you of power and rotted your brain.

Why isn't my food here already? Cheryl, please save me from myself.

"All righty. Ignoring." He picked up a rib

and sucked the meat off the bone, his lips slick as he worked it over. Portia must have made a sound because he paused and his gaze went to her face.

"Okay, you've been staring at me like I have two heads for a minute now. Don't tell me," he said, wiping at his mouth with a blue paper napkin. "My eating is uncivilized."

"Um." She was tempted to tell him what she'd really been thinking of — his lips on her body. Then Tavish's mouth pulled into a slow grin and she realized he'd understood at least some portion of that without her saying a word.

Shit.

"Here you go!" Cheryl dropped a tray in front of Portia, her smile faltering a bit as she looked back and forth between them. "Everything all right?"

"She's just eyeing my meat," Tav said. He picked up another rib and worked the meat from the bone in teasing pulls with his front teeth.

Portia was certain her face had never gone hotter. She was blushing, and Tavish was enjoying the fact that she was blushing, which made her face burn even more. She missed her days of drunken hedonism, when almost nothing could faze her. She'd lost

191

her tolerance for flirting it seemed; just the tiniest sip of one hundred proof Tav had left her dizzy.

Cheryl's face scrunched in confusion, but then a group of tourists in Union Jack T-shirts ambled up to the sandwich board menu and she went to greet them.

Come on. You've eaten men like this for breakfast — or had them eat you. Get a hold of yourself.

Portia picked up one of the fish ball skewers. "Give me one reason not to jab you with this."

"I'll give you two — one, it would be a waste of food, and two, I might like it."

She forced herself to relax. This was just talk, and she was fantastic at "all talk, no action." They were two adults, flirting, and nothing else had to come of it. Besides, he'd say something dickish soon enough, and kill the hum of attraction in her body like a mosquito on a bug zapper.

She placed the skewer down and began cutting at the fish balls with her plastic fork and knife.

"Seriously? You can't use your hands for that?"

See? Zap.

"I prefer using my hands for more enjoyable things," she said before spearing half an orb and popping it into her mouth. "Like making swords."

"Why are you here?" he asked suddenly.

"The human body requires energy to run . . ." She couldn't remember the rest of the smart-ass response she'd lifted from her friend Ledi. Something about the power-house of the cell . . . she shrugged. "I was hungry."

"No. Why did you apply for the apprenticeship? Here? And don't distract me with the spiritual mankiller tripe. You've enough experience to get a real, high-paying job. At a museum, or consulting, or anything really. But you're here, on my arse about learning how to make a sword."

He seemed to be genuinely curious and not just annoyed with her.

"Well . . . I've tried working at a museum. And art galleries. And offices. Nothing *fit*. It was like wearing a pair of too-small heels. You grin and bear it for a while, keep up appearances, try not to be a bother to everyone around you, but one day it's too much and you have to step out of the shoes or amputate your toes. Know what I mean?"

"I hope that coming here was the stepping out of the shoes and not the toe amputation part of that," he said. "But aye, I know what you mean. That's how the armory started. I was going to work in a shite office every day, hating every minute of it. Coming home to a wife who thought she'd married a reliable office jockey keen on swords, then got met with the truth — she'd married an unreliable sword jockey who hated offices."

His smile was rueful, and Portia tried to imagine him dressed in a suit, slogging to an office every day with a grimace on his face as he daydreamed of steel and battle.

"What happened?" She knew plenty of people who had divorced — it had been one of her reasons for never getting serious. Yeah, there were her parents but the data spoke for itself. Divorce was almost inevitable, but marriage didn't have to be. It just seemed like a lot of work to end up miserable and trapped. She could get that anxiety for free without putting up with an annoying partner or wedding planning stress.

Tav chuckled. "Damned if I know. After making sure I had enough income coming in from the rent here, I quit my job and started apprenticing with a swordmaker I'd met through the martial arts stuff, and it was the first time since I'd graduated that I was happy to get up and go to work.

"Greer tried to be excited for me, to care because I did, but it just wasn't what she wanted in her life — to be married to a niche tradesman. We grew apart." He looked off into the distance, then smiled and shrugged. "She's a good lassie. Living the life she wants now, just how I'm living the life I want. Which brings us back to you."

"Did my parents put you up to this?" she asked.

"What?"

"This is their favorite question for me. Asking me what I'm doing with my life, and telling me I should be more like my sister, or more like them, or like . . . . anyone but me. But I don't know what I want," she said. "I've been running from one thing to another for a long time. School, internship, school, fellowship, classes, drinking, and . . ." He didn't need to know everything. "I'm almost thirty and I have no fucking idea what I'm doing."

"I know that feeling," he said. "Everyone acts like you're just supposed to find what you love right away, and if you don't, just do something you don't love. And if you do neither of those things you're being selfish."

Portia's throat went a little tight because that was the word that lay at the heart of every discussion with her parents, whether they said it aloud or not. And when all Portia wanted to do was make people

195

happy, every insinuation otherwise was a reminder that no one, not even her family, could see through the veneer of hot mess to the real her.

"Well, what do you *like* to do?" he asked. "Besides annoy me?"

She wasn't sure anyone besides Ledi had ever asked her that. She hadn't had the answer before, but now . . . "I like figuring things out, like the website for the armory and how to get people into Mary's bookshop. I like social media — you've gained over two thousand new followers in the past three weeks, by the way. I like . . . helping people. And making things with my hands, too."

Tav shifted his bulk, leaning back in his seat. "So you're just waiting to see which shoe fits, eh Freckerella?"

She didn't quite like that comparison. People focused so much on the prince slipping on Cinderella's lost shoe that they didn't realize the real happily ever after was the moment she realized she was brave enough to go to the damned ball alone in the first place.

"I'm not waiting around for some fuckboy to bring me a shoe. I'm here, working for you. I'm finding my own shoe," she said. "Do you know how hard finding the perfect pair of shoes is? Wait, I've seen your shoes. You don't."

"Ha. Ha. All right. I've got to go make some deliveries and I have a community meeting tonight, so I might not see you at dinner later." He took a swig of his bottle of water and then stood, holding his tray. "Tomorrow is a forge day. No sleeping in."

A rush of effervescent excitement went straight to Portia's head. "Forge? I get to make a sword tomorrow? Finally?"

Her voice came out high-pitched and she would have been embarrassed if she wasn't so damn souped up.

"Aye. You like making things with your hands, right? Meet me in the courtyard bright and early because I won't wait for you if you're late."

"Yes, Sir Tavish, sir!" she said, saluting. He grinned as he walked away, and Portia sat for a moment with the carbonated happiness that fizzed in her.

She glanced at him as he took the steps up into the armory two at a time, and added Ass Man to the list of supervillain names she was compiling for him.

"Cheryl! I get to make a sword tomorrow!" She waved her hands in the air, an impromptu celebration dance, and Cheryl laughed.

"I'm not sure why you'd be happy to spend more time with that wanker, but I'm glad you get to do something that makes you happy."

"Thanks," Portia said. "Hey, do you want to do something this week maybe? Like, away from the armory?"

Cheryl's brown eyes lit up. "Of course. There's so much we can do! The Royal Mile, or a train out to the countryside, or I can take you to my parents' neighborhood, or —"

A couple of teens walked up to the window and Cheryl gave her a quick smile that implied they'd finish the conversation later, after the customers had gone.

Portia reached to grab a fish ball, utensils be damned, and her fingers slid across something sticky and slick. She looked down at her plate and realized Tav had slid the last of his ribs onto her tray when she wasn't looking.

She grinned as she bit into it, and told herself it didn't mean anything at all that it really was the best rib she'd ever eaten.

CHAPTER 11

"Okay, I was gonna get you started with something like a knife made with stock removal, but we'll do this American style. 'Go big or go home,' or whatever it is you tossers say. We're forging a longsword."

Tav stood beside the forge, hands on his hips and swagger in his voice to hide his nerves. Yes, nerves. It was fucking ridiculous. He could forge with his eyes closed — or at the very least while squinting. But even prepping the forge had felt odd, like he was using someone else's hands to gather the lengths of metal and wood, and to light the fire. That was mostly because someone else's *gazo* was on him. Portia's.

She stood before him now, tablet and electronic pencil in hand, diligently taking notes as he spoke. She was dressed rather casually, for her: a loose gray scoopneck T-shirt and black leggings. Both were made of soft fabrics that hugged her curves, and he was fairly certain that despite their casualness, they were both pricey designer items.

"Isn't stock removal the more common technique?" she asked. "Tracing a pattern onto the steel and then grinding away the excess, leaving a blade?"

"Aye, but grinding away for hours requires a certain level of stamina."

Portia's studious gaze softened to something decidedly naughty. "I would imagine so." She shook her head and laughed. "It's going to be really hard to avoid innuendo today, isn't it?"

Tav chuckled, felt the mood lighten a bit. "It's a hazard of the job I'm afraid. Don't worry, I can handle it."

"Well, since the other hazards involve accidentally cutting a finger off or burning myself with molten metal, I'll take Innuendo for $1,000, Tav."

"In that case, here's my eighteen-inch length of steel," he said, pulling the thin flat metal from the worktable.

"Dear Lord," Portia said, then pressed her lips together.

"Hey, you're the one who pressed for these lessons, Freckles." Tav gripped the steel and pointed it at her. "You had to have some idea they'd be like this."

Though he was still firmly against exploring anything with Portia, despite the banked attraction between them, they were both adults who should be able to acknowledge it and move past it.

"Oh." Her thin brows rose. "Is that why you kept brushing me off?"

Tav sighed. "No. I brushed you off because you were annoying and intrusive," he said gruffly, but Portia didn't react how she had to his previous insults. She smirked at him.

"Right."

The cheek. He really had lost his edge.

"I think you were worried about sparks flying," she said, then tilted her head toward the anvil near the forge. "Sparks? Get it?"

"I'm the only one allowed to tell bad jokes here, Freck." But he felt less nervous now that they had in a way, dealt with the horny elephant in the room. Now they could just be normal coworkers. "We're gonna start by hammering the tang, that is, the handle of the sword that's going to be embedded in the hilt. I've already cut away two triangles of metal at the end of the steel, leaving a pointed handle that will fit into the hilt."

He stopped and picked up the hammer, laying the steel down on the work surface. He'd lifted the hammer to strike the tang when she made a sound to get his attention.

"Hold on," she said, tapping at her tablet and then pointing its camera at him. "Okay, annnnnd action! You were about to hammer the tang, Sir Tav?"

It was hard to be annoyed when she called him that — hard but not impossible. "Why are you recording this?" he asked.

She rolled her eyes, as if the answer should be obvious. "Because it will get people interested in your business. Which is one of my duties as an apprentice. I'm going to post it on social media and in the next post for my sister's blog."

Tav rolled his neck, tried not to show too much annoyance. "I don't like being videoed, Freckles."

She looked up from the screen. "It's not going to steal your soul, you know. In case that was a concern. And why is this different than the exhibition?"

"I was performing then. And my face was covered." He shifted restlessly. "I just don't like the idea of people watching, making their little cool, snarky comments. I'm not entirely comfortable being reduced to a bloody hashtag."

Portia's stubborn expression softened a bit. "Oh, okay. The #swordbae thing freaked you out. That's totally understandable. BUT I need to be clear that the comments on this video will not be snarky. They will mostly be, um, appreciative, if I had to make a guess. But you don't have to do anything you don't want."

Tav remembered her comment from that first day he'd found her watching him at the grinder. He wasn't the most logical man, but it stood to reason that if she thought others would appreciate watching him, it was because she appreciated it herself.

"I'll give you thirty seconds and that's it," he said.

"Two minutes," she countered calmly.

"One," he compromised and remained stoic when she did a little gleeful jump. He kept his eyes above her neckline, too.

"Okay, and *action*! Again!"

Tav tried to frown discouragingly at her. She was having way too much fun with this.

"The tang. Yeah. Tang. Tangy," he choked out, then remembered that this was for Portia, not the annoying contraption in her hand. He straightened, and fixed her with his gaze instead of the phone. "We're hammering out the tang, aye?"

"Aye, Sir Tav!" she responded with an encouraging grin. He liked this Portia, open and teasing — the Portia he'd sent into hiding with his childish response to his attraction. He could do this silly video without complaining. For her.

"The thing with the tang, which is what keeps the blade locked into the handle of the sword for those of you who don't know, is that the angles have to be rounded. Soft." He ran his fingertip over the blunted edge of metal and because his gaze was on her face he saw the way her teeth pressed down on her bottom lip in response. "This is what secures the sword to the hilt. If you have sharp edges, it can eventually lead to fissures and cracks in the metal, and a sword that breaks off at the hilt in the middle of battle. And if that happens? You're done for. Always check for cracks at this point in the process to ensure you're crafting something that will stand the test of time."

He turned, placed the steel down on the work surface, hefted the hammer, and went at it for approximately thirty seconds, mostly so he wouldn't have to look her full in the face any longer.

He turned to her, slightly winded. "That good enough?"

She nodded, staring at the tablet, and he heard his own voice playing back. "Yeah. I think that'll go over *real* well. I'll do a photo collage of the progression of the sword, too."

She snapped a pic and Tav shook his head.

"All right, enough," he said. "Let's see if you've got what it takes to do this on your first try."

She curled her lip at him, as he knew she would. When she was in fighting form, an insult was an invitation to hand someone their arse.

While she did stop to take a photo every now and again, she was a diligent student, asking question after question, not because she didn't understand but because she wanted to know everything. He hadn't been wrong about that hunger in her. He'd expected to have to show her things multiple times, as he would with any student, but she was quick, picking up the subtleties in his motions and incorporating them into her work. When she finally held up the finished product, Tav felt real pride in her work, that had nothing to do with his attraction to her. She was on her way to becoming a fantastic swordmaker.

"Wow," she said, and the reverence in her voice pierced through the metaphorical armor he'd donned before they'd begun that morning. She was his apprentice, but if he was honest, she was something else, too. There had been a part of him that kept waiting for her to laugh, to call his work silly. After all, "wow" was what Greer had said the first time he'd forged a sword here, too, but her voice had been tinged with resentment, like she'd been wondering how the fuck she'd found herself in that particular situation.

Some part of Tav hadn't gotten past the fact that Portia — prim, proper, stylish Portia — could *really* respect what he did. But her face made clear that he'd been wrong about her, yet again. He'd been wrong about so much when it came to her.

The way she was looking at the sword was enough to start the stirrings of desire in him, despite the fact that he'd deck the next person who pointed out the weapon's phallic connotations to him.

She gripped the sword by the hilt and held it out before her. The weapon was slim and lightweight, and it seemed ornate in her long-fingered grip even though the hilt was basic wood and the cross-guard lacked any ornamentation. She was enough.

"This is . . ." She carefully swung the sword back and forth, and Tav admired the respect in her slow movements and the way she looked about to make sure she wouldn't nick anything, including him. He'd seen many a newbie hurt over the years by forgetting that a sword was a weapon.

Portia's smile was a weapon, too, gutting him as she looked up with glittering eyes.

"We made this!" she said. She was grinning like mad as she carefully placed the sword down on the forge to take a picture, then she stopped and stared at it. "You know what's weird? When we were kids, my parents would take Reggie and me to the Met. The museum, you know?"

He knew Reggie was her twin, who ran the website where she'd been writing about her adventures at the armory. Jamie and Cheryl had told him the posts were good fun; Tav wondered if she portrayed him as a medium- or large-sized bawbag.

"Reggie liked the modern art and the Egyptian tomb. My favorite pieces were the Byzantine jewelry and the Greek statues, but there's this huge room full of swords and armor . . ."

He noticed she seemed sad when she mentioned her sister, and wondered if it had something to do with being a twin. In every movie he'd seen, twins shared some weird bond. Or one was good and one was evil. He realized he shouldn't base his knowledge of twins on movies; he'd miss Jamie if he were in another country, twin or no.

Portia glided a fingertip over the smooth center of the blade. "I always wanted to go to that room, and my parents assumed it was because I liked the armored horses on display. Really, it was because I liked the weapons. I used to imagine mounting up like Joan of Arc and riding into battle, being strong enough — good enough — to defend my family from anything."

Tav could imagine it, too. Her thick curls resting about the bevor and pauldron, then flying out behind her after she raised her sword and charged. It was a magnificent fantasy, but then the real Portia's smile twitched and collapsed, rising again but as if buttressed by sheer willpower.

"After Reggie got sick, I would go sit in that room for hours — I skipped school, went there on the weekends. I spent more time there than the hospital. It was easier . . . reading all the curated information, over and over again."

Tav felt a sick embarrassment as he remembered doubting her knowledge of weaponry. *Is that how she knew so much? Christ.*

"Mostly I'd just sit and imagine being someone else, in another time, able to fight off the things that wanted to hurt the ones you loved. But a sword isn't the most efficient tool against a brain virus."

Her sadness resonated in Tav like a blow

against the anvil. He'd been obsessive about Jamie's safety, those early years when Bodotria hadn't been studded with cafes and boutiques. And Portia was a twin. He couldn't imagine the fear and pain that must have caused her, seeing a part of herself — a reflection of herself, really — on the brink of death.

She sighed. "Some sister I was, huh? Hiding in a museum while Reggie was trapped in a hospital bed."

"Portia," Tav said. He tugged at his gloves but his gaze was focused on her face.

"Sorry for the Dr. Phil shite." She shook her head and gave him that forced smile again. "I'd just completely forgotten about that. And holding the sword I remembered it. Is this some kind of fairy magic you forgot to warn me about? Is that the real reason you kept putting off the training?"

She was trying to act like what she'd told him didn't matter much, but her voice still shook. That was the thing with creating something; you put some bit of yourself into it, if you did it well, but fuck if you could control what bit of yourself that was.

"Sounds like something traumatic happened, you dealt with it as best you could, then blocked it out," he said. That was when Tav realized that his hand was resting on her shoulder.

When had that happened?

She glanced down at his hand, then up to his face, then back down at the hand, clearly wondering what he was doing. Tav was wondering the same bloody thing.

"You were brilliant today," he said. "You're gonna make a fine swordsmith, aye?"

"Probably not, but at least we made this one nice thing," she replied breezily, looking up at him with those wide brown eyes that skewered him with want.

"You don't have to find a reason to get down on yourself after you do something grand, lass," he said. He didn't know where the words came from, but he was certain he was right. It wasn't that Portia wasn't proud of her accomplishments — she certainly knew her strengths — it was that she had a way of blowing her failures up like a shield to block anyone from getting at the successes.

"That isn't what I was doing," she said. Her tone was annoyed, but her breath was coming fast and when his hand slid up the side of her neck, he could feel her pulse racing. Her hand came up and that grip of hers wrapped around his forearm. "What are *you* doing?"

Tav had no idea.

"Making sure there are no cracks," he murmured. Her throat worked beneath his palm.

She closed her eyes and her grip loosened on his arm. Tav's hand smoothed up her neck, over the soft, warm skin, and cupped her cheek.

"You're going to mess up my skin-care routine," she said, nose scrunching in annoyance as she tilted her head away from his hand. Tav's senses started coming back to him. What was he doing? With his apprentice? In the courtyard?

She was right to pull away from him.

"I'm sorry," he said, yanking his hand back.

"You should be," she said. "I have very sensitive skin." Then she pressed up on her toes and kissed him.

The kiss was not what he'd imagined. Because of course he'd imagined kissing her already, and in his fantasy she had been aggressive and take-charge, pulling him down and wrapping her legs around him. But this kiss was hesitant, though she'd initiated it, soft and just a whisper of sensitive skin rubbing over sensitive skin, as if she was prepared to pull away and run off at any second.

Can't be having that, can we?

Tav's arms slipped around her waist and pulled her up flush against him, angling his neck so that his mouth fit more firmly against hers. She moaned, and his cock thickened in his jeans and pressed against her as if urging her on.

She shifted so that her hips pressed into him — there was nothing hesitant about that motion — and her tongue slicked against his, hot and wet and searching. His hand flattened against her lower back, holding her firmly in place as he kissed the everloving fuck out of her. That was the only way to describe the ungainly, raw thrust of his tongue into her mouth, the groan that escaped him.

Her fingers were curled in the damp cotton of his shirt, bringing him down to her because, as in every other part of life, Portia was not one to let him think he could strut in and show her a thing or two, no matter how vulnerable she was at first. Now her hand was at the back of his neck, both stroking and drawing him down closer to her, like she was as afraid as he was that something would come between their questing mouths.

Tav hadn't kissed a woman in a while, and he wondered if he'd forgotten how good it was — or maybe it had just never been so good. Her tongue sparring with his, resisting his advances even as she pulled him closer, sent tingles up and down his spine. The hitch of her breath made his balls draw up tight because that might be the sound she made as he thrust into her for the first time. Her nipples were hard — *Christ, she's sensitive* — pressing into his chest, and he could only imagine how they would feel in his mouth and against his palm.

His hand slid hard up her back, fingertips dragging against the soft fabric of her shirt before sliding into her thick hair and holding her even more firmly as his tongue pillaged her mouth. She trembled in his arms and then he shivered because if she reacted like that to a slight tug of her hair . . .

Fuck, he thought.

"Fuck," she moaned, then her kissing began to slow, then stopped. She pulled away and rested her forehead against his chin. "Fuck." This time, the tone let him know something *had* come between them — reality.

She released him and pushed away, pupils wide and lips swollen.

"Of course, you would be a fantastic kisser," she said, and if he wasn't mistaken she was stressed about it.

"I'm fantastic at everything," he said,

213

ducking his head back down toward hers. He'd sipped from the Holy Grail, and now he needed another taste.

She hopped lightly out of his grasp — out of his reach.

"Except at being a boss," she said firmly. "We can't do this." She averted her gaze. "I can't do this. It's not part of the plan, okay?"

"Might I suggest an amendment to whatever plan this is?" He tried to keep the words light, but fuck if he wasn't ready to drop to his knees and beg, which meant her words applied to him, too.

He couldn't do this.

That didn't stop him from really, really wanting to.

"The plan doesn't need amendment. And I don't need this complication," she said. "In case you haven't noticed, I'm kind of a fuck-up, and I don't want this apprentice-ship to be just another mistake added to my list."

"I hadn't noticed that, though I notice you keep insisting on it," he said, crossing his arms over his chest. "But let's leave it at what it is. We were attracted to each other, we kissed, you humped my leg a little, and everything's fine now."

She gave a shocked laugh, the distress on her face driven away by the spread of her wide smile. "I did not hump your leg!"

"There was a wee bit of humping, lass," he said. He began a ridiculous reenactment of the kiss using a drainpipe as a stand-in, complete with an exaggerated dry hump. "Just a bit of 'Oh, Tavish, you great Highland beast.' "

"Stop it!" she squealed, playfully smacking at his arm. He obeyed her command, having accomplished his mission of making her laugh.

Maybe she wouldn't kiss him again. Maybe she would. Either way, she needed to know that things were fine between them.

He pulled away from the pipe, dusted off his hands. "All right, now the really fun part begins — cleanup."

They tidied the smithy, both pretending they weren't thinking of the kiss. Or maybe Portia really wasn't, but Tav was in full-blown replay mode, going over the kiss from every angle and in slo-mo like a particularly good goal in a Premiere League match.

"Thanks," she said, handing him the broom when they were done.

"Just doing my job," he said.

She nodded, then looked down to where both of their hands still held on to the broomstick. When she looked back up at him, there was that dusky rose across her cheeks.

"Back to data entry. Later!" She ran off.

"Later."

He hoped that was a promise.

CHAPTER 12

Bodotria Eagle: (left) Tavish McKenzie, Master-at-Arms at Bodotria Armory, and (right) Portia Hobbs his American apprentice. Readers of the Eagle will remember the international search for an apprentice launched by Mr. McKenzie last year, and now we're able to share the results. Ms. Hobbs made a fantastic showing at last weekend's Renaissance Faire, captivating audiences (and perhaps Mr. McKenzie?) with her impressive knowledge of weaponry and Scottish history. We look forward to seeing how the apprenticeship turns out!

Portia snuck another glimpse at the screenshot Reggie had posted on the GirlsWith-Glasses social media account.

Go, sis, go! Our favorite swordsmith in training made the Scottish papers! ♡

The message made her happy. Seeing Reggie pronounce her love and support so plainly to millions of strangers was a new experience. Her parents had always made their feelings about her clear, and Reggie had always seemed vaguely disappointed in her, too. Portia had kept her distance — it had been safer that way. Maybe she had been wrong.

"How do you know what your sister feels if you haven't asked her, Portia?"

Reggie's support was one blow to her emotions, and it had been paired with another: the photo of her and Tavish taken by the newspaper's photographer. She knew it was just silly fun, but it looked . . . perfect. His arm around her shoulders pulling her in close, both with weapons drawn in a battle stance. Tav was looking down at Portia as if he really would protect her against anything that came her way, and she was looking at him like someone had hit her upside the head with one of Cupid's arrows. It was nothing — she'd been whispering to him about marketing — but this was *before* they'd kissed. Now she couldn't help but look at it and wonder.

She put her phone down and turned her attention back to the other screen in front of her, displaying newspaper articles that were actually relevant to her work. She'd wasted enough time over the past few days thinking of Tavish when she very clearly shouldn't be.

She'd had plenty of interesting experiences with men, but none of them had involved making deadly weapons and then getting kissed like . . . like . . . she couldn't even come up with a good comparison. Tav had kissed her, and she'd never doubted she'd enjoy such a thing, but she'd clearly underestimated just how much it could shake her. In fact, her simple summation when she'd slunk into her text message group later that day and confessed to Ledi and Nya had been two words: I'm shook.

Of course, her friends had gone on a gleeful texting streak: there had been emojis, and GIFs, and GET IT GIRLs. She'd felt like less of a failure, even though she was one: she'd broken one of the cardinal rules of Project: New Portia — two if she was honest. But failure didn't feel so bad when it involved Tav's warm mouth, the scratch of his stubble against her cheek, his fingertips pressing into her hips and neck and sliding into her hair . . .

Heat warmed her breasts and she crossed her legs against the growing ache between them, making her feel like a pervert as she sat in the silent, comfortable confines of the Bodotria Library.

She could still feel his hands on her, when she closed her eyes, could even feel where his hands might have traveled if she hadn't pulled away from him. Connecting the dots from disparate information was essential to being a good researcher, and she could only come to one conclusion: Tav knew what he was doing. Her body wouldn't let her forget that.

Maybe it was because he was a little older — her hookups had tended toward young, dumb, and full of . . . imprecise applications of moves they'd picked up from watching too much porn. Or maybe it was because he was her first kiss in recent memory, and the first kiss in longer memory that hadn't tasted of booze.

"Portia, you say that alcohol helps you to relax and be open with people. Can you tell me how being open without alcohol makes you feel?"

Portia had never given much weight to her drunken escapades — that had kind of been the point. The alcohol had been its own kind of armor, protecting her from caring too much about anything. Most of the notches in her bedpost were slightly out of focus, but the memory of Tav's kiss was sharp as the blade they had forged and could cut her just as deeply if she let it.

She cleared her throat, and the librarian at the information desk raised her head from the pile of books she was sorting. For a moment, Portia was sure the dark-haired young woman knew she was having lascivious thoughts in the reference section.

"Need help with the microfiche, love?" the librarian asked. "Or a Ricola?"

"I'm fine, thank you," Portia responded guiltily, and turned back to the machine. She was totally fine. That kiss was an isolated incident, and since it would never happen again, there was no need to think about it again. She could throw all this excess energy into her research. Totally the same thing.

She was more accustomed to searching digital archives, but after a morning spent going through old newspapers, she'd gotten the hang of things. There were products to be packed and shipped — she was proud of the modest increase in sales that was resulting from her work — but Jamie had signed off on her research trip, knowing how much she wanted to get the site finished. She hadn't asked Tav; he'd been up in his office, and the risk of being alone with him had frightened her. No, that wasn't right — it had thrilled her.

She concentrated on the screen, scrolling through old copies of the *Bodotrian,* a local newspaper long since lost to the annals of time — outside of the Bodotria Library microfiche.

She was an old hand at research, but years spent on social media had prepared her for this tedious task. She scrolled by picture after picture, headlines that talked of boys going off to war and coming back, of new boats being unveiled that used increasingly complex methods of steering, of trade deals and shipping courses, and then of boys going off to war again.

She fell into a rhythm, gaze sliding over photos and words.

Giant ship with sails. Giant ship without sails. Bunch of white dudes. White dudes in front of a ship. Tavish and some fancy people. Another gia—

The hairs on the back of Portia's neck raised as she scrolled back and the picture came into view. It was grainy and black and white, but that was definitely Tavish. Or a very Tavish-like person. Talking to a woman, while holding the hand of a young boy. Their backdrop? The armory.

"Holy *shit,*" she yelped.

"Do you need *help,* love?" There was

menace in the librarian's voice now.

"No! I'm sorry. I just . . . get really excited about history, you know?"

"Ah. Well, that's fine then." The librarian smiled indulgently and nodded before returning to her work.

Portia turned and stared at the photo, then pulled out her phone and snapped a pic.

[International Friend Emporium]

Portia: <photo attachment> GUYS. I AM APPRENTICED TO AN IM-MORTAL.

Ledi: Um, is that photoshopped? Do you need me to FedEx some holy water? Holy pepper spray?

Portia: Wut is happening. I can't

Nya: Wait. WAIT.

Nya: "THERE CAN BE ONLY ONE!"

Ledi: . . .

Nya: It all makes sense! Remember the film we watched to gain knowledge of

Scottish culture before Portia left? There were Scotsmen with large swords, and beheadings, and immortals!

Ledi: You think #swordbae is . . . a Highlander?

Nya: Do you have a better explanation?

Ledi: I love you. Truly.

Portia: I'm apprenticed to The Highlander. Fuck.

She put the phone down, ignoring the texts flying by on the screen, and examined the article more closely.

ROYAL VISIT

While spending her yearly week at Holyrood, the Queen graced the waterways of Bodotria with a visit. While here, she consecrated a new ship named in her honor. In this photo, Edinburgh's Royal Duke, Douglas Dudgeon, shows her the hospital for addled soldiers he recently opened at his property, Dudgeon House. He is continuing the work of his great aunt, who opened Firth Hospital for the poor many years ago.

Portia's heart was racing as everything coalesced in her head. It could be a co-incidence that the father he'd never known had bequeathed him the property. It could be a coincidence that this man who was old enough to be his grandfather looked exactly like him. It could not be a coincidence that the man looked like Tavish, owned the same property, and had a son young enough to be Tavish's father. She didn't even need to ask Ledi to crunch the numbers on the probability of that, because it was clear as fuck: the chances of them being related was significant.

Portia: OMG It's worse.

Portia: He's not a Highlander.

Nya: Is he a vampire? Maybe I'll find my Rognath sooner than I imagined.

Portia: I think he might be the lovechild of a Duke?

Nya: EatingPopcorn.gif

Ledi: *chinhands* *like, chin is firmly nestled into my hands*

Portia: So, any advice on how to break it to someone that they're probably a member of the aristocracy?

Ledi: Wellllllllllll, I have some experience with this.

Nya: Bit of an understatement, cous.

Ledi: I know sometimes your judgment in how to present distressing news to someone can be lacking, so I'll say just gather your information, sit him down, and tell him. No contrived situations to spring the truth on him, like orchestrating an elaborate and humiliating reveal in front of a crowd of strangers.

Portia: ☹ Sorry.

Ledi: Just remember he's a human. This is his life. Unless he's completely sedated, he will have a reaction to this, and when presented with an unknown reaction in a test subject all you can do is watch and wait. And since he's not a lab rat, be there to help him through it.

Portia: I doubt he needs me for that.

Ledi: He'll need someone. You can be his someone, if you're up for it.

Ledi: I can only speak for myself, but I think I would have gone crazy after this princess shit if you weren't there to tell me how to talk to rich people and what was expected of me. You're pretty great at being a friend, Portia Hobbs. *finger guns*

Portia: 😭

Portia swiped at the real tears that had gathered in her eyes. She'd almost lost Ledi's friendship with insecurities and boundary issues. She really had lost Reggie, until just recently, by avoiding her family and their judgment. She hadn't been there for either of them when they'd needed her the most. And though both relationships seemed better and stronger now, she sometimes wondered if they weren't just pretending. Indulging the poor, misguided loser until she messed up again and lost them completely.

No.

Ledi didn't lie, and she didn't bother with emotional stuff unless she was really moved to. So Portia was left with either thinking her best friend was a sociopath drawing out some protracted mindfuck, or she had to accept that maybe, just maybe, Ledi had meant what she'd written. She allowed herself a few seconds of doubt-free joy. Sometimes it was a simple text sent from a friend thousands of miles away, a thing lots of people would call insubstantial, that felt like the most solid thing in her world.

Portia stood from her seat.

"Excuse me?"

The librarian looked up again.

"I need help now. I need to print this article and . . . do you have any books about dukes?"

The librarian's eyes went wide and she rubbed her hands together with glee. "We have a fantastic romance section," she said. "Do you need recommendations? How do you like your dukes? Grumpy? Tortured? Alpha, beta, or alpha in the streets, beta in the sheets?"

"Actually, I meant nonfiction," Portia said glumly.

The librarian sighed. "Aye. Just a warning, love — the non-fic dukes are not nearly as fun."

Portia sighed.

The librarian had no idea.

CHAPTER 13

Tavish wasn't a man prone to anxiety, but he'd spent the two hours after Portia's awkward phone call asking if they could have a meeting in a state of extreme agitation. He'd suggested they meet at Cheryl's for lunch and she'd insisted they meet in his office. He'd tried to puzzle out what could have had her in such a state, and what could be so important that she'd call a meeting, but he could only think of one thing.

She's leaving.

Though they'd cleaned together after their kiss, and agreed to act like it hadn't happened, Portia had clearly been avoiding him. She'd been quiet at dinners, though he'd caught her glancing at him. Her body had been stiff with tension, and now that he knew what she felt like in his arms, he'd wanted nothing more than to help relieve it.

Tav clomped up the steps to his office, annoyed by the way his skin felt too tight and anxiety pooled in his stomach. He'd forgotten what it felt like, being this concerned when it came to a woman.

This is exactly the feeling you wanted to avoid, you git.

After Greer — Greer who he'd loved and who had loved him, but it had all gone to hell anyway — he'd been too busy with other things to deal with feelings and all that shite. And if he hadn't been too busy, he'd been too clever, because only a fool set himself up for disappointment on a grand scale twice. He'd get an itch and he'd scratch it. He told himself that's what this was about — Portia was like a mosquito bite that he'd scratched just enough to make the itch abundantly and painfully clear. That's why his breath kicked a bit when he turned at the top of the stairs and saw her sitting pensively in the chair outside his office door in a delicate dress that had no place in his armory. That's why he was already preparing a script to convince her not to leave: *If you leave, we'll have to start the apprentice search all over again. If you stay, I'll never touch you again.*

It was then that he realized he was in deep shite. He remembered something his mum had asked him when things were falling apart with Greer.

"What are you willing to do to keep her at your side? I won't see a son of mine crawl on his knees, but if you think she's worth it, I'll be here to clean the scrapes, no matter what she decides."

Tav hadn't gone down on his knees, all those years ago. He'd politely asked Greer to stay and she'd politely declined and that had been that. He felt nothing polite in him at the thought of Portia leaving, which probably meant that she should.

"Hi," she said, standing. Her smile was friendly, but there was strain around those big brown eyes of hers.

He flung open the office door and ushered her inside, gestured toward the seat she'd sat in that first morning after nearly burning his eyes out. He sat down, laced his fingers together over the papers on his desk. He'd known how to be professional once, to sit in meetings with a bland expression, and he called on that training to keep him from thinking about how she had gasped into his mouth when he'd tugged at her hair.

"You wanted to meet?" he asked. Professional. Not remembering the slide of her stomach over his cock as she'd pressed closer to him.

"Yes." She looked worried, and Tav once

again felt that strange and unprofessional need to hold her.

He leaned forward. "Is everything all right? If this is about the other day . . ."

"No. This is something important and I'm not quite sure how to tell you."

If Tavish hadn't been well-versed in the birds and the bees, he would've started to worry that one could get pregnant from kissing. He'd nearly come in his pants from that kiss, so it wasn't the most unrealistic thing that might have happened.

"Okay." She took a fortifying breath.

"Christ, out with it then," he said. There was being professional and there was being tortured.

"So you know I've been researching the history of the building as something fun for any history buffs who might happen across the site. And I found something." She sucked in a breath and then stood, coming to stand beside him as she tapped at her tablet. She handed it over to him.

"Please don't hate me," she said. "But I would be remiss as an apprentice, and as a friend, if I didn't show you this."

Tav was caught on the fact that she'd called him a friend until his gaze tracked to the screen of the tablet, where he saw a picture of himself. No, not himself. His hair was thicker — would be wavier at that length, his nose a little less pronounced, and he had his mother's mouth. He wasn't keen on photos, but he looked in the mirror every damn day, and whoever was in this obviously old photo looked a hell of a lot like him. Tav's brain tried to process that and stalled out.

"What is this?" he asked, trying not to sound annoyed. He really didn't like situations like this, where someone already knew the endgame and he was still puzzling his way along.

She swiped the screen again and there was now the full picture, along with a newspaper clipping. There was his doppelganger, along with a little boy, and — was that the bloody Queen?? Outside of the armory?

Dread began to gather in his muscles, tensing them for some unwanted revelation.

"I found this photo at the library this morning. This is the Royal Duke of Edinburgh, Douglas Dudgeon, sometime in the late 1940s. That's his son, another Douglas Dudgeon, who inherited the property upon his father's passing." She swiped again and another image popped up, of some kind of family tree, rife with titles Tav usually came across in the old treatises he pored over for information about weapons and martial arts.

She swiped again and there was another newspaper clipping, this one more recent — from the late 1970s. A man who didn't look exactly like him, as in the other photo, but still resembled him a great deal.

Meet the New Duke! With the passing of Douglas McGuinness Dudgeon, his son Douglas Tavish McGuinness Dudgeon has inherited the title of Royal Duke of Edinburgh. He is known for his philanthropic works in the resettlement of refugees, in addition to being one of Edinburgh's most sought-after bachelors. Now that he has inherited the dukedom, the confirmed bachelor will certainly be in search of a duchess!

"Interesting," he said. "Yeah. That's . . ." He mumbled something — even he wasn't sure what. His brain was too busy spinning. "I mean, that's a pretty big coincidence."

She sucked in a deep breath. "I checked the deed again. And before it passed to you, it was registered to a non-profit organization, which upon further probing was under the umbrella of a larger corporation. Owned by Douglas Tavish McGuinness Dudgeon."

Tavish had never thought much about his father, and what he had thought hadn't been good. The man had clearly wanted nothing to do with him. Tav had been more than happy with the family he had, so there'd been no room for wishful thinking about some wanker he'd never even met.

How did he explain then, the sudden emotions whirling through him? He wanted to throw something. He wanted to stab something. He wanted to flip his desk. Not because he now had a face to put to his father, and a name, but because now he understood that his father had been a powerful man. A member of the peerage. His mother had been a scared young refugee. And this man had gotten her pregnant and abandoned her. The date on the paper didn't lie — his mother would have been well along with him when this story broke.

"The fucking numpty lavvy-heided wank stain arsepiece," Tav growled. "I'll fucking throttle him."

Portia's hand came down on his clenched fist, which he hadn't realized was shaking.

"Tav." He heard it in her tone, knew before he swiped the screen and saw the obituary.

"Well, good riddance."

"I'm sorry," she said. "I know this must be a lot for you to take in."

Tav scoffed. "Yes and no. I always knew

he was a right bloody bastard and now I have confirmation, that's all."

Her brow wrinkled and she shook her head. "I think you need to read to the end of the obituary."

He snatched the tablet, trying to concentrate on the words through the haze of his rage.

. . . as he produced no heirs, the estate and the Dukedom have passed on to a distant relation . . .

. . . as he produced no heirs . . .
. . . no heirs.

"Fuck," he said. "No. I appreciate you telling me but I want nothing to do with this scum."

"Tav, I know you're upset right now, but think about it."

"Think about being a bloody duke? Having to chat with rich arseholes like the one who knocked up my mum and abandoned her? The ones who make their little charity visits to the poor and then go home to huge estates that could house every homeless person in Scotland?"

Portia took a deep breath. "The estate is valued at basically a shit ton of money. Think about what you could do with that.

You could fix up the armory. Expand the community programs you've started. You'd be able to make an even bigger difference."

She was clever, Portia was.

He exhaled, realized that his body was taut with restrained anger, and that Portia's hand still rested on his. She was close beside him, how people hovered around brats taking their first steps. It should have annoyed him, but he couldn't remember the last time someone had been there to catch him. His family was loyal and supportive, but he'd made his role very clear: he was the protector, even when no one needed protecting. Seeing Portia look at him the way she was added more confusion to his already sparking emotions, even as he was grateful for it.

"Thank you. For telling me," he said. "I'll be honest, my head's kind of fucked right now."

She smiled. "I think that's the normal reaction to news like this, from what I've seen."

"You have experience with this?" He gave an incredulous laugh, but she did that lip licking thing he'd learned was a tell that she was nervous about something.

"Actually, I can help." She was looking at him with that pleading look again, which didn't make sense. "I don't want to be presumptuous, but I imagine you haven't had a lot of interaction with rich assholes. I have. I am one, actually, a rich asshole with years of experience who can help you navi—"

"Stop," he growled, and she flinched.

"I get it. I'll go now," she said.

"What the bloody hell, Portia? You come in here presenting this Sherlock Holmes shite, solve the greatest mystery of my life, and then call yourself an arsehole?"

She blinked at him.

"You're not an arsehole," he said.

"You don't know me well enough to say that with such conviction," she countered.

He remembered her sitting across from him that first morning.

I . . . really need this.

"Well, I guess I will soon enough. You were offering to help me with this, right?"

"Right."

"What're you charging?" he asked.

"Nothing," she said. "I'm your apprentice. It's covered."

"Charging me nothing for something I'm sure costs a song. You're right. You're a raging arsehole. Get out of my sight."

She just looked at him. Tav ran his hands through his hair, then took a deep breath.

"Look, I need to talk to Jamie. And my

mum. We have a lot to discuss, it seems. But if I do this. *If.* I wouldn't mind the help. I have to pay you, though. This is more than what you signed up for."

"I'll invoice you later." She snatched the tablet from him. "*If,* that is."

She hurried out, likely to find some new way to disrupt his life, and Tav sat alone with what looked to be a pretty clear truth: he was royally fucked.

"*Míralo,* my son has finally figured out how to use the video chat, I see."

His mother looked lovely as she always did; her smooth tan skin didn't show her sixty years, and all that she'd gone through. Behind her, he could see the artwork she and his dad had collected each trip to Santiago until they'd finally retired and made their vacation home a more permanent one. Tav focused on the art because he hadn't realized until the moment her face popped up on the screen that he was angry at her, too. Really angry, it seemed.

"*Hola, mi amor,*" she said, beaming at him.

"Douglas. *Tavish.* McGuinness. Dudgeon," he replied, the words edged with razor wire. He'd thought he'd start off with "hello" and ease into the whole "did you forget to tell me I was next in line for a dukedom?" thing, but life was full of surprises, he was discovering.

To her credit, she didn't flinch, or sigh, or react much at all. Instead, she smiled her beatific smile and shook her head like a kid caught with her hand in the cookie jar.

"*Ay dios,*" she said quietly, as if she'd forgotten her metro pass or some other mundane setback. His mother had always been good at making things seem less serious. When boys at school teased him, making fun of his mother and father and the fact that he looked nothing like them, she'd always gently said, "We know better than to indulge foolishness, *m'hijo.* And besides, the Kinley boy's mum ran off. He's just acting out."

She always had reason to forgive, and she always asked the same of Tav. One day, tired of her beatific nature he'd had the cheek to ask, "So you forgive Pinochet then?" His mother had slapped him, reflexively, then cried for days afterward every time she'd looked at him because she'd been so racked with guilt.

Tav didn't want to see her cry again, and he tried to leave his anger to cool on the sill.

"I have never cared who my father was," he said, choosing his words carefully. "My

241

biological father. Because Dad is my real father, and I love him. But I need to know. If what Portia has dug up is true . . ."

"Portia? Is this the woman your brother told me about? The apprentice?" Her eyes went wide and speculative, as if possible matchmaking might be more important than the truth around his background.

"Mum. Please."

She sighed. "Look. I was young. I was scared. I found asylum in this strange country, where I no longer had to worry that I might be tortured or killed, like so many of my family and friends." She looked around her slowly, and not for the first time he wondered if going back to Santiago meant constantly walking through the ghosts of her past. She remembered herself and looked back at him through the screen. "I'd lost everything. Then, after going through hell, I showed up in Scotland expecting the worst, and everyone was so kind! A parade met our bus as we pulled into town, and people began giving us clothing and gifts as soon as we stepped onto the ground."

She had told him this part before, in different variations throughout his life, but she had never cried before. Now the tears slipped silently down her cheeks.

"Mum," he said. This was why he hated this video shite. His teeth pressed together as he watched his mother weep on a cold, flat screen, unable to do anything about it. "I'm sorry. I didn't mean to upset you."

"I'm not crying because I'm upset," she said. "I'm crying because I was so happy and proud to be in Scotland, with these kind people, if I could no longer be in Chile. First, we had to stay with strangers in their homes, until things were sorted. And because I could speak English very well, I began to translate for the other refugees and helping the organization that was handling our care." She laughed a bit. "We didn't think of ourselves as refugees, of course. That's what everyone else called us. We just thought of ourselves as lucky."

"Is that where you met him? Translating? I saw he ran a program that worked with refugees," Tav said. "I guess he used it to troll for innocent young women, too? What a hero."

His mother wiped at the tears in her eyes. "I thought not telling you was best, but before anything, I have to say this — your father was a good man. He cared so much about helping people, and we thought we could help people together."

"Then he ran off on us," Tav said.

"No. Then, his father died. And his responsibilities fell onto him like a thunderclap from the sky." She shook her head and took a deep breath. "His father had lost most of the family's money on bad investments, and he was expected to fix their finances, join the peerage, produce an heir . . . but not with a Chilean refugee by his side."

She shrugged.

Tav was furious on her behalf. "If he really loved you, he would have fought for you."

His mother laughed. "You think that's what love is? I told you that all those books about knights and chivalry as a boy would warp your expectations."

His mother sighed and shook her head.

"He did. Fight for me, as you say. It was me who ended things. I told him it was over because I didn't know him anymore. He'd already begun to change. To grow harder. To drink more. To get angry at me when he was really angry at the world for forcing him to fill this role. It broke him, I think."

"You expect me to feel bad for him? That he was given power and property and, eventually, wealth?"

"Yes, I do, Tavish. Because I raised you better than to hate someone because it's the easy thing to do. And if you want to hate

244

someone, hate me. He didn't know about you until years later."

"Wha?" Tavish was so stunned he couldn't even hit the last consonant. He hadn't thought much about his biological father as a child — his real dad had been enough. In fact, it wasn't until he'd inherited the property that he'd first felt the sting of resentment. That was when what he'd supposed had happened to his mother had solidified into the truth in his mind — but he'd had it all wrong.

She let out a stream of Spanish he couldn't understand, then continued. "I didn't tell him because I saw what that life did to him, and I didn't want that forced onto you. And . . . I was scared. He was a powerful man who had become even more powerful, and I was a refugee. I had already learned once what the powerful were capable of. He could have done anything he wanted if he decided to keep you for himself. I couldn't take the chance of losing my child, after everything else I had lost."

Her tears had stopped and her chin was up. This was by no means an apology. It was an explanation. He felt like he deserved more, but it was simple if he thought about it. It was a lie of omission that had snowballed out of control and nearly squashed its teller. She'd thought she was doing the right thing. Tav couldn't say that she hadn't. He couldn't say she had. He was too busy being squashed by the out-of-control snowball on its return trip.

"If he didn't know about me, how did he give me the armory?" he asked. That was an easy question. Easier than dozens of others he had.

"He found out eventually. He saw us walking — saw you — and figured it out. But by that time he was married, for the second time, and bound by even more responsibility than before. The tabloid columnists were always on his tail, talking about his drinking and his mistakes, and he knew being linked with him would hurt you."

"So he was a saint," Tav said, running a hand through his hair in frustration.

"No. He was a man who wanted a simple life but was handed a complex one. And he understood that if he acknowledged you at that point, you wouldn't have that choice."

Tav felt the urge to throw things return. Goddammit, where had all these feelings come from? He needed to go forge or grind until he'd burned or abraded all his feelings away. He thought of Portia's hand resting on his trembling fist and exhaled slowly.

"This is a lot to take in, Mum."

She smiled. "I know, *m'hijo*. But you don't have to do anything you don't want to do. You are happy with your life, yes?"

Tav paused. He was generally satisfied, though stressed described the last year more accurately. Happy?

An image of Portia popped into his mind. Portia holding a blade she'd forged herself. That they'd forged together.

"I get by," he responded gruffly. "But now, I have the possibility to do more. I can expand the breakfast program, set up more programs for kids . . . do something about the shite the rich bastards are pulling in the neighborhood instead of just whinging about it."

His mother looked truly upset for the first time since the conversation had started. "You really want to pursue this?"

Tav thought of the developers ravening through his neighborhood like locusts that shit condos and coffee shops. He thought of the kids who pretended not to want breakfast and snuck muffins in their pockets when they thought no one was looking. He thought about Jamie, and Cheryl, and all of the people who voted dutifully and hoped for the best, but had no one that knew what their lives were really like schmoozing with the rich and telling things from their perspective.

"I always wanted to be a Sir Tavish McKenzie rather than Lord, but Your Grace will work," he said.

She smiled sadly.

"I know you think you hate him, but you're more like him than you know," she said. "Always helping others, and always underestimating the cost of it."

There was a knock at the door to his mother's office then, and his father suddenly appeared onscreen, holding a tray with two ceramic teacups. Tav could only see the bright green button-up shirt he wore and his dark arms holding the tray. His mother looked up. "He knows, *corazón*. And he's talking about what he could do if he claimed the title."

His father placed the tray on the desk, then knelt beside his wife to peer at Tav through the screen. His mustache was now more silver than black, but he looked well rested. "Oh I know that look," he said. "You gonna do this thing, then, son?"

"I don't know, Dad." Tav scraped his hand over his stubble. "What do you think?"

"I think the monarchy and peerage are parasites, sucking the lifeblood of the working man, but you would be my favorite parasite." His father paused and seemed to consider the possibilities. "And I have to admit, getting to have a word with the Queen would be something."

Tavish imagined his father explaining why the monarchy should have been abolished along with slavery and didn't know whether to immediately accept the title because of that or to immediately reject it.

"Do you think anyone has ever called the Queen bumbleclot to her face?" his dad asked, stroking his chin as if pondering a philosophical question.

"Henry!" His mother slapped at his father's arm, but then her hand slid down until their palms touched and their fingers interlaced. He saw his father's fingers flex, giving silent comfort though he'd cut the tension with his jokes. His parents worked well that way, one shoring the other up when necessary. In the end, he'd realized that was what had been missing with Greer. They'd never been able to figure out that delicate dance of support.

He thought of Portia offering to help him, as if it was the most natural thing in the world. He wasn't sure he was the right kind of man to take on a dukedom, but he was positive he wasn't the kind who deserved Portia's unswerving support.

"I'll see if I can get you an audience," Tav

said, then something occurred to him. "Would it bother you? Me getting involved in this stuff with my biological father's world?"

"I'm worried about you getting involved with this because I love you and I don't want you hurt. But I'm your father and you're my son, and nothing is going to change that, understand? If I could deal with you from the ages of twelve to eighteen and still love you, nothing can shake that, not even a title."

Warmth flowed through Tav's chest and he nodded. "I haven't decided yet," he said.

"What are you on about?" his father asked. "I told you I've seen that look before — it was the same one you had when you told us you were going to move into the armory place and fix it up yourself, and when you told us you were getting married, and then when you were starting the business. It's your look of stubborn determination. You inherited it from me, so I would know."

The warmth in Tav's chest coalesced into a sensation that made his eyes burn. He fought against a sniffle.

"Let us know when you figure out you've decided to do it," his father said. His mother wore a faint smile, but her brow was creased, worry creating the wrinkles time and genetics hadn't.

They traded some more pleasantries and after the call disconnected Tavish sat staring at the blank screen for a long time.

How was one even supposed to start the task of becoming a duke?

CHAPTER 14

Portia opened the copy of *Debrett's* she'd picked up from Mary and turned to the section about sending emails to members of the peerage. She had maybe been a bit too hasty with her offer of help to Tavish. She'd hobnobbed with the rich and powerful all of her life, but her mingling with royalty was relatively new, and was via one degree of separation.

She had gotten him into this, though, so she couldn't let him down. She had spent the past two days with her face stuck into the high society etiquette guide as if she was cramming for a test. In a way, she was — that is, if Tavish decided to pursue his claim to the dukedom.

He still hadn't decided, or so he'd said, but three days had passed and instead of focusing on invoices and sandpaper orders, her mind kept formulating plans for how to proceed if he decided to go for it. This was exactly what her parents had always scolded her over — *already thinking about the next pipe dream before this one has even run its course.* But to Portia, what seemed disparate to other people made perfect sense to her. For example, her parents saw her apprenticeship as a lark, instead of a way of testing the years of crafting classes, art history studies, research, and her innate talent at putting other people's best face forward. If Tav was about to become a royal duke, that was just another way in which she could help.

She ran through the list she'd created in her Brain Basura under the heading "Project: New Duke." Not entirely original, but if it worked for her it could work for Tav. She had subheadings like "style upgrade," "dinner etiquette," "not cursing at people," but she was currently staring at "contacts." She couldn't work on any of those other things — maybe ever — but she could get an email drafted and ready to go. She had to do *something.* She'd come to Scotland to learn how to make swords, and to put the Bodotria Armory on the map. This was so much more than that.

In the days since she'd told Tavish the news, the immensity of her revelation had had time to sink in. Whatever he decided, her actions had changed the course of his life, completely. Unless they perfected a memory erasing serum sometime in the next week, he couldn't go back to not knowing he was technically a duke. Whether he acted on it or not, that knowledge would be with him forever, all because of her. Her actions had consequences and she couldn't fuck up.

"You can't even manage not to flunk philosophy 101? Do you know how much we're paying for school? It's not like you got scholarships like your sister."

"Dad, I told you I'd do better next semester."

"Portia, why can't you manage even a portion of what Reggie is handling? Sometimes I wonder why —"

She closed the *Debrett's* for a moment and pressed her hand to her chest, taking deep breaths against the panic. She'd always reached for a drink whenever she'd felt this sick sensation take hold of her. It had been like a more enjoyable version of an IV drip, because once it hit her bloodstream, the tightness in her chest would release and she'd be the fun-loving Portia that people enjoyed being around. Perhaps a bit too fun-loving, as her friend Ledi had tried to gently point out over the years. But it wasn't until Portia had cut it out of her life that she'd realized it had stopped being fun and started being a coping mechanism, long, long ago.

She inhaled through her nose, then out through her mouth. Breathing through her anxiety would have to suffice for now. She had work to do. Maybe work was just another coping mechanism, but at least it was productive.

She re-opened the *Debrett's* to "How to email a royal secretary" and began composing her email. It turned out, there wasn't exactly a tactful way to say "I am writing on behalf of His Grace's secret baby," so she stuck with some approximation of that and attached her evidence.

"Oh my gosh!"

Cheryl burst into the office, the strings of her TARDIS apron flailing behind her and her phone caught in a death grip.

"What's wrong?" Portia had learned to ask before immediately going for the mace.

"GirlsWithGlasses!!!" Cheryl shouted, performing some strange circular dance routine that was maybe a reenactment of the mating dance of the flamingo. "You wrote about Doctor Hu's on GirlsWith-Glasses! And then your sister shared one of the photos from the social media account you had me create. And then THE LAT-

EST DOCTOR QUOTE-SHARED IT."

Cheryl's cheeks were pink and her eyes were glossy with tears as she stuck the phone in Portia's face.

Hoping I get to make a visit to this dimension, the food looks great.

Portia felt her adrenaline return to baseline, though she was happy that Cheryl was so happy. "That's awesome! I bet you'll have an uptick in customers —"

"Customers? Who cares about customers! The Doctor knows who I am and it's because of you!" She pulled Portia into a hug, which was apparently the culmination of the mating dance. "Thank you! You really are a superhero!"

"No, you're the hero. Um, the Food Lord, or something. Is that right? Close enough?"

Cheryl let out a peal of laughter and began clapping, and then everything happened in slow motion, or so it would seem to Portia later. The phone in its cute piglet case sliding out of Cheryl's hand, Portia ducking to the side to avoid a face full of smartphone, the crash as it collided with her laptop.

"Oh no. Oh no, oh no." Cheryl's clapping had slowed, but not stopped, and her face was scrunched in horror.

Portia heard the blip sound her computer

made when it rebooted, and turned to see the phone resting on the keyboard and the emergency mode reloading bar on the screen.

Fuck.

"Oh, I'm sorry. Christ, that looks like a really expensive computer." Cheryl was near tears again, but this time they weren't tears of happiness.

"It is! Which means it should be hard to break, and if it does, it will be easy to fix or replace because I've got a warranty. Don't worry."

They waited in tense silence as the computer loaded, Portia mostly so she could reassure Cheryl. When it did, everything seemed to be working normally.

"See," Portia said as the approximately one million tabs in her web browser restored. "Good as new. Nothing to worry about."

She glanced at the screen then and felt the sick sensation of her heart dropping into her stomach, where it was dissolved by stomach acids, which was likely to be the most pleasant thing that would happen to her that afternoon.

"Shhhhhhhhhhhiiiiiit. No."

"What is it?" Cheryl asked.

Portia simply stared at the subject of the

new message at the top of her in-box, and the snippet of the message body.

Automated message: Re: Dukedom of Edinburgh — Thank you for your inquiry. Our general response time is 12–24 hours . . .

There was no way to recall the email. There was no way to take this back.

"Tavish is going to kill me," she said, dropping into her seat. Worse, he was going to hate her. She could take being run through with a two-hander, probably, but the inevitable disappointment in his face was what would hurt the most. And what if he kicked her out, ended the apprenticeship? She'd return home a failure.

It's what everyone expects anyway.

She wrapped her arms around herself.

"What's wrong?" Cheryl knelt beside her.

"Fuck. I just messed everything up." Tears welled up in her eyes and she blinked them away. No time to feel sorry for herself. She had more unexpected news for Tavish, and though he didn't seem to be into baseball, she was fairly certain three strikes and you're out was a universal rule.

"What do you mean? I'm the one who chucked my phone at your computer!"

A deep voice cut into the conversation. "Cheryl, I thought I told you to keep your phone on a leash after the last time you got excited and put a hole through the kitchen window." Tav was leaning against the door, a slight smile on his face. The smile faded as he took in Portia's expression.

"What's with the eyes?" he asked, making his way into the room. It was a large room, but his presence seemed to crowd everything out. Even Cheryl seemed to sense it, stepping back and away from Portia.

"What about my eyes?" she asked.

"You're looking at me with those 'calf stuck in a box' eyes. What's the script?"

Oh god, she was really going to have to tell him.

She glanced up at Cheryl. "Cheryl's phone hit my computer. While I was composing a sensitive email to save in my draft folder." She took a breath so deep it made her a bit dizzy. "An email was just accidentally sent to the secretary of the Duke of Edinburgh."

"Get out, Cheryl," he said, not taking his eyes off of Portia, even as Cheryl brushed past him.

"What do you mean?" he asked. His voice was low and dangerous; it walked the fine line people usually flew past on the way to saying what they really felt about someone.

Portia tried to be professional. She'd messed up and 'fessed up on the job plenty of times. But outing Tav as a duke was slightly different than tweeting inappropriate photos of a statue's junk when she forgot to switch to her personal account.

"I was trying to be organized, so I composed an email overview of your situation. I wanted to be ready in case you decided to go ahead with this," she said. Her voice was surprisingly even. "I was just going to keep it in my drafts, but then Cheryl came in and her phone went flying and the computer rebooted and —" She glanced up at him. "I'm so sorry."

The look on his face was not "calf in a box." It was "honey badger who just gnawed its leg off to get out of a trap and is now going to beat you senseless with said leg."

"In other words, the time I was taking to decide whether I wanted to do this has been rendered moot," he said gravely. "And if I had decided no, that would also be moot."

She nodded, and noticed the responding tic in his jaw and flare of his nostrils.

"I'm —"

He scrubbed a hand over his scruff. "Yes, you're sorry. I know." Tav had said unkinder things to her before. On a scale of one to ten, that jab barely registered. But it was the way he said it — talking past her, not even able to look at her, that made it so hurtful. She would have preferred a string of blistering curse words to that mild acceptance. People only accepted what they saw as inevitable, meaning he'd known it would only be a matter of time before she screwed up.

The lump in her throat grew about three sizes, and not in a joyous Grinch kind of way.

"I was still debating, you know," he said. "Guess that takes care of that."

"I can say it was a joke," she said. "Maybe they won't even read it. They probably get all kinds of bizarre emails."

He shrugged. "Mistakes happen." His gaze lingered a bit too long on her, and she tried not to read any implications into it.

She wanted to apologize again. She wanted to smack her head against the desk. She really, *really* wanted a drink. She stood.

"I'm gonna go," she said.

"That's probably a good idea."

She grabbed her tablet then put it down.

"Yeah, maybe leave the electronic devices behind before you find another way to wreak havoc on my life."

That hurt a bit more, but she deserved it.

She deserved worse. She didn't apologize again, she simply headed past him, the pressure of her mistake ballooning to push her out of the room. It pushed her out of the armory, and down the street to the half-empty pub on the corner that she usually passed on the way to Mary's bookshop. Her body had gone on autopilot, taking her to the only familiar and comforting place in a strange land.

She walked slowly up to the bar and sat down, inhaling the familiar scent of stale alcohol and shattered dreams that permeated bars of a certain age. The place was dark and moody, the long wooden bar old and full of gouges and likely to give any patron a splinter.

She felt a sense of relief that made her ashamed.

"What can I get you, love?" the old man behind the bar asked.

Portia looked over the beers on tap; some she knew and some she hadn't seen before. She knew that one drink wouldn't hurt her. But would it be just one? And if it wouldn't hurt, it certainly wouldn't help, would it?

Do you need another reason to beat yourself up? More important, do you really need this?

She closed her eyes and took a deep breath. She was Portia Hobbs and she could solve this problem without a dose of liquid courage.

"A ginger ale," she said, settling on the wobbly bar stool.

"With . . .?" His furry eyebrows raised.

"A slice of lime."

He looked confused but set the drink in front of her a moment later, along with a bowl of peanuts.

She stared at the drink and the peanuts, which had been caressed by lord knew how many unwashed fingers. She inhaled the scent of the bar and wondered how hard it would be to get the smell out of her hair and clothing. She glanced up at the soccer game playing on the small flat screen in a corner of the bar and tried to follow the tiny colorful specks as they ran back and forth across the screen. She slowly sipped the flat soda. Anything to avoid thinking about how big of a mistake she'd just made. She was fairly certain her bags would be packed and sitting outside the armory when she returned.

"This seat taken?"

She took in a shuddering breath.

"That depends. It's reserved for people who don't know I'm a complete and utter tosser, so you'll probably have to sit over there." She pointed across the room.

"I didn't say I thought you were a tosser," Tav said, sitting beside her anyway, sideways so that he was facing her and had his back to the rest of the bar. He didn't touch her, but his presence pressed against her. She'd have to ask Ledi if humans were sensitive to particles being displaced in times of distress.

"It kind of goes without saying this time around." She took a sip of her ginger ale.

"Are you an alcoholic?" he asked, catching Portia by surprise. She coughed a bit, as the swallow of soda went down the wrong tube. Tav's big hand came to her back and patted.

"No?" she said. "I was a problem drinker. As in, I drank to escape my problems."

"Doesn't everyone?" he asked, then his gaze landed on the bartender. "A Belhaven's Best for me, thanks."

"Yeah, but I also became other people's problem when I drank." Portia realized Tav's hand was still on her back. It was just . . . resting there. Like that was normal. And it *felt* normal, and good and comforting, and all those things she'd been pushing out of her head since their kiss. "I don't even know why my friends and family put up with me."

"Probably because humans make mistakes and other humans forgive them."

She glanced at him from the corner of her eye and he was watching her. "Or not," she countered.

"You know I thought I was a pessimist, but you've got me beat in that department." His beer arrived, and he took a swig of the dark ale. "This place used to be a dive you know."

Portia wondered what he considered divey if the bar in its current state didn't fall under that umbrella.

"One night Jamie and I came here, a bit after he'd turned eighteen. Drinking together like two grown men and all that." His hand moved absently, rubbing up and down over the small of her back. "Two wankers decided to pick a fight. They didn't know we were brothers and assumed we were the next closest thing two men could be. Jamie wanted to leave. But I was the big brother, had to show him that I'd handle things, right?"

She met his gaze then. "Your wry expression leads me to believe all didn't go to plan."

"All did not go to plan. Well, I won the fight. But the next week the git and a few of his mates saw Jamie walking along the waterfront. Alone. And decided to get some retribution."

Portia turned and her hand went to his arm. "Tav."

"Luckily he didn't get stomped too badly. Blacked eyes. A couple of broken fingers. A gash across the head. Can't see it with those curls of his."

He listed the things as if from a distance, and Portia knew exactly why — everything was blurred and manageable from that perspective.

Tav sighed and shook his head. "Do you think Jamie hated me after that?"

"I can't imagine Jamie hating anyone."

"Oh, he's got a mean streak in him. It's buried deep, and those who've tapped it have gotten their due. But he didn't hate me. He didn't even blame me."

"Well, why would he?"

"Because I put those events into motion. There would have been no stomping if I had just ignored the bastards, or had defused the situation instead of trying to be the brave big brother. Mistakes happen, and some a damn sight more serious than accidentally revealing someone is a duke."

He took another gulp of beer.

For a second, Portia considered that the bartender might have added whiskey to her ginger ale. She felt light-headed and warm and like maybe she wasn't the biggest fuck-up in the world, which was basically what she'd been chasing at the bottom of happy hour cocktails.

"I really hope you were going to say yes to this," she said.

"I really hope I was going to as well," he said. "Only one reason I wouldn't have."

"Because you value your privacy and freedom?"

He snorted. "No. Because I'm scared shiteless, lass."

She burst out laughing and he joined in, his hand on her back pulling her closer to him as the silliness lifted away the dour mood that had surrounded them. She realized then that she had turned completely in her seat and her feet rested on the base of his stool. Her thighs were flanked by his. His hand was on her back, and hers rested on his arm, and their faces were so close . . .

"You know, if I have to do this I'm glad to have you as my squire," he said. His gaze was intense, the hazel green sliding over her like a velvet cloak.

"Even after this?" she asked.

"The mistake only happened because you were trying to look out for me. Like any squire worth her mettle would." He plucked a straw from a container on the bar with his free hand and traced it over the curve of her ear, and Portia couldn't hide the tremble that went through her. "I dub thee, Squire Freckles."

"I guess this is a step up from an apprentice," she said, her voice low and her body suddenly warm.

"Yes. A knight places a lot of his trust in his squire."

"Is that code for 'a knight gets to boss his squire around'?" she asked.

"Well, yes, but the squire can also make demands. It's a very intimate relationship."

Portia's breath caught in her chest. Was this chivalrous foreplay or what?

Her phone rang then, and she had to force her gaze from his as she answered.

"Hello?"

"Hello. My name is Francis Baker, secretary to the Duke of Dudgeon. I am calling to request your presence and that of Tavish McKenzie for tea at Holyrood Saturday afternoon."

"Tea at Holyrood? Saturday afternoon?" Tav was staring at her, so she mustered her best professional voice. "Why yes, His Grace would be delighted."

There was a pause, as if the woman on the other end was debating whether to challenge the use of that appellation.

"Excellent. I'll send you an email with the

particulars. Make sure you read them or you'll end up on a tour instead of at our meeting."

She hung up the phone and Portia followed suit.

"It's begun, has it?" he asked.

She nodded and he downed the rest of his beer and slid off of his seat. He extended his hand to help her down and held it for the few steps it took to get to the door, before dropping it to pull the wooden door open for her. She didn't read too much into it — he'd just admitted that he was scared. Friends could do things like hold hands during scary times, and rub each other's backs, and . . .

"So. Where do we begin?" he asked roughly. He was nervous.

Portia looked up at him.

"With some tiny sandwiches."

CHAPTER 15

"What are you wearing?"

Tav didn't have to look at Portia to know that her nose was wrinkled in distaste. He held his arms out to allow her to see the suit in all its glory. It had been her idea to go on a practice run before tea with this royal secretary, and he'd dressed up at her insistence.

She, of course, looked stunning. She wore a simple black dress that looked like something from *Breakfast at Tiffany's* and probably cost as much as a ring from Tiffany's. Her heels were high and made her legs look fantastic, and her hair surrounded her face, the curls sleek and moist. Tav felt even more like a lunkhead, but that was something he would have to get used to.

He tugged at his lapels. "You said to wear my best suit."

"Tavish." Yup. Definite nose wrinkling. "This suit is a wrinkled polyester nightmare that's about a size too small. And *what are those*?"

She pointed at the work boots he'd paired with the suit.

"My dress shoes fell apart a couple of years ago." He sighed. "I used to wear this suit to the office. I haven't exactly had need of a suit for some time."

She closed her eyes and pressed a delicate fingertip to the bridge of her nose. "Okay. We're going to George Street anyway. I'll add suit shopping to our itinerary. We have a little bit of time before the afternoon tea."

"Oh no," he said. "I'm not paying an arm and a leg for something we can get for a fraction of the price at Bodotria Commercial Center."

He was being unnecessarily mulish, but he hated this shite. He'd thought he was well done with this kind of rubbish after quitting his job, but here he was, semi-willingly allowing himself to be pulled back in. Portia was looking at him with an expression he'd seen several times before Greer had finally broken down and asked for a divorce.

No, this is totally different. He couldn't compare Portia to his ex-wife because of his own insecurities. She was there trying to help him, and Greer had been trying to help

271

him as best she'd known how.

"I'll pay for the suit, so you don't have to worry about the cost," she said, slipping her phone into her handbag. "Our SuperLift is outside."

She moved past him and made her way to the car idling out front. Kevyn sat behind the wheel. Great. So he'd have an audience for his humiliation.

He stalked up beside her and placed a hand on the car's roof. "I could have driven us," he said.

"You can drive?" She seemed genuinely surprised.

"Everyone can drive!"

"I can't. Oh, that's right, you make the deliveries . . . well, this was a simple communication error. Noted for next time. Now let's go." She slid under his arm and pulled the door open. After wrestling with the passenger seat, she pulled it down and forward.

"After you." She gave him a bright smile and he pulled a face as he smushed himself into the backseat. Portia adjusted the front seat and settled herself in.

"Hey, Kevyn," she said sweetly, and the git had the nerve to be blushing when he turned to face her.

"How's it going, love?"

"How are the wife and wean, Kevvo?" Tav

asked, shoving his face forward between them.

Kevyn grimaced. "Hey, Tav. They're good, they are." He turned his face back toward the road.

"The Armani shop please," Portia said.

"Ohhh, fancy!" Kevyn put the car into gear and pulled out into traffic.

Tav sucked in a breath. "No. I'm not buying a new suit and you definitely aren't paying for it," he attempted to whisper.

She looked back at him and his gut clenched at the annoyance in her gaze. She was rich. They both knew it. But this was not one of those moments where she needed to remind him of it.

"I know that this feels really shitty," she said, surprising him. "I've had problems with forcing my goodwill on people in the past, and I know it doesn't always have the intended result. But I have a concrete reason for paying for this suit. I'm the one who got you into this situation."

"No, technically that was Mum and this Dudgeon wanker."

"Tavish." She batted those lashes of hers, like he'd be doing her a favor by letting her buy him an overpriced suit.

"This still just doesn't sit right with me."

She gave him a look. "Tell me how you're

feeling right now. Agitated? Uncomfortable?"

"Bloody right I'm uncomfortable!"

She grinned. "Why?"

"Because I'm stuffed into this suit like a goddamn wanker —"

She held up a finger. "So. This suit makes you feel like a wanker. Going to the meeting tomorrow is going to be stressful enough, don't you want to wear something that makes you feel confident?"

"I don't see how a suit —"

She pushed her finger closer. "When you fight in an exhibition, you choose the clothing that allows you greatest range of motion while keeping you safe. Yes or no?"

He nodded and his nose brushed the tip of her finger. She blinked rapidly, but didn't move her hand.

"If this *thing* happens, you need to think about your presence. What you're projecting. If you walk in looking like a sulky child in an ill-fitting suit, they're going to treat you like one. If you show up looking like a polished, sexy man who is doing *them* a favor by bestowing his presence on them, they'll respond to that, too."

He thought about how Portia was always perfectly done up, even when doing inventory. And how he had still dismissed her from the beginning.

"So, a posh suit is a bit like donning armor," he said, and her features brightened in relief.

"Yes. I'm your squire and I'm going to make sure you're outfitted in the best fucking armor possible. You're going to need it."

She leaned back in her seat, and Tav did the same. He stared at the rust-gold curls that rested on her shoulders and wished she was sitting next to him, and that it wouldn't be strange for him to take her hand in his.

"Wait. Did you just call Tav sexy?" Kevyn asked helpfully from the driver's seat. "Because it sounded like you just called him sexy."

Portia pulled out her phone in a smooth movement and began swiping.

Tav leaned forward again. "The man asked a question, Freckles."

"Sorry, I can't hear either of you because I'm using my bawbag blocker app." Her gaze was trained on the screen and her mouth was a solemn line.

Kevyn laughed and pulled into a blessedly empty space by the curb. "Well. Here we are. Enjoy your shopping trip, Tav."

Tav reached into his pocket, which was a remarkable feat given how tight his suit was.

"How much?"

"I already paid," Portia said, waving her phone. "Technology. One day you'll catch up."

She hopped out.

"Careful with that one, Tav," Kevyn said, turning in his seat as Tav struggled to follow her. "She's a live one."

Tav recalled the morning when he'd leaned in to meet her impulsive kiss and almost drowned in her.

"You don't know the half of it."

Fine. Tavish could admit when he was wrong. Sometimes, at least. But as they walked out of the shop and he caught sight of himself reflected back in a window, he had to admit he felt . . . different. He didn't think he'd be trading in his jeans and tees for suits in the workshop, but he'd never had a suit like this before. Portia had run the shop workers ragged in a firm but polite manner, and in no time at all he'd been set up with a suit that accented all his attributes but allowed him to move freely and comfortably.

He looked . . . bloody posh.

"Checking yourself out again?" Portia sidled up beside him and Tav almost said something crass, but then he glanced at his reflection. At hers next to his. They looked good together like this. Was this the kind of man Portia was used to dating? Dressed in a suit that cost a year's rent for some people? How would that kind of man respond?

"You told me I'd have to start appreciating the finer things in life. What can I say? I was appreciating, lass." He ran a hand through his hair.

She scrunched her nose. "Oh wonderful. I've created Hobbs's monster."

"Except instead of running after me with pitchforks, they'll be after my sexy bo—"

"Oh em gee, we can turn around and return that suit right now, Sir Tavish," she said, whirling to point at the shop's entrance. "Can your ego already have grown this much? Just from a suit? I'm sure you'll be a real treat when you have your title."

"I guess my new cool and confident persona is working," Tav said. "I have done some research, you know. My mother used to have these novels that I'd read in the bathroom."

"TMI, Tavish. Rule number one of duking. Don't discuss what you do in the bathroom. No one needs to know teenage Tav's preferred wanking material."

"Right. But I learned some things while

skimming. Dukes and rich guys in suits are supposed to be all commanding and give smoldering looks to the women in their vicinity."

He narrowed his gaze on her and pursed his lips.

"You look constipated," she said, and walked off.

"Lead me to the tea service, Freckles," he said, then jogged to fall into step beside her. She muttered something under her breath.

They walked on in silence until they approached a storefront that looked like someone had taken a dollhouse and shot it with a growth ray. Through the window he could see pink walls and purple tables and gaudy silver trays and teapots.

"Here we are. Two for Tea, Edinburgh's premiere tea establishment."

"Are there seedy tea establishments? Places where they sell black market Earl Grey and chamomile that fell off the back of a lorry?" Tavish asked, and Portia sighed.

"This suit has definitely got to go."

They walked in and were greeted by an older woman who seemed like she was dressed for one of those cons Jamie and Cheryl liked, and her costume was the Queen. Her white hair was meticulously styled and her pink dress had obviously been cribbed from the royalty section of the *Looking Glass Daily.* She hustled them to a table near the window and Portia plastered on a smile.

"Do you have anything a bit more . . . private?" Portia asked, doing that lash flutter thing. "My dining partner is a bit shy."

"Oh!" the woman said, conspiratorial delight stealing through her wrinkles as she grinned and glanced back and forth between them. "I see. Yes, over here."

She led them to a table behind a veil of strung-up ceramic beads painted with little tiny teacup patterns. "We have a reservation for this table, but as long as you don't intend on staying longer than two hours, it's yours."

"Thank you so much. And we'll have traditional tea service for two," Portia said.

The woman bustled off and Tav settled onto the ornate chair. He unbuttoned his jacket as he sat. "Private? Are you planning to have your way with me?"

"Of course." She was sitting ramrod straight, hands folded in her lap, but Tav didn't miss the way her gaze tracked his fingers, or the insinuation in her tone. "I'm going to put you through your paces. I figured you wouldn't want to be in front of a window for that."

Her voice was low, and Tav imagined her bare foot sliding up the inseam of his pants leg. Or her hand reaching across the table to grab him by the tie. She was right — he did need to get more up-to-date sexist clichés.

"Apparently you Brits are really, *really,* into this tea thing. So after researching *Debrett's,* various instructional videos, and double-checking with my sources, I've made a basic *do*s and *don't*s list to get you through tomorrow."

"A list?"

She raised a brow. "It's the simplest and most efficient organizational tool. Do you want a PowerPoint presentation?"

"Fuck's sake, this is ridiculous," he said. "Why all this bloody attention to detail just to drink a cup of tea?"

"Rule number one — no cursing. And yes, bloody counts as a curse."

"You already gave me a rule number one. Don't discuss what I do in the toilet," he reminded her. "So much for organization."

He was being tetchy, but he hated all of this shite. He hated pretending to be someone he wasn't. All of those years spent making pleasant chitchat in an office when he'd wanted to hang himself by his tie. All of those years trying to figure out how to be a good husband and not being able to get it quite right in the end. A band of anxiety tightened around his chest.

"That was a rule for duking. This is a rule for drinking tea."

Tav threw his head back in frustration. "Bloody hell."

"Tavish. Please tell me the proper protocol for a knight visiting a castle in a foreign land."

He was sure she was trying to put him at ease again, but he went along with it. "Well, that depends. What time period? Is the castle in a friendly country or one where there's tension? Have they been invited? Are they there under duress?"

"So much bloody attention to detail. I wonder why that is?" She smiled as a server approached with a tray of tiny, ridiculous sandwiches. He reached for one with his fork once it was settled, but she deflected the metal prongs with her own.

"No. Use your hands for these. Using a utensil is considered gauche."

"For fuck's sake, Freckles." He grabbed a delicate sandwich between his thumb and index finger and a cucumber slid out limply and plopped onto the doily. Portia speared it with her fork.

"Rules are put in place to test people, Tav-

281

ish. They establish a baseline for respect, and people who can't meet that baseline are considered rabble that don't have to be tolerated. It's all bullshit, but if we're going to do this, I'm not letting anyone treat you like rabble. Or even merely tolerate you. You're going to be the best fucking duke this country has ever seen, got it?"

Tav stared at Portia through a space in the multi-tiered sandwich tray. She looked good in her dress, but now she was wearing that look of determination he found even sexier. And it was all for him. It wasn't quite how he'd imagined coaxing the expression from her, but it would do. For now.

He straightened in his seat and saluted her with his tiny sandwich. "Let's do this."

CHAPTER 16

A palace. A freaking palace.

Holyrood, which was indeed a freaking palace at the end of the Royal Mile, seemed to serve as more tourist trap than actual functioning home of an aristocrat, but apparently it was also used for meetings when lowly commoners showed up claiming to be secret heirs to dukedoms. Portia wondered if this weren't some form of intimidation; Thabiso had told her he usually met with Scottish peerage at the Royal Scots Club and had only been to Holyrood for events and parties. Or maybe they were going to be dragged into a secret torture chamber on the premises. Good thing she'd packed her bear spray.

After being mistaken for tourists and twice told they had to pay to enter, they'd eventually been led to the private wing of the palace, reserved for the usage of the duke and the royal family when they visited Scotland.

"Ms. Hobbs? Mr. McKenzie? Please, follow me," the butler who met them at the entrance to the private wing said.

Portia had been to homes with household staff — nannies, cleaning women, and serving staff — but seeing a real-life Jeeves reminded her that there was wealth and there was aristocracy. Even a poor duke or earl was accustomed to a certain lifestyle, and that lifestyle included butlers who sneered at guests without the decency to have titles in front of their names, or absurd wealth to make up for the lack of it.

Having worked in museums, Portia felt appropriately awed as they passed through the halls. Nearly every item, from artwork, to furniture, to molding, could have been put on display in the main touristic area.

Her phone vibrated in her purse and she was certain it was Nya or Ledi responding to the OMG I'm going to ruin everything and also if you don't hear from me in an hour have Thabiso send the SWAT team freak-out messages she'd sent to their group that morning, Scotland time. She let the vibrations comfort her. She wasn't alone. She was with Tavish. She had her friends. She could do this.

They could do this.

They entered a lavish sitting room where a man and two women sat in uncomfortable-looking chairs before a fireplace. The walls were covered in rich, floral-patterned wallpaper and large oil paintings of white dudes at various stages of life and facial hair manscaping trends.

The man, who was sitting in the most ornate chair, turned his head in their direction, and that was when Portia realized that the largest, and newest, portrait, which dominated the space above the fireplace, was him.

The two women had been in deep conversation, but then they both stood. The younger woman gave a friendly smile and adjusted the lacey collar of her dress, which looked like Duchess of York cosplay gone wrong. The slightly older woman stepped forward, a neutral expression on her face and delicate white gloves on her hands, indicating that she was above general drudgery.

"Thank you so very much for coming. We spoke on the phone. I'm Francis Baker, secretary to His Grace, David Dudgeon, the Duke of Edinburgh," she said, gesturing to the man before the fireplace. He was an average-looking dude in an ugly but expensive suit, and he stared at Portia and Tavish like they were a strange substance spilled on the last open seat in a crowded subway car. He didn't bother to stand, and looked away dismissively before Ms. Baker was even done with the introduction.

Portia had planned to be gracious, inoffensive, bland. To simply usher Tav through the meeting. But if that was how David wanted to play it, she could do genteel bitchiness, too.

"Hello, I'm Portia Hobbs, assistant to His Actual Grace, Tavish McKenzie, the Duke of Edinburgh," Portia responded, gesturing toward Tav. David curled his lip in response.

"I'm Leslie, David's sister," the other woman said. She curtsied as well, and then glanced back and forth between Tavish and David. Little worry lines creased the space between her dark brows, though she tried to smile.

"Pleased to meet you," Tavish said, walking over to the seat. He reached out to shake David's hand and the man simply regarded him for a moment, then grabbed Tav's hand and began executing some strange maneuver that didn't resemble a handshake at all. If he had tried it on a weaker man, perhaps he would have taken him off guard and shaken him like a rag doll. Instead, Tavish stood unmoved as David gritted his teeth and tugged harder.

"You okay, mate?" Tavish asked, laughter in his voice.

"I'm not your mate," David said, releasing his grip and wiping his hand on the leg of his pants as he sank back down into his seat.

"That's right. You're his cousin," Portia said. "Distant cousin."

"Supposedly," David muttered.

"Shall we be seated?" Ms. Baker asked so politely that of course it wasn't a request but a demand.

Portia and Tavish took their seats, the sound of the crackling fireplace exacerbating the tension in the air.

"Before we begin," David said, and then looked at Ms. Baker. She reluctantly pulled out a plastic case and opened it to reveal a small glass tube and some cotton swabs.

"No point in beating around the bush," David said. "It's a paternity test. If you'd be so kind as to swab your mouth."

Tav stiffened and Portia laid her hand on his knee.

"Mr. McKenzie, excuse me, *His Grace,* would be happy to take the test." Tav's knee flexed beneath her hand and she squeezed a bit. "I'm assuming you took one as well? After all, your claim to the title is much more tenuous."

Portia took great satisfaction at the way David's mouth opened and shut silently for a few seconds before slamming into a thin blanched line.

"My family's bloodline is pure and undiluted," he said after gathering his composure, barely able to look at Portia. "I didn't have anything to prove."

"Given the noted high rate of adultery and other unsavory behavior in the aristocratic ranks, a DNA test should have been carried out if that's so important to you, but we'll cross that bridge if we come to it." Portia took the cotton swab from Francis and turned to Tavish. "Open your mouth please."

Tavish's brow furrowed. "I'm no —"

"Your Grace, do you really not want to do this? It's the fastest way to make sure that certain people know their place — and yours. But you don't have to do anything you don't want to."

He gave a reluctant nod and took the swab, swiping quickly in his mouth and then dropping it into Francis's gloved, outstretched hand.

Portia glanced at Tavish, who glared at the floor. David was trying to be insulting, but only because he was already fighting a losing battle.

Portia whipped her head in the direction of their hosts. "Now, we were invited for what I assumed would be tea and a discussion of the new and exciting discovery of Mr. McKenzie's lineage. Yet we haven't even been offered refreshment. Is this some modern form of hospitality or is Mr. Dudgeon always so rude to guests?"

Leslie gasped and David frowned, but Ms. Baker jumped up from her seat.

"I'll see to it," she said, hurrying away with her sample.

Portia hoped having an American remind them of the rules of respectability would rightfully shame them.

"Well, we're not in the habit of offering refreshment to possible charlatans," David said, dashing Portia's hopes for civility.

"Mr. McKenzie?" Leslie cut in. "You make weaponry?"

"I do. Bodotria Armory makes some of the finest swords in modern Scotland."

"Replicas, I suppose," David said.

"No, they're very real," Tavish said.

"And very sharp," Portia added. She felt something on her knee and realized Tavish was now giving her the same message she had given him earlier.

Easy there.

289

She doubted he'd felt the same shocking heat spread through his body at her touch, though.

"Who exactly are you again, Ms. Hobbs?" David was looking at her with that same skeptical look people often gave her when she exerted her knowledge, or ability to speak properly, in their presence. The problem was, she didn't exactly know the answer to the question anymore. Apprentice? Consultant? Squire?

Woman blushing wildly and inappropriately at her employer's touch?

The door opened and the tinkling of a cart being wheeled in echoed through the room.

The liveried server placed out the saucers and teacups and teaspoons, the tray of sandwiches, the silver teakettle. Mundane objects that suddenly felt like a gauntlet.

The day before, Tav had done nearly everything wrong — poured milk into his cup before adding the tea, clanged his spoon around the cup like he was a toastmaster, speared the petite sandwiches with a fork. Portia didn't care, but she didn't want to give David anything to feel smug about.

Leslie took on the role of hostess, pouring the tea into the delicate china cups, passing the sugar.

"It's Darjeeling," she said. "A present

from the Queen herself."

Tav made a polite sound. "Ah, so that means technically I paid for it. With my taxes. Grand."

Portia nudged him with her knee and he shot her a devious look. She was really regretting her suit suggestion because it fit him all too well. He was sexy enough sweaty and covered in shaved metal, but in a finely tailored suit and poking fun at annoying aristocrats?

Tavish then added a dollop of milk to his tea and stirred delicately, moving his spoon up and down in a straight line — the lesson that stirring in circles was just not done had taken.

He did fine, though there was a stiffness to his movements. She could almost hear him repeating *six to twelve, six to twelve* as she'd instructed him, in the way a person who wasn't skilled at dance mentally re-hashed *one and two and three and four* instead of moving naturally to the music.

"Scone?" Leslie asked.

Tavish took one and almost picked up his knife to cut it, then seemed to remember that was a no-no.

"So exactly how did your mother meet the former duke?" David asked with insinu-ation in his voice. "He did seem rather susceptible to the charms of commoners, but he had other, more tawdry, inclinations people say."

Tavish ripped his scone in half, which was the proper technique but executed with maybe a bit more force than necessary.

"She was working as a translator for his refugee organization, one that she received help from when she arrived here from Chile," Tavish said as he spread clotted cream over his pastry. Portia hadn't been aware that cream could be spread in a threatening manner, but it most definitely could.

"And she thought that scheming her way into becoming a duchess was a perfectly reasonable step up from migrant?" David asked, sipping his tea.

"Sorry to ruin your little fiction, but she had no interest in his wealth. She turned down his proposal once she saw how detestable the aristocracy was."

"Ah. I suppose the apple *can* fall far from the tree then," David said.

Tav had picked up his saucer and been about to take a sip of the tea, but he lowered it back to the table, his expression terrifying. Portia remembered that though she didn't call him maestro, Tav was one, and spent much of his downtime studying ways to kill a man quickly and efficiently in battle.

His gaze went up to the mantel, to the sword that was hung in a place of honor beneath David's portrait.

He was on his feet in an instant, rushing for the weapon.

"Tavish!" Portia stood and hurried after him.

"Oh my," Leslie said, her hand flying to her chest.

David jumped up and ran behind one of the large chairs, putting it between himself and Tavish.

"What are you doing?" Portia tried not to let the panic come through in her voice as Tavish took down the sword and stared at it.

"I made this." The fury was gone from his face. He looked stunned. "This was one of the first pieces I sold when I opened the armory. It was a special request, made to replicate one from the buyer's family line."

He turned it in his hands, ran his finger over the ornately sculpted quillon. It had a unicorn etched into each side, similar to those she had seen in images of the dukedom's crest.

"Your father must have . . ." Portia stopped. That truth meant so many things. His father had known about his business.

He may have even communicated with Tavish himself. She couldn't imagine what he was feeling, no matter how adamantly he claimed he didn't care about his biological father.

He laughed ruefully. "I remember receiving a letter afterward, thanking me for my fine craftsmanship. And I made several more pieces for the buyer over the years. They ordered products regularly to sell in their shop, you know."

He placed the sword back on its mount. "I guess now I know why some of my orders stopped coming in," he said quietly.

He turned then, and his brows raised as he took in David, who stood clutching his chair like a shield.

"Did you think I was going to run you through?" Tav asked. His tone was amused. "If I was, that chair wouldn't have stopped me. Like she said, my swords are sharp, mate."

David straightened and adjusted his jacket.

"One never knows with someone like you," he said.

"Someone like me?" Tav squared his shoulders. "And what exactly am I like? I met you less than fifteen minutes ago, though I guess that was enough time to get your number. But you'd best not think you have mine."

"More tea?" Leslie stood, thrusting the teapot around as if a sip of piping hot Darjeeling was the key to world peace.

"That would be wonderful, thank you," Portia said, tugging discreetly at Tav's sleeve. He kept his gaze on David as he navigated his way to his seat.

The door to the parlor opened and Ms. Baker rushed over to David. She leant close to his ear and whispered something, then stood beside his chair.

"I'm guessing this is the Maury moment?" Portia asked. She sipped her tea.

"Maury?" Leslie asked.

"It's a talk show where women go on and get paternity tests done, dear," Francis said. "Quite amusing. And yes, the Duke of Edinburgh was indeed the father."

Portia choked back an inappropriate laugh. It was true. This whole wild situation was real and she had gotten Tavish into this.

"How much do you want then?" David asked, steepling his hands before him. When Tavish didn't answer, David made a sound of irritation. "To go away. How much do you want to go away?"

"Are you trying to buy me off?" He didn't sound angry about it, and Portia realized this might work out perfectly. Tavish needed money and didn't really want the aggravation and duties of the title. A payoff wasn't exactly legit, but it would solve one problem and prevent others. Tav might find it much preferable to a life spent dealing with men like David, and Portia wouldn't judge him in the slightest.

"Of course I am," David said. "Come now, do you have the slightest idea what being a member of the peerage entails?"

Tavish shifted uncomfortably. "I'm a fast learner."

David scoffed. "There are things that can't be *learned,* Mr. McKenzie. For example, you look good in a suit and can drink your tea without slurping, but do you know how to give a formal toast? Do you know the events for the season — which is already in swing, I'll have you know — the dress code for each event, the strategic social and business import of each event?" David's nostrils flared. "And that's just the beginning. I've trained my entire life for this role, waited and watched and prepared. I'm from this world, and I understand what's expected of me and what the people I represent need."

Tav was nodding along, and David could have shut up, but he didn't. Apparently, he was just getting started.

"I know what they *don't* need, too. As if this country isn't dealing with enough trash washing up on our shores. Just imagining the insult of the Queen having to share Holyrood with *you* in a few weeks makes me ill. Of *you* presenting her with the crown jewels and standing by her side at the garden party. Atrocious. I can't allow some bastard of a refugee whore to sweep in and undo everything I've worked for!" David's mouth snapped shut, as if he hadn't meant to let out all that bile but it had spewed forth of its own accord.

Portia jumped to her feet.

"Mr. Dudgeon —"

Tav's gentle grip around her arm stopped her. He stood so that he was beside her.

"I regret that I'm going to have to turn down any offer you make," he said calmly. "You'll be hearing from my lawyers to get the process of turning over the title and all it entails to its rightful owner — me. We have another engagement, so we'll be leaving. Thank you for the hospitality."

He looked down at Portia. "Shall we go?"

She didn't know the etiquette for basically saying "fuck you" and flouncing, so she executed her most ostentatious curtsy in David's direction.

"Enjoy the rest of your afternoon," she

said with a bat of her eyelashes, then she and Tav strode toward the door and out into the hallway.

"Are you okay?" she asked, placing her hand on his lower back. He stiffened, but then sighed and relaxed just before she was about to pull away.

There was a loud crash from the room they'd exited, echoing down the hall.

"Better than Davey, I suppose."

"I thought maybe you'd take the money. You said you weren't sure you even wanted this."

"I did consider it. It would have been a huge payday with no work required from me. But then I saw the look on his face when he said *refugee.* Now I know where I've seen this git's face before." Tavish sneered. "He's been in the papers putting pressure on MPs to come down harsher on migrants. Trying to get them to cut back on legal immigration, too."

"He can't make them do anything though, right? It's all talk?" She was pretty sure the Duke of Edinburgh had no voting powers. It was a royal dukedom, but like much of the Monarchy, the power was symbolic.

"No. But he can present himself as the face of Scotland and pressure the people who do. He can get in all the papers with all the historical weight a title like 'Royal Duke' holds. He can talk to the bloody Queen. If I can stop one man who thinks about other humans that way from holding *any* kind of power, I have to."

The only sound after that was the sound of their shoes tapping on the buffed tile floors, and the little voice in her head reminding her that she was in way over her head. They kept walking even when they got out of the palace, past stores and down cobblestone streets. They'd gone a couple of blocks before Tavish had even realized it.

"Thank you," he finally said as they waited for their SuperLift. He even managed a grin. "I know Davey was scared I was gonna run him through, but I think you were the one giving that serious thought."

"Eh, I'm always down to stab horrible men," she said. "No need to thank me."

"I forgot, you're the vigilante-slash-spiritual man killer," he said with a short, unamused laugh. "Aye, that's about right."

She was wavering on offended but then he looked at her, heat and something else in his gaze. "After the display David put on, I'll remind you I'm hardier than average. We're in this together, so don't worry too much about killing my spirit. I've a feeling it's a pretty good match for yours."

She couldn't think of anything to say to that so instead she just blinked up at him.

"Portia?" An apple-cheeked woman called out from the car that had pulled up. "Are you waiting for a SuperLift?"

"I call passenger seat this time if it's another numpty two-door," Tav said and strode toward the car, displaying once again just how good he looked in a suit.

Way, way *over her head.*

CHAPTER 17

Portia sensed the moment Tav's mood shifted from engaged to ennui, even with the battered kitchen table between them. He ran a hand through his hair and dropped his head back in annoyance.

"Ah, that's right. Of course I should have remembered this random inconsequential fact about fork tines. I'm a complete and utter git, obviously."

The daily "duke lessons" they'd undertaken since tea time at Holyrood a week ago hadn't been too bad, really, and sometimes they were even fun — too fun. But for the past couple of days Tav had been growing progressively more stressed, understandably so, and his ability to retain information was slipping.

He was still running a business and dealing with all that entailed on top of his lessons, and it was likely just starting to really sink in that this was his world from now on.

Going from artisan to aristocrat meant a complete restructuring of his life, from the very foundations. It would be a lot for anyone to take in, but he was also getting years of etiquette lessons and practice at social niceties crammed into just a few weeks. Her apprenticeship was only for a few weeks more, after all, and she was trying to help as much as she could before she left.

Portia hadn't thought enough about this aspect of helping Tav out. Setting out on a goal of improving herself was one thing, but trying to improve *him* felt uncomfortably like telling him something was wrong to begin with. She couldn't help but feel like an imposter for even suggesting she knew better than him.

"Okay. So. Before we continue, you shouldn't feel bad about not knowing this stuff already. Why would you know random minutiae of etiquette? It served no purpose to you before." She sighed. "You're learning skills, but lacking those skills had no impact on your worth. Your value doesn't lie in the way you hold a glass or a knife, or whether you can make a formal toast."

Portia generally kept their conversation light, but it was important to her that he understood this. She had spent years cringing her way through deportment lessons as fault after fault was pointed out for correction, and having to do the same to Tav was dredging up some unexpected memories.

Stop slumping! Enunciate! Chewing your nails is disgusting. Can you really not pay attention for more than five minutes, Portia?

Tav drummed his blunt fingertips on the tabletop, then lifted his gaze to meet hers.

"Thanks for the pep talk, Squire Freckles. You're saying you like me just the way I am, then?" he asked. His expression was wary, even though he was cracking jokes.

She lifted her brows. "If you want a compliment, all you have to do is ask. And stop cursing *Debrett's.*"

Tav made a motion that seemed to be the beginning of an eye roll, but stopped himself. "Fine, I'll behave."

"Don't get too freaked out. We're just going to review some basic etiquette skills you'll need when dealing with people like David."

Tav snorted, and then cracked his knuckles menacingly. "Think I've got the skills for that down already, lass."

"Well, as enjoyable as squaring up with David would be, the rich are extremely litigious, and the new Duke of Edinburgh being arrested for battery would make him

303

way too happy, don't you think?"

"Aye. So let's go through this again," he said, then drew a deep breath and moved his index finger toward the leftmost edge of the formal place setting Portia had laid out in front of him. "Butter plate, butter knife, salad fork, fish fork, dinner fork, service plate, dinner knife, fish knife, salad knife, soup spoon, and bloody oyster fork."

This was the easiest thing they'd gone over during their lesson, but Portia had saved it for toward the end of the lesson, when he'd be flagging and grouchy, so they could finish the day on a good note with Tav feeling accomplished and optimistic. It was something she'd adapted from a *Hot Mess Helper* video: celebrating even the smallest steps, because every small step added mileage toward reaching your goals.

She clapped with delight. "Yes! You got them all correct. Way to go!"

She reached over the table to give him a high-five which he returned a bit bashfully.

"Grand. Stuff like this makes my skin crawl, though. Everyone putting on these fake personas and indulging in these silly little rituals just to impress people. And I know I do that to an extent with the European martial arts and the exhibitions, but that's fun! This isn't fun at all."

Portia couldn't disagree, though she envied his ability to distance himself from "fake personas" and "silly rituals." She couldn't imagine moving through the world without having to do the calculations for about a million different variables that factored into how people would treat her. She felt the slightest bit of irritation that Tavish didn't have to think of all of this, then she saw the uncertainty in his eyes and sighed.

"Tavish, what did you think of me when you met me?" she asked.

His irritation slipped away and was replaced with an uncharacteristic blank stare. "Pardon?"

"Actually, I don't want to know," she said quickly, waving her hands. It wasn't too hard to figure out given his past behavior. "But when you talk about fake personas and silly rituals, remember that some of us can't opt out of that stuff. Before I even open my mouth, I'm judged based on whether I'm perceived to be pretty enough or wearing the *right* thing — not too revealing, not too frumpy, not too cheap looking, not too fancy. When I do talk, it's whether I'm articulate enough. So while you're rightfully annoyed by this, just remember that at least half of the population has to adopt these fake personas and silly rituals just to get through the day."

She expected him to push back, but he dropped his elbows to the table and stared at his hands. When he looked back at her, his brows were lifted and he looked both shocked and ashamed.

"Christ, you're right."

Portia was confused. "About what? The patriarchy? Well, yeah."

"No. Well that and the other thing about when I first met you. Don't you see? I was your David Dudgeon."

It was clear his exhaustion had finally gotten to him.

"Maybe we should take a break? Do you want some tea?"

"No. Well, I always want tea, but listen. When you showed up I acted like an arsehole to you for . . . reasons. That were no fault of your own. And then we went to Holyrood and David acted like an arsehole to me for no reason."

"Well, your taking his money and title is a pretty strong reason," she said. She wasn't sure where this was going and was slightly worried.

"I'm not being clear," he said, shaking his head. "And aye, I'm a bit knackered, but I'm not hallucinating or anything. I'm realizing. Realizing that I treated you unfairly and never really apologized for it. And that was when the only power I had was master-at-arms. If I'm going to think myself a better man than David, not being a bigoted wank stain is the lowest bar to clear. I need to do better. And I need to apologize, for real this time. So: Portia Hobbs, I'm sorry for being a shite boss and making you feel bad about yourself, and for doubting you just because I made a snap judgment. It wasn't all right, and you've my word I won't do it again."

Portia was stunned. She was usually the one doling out heartfelt apologies. She was tempted to sooth him, to tell him it had been fine.

"Yeah. That really sucked and I was disappointed and felt like an idiot. Thank you for apologizing."

They sat in awkward post-apology silence until Tav stretched in his seat.

"What next?" he asked. "Do I have to balance a book on my head?"

He gave her his normal smile, and she returned it, resetting the serious mood that had blown up out of nowhere. That had been awkward, but she felt happy. Seen. Respected. She wanted him to feel the same way.

"Actually . . ." Portia pushed out of her seat and strode around the table to stand behind him. She placed her hands lightly on his shoulders, but pulled them away when he jumped at her touch. "Sorry, I should have asked before touching you."

"No, it's fine," he said, his voice a bit gruff. "You can, erm, touch me."

His voice went low on the last two words and desire unfurled and spread its wings someplace beneath Portia's rib cage.

Touch me.

The words echoed in her head, turning what should have been something ordinary and platonic into a heated challenge.

She placed one hand on his shoulder this time, tentatively. He didn't jump, but she felt his muscles bunch beneath her palm in response. "I think you're used to bending over things, with all the grinding, and forging, and poring over medieval texts. You need to work on your posture. Pull your shoulders back, just a bit."

She squeezed his shoulder more firmly and pulled. She placed her other hand flat against the middle of his back and gently pushed up and forward. His body followed the motion naturally, his chest moving up and out and shoulders dropping back and down. She noted how the muscles of his back flexed beneath her palm, then twitched even though he was supposed to be relaxed. She pushed the thought aside — she was helping him, and she could keep any dirty thoughts about Tav's musculature to herself.

"Am I doing this right?" he asked.

"Hm, this usually works better with a mirror . . . oh! Look at your reflection in Cheryl's restaurant fridge. This is the posture you should aim for." She flexed her hands for a moment, emphasizing exactly how his body was aligned beneath them. "Imagine there's a string from the top of your head and down through your spine, and someone is pulling it up. Yes, lift your chin like that. Can you see how this posture gives you an air of power and grace?"

"Aye." His voice was rough, and she could feel his heart begin to beat faster beneath her palm. Her pulse was apparently trying to be polite, too, because it rushed to keep pace with his.

"When you walk into these events, people are going to try to intimidate you. But most of them only have their wealth, so they'll use backhanded compliments and insinuation that you aren't good enough."

"Well, they wouldn't be wrong there, would they?" He said it with a laugh and not even a forced one, but Portia felt a flare of indignation. Her hand left his shoulder and went to his chin, gently turning his face up toward her.

"Don't joke about stuff like that, Tavish. Not anymore and definitely not in front of any of these people you're going to meet."

His hazel-green gaze was hot as it locked on to hers.

"Isn't that some advice that you should heed yourself? Self-deprecation is your stock-in-trade."

"It's different for me," she responded. Quickly. Annoyed. *Because everything I say is true.* "Don't sell yourself short just because you didn't go to a fancy school or learn all the ways money can be used to make someone feel small."

His fingertips brushed her elbow, trailed up her forearm leaving a wake of goose bumps, and then his fingers encircled her wrist.

"Thank you, squire. I'll agree to that if you'll do me one better — don't sell yourself short, full stop."

She realized that she was maybe getting a bit too intense, and also still holding him by the chin like a weirdo, so she pulled her hands away and marched stiffly back to her seat across from him. She could still feel the pressure of his fingers dragging across her wrist as she'd pulled away. "Um, sorry about that."

"Sorry for trying to help me?" he asked. "Don't worry, I can handle myself."

"Look, you talk about rich fucks this, and rich arseholes that, but you don't understand how these people operate. I don't even understand. There are plenty of perfectly nice rich people, don't get me wrong."

"Oh heaven forbid I misjudge someone who can go cry into a wad of bills about it."

Portia sighed and ignored that jab. She knew he hadn't aimed it at her, but it had landed right in a sensitive spot. "All it takes is one jerk to scent a whiff of uncertainty on you. Then they have their in to bring you down a notch. If someone is going to be petty, make them work for it. Don't hand your insecurity to them on a platter."

"Is that what it was like for you?" There was concern in his eyes and this was all wrong because she was supposed to be the one helping him, but he was the one apologizing and telling her to think better of herself. She should just say "no" and move on.

She pressed her lips together. "In my family, Reggie was the smart and reliable one and I was the pretty and flighty one. That alone gave people a lot of 'ins.' I got a lot of 'don't worry, she'll find a wealthy husband to put up with her' type comments."

Tav shook his head. "That doesn't make sense. You're twins. Do you not look alike?"

"We're not identical, but we look close enough. That kind of makes it worse, huh?" She shrugged, and then decided she'd talked about herself enough. "So listen, don't get cocky or anything, but you're already pretty impressive. If you walk into a room with your back straight and your head high and your 'Yeah, I'm the new duke in town' swagger, most people will be ready to fall at your feet. It won't matter where you went to school or who your mother is."

"Not rolling my eyes is really paying off," he said lightly.

"I wasn't *trying* to compliment you," Portia said. She felt a little exposed. Tavish was looking at her in that new way he had, like he was trying to figure out what she was thinking — like he *cared* what she was thinking. She almost preferred when he'd been rude and hell-bent on ignoring her.

"Even better," he said. Her forearms rested flat on the table in front of her and he reached out and brushed his fingertip over the back of her hand. That soft touch sent a thrill up her arm that left raised hairs in its wake. "Thank you. For all this. I —"

"Special delivery!" Jamie announced as he shuffled into the kitchen lugging a huge trunk behind him. Portia quickly pulled her arms back across the table.

Tav stood up and glanced at her. "Always stand when someone enters the room," he said in the exaggerated posh accent he used to mock his etiquette lessons.

He made his way over to Jamie, somewhat reluctantly, and she got up to follow. She should have been happy for the interruption, right? They didn't need to keep finding reasons to touch one another.

"Here you go, Your Grace," Jamie said, bowing at Tav as he presented the trunk. He was super enthusiastic about Tavish's news, and apparently the novelty hadn't worn off yet.

"Don't call me that," Tav snapped, shocking Portia with his sudden mood change.

"I was just joking, bruv," Jamie said, but he looked surprised too, and a little hurt.

"It's not really funny is it, Jamie?"

Portia had noticed the way Tav seemed to stiffen up every time Cheryl and Jamie said the word *duke*, which was admittedly a lot, but they were his biggest supporters. Jamie had started doing much of the non-artisanal labor so deliveries wouldn't fall behind, and Cheryl and Kevyn had been leading some of the kids' classes. Portia always felt a bit of shame seeing how they threw their support behind Tav, remembering the one crisis her family had gone through and how she'd run off instead of helping her parents or spending more time at the hospital. She couldn't understand why their enthusiasm angered Tav.

Jamie's hurt expression morphed into one of annoyance — perhaps the first time Portia had ever seen it on his face. "I don't see what the problem is. Unless you're planning on cutting and running, that's your title, aye?"

"Give it a rest." Tav glared at him as he ripped at the tape surrounding the trunk and pried it open. "It's bad enough other people will call me that. I don't need to hear it in my own home."

Jamie's mouth twisted. "Oh, you mean the home that you got from your father the duke, along with a title, power, and who knows how many millions of quid?"

"Hey, guys," Portia said, stepping in between them. Two large men who knew how to grapple and use swords arguing was a little frightening, even if she knew they'd never hurt one another. Physically, at least.

"Oh, don't tell me you're jealous," Tav said, ignoring her. "You think I asked for any of this?"

Jamie exhaled a frustrated noise and ran a hand over his face, before using it to gesture in Tav's direction. "Obviously I'm jealous. Who wouldn't be jealous of someone who had won the absentee father lottery? But that's not the problem here. Your whinging all the damned time is the problem!"

"Whinging?" Tav seemed to choke on the word and Portia stepped back from between them.

Jamie's face scrunched up. "For years, we've all had to hear about how little you care about this building, even though you encouraged me and Cheryl to invest our livelihood in it. As if being gifted a grand old building was a burden. And now you've been given a title and money and power and all you can do is complain about that, too! Fuck's sake, Tavish, you really are a wanker, you know that?"

Jamie turned to go.

"Jamie. Jamie!"

Jamie stopped. His hands went to his waist, his shoulders slumped, and his head dropped forward. "Yeah?"

"I'm sorry. Guess I've kind of had tunnel vision about all this. Or wankervision."

Jamie chuckled a bit, then sighed and turned around.

315

"Come here, bruv." He held his arms open and beckoned Tav with his hands. "You know I don't like arguing. Family have to stick together. Bring it in."

Portia watched as Tav lumbered over and clapped his baby brother in a hug. Just like that, all the angry energy between them dissolved like cotton candy under a sprinkler. If there was anything to be jealous about, it wasn't Tav's title.

She glanced over at the trunk. "Oh, your clothes have arrived!"

She busied herself pulling out the various slacks, jeans, sweaters, and suits and laying them carefully over the backs of the kitchen chairs.

"Clothes?" Tav and Jamie said at the same time.

Portia grabbed one of the shirts, a blue houndstooth button-up that was impossibly soft, and walked over to Tav, holding it up against his chest. "They're from a service that delivers clothing. You try it on. If you like it, you keep it. If not, you send it back with the trunk. No need to go to shops."

Tav rubbed the material of the shirt between his thumb and forefinger. "Hm. You know, I can't even take the piss out of this. Doing the whole fitting mess without leaving the house? I could get used to that."

"Try it on, Tav!" Jamie said. His anger was gone, and he was already excitedly digging through the clothing, picking out items he thought would look good.

Portia's phone vibrated on the kitchen table. "I'll give you some privacy. But Jamie, take a photo of every outfit so I can check them out later."

"You're not going to supervise?" Tavish said with a quirk of his brows.

"I trust your judgment," she said quickly. She didn't really, when it came to clothing, but the last thing she needed was to be in a room with a half-dressed Tavish. The kernel of a crush was a full-grown stalk, budding ears of corn that could not be harvested. She swept up her phone and turned her back on Tavish and his inviting brows. Besides, one of her parents was on the phone and she was certain she couldn't hold a conversation if Tav was stripping down in front of her.

"Hello?"

"Portia Monique Hobbs." Her mother's voice was sharp on the other end of the phone. "Why did I have to find out about this duke business from your sister?"

"Reggie told you?" Portia was blindsided. She'd told Reggie because it was pretty huge news and Tav had agreed that she could announce it in the travel column she'd been doing for Reggie. Low key, high visibility, totally in their control. She hadn't expected her sister to run and tell her parents, but then again, Reggie had conversations with them that consisted of more than flailing defensively.

"Well, she stopped by the office and Vanessa started talking about your little trip, since she'd seen some stuff about it on Reggie's site. Vanessa then started talking about some photo of you with this man you're apprenticing with, and when I asked if the only reason you'd gone was to 'hook up' with some Scottish man, Reggie explained what was going on."

Portia couldn't even muster up the energy to be angry at her mother's assumption, though she was sure it would come eventually.

"I told you that I took this apprenticeship because I was interested in helping build this business and in learning this craft. You really thought it was possible that I came here to chase after a man?"

"Portia, I never know what's possible with you. Then Vanessa started showing me all this gossip on social media and I didn't know what to think."

Tears stung Portia's eyes. The anger had

arrived earlier than she'd imagined. "What do you want, Mom?"

"Well, I just want to know what was going on." Her mother's voice was suddenly warmer, friendlier, than she'd heard it in ages. "And if these rumors were fact. Because if what Vanessa said is true and if what Reggie said is true, well . . . your father and I wanted you to come fill this position, but we'd certainly be proud to have a duchess in the family instead."

Portia felt actual nausea building in her stomach, but her mother kept going.

"I know you've never clicked with any of the men your father and I tried to set you up with, but we always thought it would be best if you had a good man to look after you, and why not a duke?"

Portia hadn't heard this tone from her mother since she was sixteen and had just slipped into her frilly white debut dress. It was a tone of pride, and the only thing that had brought it out half a lifetime later was the possibility of Portia marrying well.

"My duties have taken on a wider scope since the discovery, but I'm his apprentice and that's it," Portia said. "It's really hard work, not a dating service."

"Is there any reason why now you're suddenly fickle when it comes to men? You've always been like this. Happy to do something until I make a suggestion. Reggie always had her own goals and plans, but yours seem to be just whatever it is that your father and I don't want."

Ouch. Portia had no regrets about her past, but having her mom throw it in her face fell under the "probably need to talk to my therapist" column of life.

"That's not true." Sure, she hadn't lived up to their expectations. And somewhere around her second semester of college she'd stopped trying to — that had been the easiest thing for everyone involved. But she *had* tried.

Portia thought of the hours of ballet classes and deportment lessons, and cotillion practices, all the things she'd done to please her parents that had never added up to enough. Of the awful sinking feeling that had come over her when her parents rushed Reggie to the hospital, when she'd realized something awful was happening, and for some illogical reason it was happening to Reggie and not to her, who deserved it . . .

"Check me out, Freckles!" Tavish strutted out into the hall wearing a green button-up shirt tucked into sharp black slacks. "Forget the photos, you need to see this in all its glory. What do you — oh, sorry, you're on the phone."

"I have to go, Mom. Bye."

"Por—"

She hung up, not wanting to hear anything else her mother had to say, and pasted a smile on her face. "I love it. David's going to be even more jealous when he sees you."

Tav dropped his arms.

"What's up?" He motioned around his own eyes with his index finger. "Calf box eyes."

"It was my mom. Doing mom things." She shrugged and hated that the breath she exhaled was shaky.

Tav's brow creased. "Mum things are not good, I gather?"

"Not when it comes to me. I'm sure if you talked to Reggie, they would entail constant praise and normal fun conversations."

"Oh," Tav said, rubbing a knuckle over his stubbled jawline. "Ohhhhhhhhh. I see."

"Yeah, everyone does eventually," Portia muttered. It was childish, wanting to cry over her mother's occasional barbed comments. She was an adult. It didn't matter.

"So this is where it comes from. All the 'I'm a fuckup' hogwash?" Tavish chuckled, and Portia narrowed her gaze at him. "Come now. This is classic Dr. Phil shite. I value my life enough not to say anything

321

bad about your mother, but as someone who just apologized for being a jerk to you myself, maybe you should consider that she's wrong?"

Portia *had* considered that. But there was considering and there was believing.

She sucked in a deep breath and remembered that she was New Portia. New Portia couldn't let anyone sap her energy, even if that person had given her life.

"Hey," Tav said, snapping his fingers to get her attention. "I need your opinion on a suit. Is that all right? You can tell me about erm, thread count and the cut of the lapel, or whatever."

Portia almost did cry then. He was trying to distract her. It was clumsy and he was perhaps confusing suits with linens, but her chest tightened a little.

"I'm an excellent judge of lapels," she said. "Go try it on. I'll be right there."

Tav gave her one of those full smiles then. "Grand. Don't stay out here beating yourself up or anything. I expect my lapel critiques promptly."

Portia took in a deep, trembly breath. Her mother's words had hurt because, as always, they were just a bit too close to what she wished for herself. It was like her mother always saw her dreams as reflected in a fun house mirror.

A burst of deep brotherly laughter sounded from behind the door and Portia followed it. She had lapels to judge.

CHAPTER 18

Struggling to balance the workload of the armory along with duke lessons was tiring as fuck. He'd always made fun of the aristocracy, but Christ he was glad he hadn't had to spend an entire lifetime bound by these arbitrary rules. *Smile like this, laugh like that, toast like this, sit like that.* Tav was well and truly knackered, but not as much as he should have been, since Portia was running herself ragged trying to make things go smoothly for him.

"I'll be right there." He'd nearly closed the space between them in the hallway when she'd said those words so guilelessly, as if that was something she could offer him simply and without a second thought. It had hurt, because it wasn't true in the long term. Apprenticeships ended, as did visas. In the meantime, she was doing exactly that. Being there for him.

She'd contacted her princess friend —

because of course she hadn't been joking about that — and found a lawyer perfect for the job of navigating all the aristocratic bullshit and transitioning the title, and all the land and money and prestige associated with it, to Tavish. The mere thought of it made him feel like he'd been kicked in the chest. She'd taken over his emails and begun answering the inquiries that had started to trickle in — Tavish assumed there would be a tidal wave once word really got out. There were the lessons of course, and in her spare time she was still putting the finishing touches on the armory's website and running the social media.

He'd brought on an apprentice but gotten a force of nature instead.

He finished up his work for the day and headed to Portia's room, in what had become the norm for them. He'd gone from avoiding his apprentice to spending every free minute with his squire. The flurry of anticipation that built in his stomach as he approached her room had also become the norm. Tav had thought the infatuation would fade away, or that her drills on social interactions and small talk and how to act like a rich git — reminders that she was one — would have turned him off. As with everything when it came to Portia, he'd been wrong.

He remembered how wrong he'd been about her kissing style, how she'd been shy and vulnerable, growing bolder as their tongues tangled. Even with all that had happened in the weeks since she'd arrived, it was that kiss by the forge he couldn't stop thinking of. His entire world was on the precipice of change. Life as he had known it was about to fall and smash to pieces on the cobblestone below — was in fact already tumbling toward the ground — but he was too busy fixating on the memory of her mouth and her hands and the way she'd moaned . . .

What a tosser you are, Tavish.

He pushed the thoughts away as he raised his hand to knock on the door. There was no response and he waited, then knocked again. Finally, he heard the shuffling of sheets and a groggy "Come in."

When he stepped into the dim room, the first thing that hit him was how her territory seemed to be marked by smell — a fragile floral scent that told intruders this space was hers now. The second was that she looked . . . well, she was lying across her bed, hair wild, the skirt of her black dress wrinkled and hiked up in precarious folds just above her knees. Her feet dangled off of the edge of the bed, and her heels were still on. It was like walking into a boudoir fantasy until Tav noticed the dark circles under her eyes and how out of it she seemed.

He stalked over to the bed and sat down, ignoring the warning creak emitted by the frame.

"You look like hell," he said, and no, that wasn't exactly what she wanted to hear judging from the glare she shot him. It was a sleepy glare, bordering on adorable since he could see both of her hands and she wasn't toting any weapons.

"I feel like shit," she said. Her voice was hoarse, and not sexy, Kim Cattrall hoarse. Worry tumbled Tav's stomach.

"Are you ill?" he asked.

"I think I'm just really, really tired." She shook her head ruefully and wiggled down further into her duvet. "I sat down for a minute, and I passed right out."

She had taken on so much — much more than could be justified with this talk of apprenticeships and squires. He would pay her, once things were settled and he had the money that was supposedly his by virtue of blood.

"You're toast, lass. Burnt," he said. His hand went to her hair, sweeping the curls back and out of her face. "Setting off the damned fire alarm in the kitchen, even though some knob's taken the battery out." She laughed softly.

"I just needed a nap. I'm fine now . . ." She started to sit up and Tav laid his hand heavily on her shoulder to keep her down, and then she flopped back onto the bed and looked up at him with wide eyes.

"Here's what's going to happen tonight," he said, speaking in an exaggeratedly slow tone. "You are going to take a break."

"I promised to help you," she said, and Tav felt something in his chest region that was probably similar to what a man run through with a sword felt before he gave up the ghost.

The look in her eyes was dangerous because it was ridiculously pure, despite the fact that he'd spent a good portion of his time around her at between a six and a ten on the wanker-ometer.

"Helping me shouldn't leave you feeling like shite. You know that, right? And like I said, you look like —"

"Hell. Yes. Got it." She pulled the duvet up over her head.

"Glad we're on the same page. So instead of teaching me how to curtsy or hold a damn fork or whatever you had planned for this evening, how about you sleep? Just relax?"

She let out a soft laugh, and shook her head beneath the duvet before pulling the cover back down. This was basic peek-a-boo shite, but Tav couldn't help the strange spike of happiness when her face was revealed again.

"I don't think I can go back to sleep now," she said. She rolled over and picked up her tablet, which was never far from her reach. "It's cool. I have to —"

Tav plucked the tablet out of her hands and tossed it onto the sofa across the room.

"Careful!" She leapt up and he held his forearm across the front of her, feeling the delicious press of her breasts as she dove for the tablet, which was resting safely atop a knit jumper.

He expected her to pull back, but she didn't. Her head swiveled toward him, but the soft globes of her breasts rested against his forearm, the weight of them pure temptation. Her eyes were wide and he could feel her heart thudding where he held her. His own heart was giving hers a run for its money because his pulse rushed in his ears, drowning everything out except for the voice shouting *Kiss her.*

Tav swallowed.

"You're my squire, aye?" It was a reminder to himself. She'd already said that anything more than that wasn't on offer, even if her pupils were wide and those lovely pinky-brown lips were parted in anticipation.

"Yes," she said. The word came out on a wary huff of breath.

"That means this isn't a one-way street. I get to look out for you, too, remember? I think you need a break tonight and I'm going to have to insist on that."

Her lashes fluttered. He wanted to feel them against his cheeks as she kissed him.

He couldn't.

"Oh. Okay." She leaned back, taking the glorious press of her bosom from his arm.

"I'll just . . . not do anything then." She glanced longingly at her tablet and Tav knew if he left her to get sleep she would just jump back into work as soon as the door shut, researching, sending emails, and whatever else she could do from bed.

"Can you be ready to go in half an hour?" he asked.

Her head tilted to the side and Tavish wanted to cup her face in his hands, to run his tongue over the seam of her mouth. *That wouldn't exactly be restful for her.*

"Sure," she said. "To go where?"

"To have your mind — and your taste

330

buds — blown."

The restaurant was smaller than Tavish remembered. He hadn't been in years — the last time had probably been that awful dinner with Greer when he'd sat searching for words that never came and the realization that it was well and truly over had settled on him. But when he'd sat on the edge of Portia's bed, watching her rationalize how to sneak in some work, he'd had a craving for the taste of home. That he'd wanted her to taste it with him was something he'd worry about another day.

Across the table, she was biting into her fourth empanada, eyes fluttering closed and smile resting on her grease-slick lips.

"This is so good," she murmured. Bits of the flaky pastry clung to her red-stained lips, and she licked them away.

The restaurant was small and dark and not much to look at, but the chef could make Portia smile and moan in a way Tav wasn't able to, so it had been the right choice. He'd worried when he led her into the alley, and then down the flight of rickety stairs to the basement, that she might scoff or pull a face. He didn't know why he kept expecting these things — Portia had never done anything to make him think she'd react in such a way.

Maybe it's because life would be much easier for you if she did act like the annoying imaginary version of her you conjured up.

"You should taste my mum's empanadas," he said. "Makes these taste like deep fried dust."

"I'm gonna hold you to that," she said. She stopped and pulled out her phone with her free hand.

"Hey," he said menacingly. "No working, remember?"

"I'm sending a picture to my friends," she said, tapping away at the phone with a smile before tucking it away. "Evidence that I am actually taking a night off. You're not the only one who's been on my case. Also this deliciousness deserves to be preserved for future generations. One day I can show this picture to my grandchildren."

Tav smiled.

"The owner of this place is friends with my mum," he said. "We used to come here all the time when I was younger. Had birthday parties and community events here with other Chileans who'd had to come to Scotland. I thought you might like it."

"I love it," she said. She licked at the tip of her thumb, which he was sure wasn't in any etiquette book, and that made it all the more alluring. When she caught him staring at her, she sheepishly picked up her napkin.

"Do you *enjoy* the etiquette stuff?" he asked. "I hope so because it'd be a hell of a waste to spend so much time learning and teaching something you didn't."

She shrugged. "I'm ambivalent. It's what my parents thought I was good at. My sister — the smart twin — was more focused on school and I liked artsy stuff and clothes and attention. I was eager to please, while Reggie generally didn't give a fuck about that as long as she achieved her goals."

The paint-by-number portrait of Portia's family situation was getting slowly filled in, but Tav couldn't quite understand how the woman across from him could be seen as anything less than brilliant.

"So this Reggie is a genius? Because she would have to be pretty fucking intelligent to hold the title of 'the smart twin' between the two of you."

"I know I'm smart. But you know how it is." Portia shrugged. "My parents sent me for deportment lessons and entered me into local beauty contests."

"I can't believe you've been holding out that you were a beauty queen, Freckles." Tav wasn't exactly surprised, but was still strange to think of Portia parading herself around to be judged. His jibes had hurt her so easily.

She shook her head. "I was a contestant. You have to win to be a queen. But yeah. I had a debut, with the frilly dress and everything, too. I think they were training me to be a good wife since I was so uneven at school and they didn't think art or hanging on the internet were viable careers. Not their best investment."

She gave him something between a grin and a grimace. The waiter arrived then with *pastel de choclo* for her and *lomo a lo pobre* for him.

"Anything to drink with your meal?" the waiter asked.

"I'll have another glass of red," Tavish said.

"And sparkling water with a slice of lime for me," Portia added. The waiter went off on his way.

"Does it bother you? My drinking?" he asked. "I can just have water, too."

"No, it's cool," she said, cutting into her corn and meat pie. "I can have a drink and be fine. I don't crave alcohol and I don't binge drink every time I have it. I decided not to drink because I wanted to see what I'm like when I'm not setting myself up to be a hot mess."

She shrugged and scooped some of her

food onto her fork awkwardly. She was uncomfortable.

"Well, good on you," he said, but something she'd said snagged annoyingly in his mind. "I don't know what you were like before, but you're the furthest thing from a hot mess I've seen. Without you I would be completely lost."

Another shrug. "Without me you wouldn't be dealing with this to begin with."

"Portia."

She shoved a forkful of food in her mouth.

"Portia. Hey, lass."

She looked up at him, chewing apprehensively, and he folded his hands together and regarded her with as serious an expression as he could muster.

"Has anyone ever told you that you're shite at taking compliments?"

Her hand went to her mouth as a squeal of surprised laughter escaped.

"Like *really* shite. Jesus Christ." He was rewarded with more laughter.

Her hand was still in front of her mouth, blocking it from view as she finished chewing. "Sorry."

"Don't be sorry. Just take the fucking compliment. Do I seem like the type who goes about doling them out to every Tom, Dick, and Mary?"

She narrowed her gaze at him. "Actually, your dirty little secret is that inside all that armor you've outfitted yourself with, you're a squishy marshmallow."

Tav growled and shoved the deliciously seasoned steak and chips into his mouth instead of replying. He was used to being described as cold and rude, not *squishy* for fuck's sake.

Portia chuckled. "I guess I'm not the only one who can't take a compliment, Lord I-Turned-Down-a-Shitload-of-Cash-Because-David-Insulted-Refugees."

Tav pushed a chip to the edge of his plate with the tines of his fork. "Do you think I should have accepted his bribe?"

Do you think I don't have what it takes to be a duke?

"I think you could have, but I really don't see you as the type to take hush money from an asshole like that, even if it's the easy thing to do."

He wanted to ask her just exactly how she saw him because every morning he looked in the mirror and tried to tell himself he was a duke now, an important man, and every morning he failed spectacularly.

"I keep wondering, who the fuck am I? To think I deserve the titles and properties and everything that comes along with this?"

"The fact that you're even wondering is a good start," she said, waving her knife in his direction — something he wouldn't have trusted her with before. "There are people out there who will do anything for money and prestige, even when they already have it. Your reservations are a good sign."

Tav sighed. "It's just . . . When I talked to my mum, I was so mad at this Dudgeon prick, but she loved him at some point. And he loved her. He was dedicated to helping the downtrodden, by all accounts. But she said becoming a duke changed him, and not for the better. I can't stop thinking what if . . ."

He thought again of the sword above the mantelpiece. It had done something to him, knowing his father had commissioned that first big piece. Like he'd been watching from the wings, and had maybe been proud. Had maybe even cared.

"Tavish, you don't have to become your father," Portia said. "You're your own man. And let's keep it real – you can't be worse than David. From what I've read, he's spent more time using his new status to pick up women and bash migrants than he has doing anything else."

"That git was using the title to pull birds? Of course, he was."

Portia took a sip of water, and trained her gaze on her plate. "I guess that's one benefit you haven't taken into account. A duke is not going to have trouble in the dating department."

Tav didn't know what to feel about that, mostly because he hadn't thought of another woman in weeks. He tried to imagine it now, some playboy aristocrat lifestyle where he kicked beautiful women out of his bed every other morning and traded them in for new models. Unfortunately, his mind could only conjure images of Portia, the feel of her mouth against his and the heat of her hands pulling him close. Kicking her out of his bed played no part in that ongoing fantasy, and therein lay his problem.

"So, I'm to be a rake now? Don't quite know how I feel about that. Raking seems like a lot of work. All that seducing and being charming. You know charm isn't my strong suit."

She pursed her lips as she chewed and swallowed.

"You joke, but I've already started getting formal inquiries as to whether you're dating anyone and the news isn't even fully out yet. A handsome newly minted duke is apparently irresistible, so you'd better figure out your thoughts on the matter soon." He wanted the words to be flirtatious, but she was still looking everywhere but at his face.

"Is that a general statement or a personal one? The bit about me being irresistible?" he asked. He leaned forward a bit and his knee brushed hers beneath the table.

"Oh, come on. Don't tell me you haven't thought of how women will react," she said, avoiding his question. The grimace on her face revealed something else: she had thought of it, and she wasn't keen on the idea. "When the internet finds out #sword-bae is also #dukebae, your DMs are gonna be lit."

"Well, I don't know what that last bit means, but I've not been thinking about hypothetical women. I've been fairly focused on other matters." He kept his gaze on her, wondering whether the anticipation pooling in his stomach was a one-sided thing. Her brown eyes were wide, gathering the flickering candlelight in their warm depths.

"Did you see the new exhibit at the Medieval Museum?" she asked suddenly. "I know we've been busy, but I was thinking I could talk to someone there about doing an exhibit of some of the interesting pieces you have in your collection and on modern swordsmithing. 'Modern meets Medieval: A return to classic Scots swordmaking' or something like that."

Ah. Conversation change. Tav would respect that. She'd already told him she didn't want anything and this night was about helping her feel better, not an opportunity to force the issue of their clear chemistry.

He shouldn't have pushed, even though his push had mostly been a steady gaze and a one-track mind. He didn't drink the rest of his wine. He was sober, but he didn't want the excuse of lowered inhibitions to let his growing feelings for her slip. His feelings weren't something else of his for her to manage.

"That sounds brilliant," he said, settling against the back of his chair. They finished the dinner talking about everything but dukedoms and dating. Portia dragged him down a rabbit hole that led from medieval swords to ancient Etruscan sabers to Byzantine architecture to the basic structure of a web page, and Tav loved every minute of it.

Dating after his marriage had always ranged from "She's a fun lass" to "this will work for now," but as they sat eating the food of his childhood and opening up to each other, Tavish felt something come into alignment.

He'd been attracted to Portia before that

night. He had grown accustomed to her presence. But the churn of emotions staging a tourney in his rib cage was more than those two things — he *wanted* her. He was well aware that he couldn't and shouldn't but he did, and Christ's sake was he ever screwed.

"Is there . . . ?" She motioned around her face.

"What?" He tried to pull his focus back instead of staring at her like she was a sword he was grinding.

"Last time you looked at me like that there was something on my face," she said, pulling out her compact. She dabbed at that red lipstick that miraculously hadn't budged though they'd just eaten, and Tav watched her finger brush the sensitive skin on her pouty bottom lip.

Over her shoulder he noticed one of the waiters begin to flip chairs over onto tables, the universal sign for "you don't have to go home but you can't stay here."

"We should probably pay." He stood and she followed him, thankfully not protesting when he paid the tab at the register. He wasn't trying to be a chauvinist; it was the least he could do to repay her for her help.

"It's not what I'd call a warm summer night, but it's not raining. Let's walk back," she said once they'd left the alley. The salty scent from the firth was carried by the strong night wind, and she closed her eyes as if savoring it, just as she had with the food. He'd once predicted that she'd be picky, but Portia was a woman who savored trying new things.

They walked and talked, Tavish trying not to think too much about how much he wanted to kiss her. This wasn't a date, it was . . . a man and a woman who were attracted to each other sharing an excellent meal and conversation.

Oh hell.

"What is that?" she exclaimed when they were nearing their neighborhood. He followed the path from her tapered fingertip to the huge old ship anchored along the waterway. It was painted with stripes and blocks of different colors and patterns all contrasting. "It's like a drunken Mondrian."

Tav didn't know what a sober Mondrian was, but he did know about the ship; he was so used to it, he hardly ever noticed it anymore. "It's a dazzler. During the Second World War, German U-boats would patrol and sink ships in the bay, but when they saw a ship painted like this against the horizon, they couldn't make them out. Apparently, the best camouflage was to be bright and beautiful."

She stood looking at the ship and he stood looking at her, in her red lipstick and red blouse and red-bottomed heels.

She glanced at him from the corner of her eye and pursed her lips.

"Enough with the Dr. Phil shite," she said and Tav burst into laughter, jogging to keep up with her as she stalked away. A smile hovered on her lips when he caught up to her, though.

"This is really your first time seeing the dazzler, then? I guess the camouflage really does work well."

She shook her head. "I haven't walked much along the water."

"What have you been doing?" he asked, then pulled a face of mock surprise. "Ah that's right, solving mysteries and getting my life in order. You're like an American Mary Poppins, but more smartly dressed. And more —"

She made a scoffing sound. "No —"

Tav turned and stood in front of her, walking backward. "Hey now. You can't refute a compliment I didn't give you yet, lass," he said.

She smirked up at him. "Watch it."

"Or what?" he asked, and then something metal and cold hit him across the lower back. Portia grabbed him by his belt and tugged him forward.

"Or you fall into the water and meet your death," she said. "I can't swim."

"You can't drive and you can't swim?"

"Yup, that's me. Master of none." She said it in a breezy tone, but he knew her well enough to understand that she believed that tripe.

"There's at least one thing you've mastered quite well," he said. Her hand was still on his belt, knuckles pressing into his abdomen.

She rolled her eyes. "What's that? Annoying you?"

"No. Dazzling."

She was looking up at him, her delicate brow furrowed and her lips parted as if she might protest. Knowing *again* that he shouldn't, Tav leaned down and pressed his mouth to hers. She made a sound, but it wasn't one of protest.

"Mpf," she breathed against his lips, and there was lust and relief and humor all rolled up into that sound, like she'd been waiting for this moment without knowing it, too. She licked into his mouth hungrily and sensation clanged up his spine. Yes, she'd been holding herself back, and now that she wasn't Tav had no reason to either.

Their tongues darted and clashed and *bloody hell* he hadn't realized how spot-on his little spiel about delayed gratification had been. He'd waited and denied and fantasized and now that she was in his arms again, it was even better than he remembered or imagined.

Her kiss tasted of the rice dessert they'd eaten, cinnamon sweetness. Her grip tightened on his belt as his hands clenched on her shoulders. Her shirt was silky smooth under his fingertips, but not so much as her tongue as it slid over his. He traced his fingertips over her shoulder blades, then flattened his hands and brushed down, down, until the curves of her ass filled his palms.

"Oh dammit," she moaned against his mouth, pulling away.

"I'm sorry," he said.

"I'm not." Her gaze was dark, intense and her lips were full and moist. "Look, I think this isn't going to go away. This thing between us."

He wondered if by *thing* she meant "excruciating need to fuck each other senseless."

"I think not," he said carefully.

"In fact, I only know one way to get rid of a persistent *thing,*" she said. Her expression suddenly went shy, her gaze softening as she shifted from foot to foot. "Let's do it."

"Do what?"

She glared up at him, but it was a vulnerable glare, somehow.

Tav laughed, caressed his hand up her silk-clad back. "Are you sure? I don't want you to think . . . I didn't take you to dinner because I expected this to happen."

"Why *did* you take me to dinner?" she asked.

Tav wasn't the smoothest talker, but he could have pulled out some line designed for seduction. He decided to tell the truth instead. "Because I like spending time with you. I like *you*. And I wanted to make you feel good."

She suddenly looked away from him, as if she could see out into the darkness where the waves rolled in from along the horizon to slap against the docks. When she met his gaze again, there was challenge in her eyes and her response was sharp. "It is a truth universally acknowledged that chemistry like this never lives up to the hype. I've scratched enough itches to know."

Ah. She'd already told him she wasn't looking for more. These were her terms and conditions. No more *I like you*s, then. This was a lark, she was telling him with her careful avoidance of his confession, and although it was something he'd likely regret, he decided he'd just go with the flow. After all, he didn't want a relationship either. He wasn't stupid enough to allow his heart to be drawn and quartered a second time.

Just sex. He could do that.

Aye.

"You know, you're right," he said. "I've scratched a fair few itches myself and never quite felt a need to go back for a second helping."

It felt wrong, comparing her to past lovers, but that's how they were playing this. Cool. Casual.

Ach, he was too old for this shite.

"You're mixing your metaphors," she said, running her hands over his chest like she'd finally been extended an invitation. It felt bloody good, just that quick, warm press of her palms through his shirt. Tav grasped her hands with his own, stopping their motion.

"Well begging your pardon, but most of my blood isn't in my brain right now. You'll deal."

She giggled. "I'll deal." She stepped forward, her right thigh notching between both of his as she pressed against him. The weight of her breasts pushed against his torso, her stomach grazed over his erection, and that delicate scent of hers mixed in with the salty air off the firth. "One and done?" she asked, mischief and lust pushing away the shyness she'd displayed a moment ago.

He wasn't sure if she was declaring that to be the arrangement or asking whether it was even possible between them, but he didn't clarify because she was close and desire danced in her eyes and he needed to taste her again.

He caressed her face once, twice, and then molded his lips over hers. He kissed with his eyes open because he wanted to see that freckled nose wrinkle in concentration — and so he could start navigating them back to the armory and not into the firth, though even a dunk in the cold sea wouldn't cool him down now.

Portia had thrown down a challenge that had nothing to do with class or etiquette or fake posh shite. He didn't suppose there were rules in *Debrett's* for what they were about to do, but all the better. A wild, passionate energy was flowing between them, and Tavish doubted either of them planned on being polite.

CHAPTER 19

Having sex with Tav hadn't been in her plans — in fact, she'd had specific rules against this very situation — but then again, neither had revealing him to be a duke. Plans changed, she reasoned, and it wasn't like this was impulsive. It was inevitable, it seemed. She'd felt the urge to jump him upon their first meeting, which was midmacing, and had been fighting her attraction ever since. This, whatever was happening between them, was kind of a foregone conclusion. She'd regret detonating this foundational pillar of Project: New Portia later; for now, she'd glory in the explosion.

They crept up to her room instead of his office. Jamie and Cheryl were out at a pub quiz night — he could be the one risking bumping into them afterward.

They'd kept their hands to themselves on the way back to the armory — after all, she didn't need Mary or any of the other neighborhood familiars catching Tav's hand up her shirt. Both of them had been on the verge of breaking out into a trot and had kept giving each other heated looks, their intent likely clear to anyone who paid attention, but none of that mattered once she closed the door to her room and shoved Tav up against it.

"That was the longest walk of my life," he groaned as his hands came to her hips and tugged her close against him. The blunt tips of his fingers pressed into her hips and she swallowed a soft moan. She loved how strong his hands were — strength that came from grinding and fighting, from artistry and dedication. Each time he held her it sent a possessive thrill through her.

"Not gonna lie — I scoped out a few dark corners on the way in case we couldn't make it," she said.

Laughter rumbled through his chest. "I'd be amenable to testing out dark corners sometime."

Sometime.

I like you.

No. Taking his words seriously was asking for trouble. She would operate as she always had; no catching feelings, no getting hurt. She was a damned expert at that. She ignored what he was insinuating and focused on his mouth, his firm lips, his hands sliding into the waistband of her pants in search of the hidden clasp that would release them.

"How are these secured?" he growled, tugging at the waistband. "Magic? Are these chastity trousers?"

She grinned against his mouth. "Mmm, yes, they're enchanted. Only the chosen one can get into them. Pantscalibur, or as they were known in Middle Welsh, *Pantsvich*—"

"Very funny. Oh, what's this?" His fingers found the eyelet hook along the side of the pants just then and deftly unhooked it, then grasped at the pull of the zipper and tugged slowly. He kissed her again as his fingers worked. The pants were too tight to fall to the ground, but now there was room for his hands to slip inside, for his palms to glide over her silk underwear and his hands to cup her ass.

She shuddered and moaned into his mouth.

"It appears I'm the chosen one," he said, his mouth moving from her lips to press hungry kisses along her jawline and down her neck as his hands held her firmly in place. "Yay, me."

"I'm trying to come up with a dirty sword in the stone double entendre but fuck your hands feel amazing," she said, and maybe that was even better than a joke because he exhaled harshly against her neck and the tightened his grip on her, the combination rapidly unraveling her control.

No.

Her hand went to his belt again, this time to tug it open, and her other hand slid up under his shirt, following the trail of hair from the taper at the waist of his pants to where it spread over his chest. She kissed at his neck as she undid his belt and his aggravating button fly jeans. Finally, finally, her fingers encircled his thick, warm cock and he groaned and . . . it was in that moment that Portia realized she had no idea what she was doing. Well, she knew what she was *doing,* but she was usually loosened up by a drink or two while doing it. When was the last time she'd given a hand job totally sober?

Without the inhibition-loosening effects of alcohol, little annoying thoughts started to eat away at the lust and frenzy that had propelled her through the streets of Bodotria and toward her bed.

Does he like what you're doing? Are you pulling too hard? Not hard enough. Should you just get on your knees? Yeah, yeah, do that. Every guy likes that, right?

She started to drop down, eyes locked on Tav's, but his grip slid up to her shoulders and tightened, sending a thrill through her but also confusing her because he was holding her in place.

His gaze on her was still intense, hot, but he seemed to be searching her face for something. His expression was so serious that for a second Portia was mortified, certain she really had given the worst hand job ever and he didn't trust her teeth anywhere near him, but then he grinned and shook his head.

"I thought we agreed that I'm the chosen one here, love. That means I get the reward and I have something else in mind, if it's all right with you."

He began walking her back toward the bed, his hands sliding down the front of her blouse and undoing the buttons one by one. He slid the shirt back over her shoulders and they both stepped over it when it pooled on the floor. Now she was in just her lace bra and tight pants and heels, a style Tavish seemed to appreciate.

He leaned down and kissed her again, an action that seesawed between harsh and gentle, desire and denial. One of his hands smoothed down over the curve of her breasts, over her stomach, until his fingers had notched into the vee between her thighs. Those thick fingers she'd admired since the first morning she sat across from him in his office began to move now, circling over the fabric of her pants and underwear. The pressure was steady and firm, with no tentative fumbling as he searched for her clit. He zeroed in fast and hard, leaving her gasping with the sudden onslaught of pleasure. He was good with his hands in every situation, it seemed.

Her hips rolled and her head dropped back as she pressed into his touch.

"Do you like that?" he asked, rubbing faster, pressing deeper. Pleasure washed through her in time to his motions, rippling out from her clit to her toes to her fingertips in tingling waves.

"Yes," she managed before pressing her teeth into her bottom lip to keep from crying out — they weren't supposed to be doing this after all. Tavish's laugh rumbled as he alternated the speed of his caressing.

"Good." He tipped her back onto the bed, a move that was just a step below gentle, and followed her down as she fell backward onto the mattress, one hand still working. The other hand pressed her shoulder down into the mattress and Portia shuddered at the weight of it, which gave her pleasure just as much as the hand between her legs did.

Then he was kissing her as he rubbed, and though they'd been at it off and on for the last half hour, he kissed her like a lover who hadn't seen his beloved in months. She wasn't one for romanticizing, but he kissed with the lush, seductive artistry of Klimt, dark passion hidden beneath rich, solid strokes. His fingers pressed and his tongue caressed and she knew when the moisture of her desire had seeped through her pants because he *Mmmm*ed into her mouth with a devilish delight that made her toes curl.

"Fuck, Tavish," she whispered.

He was settled between her thighs, mouth fused to hers as he got her off with one hand. His other hand tugged at her bra straps, pulled the band roughly down over her stomach before his palm scraped over her breasts, the calluses and scars of his trade adding to the friction. He licked into her mouth, and then his thumb and index fingers closed around her nipple and pinched just hard enough to make her gasp and buck up beneath him.

He pulled his mouth away and his hand stopped moving, making her realize she'd caught his rhythm and had been riding it like she was in was the most important dressage competition of her life. "Too much?" he asked.

Somewhere in the back of her mind a voice told her she was supposed to deny liking such things, but instead she licked her lips and shook her head.

"Not enough."

Tav groaned a laugh and then his lips pressed into her neck, then her collarbone, and then clamped around her nipple. He lashed it with short, hard strokes of his tongue. Her hands dove into his thick hair as she writhed and fought against the cry rising in her throat.

She didn't know if it was his added years of experience or just innate talent, but Tav seemed to know exactly what pushed her buttons. His grip was strong and sure and his mouth and tongue moved with one mission: to drive pleasure into her. He gripped her nipple lightly between his teeth and tugged, as if reminding her that he could pleasure with any part of his body he so chose.

"Oh fuck." Her body slid wildly against his and he did that thing again — pressing her down into the mattress with one hand to keep her in place. She let out a moan and he grinned, eyes on her and other hand at the waistband of her pants.

"More?" he asked, and waited for her shaky nod to tug her pants and underwear both down with one hand. His fingers slipped against her clit without the barrier of fabric, sending sparks of pleasure zipping through her. He wasn't any more gentle than he had been, but it was exactly what Portia wanted from him. He rubbed hard circles into her wetness, still holding her down by a shoulder.

"I can feel you trembling. Are you close, love?" He slowed the motion down so he was moving his fingers in deep, torturous circles over her sleek nub.

"Yes, Tav," she choked out. *So close.* She reached out to grip the length of him where he bulged against his boxer briefs. He grunted a curse as she pulled him through the flap. She stroked him as he stroked her, and watching the muscles in his jaw tense and his eyes squeeze shut almost pushed her over the edge completely.

His gaze was intense as it rested on her face and he pumped into her hand. She picked up the rhythm of his touch between her legs, matching the slide of her hand against his cock. Portia was overcome with sensation, she was so close but she couldn't . . .

Then Tavish's hand slipped from her

shoulder to her neck, his fingers loosely encircling it, palm resting on her collarbones. His brows raised and she nodded, and then he increased the pressure just the slightest bit. It wasn't enough to impede her breathing, but the weight of it paired with the two fingers he slid inside of her at the same moment were enough.

"Oh, fuck! Tavish!" Her back arched and she grabbed on to his forearm with both hands as she clamped around his fingers and rode out the impossible sensation flowing through her. Sparks from an anvil, fireworks — all of that good shit — flashed behind her tightly squeezed eyes as her orgasm crested over her. She didn't know how long she writhed and bucked — and how long he held her down through it — but when she finally opened her eyes, panting and short of breath, he was staring at her hard.

"Okay there, lass?" His voice was hoarse with need.

She responded by tugging him onto the bed beside her and kissing him, her hand frantically searching out his cock and closing over his own — he'd been working himself as he watched her fly apart beneath him.

She leaned back, taking a breath from

their frantic pace, and watched him stroke himself. The kernel of a crush in her chest that had grown into a cornfield all simultaneously popped into popcorn from the heat of it. Fuck. She'd already thought him sexy, but now she'd be stuck with this image of him lazily touching himself, invitation in his hazel gaze, whenever her brain wanted to mess with her.

She reached into the toiletry bag beside her bed to pull out a condom, knocking his hand out of the way to slide it onto him. He chuckled at her rush, a sound that was cut short as she slid the condom down. She waited a moment, until he pumped up into her fist impatiently, and then knelt over him and followed suit with her body.

He wasn't lacking in the girth department, and Portia rested on the tip of his cock for a moment, gaze locked on his as she slowly took him into her. The slow, deep stretch of him felt more intimate than anything Portia had ever experienced. He leaned up on his elbows to watch her, them, though the more she took in, the more tightly his eyes squeezed shut.

She squeezed his torso between her knees as she rode him, loving the thick friction of him inside of her, relishing the way his hips moved as he pushed up to deepen their joining. Her hands rested on his chest as she met his shallow stroke with a deep one, pulling a moan from both of them.

"Jesus, Portia."

After that there was just the slap and slide of their bodies against one another, their hushed moans. He leaned up, one hand sliding into her hair to hold her gaze with his and the other gripping her hip as he pumped up into her.

"You're . . ." His eyes closed and he grit his teeth. "You're driving me crazy. You beautiful . . ."

His words trailed off as she swiveled her hips in his lap, meeting his upward thrusts from a new angle. His hand in her hair guided her mouth to his for a bruising kiss and his hand gripped her hip enough to cause sweet shocks of pain.

"Tav, I'm gonna —" Then she cried out into his mouth as her body went taut with ecstasy. He let out a series of curses as he pounded up into her and then they both toppled over onto the mattress, a tangle of sweaty limbs and heaving chests.

Shit, Portia thought. *Now what?*

Of course she hadn't thought ahead to this part. After the hookup. She would usually get up and go now, but this was her room. They lived in the same building.

And I don't want to.

"Fuck's sake," Tav drawled miserably, and Portia steeled herself.

"This bed really is uncomfortable." He shifted around a bit until he was cradling her in his arms. "Why didn't you tell me you were serious about that?"

She let out a snort of disbelief and he nuzzled into her neck.

"And you called me a princess," she asked.

He nuzzled some more — he was a cuddler apparently. She tried to ignore how good and natural it felt to be with him like this.

"Eh, so about that simmering and itch scratching and hype and what not?" His voice was only a little playful.

"We'll see how we feel in the morning," she said carefully.

His hand slid up her waist and cupped her breast. "Morning's a long way off," he mumbled into her neck. Portia allowed herself to sink into his touch. He was right; sometimes it took a few rounds to *really* fuck a man out of your system. By the time the sun filtered through the fog of Bodotria, they'd be over each other for sure.

Totally.

CHAPTER 20

Tavish was sleeping; Portia was not. He had his arms around her and was holding her close and, honestly, who slept like that? Holding another human being like a koala hugged up on a eucalyptus tree. Ew.

She batted at her pillow and Tav's arm tightened around her.

It wasn't *bad* exactly, it was just that he was so warm. His chest hair tickled her back each time he inhaled and exhaled. He smelled — it was a good smell, but still. If she was a man-sweat sommelier, she would say it had hints of steel, citrus, and essence of Tavish. But she had never cared about a guy's smell before unless it was a rando crushed against her on the train. It bothered her that she was sneaking whiffs of Tav's elbow, partly because there would be no further elbow sniffing.

One and done. He was supposed to be out of her system. She was supposed to be sliding out from beneath his arm, then firmly but politely shoving him out the door, both of them much too mature to feel anything other than a bit of mischievous pride.

She nestled into him a little closer. Inhaled.

"Why is it you don't allow yourself to become attached to any of these men, Portia?"

"It's just easier that way. No muss, no fuss."

She'd made a lot of mistakes in her life, but maybe none so grave as the three words she'd spoken the night before.

Let's do it.

A chirping sound filled the room and for a moment she thought it was the morning birds, but as it grew more insistent she realized it was the sound of an incoming video call.

Oh shit.

She'd forgotten Ledi was on a flight to Thesolo and had said she would call at some godawful time. Portia slipped out of Tavish's hold and smiled at the way he grumbled, then caught herself. She glanced at him, against her better judgment, and her breath caught for a moment.

He didn't look boyish, with his disheveled salt-and-pepper hair and crow's feet, and he didn't look serene. He looked like he was dreaming about something salacious, a sly grin quirking a corner of his mouth and creasing the stubble on his cheeks, and the *want* that should have burned away with hours of sex flared up again, stronger than before.

She pulled on a T-shirt and grabbed her phone, slipping in her earpiece as she accepted the call.

Ledi was staring sleepily at the screen, her braids pineappled atop her head and poking out from her silk scarf. "Hey, girl." Ledi's brows went up. "Heyyyyy, girl. No headscarf. Crazy tangled hair. Yesterday's makeup still on, kind of. Am I interrupting something?"

Portia's gaze flicked guiltily toward the bed. "What had happened was, we went to dinner —"

Ledi burst into laughter and shook her head. "I knew it! I knew it! Biso, you owe me twenty dollars."

The camera jostled and swiveled and then Prince Thabiso was on the screen, brows jumping suggestively over sleep-hooded eyes. "Got down and dirty with the duke, did you, Portia? How could you do this to me? I had twenty dollars that said you could resist his charms."

"You guys bet on me?" Portia wasn't sure

how she felt about that. Actually, she did know, and it wasn't great. "And only twenty bucks? You're royalty!"

"I have to reinvest my money into my country, Portia, I can't go throwing it about gambling on sex acts," Thabiso said gravely. "Besides, you know how cheap Ledi is. She wanted to bet five."

Ledi appeared in the screen again, elbow first as she shoved Thabiso out of the way. "I showed Biso that video of Tavish pounding away on the anvil, and said if I were in your shoes, that metal wouldn't be the only thing getting hit at the armory, so I didn't know how you were holding out. This wasn't some judgment on your character. It was vicarious living."

"How is it that you've become more crude since you became a princess?" Portia asked, mentally smoothing her ruffled feathers.

"Portia, if the last few weeks has taught you anything, it should have been that the aristocracy is crude as they come," Thabiso cut in. "The parties and jewels and ceremony are all to distract the rabble with shiny things while we engage in indecent behavior."

"We?" Ledi asked archly.

"Sorry, I slipped into French. Must be because I just finished talking to Johan.

They." He winked at Portia through the screen, then his eyes went wide. "Did you say she called him Ass Man, Ledi? That *is* a spectacular ass. Shield your eyes."

"Here, we have a male engaged in the rarely captured walk of shame," Ledi said in a faux nature show host voice, pushing Thabiso's hand away. "The male is confused by awakening in a strange habitat. Human males are creatures of routine."

Something pale moved behind Portia in the inset video on the phone and she turned to find a naked, spectacular-assed sword-maker blundering around her room searching for his boxers. She let out a horrified laugh and immediately swiveled the phone away.

"Morning," he grumbled. "I have to go practice with the weans for the exhibition. It's their first so I want to make sure they're good and ready."

"Oh! Great! I'm on a call!" Portia didn't know why the words came out as high-pitched squeaks. Probably because her boss had just mooned her friends. Because he was naked in her room. Because she'd spent a hedonistic night with him.

She cleared her throat. "I'm on a call with Ledi and Thabiso."

"Princess and her prince?" His voice was

rough with sleep — his burr more pronounced — and Portia felt a pang that they hadn't woken up earlier. She wanted to feel the rumble of his growl between her thighs one more time. But that wasn't part of Project: New Portia, Electric Boogaloo, with the one-night stand amendment.

"Yes. You've officially mooned royalty," she said.

He chuckled. "Ah. Dad will be so proud."

"Unplug your headphones so we can talk to him," Ledi urged.

"No. He's not even wearing any pants," Portia said. Besides, it would be too weird, her best friend talking to him. Ledi had never met any of Portia's conquests, apart from being at a bar with Portia when she encountered them. Though Tavish wasn't a conquest. He was her boss . . . and her friend?

Portia's brain was muddled. Maybe she had OD'd on sex endorphins during the night.

"My friends want to chat with you," she said, surprising herself.

Tav scoffed as he pulled on his pants. "Your friends can get in line behind my mum and dad. You know I don't like video, Freckles."

Portia tried not to let her disappointment

show. Why did she care? It would have been weird, and they didn't need weirdness. They needed for him to leave and for both of them to act like the night before hadn't happened.

"He doesn't like video chatting, sorry guys. Your dreams of conversing with a semi-nude duke have been dashed." Footsteps approached and then Tav's jean-clad legs appeared onscreen beside her. She saw his hand heading for her shoulder before she felt the weight of it, before her brain remembered all the things that hand had done to her the night before.

"Hello friends of Portia," he said much too loudly, as if he was trying to shout toward their plane wherever it was in the sky. "I have to go serve the youth of Bodotria right now, and I also don't want to overwhelm you with my devilish good looks, but nice meeting you. Cute scarf, Princess. Sweet robe, Prince."

He ruffled Portia's hair — *what the hell? A hair ruffle?* — and turned and left.

"Oh, his voice is even dreamier all gravelly like that," Ledi said. "And the way he rolled the *r* in *princess* . . ."

Ledi sighed.

"I have an accent, too," Thabiso said petulantly.

"You have the *sexiest* accent," Ledi said, leaning her head on his shoulder and looking up at him. She had once been super reserved, but was so open with her affection now. Portia assumed it was because of Thabiso, and then felt a flash of envy. She wouldn't have that with Tav. She was helping him get a handle on his life, and then she'd be on her way. Mary Poppins, indeed.

"I'm still here, guys," Portia said.

"Oh sorry," Thabiso said, his mood much improved. "I was going to tell the Duke of Assman that my friend Johan is going to be in Edinburgh and he owes me a favor. He can stop by to give him some advice."

"Prince Johan? The Liechtienbourg guy?" Portia asked. "I mean, speaking of asses, his was on the cover of every tabloid after he got caught playing strip poker. Is he the best person to be giving Tav advice?"

"He's not technically a prince, though that situation is rather awkward. Best not to bring it up when you meet him," Thabiso said. "But yes, that Prince Johan. He's a good guy, really. Really . . . insightful, I'd call him. Don't believe everything you read in the papers."

"So that wasn't his butt?" Portia asked.

"Oh, it definitely was, and you should have seen the photos that didn't get published," Thabiso said. "His family paid a pretty penny to keep those under wraps."

"I've seen them," Ledi said primly. "Thabiso is already mad at me, so I won't comment any further. But Johan's actually a cool guy . . . beneath all the other stuff."

"I could use some help actually. This is above my pay grade. Thanks for your help, guys."

"We would have come ourselves but there's a new energy plant opening — the one with the waterfalls that Thabiso had prioritized — and we need to be there. Optics." Ledi said the last word as if it was a horrible disease.

"I know all about optics," Portia said, fighting a sudden pang of homesickness as the end of the call neared. It tightened around her chest and tugged, pulling her toward the familiar. The reliable. "I miss you. The past few weeks have been . . . a lot."

Taking the night off to enjoy herself — and all that had come with that — had given her the space to realize just how hard she had been working. Now she was *thinking* and *feeling.* She should have never let Tavish take her tablet away.

"Do you need me there?" Ledi asked. It was a ridiculous idea — they were en route to Thesolo — but Ledi was completely serious. She *would* come if needed, and that was enough for Portia.

"No, I'm okay. Gonna go shower."

They said their goodbyes and Portia padded into the bathroom and stepped beneath the hot spray, ignoring the sore muscles that urged her into flashbacks of the night before. She took longer than usual in the shower, washing her hair, exfoliating her skin — trying to rid herself of that scent that she knew still lingered in her sheets. Trying to wash away the feel of Tavish's hands and mouth on her body. She would be scrubbed free of everything that had happened between them the night before, his trusty platonic squire once again. That was all that she wanted to be, and that was all she would allow herself anyway.

She threw on her pink dry-tech workout pants, a T-shirt with the armory's new logo emblazoned on it, and her matching pink hoodie, then grabbed a coffee from the kitchen before heading to the gymnasium. She'd snap some pics of the kids' morning program for social media and then do Jamie's Extreme Defending the Castle workout, which she needed more than ever.

When she got into the gym, Tav was working with Syed and some of the other children on a demonstration for the next exhibition. They had broomsticks with papier-mâché horse heads fixed on one end between their legs and were practicing jousting. She watched Tavish laugh and clap Syed on the back and felt a pang of longing.

This will pass. For sure.

"He's great with kids. I wouldn't have expected that."

She looked beside her to find Leslie, David's sister. Leslie was wearing Prada from head to toe, and there wasn't a single strand of hair out of place on her head, though Portia could hear the wind howling off of the bay. Portia felt like a knight who had showed up at the tourney field in her thinnest, schlubbiest armor. She'd muddle through.

She stood straighter, made sure to turn the consonants in her words into sharp edges when she spoke, the better to wield them like daggers.

"Why, Leslie, how lovely to see you. May I ask what brought about this unexpected visit?"

Leslie looked away from Tavish then, and there was misery in her eyes, so plain that Portia wondered if she was even trying to hide it.

"I'm here to seduce a duke."

"Pardon?" Tavish asked, unfettered confusion scrunching his features. They were up in his office now, sipping tea. Portia noticed that Leslie stirred her tea in a circular motion, almost defiantly.

"Well, technically I am supposed to offer you my assistance," Leslie explained, her voice flat and refined. "You know, the season is wrapping up, and there's the ball at Essexlove House two Saturdays from now, to mark the official turning over of the title and properties and David's farewell to the peerage."

Tavish glanced at Portia, but she was already pulling out her phone and scanning emails. "Oh. Ms. Baker sent an email invitation last night," she said. "I missed it. Because."

She cleared her throat. A flush cupped Tav's cheekbones.

Leslie reached into her bag and pulled out a paper invitation. "Yes. And I brought the paper one. There's also the matter of the Queen's garden party to kick of her arrival at Holyrood, which you co-host with Her Majesty herself. Three Saturdays from now."

"Bloody hell," Tavish said. "The weans

have their exhibition that day."

"Well, you'll have to skip it. Queens over weans, I'm afraid," Leslie said matter-of-factly. She handed off the invitation to Portia. "I was also supposed to see if you'd like to take me as your date to the ball."

"Me?" Portia asked.

"No, though that would be lovely. Tavish. A night spent together at the ball, an offer of aid that would draw us closer — things that would of course lead to our eventual union."

"There are many problems with this plan, but first — aren't we cousins?" Tavish asked, brow furrowed.

Leslie tilted her head and regarded Tav. "Oh dear. You really don't know anything about the aristocracy at all. How adorable."

"Why are you telling us this?" Portia asked.

"Because I'm tired." Leslie picked at her cardigan. "David doesn't have a wife. He was looking into some heiresses, and there was a music producer's daughter, too. I've spent the last year doing all those duchess things for him — managing the estates, setting up parties, being friendly to people while he was off having affair after affair or stirring the political pot. Before that, as soon as it became clear that your father wasn't going to have any children, my parents became obsessed with David and his eventual entry into the peerage. No one cared about what I wanted."

She glanced at Portia and her expression became guarded. "I don't want to date. Or to marry. Anyone. I'm not . . . wired that way, I suppose. David said since I didn't want anyone else, that it should be no matter to marry Tavish. That it was my *duty* to the family."

Portia knew family expectations could be painful, but her family had always wanted her to be happy and secure, even when their words hurt her. David didn't seem to care about Leslie's happiness at all.

"Doesn't he think I'm a disgusting social climber?" Tav asked.

"Yes, but only because you didn't go to Eton," Leslie said. "That's where proper social climbers meet, you know."

"And the refugee trash part?" Tav added.

"I don't want children, and suddenly what I want matters if it means the family name won't be 'tarnished by the fruit of miscegenation,'" Leslie replied, a grimace on her face. "David's taken everything into account it seems."

"I'm sorry," Portia said. "I'm sorry your brother would do that to you. He's supposed to protect you."

Sudden emotion clogged Portia's throat as a realization hit her. *That* was what she had drank and studied and fucked away from for all these years. She hadn't protected Reggie, illogical as it was. How could she have protected someone from an illness? She couldn't have. That hadn't made it hurt less. And then she hadn't even lived up to anyone's wishes and dreams, compounding that failure.

Portia took a swallow of tea. This wasn't the time for plumbing her emotional depths, though maybe she should call Dr. Lewis after throwing her goals away for a night in bed and having traumatic revelations.

"Honestly, I knew he was an asshole, but this is horrifying." She fixed Leslie with a stern look. "You don't have to do anything you don't want to do, especially not seducing someone you aren't attracted to. You do understand that, right?"

Leslie's glossy eyes met Portia's. "See? That's it. I saw how you defended Tavish, how you looked at David like you would rip him in half when he insulted him, and it all fell into place. No one has ever . . ." A stray tear slipped down her cheek and she dashed it away. "Oh. Pardon me. Your sister must feel very lucky to have you, is all."

"Not sure she feels that way, but thanks," Portia said, then realized something. "How do you know I have a sister?"

Leslie did her head tilt thing again. "You two haven't the slightest idea what you've gotten into."

She stood, threw back the rest of her tea like it was a tumbler of whiskey, and straightened her dress. "The offer still stands of course. I can be your date to the ball, and more, if you want, Tavish."

"But. You just said you didn't want to?" Tavish looked as confused as Portia felt.

"You will soon understand that one must do a great many things one doesn't want to. David gave me a command. I wanted to give you a choice. We could figure something out, if you wanted to make it work." She looked between him and Portia, then breezed out of the office.

Portia's phone vibrated in her hand, a message from Reggie on the screen.

💣 Incoming. We got scooped. #swordbae's duke news is the Looking Glass Daily's breaking news. Your notifications are gonna be a mess.

Portia clicked on the link and held her breath — the *Looking Glass Daily* was world renowned for its sensationalist, lie-riddled stories — but this one was mild. It listed basic information about Tavish in a bullet point format, discussed the #swordbae meme, and talked about the Scottish peerage in general and what being a duke meant. There was the picture of them from the *Bodotria Eagle,* but the caption read "The new duke in town, and (more than?) friend."

"You might want to see this," she said, handing the phone to Tavish. She hated his frown when he saw the still from the video she'd posted and how it deepened as he read.

He took a deep breath and exhaled through his nose. "This is only the beginning, isn't it?"

"Probably."

He threw himself back into his chair. "What do we do now?"

Portia felt momentary confusion at the "we." Not at the pronoun, but at what it connoted. Tavish was still the Duke of Edinburgh, but where did she stand in relation to him after last night?

"I really am going to have to pay you a million pounds for helping me manage this shite," he said irritably, and Portia cringed. It was ridiculous — so ridiculous. She was the one who had said there couldn't be anything more between them, but still, nothing clarified your relationship to a man better than an offer of pounds sterling for your services.

"We'll post a statement on the armory's social media sites," she said, already trying to figure out what angle to take in the wording. "I wrote up something fun and charming for Reggie's site, and she's likely hitting publish now if I know her well enough. We'll play this calm and casual. It was a surprise. You're an underdog. Who doesn't love an underdog?"

He looked over at her. "Okay. I can write the statement. You don't have to take care of everything."

She thought about what Leslie had said. And Tav's offer.

"Since you're talking about payment beyond the apprenticeship stipend, maybe you should consider getting a publicist. Or someone who actually knows what they're doing." She felt silly saying she didn't want his money. Her entire trip to Scotland had been predicated on taking his money, though she was now going above and beyond anything she'd imagined her apprenticeship would entail. She was working hard and deserved payment for her work. But it felt . . . not great. Which was one of many reasons why she shouldn't have slept with her boss.

"I don't want anyone else," Tav said, so quickly and definitively that her pulse raced to catch up. "But I understand if this is getting to be too much. It's too much for me and it's *my* life. Just let me know. We can go back to the original terms of the apprenticeship."

His gaze searched her face and she tried to reveal nothing, like confusion as to why she would stay on as an apprentice — or anything at all — if he hired someone else. She didn't think there was any going back to before, but she didn't want to get into that.

"I don't want to mess anything up," she said. That was the truth, if not the whole truth.

"I don't want you to assume you will," he said. "It seems we're at an impasse."

"Tavish, this is serious," she said. He didn't know any better and was relying on the fact that she was already there. "This is your life. I don't want you to put it in my hands because it's the easy thing to do."

"I think that's exactly the reason I should put my life in your hands. It's scarily easy for me. There's that impasse again."

A thought that had somehow been lost beneath all the madness pushed its way to the front, putting everything into a perspective of sorts.

"There are only a few weeks left in this apprenticeship," she quietly reminded him. "You need to start thinking about what you're going to do moving forward."

When I'm gone. In a few weeks she'd likely assume her position at her parents' company, cementing herself in her new, serious life and forgetting this had ever happened. Or pretending it hadn't. Forgetting didn't seem likely.

They stared at each other, and Portia was overcome with the urge to be hugged. It was the same feeling of homesickness that had overwhelmed her while talking to Ledi and Thabiso, except the hug she wanted — needed — was from Tav, who was about as far from home as she could get.

"How's your system?" he asked. His gaze was weighted, and not by frustration as it had been a few minutes before.

"What?"

He swiveled back and forth in his office chair. "Your system. Am I out of it? We didn't get to discuss before I flashed your friends and was almost seduced by an aristocrat."

She should've given him a definitive "Yes" and continued about her business. But she'd mixed business with pleasure and, despite

381

her intentions, after just one night they'd become hopelessly tangled. And like she'd just said, there were only a few weeks left of the apprenticeship. Whatever it was between them had an expiration date. It was only a question of sooner or later.

"I think — I think there are still some trace amounts," she said.

She couldn't even lie and say that she hoped pulling at this string would undo the knots last night's roll in the hay had created. She knew very well that she was taking the express train to "Why the fuck did I do that?"-ville, but it was a very pleasant ride that made up for the final destination.

She wanted Tav's mouth on her again, no more, no less.

"The thing with all these treatises I studied is that you have to be very specific when brokering a deal," he said. "We were not very specific. Our agreement could technically be read as one *day* and done, right? It hasn't even been twenty-four hours yet."

"That's one way of looking at it," Portia said. "But we have to work on your statement. And —"

"It can wait. Come here," he said, then added, "Please."

He leaned back in his chair, but it wasn't imperious. It was vulnerable somehow, the way he sat back just a bit awkwardly and hoped that she came to him.

"How polite of you." She walked over slowly, placing her tablet down on the seat in front of his desk before making her way around. He reached out and tugged at the waistband of her workout pants. She thought he'd pull her into his lap, but instead both of his hands went around her waist and he marched her back until her ass was against his desk.

He leaned down and pulled off her sneakers, then her ankle socks, tugging them off slowly and stroking the bare skin of her feet. She ran her hand through his hair.

"Is this where you reveal you've got a thing for feet?" she asked.

He glanced up at her, smirk on his lips and gray at his temples. Damn, he was handsome. "I'm discovering I have a lot of 'things.' Feet. Ass. Collarbones. Nose. Freckles. One common denominator, though."

Portia swallowed hard.

He stood, his hazel-green gaze boring into hers, then his mouth was on hers, lush, warm, tasting of coffee and pleasure. His hands skimmed over her chest, unzipping her hoodie and smoothing over her breasts, constrained beneath her sports bra. Even the specially designed elastic couldn't suppress her hardening nipples, and he teased them through the fabric, rubbing his thumbs over them achingly slow before pinching, then repeating, lashing at her gasps with his insistent tongue all the while.

"Tavish," she whispered, and his hands dropped back to her waistband.

"I'm gonna take these off now, love," he said. She nodded into the rough kiss he pressed against her mouth before pulling away.

He hooked his fingertips into the waistband and pulled, dragging the material down to her ankles and off, finishing in the kneeling position. "See how easy that was after I was chosen by Pantscalibur?"

His voice was too low to carry the joke, and his intent gaze rested between her legs. His hands went to her knees and pushed them apart.

"Tav," she whispered as the first soft kiss landed on her inner thigh. A shiver went through her at the scrape of his stubble against her sensitive skin. His hands slid up her outer thighs and up to her ass as his mouth and stubbled cheeks worked their way upward, upward until she could feel his breath hot against her mound.

"Tavish." She couldn't quite whisper

anymore. Or say anything other than his name.

He pulled her forward, closing the space between them, and then she knew for certain she'd get no response because his mouth was busy giving her the best head of her life. Long, hard licks against her slit, followed by soft suckling of her clit that grew stronger and stronger until she was gripping the desk and grinding against his face trying not to shout.

Her toes curled and her abs flexed convulsively to some innate rhythm as Tav nuzzled deeper into her folds, alternating between soft and hard licks against her sensitive nub.

"Fuck, fuck!" She ground her teeth together and bucked up against his face as she came, maybe quicker than she ever had, just from the pleasant surprise of his intense focus.

She tried gathering her senses, which had been scattered like billiard balls after a wild breaking shot, but it was a fruitless endeavor. When she opened her eyes, Tav was watching her, cock in his hand as he rolled on a condom.

He approached, stroking himself as he bent over to kiss her. His arm brushed against her side as he placed a hand onto the desk for balance and pressed against her opening.

"God, we're such a cliché right now," Portia muttered. "Banging on the boss's desk."

"You know what a fan I am of dated clichés," he said and pushed into her, eliciting a gasp. Her arms went around his neck and her head dropped back. Her hips swiveled to meet his short, controlled thrusts.

"Oh god, okay this is one cliché you can keep," she groaned, and he chuckled and kissed her. They had spent the entire night together, but something about their joining felt urgent. He didn't take his time, as he had the second, fourth, and fifth time they'd come together in her bed. He thrust fast and hard, plunging more deeply each time, and groaning to match the muffled squeals of pleasure Portia released against his lips as she held on for dear life.

His desk began rocking loudly, slamming with each thrust, and then Portia felt his hands scoop under her and lift her up. Her legs wrapped around him, and she used them to lever herself up and down as he lifted. The new position provided a different and deeper kind of friction, and she rocked against him, taking his mouth with her own, not thinking of anything but her tongue against his and his hands holding her tight

386

and his cock sliding against a spot she hadn't known existed.

"Fuck, Portia, I'm so close," he said, and the strain in his voice as he tried to hold back — and one frantic, solid stroke — sent her spinning into her next orgasm, shuddering against him as he groaned and tightened his hold on her.

He dropped into his chair and they rolled back until they hit the shelving behind his desk. There was nothing but the sound of their heavy breathing and cold summer rain pattering against the window. She realized she would miss the rain and cold when she left, even though she missed the heat and humidity of New York. She would miss Tav holding her like this even more, which was why she needed to end this, now. Why she shouldn't have ever convinced herself to start it.

"About this ball," Tav said, breaking the silence. "I'm gonna need a date, I figure."

"You can go with Leslie," Portia said. In that moment, she was deep in her head, had already pushed him away. She was already gone.

Tav's exasperated sigh shifted her from her comfortable position on his chest. "Fuck's sake, can you wait until I pull out before fobbing me off on another woman?"

Portia twisted her head so that she was looking up at him. "Oh. You were asking me."

She hoped he attributed her quick heart-beat to the impromptu workout they'd just had. She hadn't defended her castle well at all. She'd let down the drawbridge and invited the invader in, and now he was wreaking havoc on her heart, and not just with his heavy, long two-hander.

Tav shrugged, not knowing that she was already deep in PANIC! EJECT! mode. "It's the kind of thing you like, right? Fancy clothes and dancing and all that shite. Who else would I bring?"

"Oh, you hopeless romantic, Tavish." She didn't know why she was disappointed. He wasn't her boyfriend. This wasn't some fairy tale where he would get on one knee and beg her to go to the ball. He was being practical, and so should she.

"Maybe you want to bring someone else?" he asked. "That's fine, too. I know you don't want anything serious. I just thought it could be a bit of fun in all this madness."

She drew back and glared at him. He had crossed the line from practical into annoy-ing. "Remember that 'still inside me' thing from a few seconds ago?"

She stood slowly, separating them, and

grabbed her underwear. "I don't have a date. I'm going with you. As your squire." She had to rebuild those boundaries and this was as good a place to start as any. "I'll go work on the statement and then we'll figure out what you need to get prepped for the ball."

"Sure thing," he said. His voice was flat. There was barely any burr on the *r* in sure. She felt awkward and stiff as she pulled on her pants, and she fumbled her tablet as she snagged it from the seat.

"Well. I guess our systems have been flushed," she said in what she hoped was a carefree and casual voice. They had wanted to cut the attraction between them, it had worked, and now she wanted to be as far away from him as possible.

"Mission accomplished," he said darkly.

This was good. Right?

"Later."

Tav grunted in response. She didn't look back as she hurried out the door. She had a second shower to take, and maybe this one would succeed at washing him from under her skin.

CHAPTER 21

Tavish watched Portia across the breakfast table. A few weeks ago he would have called her rude for constantly swiping her finger across the screen of her tablet and typing away at her tiny keyboard as she picked at her beans and toast. Now he knew she was handling online social media responses to his statement. She was responding to requests for interviews. She was answering private messages, emails, and public posts in a witty, engaging, and professional manner. And she was doing it all without breaking a sweat and without complaint.

She can't do this forever.

The low-level panic that had gripped him since she'd left his office the other day seized Tav. He was struck with dual realizations, like two attackers coming at him from different angles and impossible to fend off. One: for him, being a duke was completely tied to Portia. Spending time with her, learning from her, watching her nimble mind come up with new ideas, was one of the only good things that had come of the revelation. Would he be able to do it without her? Two: outside of the duke thing, he liked her very much. VERRA much. Was it really possible to separate his feelings for her from her helping him? Was it possible for her to be in his life without helping him? Because when he thought of her now, it wasn't as an employee. He had thought of her as more than that for some time now.

Sweat broke out at his temples as he wrestled with where exactly Portia fit in his life, and the fact that in a few weeks she would be out of it given their current plan.

"Bruv. Tav. Tavish!"

He pulled his gaze away from Portia to find Jamie regarding him with a look of annoyance. "Hullo. Did you hear anything I said?"

Tav considered lying, but Jamie's rare scowl wasn't something that could be overlooked.

"No, sorry —"

Cheryl huffed. "He said what is he supposed to do about the media calling us all hours of the day and night?" She stormed over to the window and peeked through an opening in the curtains. "Look! There's one of them right now, loitering about. I'm tempted to go wave a sword at him, but I'd end up on the cover of the *Looking Glass* with some bloody awful headline."

Tav looked out the window and saw a man dressed in black, leaning against a pole. He was smoking lackadaisically, but one hand rested on his camera, ready to spring into action. Tav wanted to smash it, but it didn't matter. The photo that had run in the *Bodotria Eagle* had already been purchased by news outlets. Once word had gotten out how exactly it had been discovered he was a duke, the story had spread like wildfire, along with conjecture about every aspect of his life, including who Portia was to him. He wouldn't have had a good answer for that, even if they'd bothered to ask him instead of creating stories likely to grab attention.

"One of these guys left a message asking about my police record," Jamie said. "I don't have a record, unless they mean the cops almost arresting me that time because they were bloody racist and wrong."

"They're just making shite up, now. I don't want these people trying to paint him as the dangerous thug brother of the new duke," Cheryl said. Her voice was trembling, which it only did when she was furious.

"You think *I* want that?" Tav snapped, the rush of anger stiffening his neck. Part of the reason he'd thought the duke thing worthwhile was that he might be able to ensure his family's security in a way swordmaking never could. There was that idea gone.

"Well, you're the one who brought this on us, you need to deal with it," Cheryl said. "You've already broken the kids' hearts by abandoning them at the exhibition. Can't you spare a moment from your aristocratic time to take care of this?"

Christ. As if he didn't feel shitty enough. "I'd love to be at the exhibition, but I literally have to throw a party for the Queen. The fucking Queen. Trust me, I'd rather be with you lot."

Ms. Baker had reached out to Portia and handed over the planning for the Queen's garden party, which was traditionally hosted by the Duke of Edinburgh. Tav didn't care for royals, but the thought of meeting the Queen filled him with a nervous dread. What if she treated him as David had? What if she shunned him, publicly? What if she told awful racist jokes and expected him to laugh?

"I'll try to take care of the paps," Tavish

said, though he had no idea how to do so without threatening them. He only knew how to ask Portia what to do, and she was already stretched thin and holding herself away from him since the afternoon they'd ruined him being able to spend more than five minutes at his desk without a naughty thought.

Cheryl continued her uncharacteristic rant. "And you might also tell the paparazzi if they're going to ruin my business by gathering in front of the armory and scaring customers, the least they can do is buy lunch!"

It was when her voice went shrill that Tav realized what was fueling her: fear. Having a duke for a brother-in-law had seemed fun at first, but now that reality was setting in, Cheryl was likely reconsidering her earlier excitement.

The click clack of Portia's fingers on the keyboard stopped. "Everyone needs to calm down."

"That's easy for you to say, no one's about to make you out to be some kind of gangster in the papers," Jamie said.

"Gangster? I've been called an American con artist who falsified paternity tests and Tav's pregnant mistress. And unlike you, I have an internet presence, a semi-famous sister, and wealthy, prominent parents whose business could be affected by negative press. I've had to deal with the blowback for myself, my family, Tavish, and both of you. I've been the one dealing with everything. *Everything.* You want to tell me that's easy one more time?"

There was steel in her voice — Tav heard it loud and clear, but Jamie and Cheryl were used to nice, accommodating Portia. Or they were too panicked to pay attention.

"Well, it will be over for you eventually. You get to skip away from all this soon," Cheryl said. "That's why you get to sit there all calm, even though you started this mess."

Portia's usually expressive face went blank, her eyes desolate. That had hurt her, and Tav's urge to protect everyone found its focus.

Tav stepped between them. "Hey now, it's not her fault. Maybe you want to take it up with your mother-in-law instead of an easy target. Or have you forgotten about all that *sensitive* shite you talked the other week?"

"No, she's right. I do leave soon." Portia was still looking at her screen and her voice was strangely dull when she spoke again. "Leave and spend every day hoping that I didn't ruin all of your fucking lives by going to the library and meddling in the past. So I understand that you're stressed, but I can't be stressed right now. I don't have that option. There's a ball in a few days and Tavish doesn't even know how to waltz. Every news outlet from Buzzfeed to *Horse & Hound* is in our in-box. There are two hundred and forty messages on the armory's voice mail and I don't see either of you volunteering to log them, let alone get back to anyone with a coherent answer. So. I am going to need you to *calm down.*"

Cheryl sucked in a deep breath, as if emerging from a well of panic. "Oh my goodness. I'm sorry, Portia. I just — this is a lot to take in."

"I know," Portia said. "I know. It's okay. Everything is going to be okay."

She finally looked away from her screen and tried to give Cheryl a smile of reassurance, but her expression was tight and Tavish could feel the tension vibrating from her.

Fuck all this.

"Freckles."

She didn't look at him.

"Freckles McGee, there's something I have to show you."

"I don't have time," she said in that strange voice. He stood, walked around the table, and placed his hand on the back of her neck. She stiffened, then relaxed into his hold, and he felt her release a shuddering breath. Desire tickled his palm, along with the curls at her nape, and traveled through his system, but that wasn't what this was about.

"I must insist that you make time, squire," he said, trying to remind her that he was supposed to take care of her, too, in whatever this relationship was. "Let's go."

She sighed and stood, her movement forcing his hand away.

"Go get one of your sporty little hoodies. We're going for a walk."

"This has been here the entire time?" Portia asked, as she picked her way along the path. They'd walked in silence since Tav had driven them to the wooded section of the Bodotria Trail, which passed from the gentrifying industrial area of the docks, on past the brick town houses, and through old railroad tunnels and over abandoned tracks. The greenery expanded from moss on the rocks along the river, to bushes, to this lush — though compact — wooded gorge.

Tav had let Portia walk in peace, watching as the weight seemed to lift from her shoulders and brightness crept into her eyes. She asked questions about the area every now and again, and he enjoyed being the one who had answers for once.

"This is so beautiful," she breathed. A couple of small brown birds chirped as they chased each other through the branches of chestnuts and beeches. "And peaceful. It reminds me of going to Central Park and finding a space that seemed magical in the rush of the city."

Tav nodded. "I used to come here when I was a lad and play at being a knight. There was a lot more rubbish about back then. Mum was always warning me not to touch any strange needles. But this place cleans up well."

"As do you. We have to think about what you'll wear this Saturday, by the way," she said, and he noticed her brow wrinkle just a bit.

"It's a Highland ball. I'll be wearing a kilt," he said easily. "I may not know much about suits, but I've a very fine formal kilt and hose and all that. Don't stress."

He realized that the last bit would fall on deaf ears — Portia was always stressing. Maybe she should have been the one taking this post. She was certainly working harder for it than he was.

A duke needs a duchess . . .

Leslie's words came to him as Portia

stepped into a beam of sunshine filtering down through the leafy overhang and turned to look at him. The sun hit the strands of bronze in her hair, coaxed the golden undertones of her brown skin to the surface, and Tav was struck with wistfulness like an anvil dropping from the sky. He'd tried, and failed, at marriage, and it wasn't something he was eager to try again. And his feelings for Portia were inextricably tied to the duke shite.

But he didn't think that was what made his heart beat faster as she stood looking at him like some freckled nymph caught frolicking along the banks of the Bodotria. He didn't *think* — but he wasn't sure, and it was that lack of surety that meant he should push all thoughts of duchesses out of his mind. He'd married Greer for the wrong reasons, he'd realized much too late, and though he'd loved her, love wasn't enough.

"*Do you love her,* m'hijo?"

"What about dancing?" Portia asked, that wide mouth of hers pulling into a grin.

Not yet, but oh fuck, could I. Shite.

"What about it?" he asked, stepping closer.

"Do you have two left feet, or three?" she asked.

"I'll let you judge that." He reached out a hand for her and she took it, tugging him close. He laughed. "I'm supposed to lead, Freckles."

"Says who?" she taunted, tugging his arms out into a waltz position and slowly beginning the steps. Tavish fought against everything he'd learned, stumbling as he followed.

"I know a thing or two," he said, pleased because she was pleased with him. "But this is a Highland ball, lass. There won't only be waltzing."

He stopped their movement, feeling the pull of her for a second, and when she relaxed and looked up in confusion he skipped into a reel, tugging her lightly along with him. He slowed to show her when to point her toe, when to lean back, when to turn, and when to bow. She picked up quickly and within a few moments they were whirling and hopping across the grass and mossy rocks, her laughter riding on the rustle of the wind through the trees like some kind of goddamned fairy song.

Do you love her?

They came to a panting sweaty stop and Tavish stared down at her as she threw her head back, letting the sun filtering through the trees warm her face.

I really could. Maybe I already do? This is not *good.*

Some part of him had known this was possible since the moment he'd seen her, mace and all. So he'd been a wanker in the hopes it would keep that distance between them. He should have still been pushing her away, but instead he sat down on an old tree stump and looked at her, willing her to come to him.

Her eyes narrowed and she strutted toward him, all of the stress from earlier in the day gone.

"Mind if I join you?" she asked, brow raised. He circled her wrist with his thumb and forefinger, giving a slight tug in his direction because she'd shown she liked that and Tav noted what made her happy very carefully these days. She swung her leg over his thigh and straddled him as if it was the natural thing to do. The weight of her against him, and the smell of her, and the press of her hands against his shoulders? That felt natural, too.

"That was fun." Her eyes were glinting and a dusky blush spread over her cheeks.

"Good. You need some fun in your life," he said.

"I've had my fair share of fun, don't worry about me." Another smile, but her eyes had lost a bit of their shine. She was doing that thing, where she parried good things by reminding others — and herself — that she was bad. Bollocks to that.

"Look at me, Portia." She reluctantly brought her gaze to his. "You've been having me do all this stuff so that I can walk into any room and know I belong there. I need you to do the same for me now. Repeat after me."

"This is silly," she said, shifting in his lap.

"My name is Portia Hobbs, and I'm bloody magnificent." Tav bounced his knees. "Say it."

"My name is Portia Hobbs, and I'm bloody magnificent," she muttered.

"I'm smart as fuck, and can do literally anything I put my mind to. Now you say it."

"I'm smart as fuck and . . ." She trailed off and dropped her gaze. "I feel ridiculous."

"I'm going to say something so pathetic that I will vehemently deny it if you ask me about it later." He slipped his hands behind her back and wove his fingers together, resting his hands at the dip of her back.

"Are you secretly a Dr. Phil stan?" she asked, clearly trying to distract him. He didn't go for the bait.

"I wish you could see yourself through someone else's eyes. Mine. You can think what you want about yourself, but I've two eyes and a brain in my head and the view right now? It's bloody brilliant."

He might turn out to be a shite duke. He might spend the rest of his days wishing he'd never found out the truth about his father. But Portia's gaze popped up to his and her palm came to his cheek and she smiled so brilliantly that Tavish could never regret wearing his heart on his chain mail sleeve.

"Have you forgotten that you're supposed to be a wanker?" she asked as she rocked forward in his lap.

"I haven't forgotten, but maybe you're rubbing off on me."

"Rubbing off? Is that what you call it here?" She rocked forward again, her hips moving in a sinuous motion beneath his arms. Sensation shivered up Tav's spine then vibrated against his thigh . . . then vibrated again.

Wait.

Portia huffed, pulled back, dug into her pocket, and tugged out her phone.

"Hm."

Tav gave her a quizzical look.

"Apparently, we have company," she said.

"Who is it?" Tav husked.

"Who are *they.* Someone named Greer? And a guy who showed up with her."

"Ah. My ex-wife. And her husband, I suppose." He looked at her closely, gauging her reaction.

Portia made a considering noise. "I haven't checked the *Debrett's* but I'm pretty sure leaving your ex waiting while you dry hump your squire in a fairy wood is just not done, Your Grace."

There was slight disappointment in her voice, but nothing more, as she stood and began tapping her response.

"Back to reality," he said.

"Your reality is other people's fantasy," she reminded him gently.

Tav knew what his fantasy was and it had just been disturbed.

"Aye? Well, other people need better imaginations."

CHAPTER 22

It had been a bit of a day. Portia had gone from bordering on the edge of burnout, to lap grinding in the forest, to sitting awkwardly in the armory's living room sipping tea with Tavish, his ex-wife, Greer, and Johan, the Prince of Liechtienbourg. She'd come to Scotland for excitement, and she was certainly getting it.

"Well, this is cozy," Johan said in his deep Franco-Germanic accented voice, pushing a lock of auburn hair from his face. His keen gaze danced between Portia, Greer, and Tav, and then he took a sip of tea.

"Yes. Quite," Portia said, surprised to find herself a bit flustered. She didn't get the urge to climb him as she had when she'd first seen Tav, but Johan was kind of attention grabbing.

She'd seen him in tabloids and thought he was okay — too pretty for her taste — but in person he was . . . harshly beautiful?

He looked like a fairy prince: tall, lean but muscular, and oozing refinement. Big blue eyes and long lashes and a semi-permanent smirk evened out by a strong jaw, as if he was always faintly amused. She would have mistaken him for a polished aristocrat if she hadn't seen his ass in the news more than once.

Greer shifted on the sofa, visibly uncomfortable. She had long black hair and warm gray eyes that were dimmed with worry. Her nails were polished and unchipped, and she still worked at the same company she had ten years ago and owned a house in a nice neighborhood that wasn't a gift like Portia's properties were. She wore a brown knit sweater, jeans, and a stiff smile, and she was the woman Tavish had once thought he'd spend forever with.

Portia thought back to their dancing in the woods and wondered if he'd ever made Greer feel like she was the center of his world, and everything would work out fine if she'd step into his embrace. Portia bit her inner cheek lightly to chase the thought away. Of course, Tav had made Greer feel good. He would have been a terrible husband otherwise. But they'd still grown apart, eventually.

If she wasn't enough for him, this portrait of

domestic stability, why would he stick around once you start making mistakes left and right?

No. None of that. *I'm bloody magnificent. I'm also leaving in a few weeks.*

"Sorry to be a bother," Greer said. "I just didn't know what to do. I tried calling you, Tav, but your voice mail box is full."

"I've been meaning to check it, but I forgot the pin and then I forgot to change the pin and things have been busy . . ." Tav's shoulders rose up toward his ears as he struck an apologetic pose.

Greer chuckled and shook her head. "I've heard that before." Her tone was nostalgic, not bitter, and Tav chuckled, too. There was an affection between them, a familiarity, and Portia tried not to imagine them in love in this very building years before. Acknowledging someone's past was much easier than visualizing it.

"Aye. You know how it is. How I am." He ran a hand through his hair, and Portia picked up her tablet and added "Tavish haircut" to her to-do list, which was his to-do list. "Portia has been handling pretty much all of the communications, bless her, but not my cell phone."

Greer glanced at Portia. "He's the worst, isn't he?"

There was something shy in the way she

407

said it, searching, and Portia realized that Greer was extending some "This is awkward, but we're cool, right?" feelers. As if Portia were Tav's girlfriend, instead of his apprentice or squire, which at this point, she wasn't too clear about either.

Portia nodded and returned her smile.

Greer turned her gaze back to Tavish. "I'm here about this duke business, which is something I never thought I'd say to you of all people. My goodness, your father must be livid."

Johan raised a hand in the air. "I'm here for that, too. I was just in town for a charity polo match and Thabiso asked me to stop by and offer my vast expertise on being famous for no good reason." He glanced at Greer. "Thabiso is my friend. He's a prince."

Greer nodded, her eyes widening as they did every time she glanced in Johan's direction.

"I have to admit this is all a bit much. Tavish is a duke, there's a prince in the parlor." She looked at Portia, then Tav. "I'm not used to this. And that's why I'm here. The paparazzi have been hanging about. They've snapped photos while I'm taking the kids to school, and shown up at my work and Christopher's, trying to get dirt on Tavish. They won't listen when I say I don't know anything and it's a bit frightening."

Tav made a sound of frustration. "I'm sorry, Greer. I never meant for you to get caught up in this."

"It's not your fault. It's just . . . a lot. They shout things like 'Do you regret divorcing him now that he's a duke?' Christopher's been taking it all in stride, but the kids are frightened and it's a bother to our neighbors and other parents at the school."

Portia put down her cup. "I've been researching British law to figure out where we can draw the line with these people, and what's actionable and what's not, but with everything else going on I dropped the ball. Sorry."

"Are you running Mr. McKenzie's security detail? Or are you his lawyer?" Johan asked in a tone Portia couldn't parse. "Thabiso told me you were an apprentice swordmaker."

She *could* parse that. Johan's tone was somewhere between polite inquiry and not so subtle judgment.

"I am an apprentice. I've been handling other matters, though." She gave Greer an encouraging look. "I'll try to figure this out."

She tapped open her to-do list added *Fig-*

ure out how to stop paps and *Security detail for Tav.*

She swiped to her emails and beside her Tavish heaved a sigh. "They've been after Jamie and Cheryl, and bothering folks in the neighborhood. I didn't think they'd bother you, though. It's been ages."

"That was a mistake," Johan cut in. "Everything is carrion for these vultures now. They'll search out your first kiss, your teachers, your plumber. There are now people out there intrigued by what dental floss you used just because you have a title in front of your name. *C'est das leben.*"

"So there's nothing to be done. How comforting," Tavish said, narrowing his eyes in Johan's direction.

Johan shrugged. "I wasn't sent to give you comfort. You already have someone for that." He nodded in Portia's direction and her face went warm. "I'm here to help you navigate your new career."

"I already have a job," Tav said.

"And now you have two," Johan replied. "Portia here seems to have several more than that so no complaining unless you're not as capable as your apprentice."

Tav looked a bit flustered. "Well, it seems a bit rude to point this out, but aren't you on the cover of damn near every tabloid?

Not sure you're really going to be helpful with the career navigation."

Johan looked at Tavish the same way one would a chick chirping mindlessly. "Do you happen to know what my brother, the actual crown prince of Liechtienbourg, looks like? Or what he does on a daily basis?"

Portia racked her brain. Prince . . . Luca? Was that his name? He was still in high school. She thought he might have blond hair . . .

"I'm drawing a blank," Portia said.

"Me, too," Greer added. She kept her gaze pointedly away from Johan and Portia was sure the woman was thinking of some debauchery or other that she *had* seen.

"No clue," Tav admitted.

"Well, then you can understand that there are many ways of handling the paparazzi. I use one that works well for me, and to do that I need to know how they operate. Do you think one just ends up on every tabloid cover — not damn near every — by chance?"

"So . . . you play them to your own ends?" Tav asked.

"*Ouay.* They focus on me, and they leave Lukas alone. If you don't think that's help-ful to you, I can go."

"I need all the help I can get if you hadn't

noticed," Tav said ruefully. "Thank you for offering and I accept."

Portia glanced at her texts and noticed she'd just received an influx of them — there was a string of messages from her various social media accounts notifying her that attempts had been made to change her passwords. Panic seized her.

"Someone is trying to hack my social media." The thought of her private messages and private photos being stolen, or worse, shared, filled her with tension.

"What?" Tav said.

Johan sighed. "You have two-step activated, I suppose?"

Portia nodded as she hopped apps, checking that each was still in her control. Her heart was pounding — even though this wasn't a physical attack, it was an intimate one. Her privacy was being invaded before her eyes by unseen forces.

"Change all of your passwords to be safe. Tavish, you'll have to change your passwords, too." Johan turned to Greer. "There's a service for people who prefer a more direct approach to ridding themselves of insistent paparazzi. Former rugby players in possession of very thick necks and a thorough knowledge of British law. If you provide me your phone number, I'll have them contact you. Don't worry about the cost."

Portia glanced at him, surprised. She'd wondered why Thabiso was such good friends with a known troublemaker, and now it was starting to make sense. He was a fuckboy with a heart of gold.

Greer stood and took the card Johan had smoothly proffered. "I'm going to go; have to pick up the kids. Thank you, um, Your Highness."

"Please. Call me Johan." He stood, taking her extended hand and bowing regally over it. Pink bloomed on Greer's cheeks.

"Oh, um, yes. Johan. And nice to meet you, Portia. I hope you get everything sorted with the hacking. We'll all have to deal with the invasiveness for a bit, it seems."

She didn't sound bitter, but the words landed heavily between them. Little did Greer know that all of this was Portia's fault. If she hadn't gone into hyper research mode for no damn reason, none of this would be happening.

"I'll see you out," Tav said, standing to follow her.

Johan turned his gaze to Portia and she raised her brow in a silent "what?"

"Thabiso is a shameless gossip but he didn't tell me you and the new duke were

413

an item."

"We're not," she said, training her face to an impassiveness that almost matched his own. She and Tav had barely spoken to each other in his presence — how had he picked up on anything?

"So, you're just friends with benefits? All the better. Best to get over him now and get out while you have a chance." He said it nonchalantly, as if he'd commented on the weather before taking another sip of his tea.

Portia's mind-your-business hackles activated and stood at attention. "This is super inappropriate. I know you're Thabiso's friend, but you know literally jack shit about me."

"Ach. Sometimes I forget that Liechtienbourger forwardness can be considered rude by Americans. Ironic, yes?" He presented her with a smile meant to disarm and swept that lock of hair from his eyes. "I know a little about you. I don't say this to brag, but I'm very good at reading people. I don't usually call things to their attention unless I think they're in danger."

Portia scoffed and laughed at the same time — scaughed? — and shook her head. "Did you literally 'Portia, you in danger, girl' me?"

Johan deigned to show confusion. "What?"

"*Ghost?* Whoopi? As in a charlatan psychic?" Her annoyance grew, fed by her fatigue and her anger that even a stranger could take one look at her and tell her she was silly for expecting someone to care about her. "Ooo, do I get to be the 'close acquaintance' who calls the *Looking Glass* to inform them of Prince Johan's psychic powers? I don't really need the money, but it would be an upgrade from the usual stories they write about you."

His confusion faded and he set his mug on its saucer. "You are a people pleaser. You worry about failing those around you to your own detriment, and you don't stop to think about what you're getting into until you're past the point of no return." He opened his mouth as if to say something else, but then caught himself, pressing his lips together.

She put her phone down in her lap, trying to hold his gaze even though she felt as exposed as she had by the hacking attempts. "Is it my turn to play this weird party game?"

Johan did his hair toss, and angled his face so that she got an eyeful of sharp cheekbones and pouty lips. He was trying to distract her with his beauty, likely out of sheer habit. His eyes held no hint of flirtation — they were serious and somewhat cold. She thought of the dazzler Tav had explained to her. "Party games are fun, or the ones I'm used to are, and this isn't. I think you know that, as you've been scanning the room trying to figure out what people needed and how you could give it to them since you met me."

What the hell was this? She wanted to tell him that he had it all wrong, that she was selfish and didn't think of others, except he wasn't. She *was* always trying to figure out how to please people. She *was* always running low level scans making sure there was nothing for her to do. It was exhausting, now that she had put her finger on it. Now that Johan had, rather.

"Is there a point to this?" She took back whatever kind thoughts she'd had about the prince, and about Thabiso for sending him.

"You're a comfortable person to talk to. Has anyone ever told you this?"

Portia blushed despite knowing he was buttering her up, but then he kept going.

"Because of that, I will be to the point. If you have a choice, and you do have a choice, you should run far and fast from this situation."

"And why would I do that? Because some bored royal is trying to mess with my head?"

Johan dropped his gaze into the bottom of his teacup, and when he spoke his voice was as bitter as the leaves at the bottom of it. "My mother was my father's secretary. Their love story is very famous. There are even films about it! The bachelor king falling for his commoner assistant."

"I'm not exactly a commoner," Portia said, slightly offended. "I'm the wealthy American teaching Tav how to maneuver through high society. It's not like I'm powerless."

"Even more reason to run. You don't need him." Johan caught her gaze with his and she could see that his concern was genuine. He wasn't playing some aristocratic mind game with her. "You were hired as his apprentice, yes? I read your blog posts on the way here. When did you last make a sword? What are you getting out of this?"

Portia had asked herself the same questions, but hearing them come from a complete stranger was bracing.

"That's none of your concern," she bit out.

He nodded thoughtfully. "That may be true, but please ask yourself — where does your work stop and your relationship begin? My mother dedicated every bit of herself to supporting my father. To making sure she lived up to this great man who had chosen *her* of all people, and taken in her son as well. And, this part you may know, if you've seen the movies or books or commemorative plates — my mother is dead."

Before Liechtienbourg had a wild semi-prince, they'd had a beloved queen. Her passing had been covered extensively by the tabloids, too, but Portia had been a kid then, and she'd purposely avoided it. It had reminded her that her own parents were mere mortals. If a kind queen could die, couldn't they? Couldn't Reggie? She'd remembered that fear as she sat next to Reggie in the hospital and felt a wave of guilt. Maybe she'd caused her illness with her constant worry . . . .

"I did know that. And I'm sorry for your loss."

"As am I." The look he gave her now was sheepish, real, and not something contrived by a manipulative tabloid prince. She wasn't the only one feeling exposed. "That is why I am being completely rude and warning you off. I see the way you look at him, so ready to make his life easier without regard for your own, and it's much too familiar to me."

Portia was suddenly aware of how she'd been pouring her energy into others for weeks. The pressure she had placed on herself to get Tavish ready, to cover all the bases, to make up for being the one who had brought this on to him and turned his life upside down. He hadn't asked any of this from her, had tried to muddle through on his own, but could things ever be different between them? Could she ever be simply Tav's partner, and did he even want her to be? Did *she* want to be?

Her head was spinning, reminding her why she shouldn't have broken the rules of Project: New Portia.

Johan sighed. "I don't say this to distress you, *poulette.*"

"I don't quite think we're at the nickname stage yet," Portia said, holding up a hand. "Is this part of the Liechtienbourgian forwardness?"

Johan grinned. "It's Liechtienbourger. And it's a habit of mine, *but fine,* no nicknames. I'll simply say I did not have a choice in my station in life. You do. While relationships are about assisting each other, with your inclination, you can be his assistant or you can be his partner. You should not be both. *Das ist tout.*"

Tavish walked back in then and Portia jumped guiltily as he dropped onto the chair beside her.

"This is mad! Some guy jumped out from

behind Cheryl's stand and snapped a photo as I hugged Greer goodbye." He dropped into the chair beside Portia.

Johan sighed. "Ah, so tomorrow I'll have to share the front page of the paper with you. I suppose I should be offended, but you're better than the reality show star who's trying to crowdfund their own country."

Tavish snorted.

"Is everything okay with your social media accounts? Do you need help with anything?" he asked, surprising her. He usually didn't care about internet shite, as he called it.

"Yeah, I'm just a little freaked out. I have to change my passwords. I can change you —"

Johan loudly cleared his throat and stood up, and Portia caught herself. Tav could handle changing his own passwords.

"I must be going. Will you be free tomorrow at the same time?" he asked Tav.

Portia felt Tav's gaze land on her, but she kept her eyes glued to her phone.

"Aye," he responded when she made no move to answer.

"Excellent."

Tav made another trip to the front door, and Portia flopped back in her chair.

She'd expected Johan to be frivolous, but

he'd walked in, spotted her biggest worry, and turned a floodlight on it. She couldn't keep this up — she couldn't downplay it as a crush or something that would go away. She'd fallen for her boss, and her work had taken over her life, and everything was a mess. She'd come to Scotland to escape herself, but she was falling right into the same cycle that had gotten her into trouble with Ledi and her family.

She didn't wait for Tav to come back to the parlor; she went up to her room with her phone in hand and scrolled down to a number she didn't think she'd need while on the trip.

The phone rang and was answered by a human instead of going to voice mail.

"Hello, Dr. Lewis speaking."

"Hi. It's Portia Hobbs. You said if I ever needed to talk . . . well, um, I've been having some boundary issues again. And some family issues. And relationship stuff and just . . . Do you have any appointments available?"

CHAPTER 23

This Johan guy is a piece of work.

It was their third meeting in three days — meetings alone, because Portia had made herself scarce. Last he'd seen, she and Cheryl had been squealing over some nail polish that had been sent to the armory for promotion, which had seemed strange to him, but Portia explained it meant he now had "internet capital." She hadn't explained more than that though, as she hadn't spoken to him about much since they'd returned from the Bodotria Trail. She'd been strictly business since he'd come back to an empty parlor after walking Johan to the door.

At first, he'd thought something had happened when he'd left her and Johan alone — the guy was closer in age, after all, and charming and fit. He'd wondered if he was officially out of her system, which should have been the best-case scenario for both of them but the possibility alone made him

422

feel like utter shite.

She'd finally sat him down and talked to him that morning.

"We need some boundaries," she'd said, cutting to the chase unlike the last time she'd held an impromptu meeting. "Right now, we're too enmeshed in each other's lives, or rather I'm too enmeshed in yours, since you don't know very much about my life at all, actually."

Tav had wanted to argue otherwise — he knew about her parents and her sister, the pressures her family exerted on her and the even greater weight she placed on herself. He knew a lot about Portia, but in the end it wasn't the same as the way his entire life and family history had consumed her time. He'd been worried for weeks but hadn't pinpointed the reason why: Portia had given him much more than he had given her, though he was supposed to be her instructor.

She'd continued, looking ill at ease. "I came here to find myself but I feel like I'm losing myself instead. So, factory reset time. Our only official relationship is swordmaker and apprentice, and maybe knight and squire if we're feeling frisky, and we're going to have to stick to that. I'm leaving soon, after all."

Tav had been hurt by the matter-of-factness in her tone, and surprised by his hurt. But he hadn't said more than "Aye. Whatever's best for you, lass." What else could he say? The apprenticeship was over soon, and it had been a failure. She'd made one sword and gotten nothing but headaches and piles of work that had nothing to do with the armory.

A crumpled crisps wrapper bounced off of Tavish's forehead and onto his lap. He rerouted his train of thought back into the parlor, where Johan sat across from him with his brows raised.

"Oh, did that manage to get your attention?" Johan was rightfully annoyed, though it was a quite refined annoyance.

Tav was having trouble following along because, well, nice as he was, Johan was no Portia. Tav hadn't realized how easy she'd made all those lessons for him. Johan had zero interest in humoring him.

Tav grabbed the crisp bag and lightly tossed it onto the table. "Sorry, mate, I drifted off. What were you saying I should know about the Queen?"

"That she enjoys challenging people to impromptu arm wrestling matches and can beat most of the peerage fair and square. Don't underestimate her — she has a pull-up bar installed behind her throne."

Tav rolled his eyes. "Okay, I get it, I'll pay attention. It's rude of me to waste your time."

"Almost inexcusably rude — almost! — but understandable. We've been going for hours."

"I honestly don't even know what day of the week it is," Tav said wearily, pressing his palms to his face and dragging them down. His stubble was dangerously close to "creeper beard" but he'd been too tired to shave.

"It's a great day to pay attention to your better," Johan said with a faux haughty smile that undercut his words.

"Aye? When is this better arriving?" Tav asked, which got a chuckle from Johan. The prince stood and stretched, a reminder that though he was making jokes he was also doing work. So many people were spending time and energy to help him. He needed to push himself harder.

"All right. I'm focused now. We can get back to this weird role playing because I need to be ready."

He couldn't disappoint Johan, or Jamie or Cheryl or the weans. He most definitely couldn't let down Portia, who'd run herself ragged on his behalf.

"When I was a child, my advisors told me that learning to make small talk with the aristocracy is the same as picking up another language. It requires practice and time. I think that's nonsense, though." Johan stroked his sharp jaw and regarded Tav through narrowed eyes. "All you have to do is channel your international man of mystery."

Tav scoffed and tugged at a lock of hair. "International? The last time I traveled outside the UK there was no gray in these strands."

"Okay, your national man of mystery. Just be smooth, charming, and playful, like when you were flirting with Portia at lunch today. And yesterday. And the day before." Johan's smile had an edge to it now.

"I don't flirt," Tav grumped. "Man of mystery. What a laugh. This would be easier if Portia could just tell me what to say to these gits. Like Cyrano, but wooing aristos instead of a woman."

"If you can't even hold a conversation without Portia by your side to guide you, you have more problems than I can help you with." The edge had crept from his smile into his tone, and his eyes were suddenly serious.

"I can chat just fine — I've managed it for

most of thirty-eight years, mate. I'm just tired," Tav said.

Johan *tsked.* "You're going to be tired all the time in this new life of yours. Do you know who bears the brunt of it when a man given power gets tired?"

"Christ, look, if you have something to say, just say it. Out with it." Johan exhaled deeply, as if he'd been waiting for Tav to ask.

"Portia is not your walking stick, McKenzie. If you cannot do something without her, that means that when you do something *with* her, you're bearing down on her with all your force. You're a large man, and every walking stick has a maximum load it can take before it snaps. Adding romantic liaisons only decreases the loadbearing capabilities."

"Fuck's sake, what are you on about? We're talking the physics of walking sticks now? Portia and I are adults, and we'll deal with whatever happens." He didn't need a lecture from a guy whose exploits could make a list as long as St. Nick's.

"I don't do love or any of that foolishness," Johan said. "But relationships don't *just happen.* You both are making decisions, even when you pretend you're not. Ignoring that fact is a fantastic way to get hurt, or hurt her."

"Aye, well, I don't think there will be any hurting, okay? Our relationship is strictly professional for now."

"For now? *Schiesse de merde.* That's cute, but I have intruded enough. Is there anything else you want to talk about while you have me trapped in this dank excuse for a parlor?"

"Nope. I'm about talked out."

"Great. Back to work." Johan stroked his chin thoughtfully, then snapped. "Oh! I just thought of something *I* wanted to talk about."

"You're a terrible actor," Tav said with an aggrieved sigh.

Johan ignored him. "You know what I found very taxing when my mother became engaged to the king? Being in the public eye. There was all this talk of how to handle a step-prince, what my behavior was like, my physical attributes. I wasn't prepared for it all, but I wouldn't talk to anyone because I didn't want to seem ungrateful."

He glanced at Tav with a knowing look.

"I said I was talked out," Tav sighed.

"I know. That's why I'm talking." Another smirk.

In the treatises and medieval texts Tav had studied, Liechtienbourger knights were generally described as haughty, outlandish, and unexpectedly deadly because they were unmatched in persistence. It seemed this trait was still in the gene pool.

Johan was maybe the only person in Tav's orbit right now who might understand how he felt. Jamie tried to be supportive, but he mostly thought Tav's complaints were whinging. Cheryl was stressed about all the changes to their lives. Portia was too busy trying to make sure everything went smoothly for him. If Johan had something else to offer besides steering him through social situations and commenting on his love life, Tav would take it.

"Fine." Tav poured himself more water.

"Oh, is something on your mind?" Johan asked like the cheeky bastard he was.

"I just don't know how to take this all in," Tav said. "I was just an average guy before and now —"

"I'm sorry, you make swords and travel around Europe to battle strangers at tournaments. That's not quite average."

Tav rolled his eyes. "Okay, I was a not-famous guy. Now I'm a meme on social media, whatever meme means. I'm in the papers. They've started calling me the patron saint of refugees, talking about my mum and everything that happened to her, and how I grew up in this diverse family that represents the best of Scotland, or the worst of it depending on who's telling it. They've already started telling this *story* about me that doesn't feel like me at all. What if I don't live up to it? Or what if the story changes for the worse? Or what if everyone I'm close to gets hurt?"

"Those are all eminently reasonable questions that I do not have the answers to," Johan said sadly.

Tav stood and walked over to the sandpaper and unfinished blade he'd been working on before Johan had entered his office. He started working the grit over the metal, but even that familiar, usually calming motion brought him no pleasure. It reminded him that though orders had gone through the roof, he was too swamped to get into a solid production mode and his apprentice was still a beginner because he'd been shite at training her.

"How does this all shake out, long term? I know it's different for you, because I'm a lowly duke and you're a prince."

Tav was cut off by Johan raising a hand. "That isn't true. You have more social standing than me, Your Grace. I'm not a prince. Though I am your better, I'm the stepson of a king and the stepbrother of a prince. I'm not in the line of succession, so the only title I actually own is Prince of the Tabloids, and that's responsibility enough."

"I'd honestly forgotten," Tav said.

Johan scrubbed his knuckles over his jaw, the movement at odds with the refined and aloof air he usually had. "People only seem to remember at the most inopportune times. But keeping up the fantasy isn't so very hard. The public wants a wild and carefree European prince to project their fantasies onto. I saw the position was open, and I took it."

"So you lie then? Is that what I have to look forward to?"

"Some call it lying, I call it sculpting perception. I'm rather like one of the Renaissance masters if you really think about it."

"The only thing you have in common with the masters is that they were also famous for bare asses plastered in public places," Tav griped, and Johan barked out a loud, deep laugh, losing all pretense of refinement; it was the first time Johan had really let his guard down in their three days together.

Johan looked up at him, cheeks ruddy. "Okay. For that brief moment of joy, I'll trade you perhaps the most important piece of advice in my arsenal."

Tav leaned forward.

"Don't eat the brussels sprouts at Buckingham Palace. They're soggy, with not even a hint of bacon fat to give them some flavor, and they give you atrocious gas."

"Johan."

"Oh wait! That wasn't the advice. This is it. Every person in your situation has to find the style in which they will wear the mantle that has been placed on them. Me? I court attention, I give the public something that they lap up like thirsty ostriches, but I don't give them *myself*. I took that lesson from my mother's example."

Tav's head was spinning. "Fuck's sake. This really is like a full-time job."

"People have expectations, Tavish. What you need to focus on isn't how to fit in with the aristocracy, though it is a helpful tool. You need to figure out what you are able to give to the public, and what you must keep for yourself. Unfortunately for you, I still retain the title of hottest royal bachelor, now that Thabiso is married. What do you want?"

There was really only one thing Tav wanted, one person, but she seemed increasingly out of his reach. Was this how his biological father had felt, watching the woman he loved get crowded out by his title and responsibilities?

Tav closed his eyes for a minute. He'd thought he'd had what he wanted in the past — his swordmaking business. His family. His community. But now he had the opportunity to do so much more, even though the cost would be higher — emotionally, not financially. He'd once thought losing the armory was the biggest problem he could face, but now he was at risk of losing himself.

Portia's face popped into his mind, wearing the expression she always made when trying to explain some internet shite to him. He thought of Jamie's smile as he excitedly described his hopes for the future, and of Cheryl making her living with the culinary knowledge that'd been passed down to her from her parents. He thought of Syed, and his mother and father. Of Johan, who seemed so carefree and spontaneous on the covers of tabloids, but who rarely laughed.

Something was coalescing in his mind. He jumped out of the chair and went to the circular window in his office. Down below, he saw two paparazzi leaning against the building across the street.

"You know what I like to do when I need to think?" he asked.

"Throw logs, or something of the sort?"

Johan ventured.

Tav turned to him. "I like to make weapons. Outdoors at the smithy. Get all sweaty and the like. A wise person once explained to me that the public found that sort of activity appealing. That sharing it online was called a 'thirst trap.' You ever make a sword before?"

Johan smiled with devious pride. "No, but I'm an expert at thirst traps. I'll probably have to take my shirt off in this oppressive Edinburgh heat. It'll look better on the front page."

Portia had told Tavish he was a quick learner. He could only hope that this application of her lessons, with Johan's advice, would go over well. He was a swordmaker. He was a duke. He had a lot to think on, but if he needed to create a version of himself that gave the public what they were after and honed what he wanted them to think of him, he'd forge it himself.

When he glanced up, Johan was already out of his blazer and unbuttoning his shirt, then he paused. "Wait, I'll disrobe outside, lest we start an entirely different conversation than we intended by leaving the building in a state of undress. The last thing we need right before you're officially given your title is a rumor that I've debauched you."

"Aye. I don't need your jealous fans coming at me on top of everything else," Tav said with a laugh.

Tav cared piss-all about rumors, but there was only one person he wanted debauching him. He had to figure that out, too, and hoped some time hammering away at the forge would help him figure out just how to make it happen.

CHAPTER 24

Tavish could tell he looked fit in the suit he'd picked out for himself. The journalist seated across from him had given him the eye twice, and Portia wouldn't meet his gaze as she sat in a chair off to the side. He'd had his hair cut the day before, something the stylist had called "classic but modern" and he'd thought showed too much of his gray; he'd changed his mind when Portia had barely been able to tear her gaze from him as he'd fielded practice questions from her and Jamie and Cheryl.

She was only a few feet away from him as he used that practice in his real interview, but the distance between them had grown over the last few days. Even now, the day before he was due to make his debut before the peerage, he hadn't figured out how to close the ever-widening gulf.

This is what happens when you don't check for cracks, he thought miserably. He'd been so busy trying to pretend he didn't care about longevity that he'd allowed himself to create a flawed product, and now he'd nicked himself hard on it.

"After having toured your armory and the neighborhood you grew up in, it's abundantly clear that you've lived a very different life from most of your fellow peers," the journalist said in her meticulously smooth voice. It was soothing, familiar; Tav had watched Effie Wilson on telly for years, but now she sat across from him, as if he was someone interesting. There was a twinkle in her eyes, likely caused by the ratings dancing in her head, but she was good at her job and highly professional. Johan had brokered the interview — Tav had never thought about being *paid* to talk about inheriting money.

"Aye, but I wouldn't say that's a bad thing. I practice European martial arts and make Scottish weaponry for a living — I obviously understand the appeal of tradition. But sometimes you need to change things up a wee bit. If you base everything on how things worked in the past, then we'd have no innovation and no change." *Christ, I sound like a pretentious git,* he thought, but he couldn't very well get up and walk out of the interview. "I won't presume to know

437

what Scotland needs, but I can't possibly do worse than these blue bloods who don't even know what the average meal is, let alone the average median income."

He resisted the urge to glance at Portia and focused on Effie, who was wearing the same ambivalent semi-smile she had for most of the interview. He couldn't tell if he was spouting the most ridiculous tripe she'd ever heard, or she thought him brilliant.

"From what I gather, you aren't happy with the stance of some of these 'blue bloods,' particularly when it comes to immigration. By all appearances, you're a bit of a crusader for the migrants," Effie said. Again, he couldn't tell if she thought this was good or bad.

"I wouldn't call myself a crusader," Tav said. "Though if you want to talk about people invading countries and destroying cultures, the Crusades are a good point of conversation. Except no one likes to talk about that because the people doing the invading that time weren't brown."

The interviewer smiled tightly. "Ah, quite. But is the migrant question not your cause?"

Tav almost ran his hand over his stubble, now trimmed to acceptable rakish length, but then crossed his hands in his lap and drew his shoulders back instead.

"Well, all right. You know what? I will say I'm a crusader. For basic human rights, and human dignity. But instead of asking me why I'm fighting for people to have access to safety and education and affordable housing, maybe you should be talking to the knobs who *don't* want people to have those things." Tav remembered David, sitting on as close to a throne as he could get and unable to hide his disgust for people running from war and famine and terror. "I mean, honestly what kind of wanker is fine with turning away people in need, or looks down on those they should be lifting up? What an utter fucking tosser must you be to see someone crying out for help and think 'Right, I'll kick them in the face with my fancy loafer instead of giving them a hand'?"

Tav's face was warm and he realized he was bent forward in his seat. He leaned back and took a calming breath before speaking. "I just don't understand why people hold on to power as hard as the peerage have if not to do something bloody useful with it."

"Thank you, Your Grace," the journalist said. She turned toward the camera designated for her with a warm smile on her face. "And thank you for joining us to meet Tavish Arredondo McKenzie, Duke of Edin-

439

burgh, Scotland's newest duke."

As soon as the camera's stopped rolling, actual human emotion suffused Effie's face, and when she spoke she lost a bit of her posh accent. "Oh, that was fantastic. That last bit? Going to make the perfect teaser."

Tav felt a mix of pride and embarrassment.

"Ta, I guess."

"I should be thanking you. I grew up in a neighborhood like Bodotria, you know. Working class, down on its luck. I can't imagine what it must have been like for the kids to find out their neighbor was a duke. To know that potential was amongst them."

"I haven't done anything, though," Tav said.

"That's the beautiful thing. Like the rest of the peerage, you're not expected to work. But unlike them, your existence alone might make a difference for someone."

Effie and her crew packed up and left, and Tav glanced over at Portia.

Portia smiled up at him. It was a reserved smile, but there was pride in her eyes. "You did great."

"That was weird," he said. He tried to shove his fingers through his hair but it was sticky with hair gel. He sighed. "The cameras and the makeup and the smoke she was

440

blowing about my existence making a difference."

Portia dropped her head back on the sofa so she was looking up at him. "You've read Arthurian legend. You get the appeal. Arthur was the chosen one, the one who could pull the sword from the stone. But every kid who's heard that story from the middle ages until today has thought 'That could be me.' And now you're Arthur. These kids might not want to become a duke, but they know it's *possible*."

Tavish sat beside her on the sofa, leaving a space between them. "Aye. No one ever talks about how Arthur felt holding that sword, though. And I'm not complaining, but it's a mite heavy at times."

"Heavy is the hand that wields *Caledfwich*," she joked. Tav tried not to remember Pantscalibur. Oddly, it wasn't the sex he missed the most. That was grand, of course, but he missed the weight of her in his arms. He missed the banter and the openness.

"Portia —"

"My parents offered me a job," she said. It was like she'd sensed he was about to make an arse of himself. "A few weeks ago, but I have something lined up for me once the apprenticeship ends."

About ten different emotions collided in

Tavish's chest but he tried not to show it. "Aye? I was hoping . . ."

Her head whipped in his direction. Her usually expressive brows rested in their natural place, and her deep brown eyes revealed nothing.

"I was hoping we'd have more time to make swords after this mess died down. You only got to make the one."

She looked down, and though her body didn't move, Tav felt as if a shield had just been thrown up between them.

"It's okay," she said calmly. "You can teach your next apprentice. I'm sure things will be less exciting the second time around, unless you have any other wild family secrets."

"I fucking hope we don't," he said, trying to lighten the mood. "And I wasn't planning on finding another apprentice."

"You need to. Who's going to make the swords while you're off crusading?"

There was melancholy in her voice, and in the space between them on the sofa, and Tav didn't know how to dispel it. He couldn't really ask her to stay, could he? She had a job lined up and who in their right mind would give that up to be stuck with a grumpy Scotsman flailing about as he pretended to be something he wasn't. If she stayed, she'd break from him leaning on her too hard. Worse, she'd grow to resent him and whatever it was between them would slip away.

No.

It was better for things to end like this: fast, easy, and with his heart only marginally battered. He'd get over it soon enough.

"Are you sure, though?" She gave him that inscrutable look again. "About not making any more weapons? I was thinking we could fire up the forge tomorrow morning. I know how important that was to you."

She shrugged and stood, looking down at him. A faint smile graced her lips. "No, I was just being silly. Besides, it's not like it's a skill I'll need while doing real estate investment."

She emphasized the last three words, and seemed to be waiting for some response from him.

"Is that the family business then?" he asked.

"Yup. Just some rich assholes buying property in emerging neighborhoods and making a profit by selling at a higher cost."

Ah. He saw what she was doing now. She looked calm, apart from the challenge in her eyes, but this was a berserker's move; she was swinging her weapon wildly to keep him away from her. He hadn't known what her family did. He didn't know if it was the same as the gentrifying companies ravening through Bodotria. But he did know that she was pushing him away and he needed to respect that, even if he didn't agree.

"Sounds like loads of fun," he said with a shrug. "Maybe not what I'd imagined you doing with your life, though."

"And what did you imagine exactly?"

Tav hadn't really allowed himself to explore those unlikely paths because given the least leeway, his imagination was off and running. Breakfast in bed, cycling along the docks, sharing dinners and dreams and a shared hope for the future. Tav couldn't lay that on her. Not when she'd already decided to go.

"Nothing," he said. "I'm sure the job will be grand."

"I'm going dress shopping with Cheryl. Later."

"Later," he mumbled as she walked off.

There was no promise in the word for him any longer because she'd be gone, and soon.

CHAPTER 25

Portia was a pro at balls, dances, galas, and other synonyms for "rich person excuse to show off," but she lay on her uncomfortable bed on her scratchy duvet and wished she could just stay at home. The fact that the armory was what she thought of when she thought of "home" now made her slap a hand down on the bed in exasperation. She'd let her impulsiveness get the best of her again, and now she was drowning in a field of popped Tavcorn.

Her phone rang and she squeezed her eyes together.

Great.

"Please just be cool," she muttered as she picked up the phone. "Hi, Mom."

"Hi, baby. Your father's on the line, too."

"Is everything okay?" Fear briefly turned her stomach as she remembered being called to the school office and told that Reggie was in the hospital, and that it was very serious.

Her mother heard the panic in her tone. "Nothing to worry about. Everyone's okay. Well, there is one thing."

"Marvin Dixon's daughter is apparently looking for work," her father cut in. "You know Narisa? Who interned here for three summers in a row?"

Portia didn't know her . . . because she hadn't paid attention to what happened at Hobbs Capital until very recently.

"Um, yeah. She was nice."

"She was, and a really sharp analyst, too," her dad cut in. "She got let go when her company downsized and had heard about Reggie leaving, so she checked in with us."

Portia realized she still hadn't looked through the research her father had sent her weeks ago. It had just . . . completely slipped her mind. She thought of the important/priority matrix she'd learned about from one of the *Hot Mess Helper* videos. The job research had been nowhere on that matrix, had simply fallen off the edge into the abyss where all of Portia's forgotten obligations went to die.

"That's interesting?" Portia had a not-good feeling about this.

"What your father is trying to say is that, after some discussion, we've decided to offer the job to Narisa. She always got along great with everyone and worked really hard, and we think she's a good fit."

Portia read between the lines: *you aren't a good fit with us, your own family.*

She didn't know why it hit her like a fist around a brick — it was the truth. She hadn't ever wanted the job. She hadn't even bothered to look into it. She'd just spent half a session telling Dr. Lewis how the job offer itself had made her feel awful and inadequate, and how she needed to talk to her parents about her possible ADHD diagnosis and how that would affect her career choices. But some small part of her, behind the fear of disappointing her parents, had been surprised and pleased that they'd considered her, without even being informed that a good portion of her mistakes were possibly the result of not knowing how her brain was wired. That, knowing how prone to flightiness and error she was, they'd decided to take a risk. And now they'd rescinded that offer.

It wasn't surprising; she hadn't even been able to give them the reassurance of checking in, of providing a start date, of showing enthusiasm. And they'd chosen someone who would make their lives easier instead of harder. That was what would always happen when it came to her.

"All right. I understand. Thanks for letting me know."

It would be better this way. She wouldn't mess up the family business, or be a constant reminder to her parents of how unreliable and untalented she was compared to her sister.

Tension grew in her neck and pressure expanded in her sinuses.

"See, I knew she'd be fine with it," her father said, apparently to her mother. "Your mom saw all that stuff in the press and figured you might as well stay there since you're all lovey dovey with the duke anyway. Is it true he was spotted ring shopping?"

Oh fuck.

Portia tapped at the tears forming in the corners of her eyes before they could ruin her makeup. How humiliating. It made more sense now; her parents decision to rescind he job offer had been at least partially spurred by the mistaken belief that she had someone else to look after her now. It hadn't occurred to them that if they didn't want her around, Tavish wouldn't either.

"Probably not, but way to ruin the surprise if that was the case," she said cheerily. "We're actually heading out to a big event, meeting the Scottish peerage, so I have to go."

"All right! Have fun, baby!"

Her mother sounded prouder of her than she had in years, and oh did it burn.

There was a knock at the door. "Are you coming to get your nails did, Portia?" Cheryl asked excitedly. She'd offered to help fix the chips in the manicures they'd given themselves the other day.

"Coming!"

"Okay! Meet you in the parlor!"

Portia dropped her phone, checked her face and dress in the full-length mirror. She had been rejected by Tavish, and her family, but at least she looked like a goddamned princess. She would put on a happy face and pretend everything was all right because this was Tav's big night and she wasn't going to ruin it.

Portia had always assumed that riding up to a castle in a queue of carriages would be magical, but she was too nervous to appreciate the fairy tale she was acting out. Each clop of the horses' hooves as they approached the squat, foreboding building made her stomach flip. Maybe this was what Cinderella had felt like: filled with dread and unable to tell if she was light-headed from nerves or because the bodice on her dress was too tight.

This was different from a fancy fundraiser or any of the numerous black-tie events she'd attended throughout her life. It was Tavish's debut, and she needed to make sure it went well. If she got him started on the right foot, perhaps everything else would fall into place.

She pushed away thoughts of Tav flourishing or failing after she left. Of their discussion and how he'd seemed resigned to the fact that she *would* leave, as if he had no input on the matter. His well-being wouldn't be on her agenda anymore, and he'd made it clear that his biggest concern was how he'd mishandled her job, not her heart. That was all he saw between them in the end: an apprenticeship. Well, an apprenticeship and some major chemistry and the best sex of her life. But chemistry faded and apprenticeships ended — it wasn't even a full-time job. Despite that, it had taken over her life.

"This portion of Essexlove was built to repel invaders in 1575," Portia said when the itchy tension started at the base of her neck. "It was renovated with a more modern look in 1912, though on this side you can still see the high, thin windows to prevent the English from storming the castle."

"I should make sure David isn't on the battlements with a pot of boiling oil," Tav said drily.

The carriage moved forward in the line and she felt so nervous her head spun. They had worked hard in preparation for this moment, and now that it was here she felt totally out of it, as if she was watching it play out from a distance. All she could think of were the things she should have focused on with Tav, of her phone call with her parents, of the fact that no matter what she did, it wasn't good enough. Her chest went tight and pressed back into her plush carriage seat.

"The stone was all locally sourced and the newer wings —"

"Relax, *poulette,*" Johan said. He was seated across from her, sporting a kilt that seemed perhaps a bit shorter than standard. He seemed quite comfortable, given his dangerous manspreading on his side of the carriage. He'd already announced he was playing a game of Liechtienbourgian roulette by going sans underwear, so Portia kept her gaze above his waist. "If you start to feel inadequate, just remember that you two will likely be the only people there tonight who make an actual contribution to the world, apart from the staff."

Portia noted that he didn't include himself in the positive contributions to the world column. "What about you?"

He ran a hand through his floppy ginger locks and shot her a devilish grin. "I'm semi-royalty. That's even more useless than actual royalty."

"Hey, you do good things. And you just spent days helping complete strangers because a friend asked you to."

"I needed something to keep me occupied while in this dreadful country," he countered, as if he hadn't come explicitly to help Tav.

Portia started to protest but Tav sighed loudly.

"Christ, the two of you. Now can you see how frustrating it is trying to give you a compliment, Freckles?" Tav asked, shifting closer to her as he tugged at his kilt. Part of her was taken aback by his gruff words, but then his fingertips brushed over the back of her hand and she realized that someone being annoyed because they thought you were greater than you could imagine was perhaps not the worst situation one could find themselves in.

But having that and losing it was, and this was a game she'd already lost.

"And can you see how frustrating it is

when you pretend she isn't your lady love?" Johan chimed in with a smile. "I can say from experience that the *Looking Glass Daily* isn't always *entirely* wrong."

Tav drew his hand away and Portia swallowed against the roughening in her throat.

She shot Johan a dirty look, and he raised a shoulder. He knew something was up between her and Tavish, and his little pokes weren't helping. *Lady love.* Pfft. Lady close to hand was more accurate.

Portia kept thinking about Tav's complete lack of reaction when she'd told him about her next job. How he'd accepted it so easily. Because she wasn't the kind of person people kept around.

Enough overthinking.

The carriage stopped and the door was pulled open by a liveried footman. Portia and Tavish looked at each other for a long moment.

"Ready?" she asked.

"Remember, you're an international, *ahem* national, man of mystery," Johan said from across the carriage. "James Bond, minus the taking advantage of abused women, plus a sword and whatever medieval affectations please you." With that, he leapt down from the carriage, seemingly not caring at all that it was a gusty night and his kilt was flapping dangerously.

"You've got this," Portia said.

"We've got this," Tavish replied, giving her hand a squeeze before letting it go. "All right, on with it."

He stepped out of the carriage and then turned to guide her down, and Portia's heart squeezed. It should have been a perfect moment: Tavish in his Highland best, her in a buttery yellow princess-style gown. The look in his eyes. The incomprehensible feeling that welled up in her chest and made her eyes suddenly dangerously moist. But like in any fairy tale, a night at the ball had a catch. She wouldn't turn into a pumpkin at midnight, but she had an expiration date.

This was Tavish's happily ever after, not hers — she was just a helpful woodland creature, or maybe a fairy godmother if she was more generous with herself, who worked her magic and then faded to the background while the hero continued his journey. If she'd thought otherwise, she could only blame herself for the confusion.

"Portia?"

She took his hand and made her way carefully down the carriage steps. She couldn't meet his gaze — she didn't know what he would see there and she couldn't let her ridiculous feelings ruin the night.

Tavish tucked her arm beneath his, as they had practiced.

"You're shaking," he murmured.

Great. She was supposed to be here to support him, not distract him, and she couldn't even do that.

"I'm fine. I forgot to eat," she said. It wasn't a lie, she realized, but she needed to pull it together. "Don't worry about me. Pretend I'm . . . an accessory. Like your tie. Part of the ensemble but nothing you really need to pay attention to now that you're at the event."

Tav grunted. "What? If you think I could focus on something besides you, or would want to, then you really do need a bit of haggis to set you right."

Great. She was making a scene and he was trying to make things better.

"This is your night," she whispered. "I don't want to —"

"Let me guess. Mess things up?" He chuckled. "I'm the one who'll be making the cock-ups tonight. And if I do, it will be fine. And even if somehow you did, that would be fine, too."

It was both exactly what she needed to hear and exactly what she didn't. She was being selfish again. She needed to think

455

about her job, not her emotions. She needed to be professional.

"Right. Here we go. Don't forget not to curse anyone out or physically attack anyone."

"I think I'll manage," Tav said.

She held her breath as he greeted the people in line before them, only releasing it when the cordialities had passed successfully and the older man and woman seemed suitably charmed. The line moved quickly and soon they were at the top of a ridiculously long flight of stairs.

"His Grace, the Duke of Edinburgh, Tavish McKenzie!"

The crowd went silent, so Portia should have been able to hear herself and Johan being introduced, but she was busy scanning the room, taking in the breadth of reactions to Tavish. There were many, many faces — most of them white, many of them wrinkled — but only about three sets of expressions that she could make out: outright disdain, curiosity, and blatantly-wondering-what's-under-that-kilt. Curiosity far outnumbered the other two. Portia felt a bit of the tension leave her. They could work with this.

Johan took her other arm as they descended the stairs, and she understood that for all his attempts to come off as a devil-may-care-aristocrat, his arm through hers was lending them the power and presence of the Kingdom of Liechtienbourg. Johan didn't think much of these people, but his family and their wealth made everyone in the room think a lot of him.

"Want a shot? Whiskey? Tequila?" He raised his brows suggestively. He'd only drunk tea while at the armory, so she was a bit surprised.

"I don't want a shot and you don't need one," she said. "Thank you, by the way."

"Very true," he said, ignoring the last part. "I'll have a Manhattan, in your honor."

He stepped away with a wink — and several admiring glances at his legs trailed in his wake.

"He's not a bad type, that Johan," Tavish said. "Too bad he isn't Scottish."

"Oh, I'm sure everyone is saying the same about you." David had a smile on his face as he approached Tavish and held out his hand, but his gaze was flat and his eyes ringed with dark circles.

Tav ignored his hand and clapped him on the back. "Not falling for that trick again, etiquette or no. And I was born and raised here, same as you, except I didn't have a silver spoon up my ass."

Leslie hurried up to Tav, looking lovely in a gauzy pink gown. "Your Grace. So very good to see you again."

David bristled, and the slightest smirk lifted the edges of Leslie's mouth. "I hope your trip here passed well and the carriage ride was acceptable."

"It was lovely," Tavish said, gracing her with a smile. "Nothing like the smell of manure to get you ready for a night with the peerage."

David seethed. "Perfect. Absolutely perfect. *This* is who gets a seat at the table now."

"Quite right," Tavish said. "And I have a tradesman's appetite, too. Plus I'll likely invite my friends and family without permission. You must understand that people like me can't help ourselves."

Portia glanced up at him. She'd expected him to be nervous, but he seemed calm, cool. Like himself, but with a bit of charm rounding out his rough edges. He wasn't exactly Tavish — he was the Duke of Edinburgh now, testing out the persona that she'd helped craft. She couldn't help but wonder if that was good or bad.

An older man who had been standing behind David shuffled into the circle, rheumy eyes squinted as he blatantly examined Tavish. He scowled, but then a bit of laughter escaped from his mouth.

"Well, if you aren't the spitting image of your grandfather."

"May I present Lord Washburn," Leslie said, and Portia made a mental note of his name and face, then realized she wouldn't need to know his name for future events.

"He had a sharp tongue too, you know," Washburn said. "Got him into heaps of trouble, but always made for an amusing time. Some people prefer mealy-mouthed brownnosing, but my god things have been boring until the last few weeks."

David sneered. He was likely having the worst night of his life, so Portia couldn't blame him.

"I'm glad I could amuse you," Tavish said. "Are you the Washburn who's been advocating against sanctuary for immigrants? I imagine you won't find me amusing for long."

Portia felt a surge of pride at his quick response, but Washburn seemed to take the threat in stride. "Oh right, that's to be your pet project it seems. Let's talk a bit when you've settled into the role. I'm always up for a spirited debate."

The man shuffled away.

"A debate. That's what this is for him, the

git." Tavish shook his head.

Portia felt a trickle of relief. He was still Tav.

"Well, he's as far as you'll get. You see, for most of us, there is no debate," David said.

"Do you practice saying ridiculous shit like this in a mirror?" Portia asked, making sure she smiled politely so anyone watching would assume their conversation was convivial. "The former duke would have hated everything you stand for."

"The former duke was a promiscuous drunk who squandered his power," David said, his face flushing red.

"Well, he managed to do two things right," Portia said. "And neither of them was allowing the dukedom to be passed down to someone like you. Good thing now *you're* the former duke."

"I'll take you around and make the introductions," Leslie said to Tav politely, as if Portia and David had been discussing the weather. Polite sniping was common, so Portia was sure she'd seen much worse.

Tavish turned to Portia and held his arm out, but Leslie slid her own into the opening. "It's best if I bring you around. Portia, lovely as she is, would raise questions and distract from your integration."

Portia knew Leslie wasn't trying to be

rude — and that she was correct — but it still made her stomach hurt. She'd been replaced, just like that. Her parents had Narisa. Tav had Leslie.

No one really needs you.

The brief panic on Tavish's face spoke to just how important it was that he learned to do this without her at his side. And she needed to be proud of him for not needing her.

"Go ahead. I'll go find Johan," she said cheerily.

His expression cleared, his man of mystery swagger returned. "I'll nip back round and find you in a bit."

Leslie was already pulling him away, so he threw her a beleaguered grin over his shoulder. Portia had to admit they made a lovely couple; they'd certainly grace many magazine covers if Tavish took Leslie up on her sad offer. She couldn't imagine he would, but maybe it would benefit them both. Maybe after a few months mingling with the elite, he'd see that Leslie's idea wasn't so far-fetched, comparatively speaking.

A sudden hard grip on her arm shocked her. When she tried to pull away and couldn't, she felt the beginnings of panic. She looked up into David's face, which was placid, as if he weren't squeezing her arm like a vise.

"Let go of me." She reminded herself that she was in a room full of people. That he couldn't hurt her — could he? The fact that he didn't seem to care if anyone noticed chilled her. This man had until that very night been wielding an inordinate amount of power. After the night was over, he'd still have the power of his wealth and connections. He thought nothing of using that power to intimidate a woman seemingly just because he could.

He tugged her closer to him, and Portia stutter-stepped forward though she tried to resist.

I should scream, she thought. *I should say something.*

She looked up at him and didn't say anything at all.

"I don't know what your plan is or how you talked him into this, but you and whoever sent you to do this to me are going to regret it," David said.

"Sent me?" She didn't know what he was talking about.

"Don't play coy," he growled. "You think I don't know who you are? Who your parents are and the inquiries they've been making? Oh, the daughter of real estate venture capitalists just happens to get her hooks into the love child of a duke."

Portia snapped out of it. She could do the genteel thing, and politely move away, but not when a strange man was holding her arm and muttering paranoid threats at her. She wouldn't put up with that in a subway car or night club, and she wouldn't accept it from some bawbag in middle-of-nowhere Scotland. She couldn't reach her pepper spray, so she pivoted toward David, placed her hand gently on his chest, and kneed him in the balls.

He emitted a muffled squeal and lurched forward, but she grabbed his shoulder before he sank to the ground, holding him upright.

"One of the benefits of this ridiculous skirt is that it conceals the movement of the legs," she said close to his ear, which was as red as his face.

The sudden scent of whiskey made her stomach turn a bit, but the long, muscular legs covered with gingery hair that accompanied the scent gave her some relief.

"Johan." She turned and smiled pleasantly at him. "I was just leaving Mr. Dudgeon to his business. Do you mind escorting me to the other side of the room?"

Johan was usually playful, but his stance and expression made it clear that behind his charming demeanor was a man who would gladly throw down, and was possibly looking for an opportunity to do just that.

"Is there a problem, *putain*?" he asked, gaze not moving from David.

"I think we're good here," Portia said, tugging Johan along by his sleeve. Her breath was coming fast and she felt a little shaky, but she just wanted to get away from David. "Please. Let's go."

Johan shot David a glare, but escorted Portia away.

"What happened?"

"Oh, it was nothing. He thinks I'm part of some conspiracy. As if I would have willingly dragged Tavish into this mess."

"He was trying to hurt you, friend. That is not nothing."

Portia sucked in a breath and realized she was shaking — he was right. Why was she downplaying this? She didn't have to. David should never have touched her.

"You're right. I was scared. I just don't want to make a scene."

"I hate these people," Johan said miserably. "Cruelty is so normal to many of them."

"How many shots did you have?" she asked.

"Only two," he said. "For fortitude. And

some whiskey."

His gaze scanned the room, a troublesome glint in his eyes. She felt a sudden, sad kinship with the redheaded step-prince. She decided to do what she would have done to Old Portia if given a chance.

"You know what, I really need something to eat. Let's go get some appetizers and non-alcoholic drinks. We have a long night ahead of us," she said. They'd hydrate and wait for Tavish to return or for the night to be over — whichever happened first.

CHAPTER 26

Tavish was exhausted. He could spend hours practicing parries and thrusts, or bent over a forge, and be good to go, but his interactions with the peerage drained him in a way physical labor didn't.

"That went well," he said to Leslie as they walked away from an elderly duchess smoking a long, thin cigarette.

"I think it went well, though most people are away at the yacht races this weekend. It's a major event. I'm fairly certain David planned it this way on purpose."

Tav listened while scanning the room for Portia's rust-gold ringlets and yellow dress. He'd read a thing or two about codependency after Johan's walking stick analogy and his subsequent talks, or non-talks, with Portia. It worried him how much he itched to see her, to be next to her again, but he didn't want her advice or assistance. He wanted her. How in the hell was he supposed to differentiate between over-reliance and love?

Love.

"Fuck's sake," Tav said aloud as the realization hit him.

"Yes, it is a pity," Leslie continued the explanation Tav's thoughts had interrupted. "But don't fret, you'll meet everyone at the Holyrood garden party."

"Ah, yes. Along with the Queen."

"In a week," Leslie said, then stopped walking, halting their progress. Tavish's gaze went from scanning the room back down to her.

"Honestly, Your Grace? You're not ready. I know you have some type of arrangement with Ms. Hobbs, but if you're serious about this title, you need to find someone else to help you. More importantly, you should do so if you're serious about her."

Irritation walloped through him, mostly with himself. Two people who barely knew either of them were warning him off, and Portia had pulled away, too. Maybe this title was already turning him into an arsehole and this was everyone's way of telling him.

"If you're trying to muscle your way into the job, insulting Portia isn't the way to do it, lass."

Leslie shook her head. "I'm not trying to

467

insult her. I'm being frank, because I thought you appreciated frankness. She's American. She has little experience with the peerage. Worst of all, she loves you."

"What does that have to do with anything?" Tavish said, though his irritation was being replaced with a hope he tried not to show. "Things are not like that —"

"She's willing to give her all to make this work for you, even if she can't. If you felt the same, would you let her? Because I have to tell you, after years of making everything go smoothly for David, love is the last thing I feel for him."

"Oh, that's sorted. Her apprenticeship is almost over," he said. "It was always going to be three months. We've already discussed replacing her."

"Oh dear," Leslie sighed. "You really don't know what you've gotten yourself into."

"Look, I get it. You think I don't fit in with any of these people and I'm going to make a fool of myself."

Tavish thought he would, too, but he was starting to understand how he needed to move forward.

"Well, possibly. But I was talking about with Ms. Hobbs." She patted his arm. "Give me a call next week and we can discuss finding you a secretary when she goes. Possibly me, or someone else if you'd prefer that."

"Why is it that everyone seems to know what I need more than I do?" Tav asked irritably.

"Why is it you're waiting for someone to tell you?" Leslie countered, and something else clicked into place for him. He'd told Portia he'd replace her, that she should go. He was so thick he'd thought that was giving her space, but maybe there was such a thing as too much space.

Bloody hell. Tav had said he'd likely be the one to cock up, without realizing he already had.

"You're lucky I like you, cuzzo," he said and was rewarded with a brief smile, one that faltered.

"Be careful, Tavish. I know all of this seems frivolous and silly, but some people take it quite seriously. There's Ms. Hobbs by the way."

Tav turned and saw Portia chatting with Lord Washburn. Johan strolled up and handed her a glass of punch, like it was his duty, and jealousy twisted in Tav's stomach. He ignored it — ignored the fact that Johan was already rich and wouldn't need things explained to him like a child. Johan had been nothing but a friend to him and he wasn't going to repay him by using him as a convenient target when he was angry with himself.

Portia nodded politely as Johan and Washburn talked, but her head swiveled every few seconds. She was looking for him, too, he knew, and then she found him. Her gaze latched onto his and he felt the connection between them like a physical thing. Molten metal waiting to be shaped; if he let it go cold, it would become an ugly, useless lump instead of the beautiful item he knew they were capable of creating together. She was a claymore's length away from him and it was still too far.

"Save a reel for me, Tavish," Leslie said, then headed off. Tav didn't take his eyes from Portia, just walked straight to her.

"Hullo," he said. She smiled, looked up at him from under her lashes.

"How is the evening treating you, Your Grace?" she asked.

"It's treated me well so far, but I find I need a breath of fresh air," he said. "Leslie was telling me about the gardens."

He held out his hand to her and she took it.

"I assume I'm not invited," Johan said pleasantly.

"Of course, you are," Portia said.

"Of course, you're not," Tavish echoed.

"We won't be gone long."

"Don't worry, I'm used to being cast aside. Lord Washburn here will keep me entertained, I'm sure." He didn't sound like he found the man entertaining, but he winked at Tavish and began talking to the elderly lord anyway.

Tav led Portia through the crowds and out into the sprawling garden. Summer was evident in the blossoming canopies overhead, and the flowers carpeting the grounds. The air smelled green and fresh in a way Tav didn't often encounter in Bodotria, outside of the river walk.

"Everything okay?" Portia asked.

"I figure. It seems like I'm being received well enough, but we're all pretending to like each other so it doesn't matter in the end." He shrugged.

"I kicked David in the balls," she said casually, "after he had the bright idea to grab me and threaten me."

Tav was already turning around and heading back toward the building and throttle the bastard, but a blast of cool air where there shouldn't have been any stopped him. Portia was tugging at his kilt to keep him in place. She slid her arm through his and pulled until he started walking alongside her again. His heart was beating fast and a

471

fury he hadn't felt possibly ever throbbed in his blood.

"I handled it," she said. "So just pretend I never told you anything. But after I go, be careful. I don't trust him. I don't know if you can trust Leslie either, though she seems nice."

"You expect me *not* to knock him across the room as soon as I get back in there?" he asked.

"I expect you not to give him the satisfaction," she said. "He's already saying all kinds of horrible things about you. A public display of masculinity will just validate him. And piss me off. You need to be more devious."

He slid his arm around her shoulders. "I can be devious when the mood strikes," he said. "That mood isn't now, though. I was so busy being a Cro-Magnon that I didn't ask the most obvious question. Are you all right?"

"I'm fine," she said, but her voice was a little shaky and her smile was halfhearted. He could feel the hunch of her shoulders beneath his hold.

"Portia, tell me the truth. Your well-being is not a bother to me."

"It's silly. I've had guys try worse, trust me. It just freaked me out how angry he was, and how much it hurt when he wouldn't let go."

A sick sensation roiled through Tav's stomach at the thought of David and unknown men frightening Portia. Hurting her.

"I'm sorry. What do you want me to do?"

"Exactly what you're doing right now. Hold me for a minute, okay?"

Tav realized Portia had asked him only three things since he'd met her. For a chance to prove herself, how she could help him, and, now, to be held. This was one thing he could do right. He enveloped her in his arms, inhaling her faint floral scent.

"Don't say anything to him tonight," she said into his chest. "It will make a scene, and I'd prefer to keep things positive."

"Well, I'd prefer to break David's fingers. That sounds pretty positive to me." She tensed in his grip and he rubbed a hand over the exposed skin of her back. "But I won't. I won't do anything you don't want me to do. I will be talking about this with someone later though, if that's all right."

She sighed against him. "Sure. I bet you weren't expecting all that when you lured me out here to have your way with me, in preparation for your role of newest rake in town. Ravishing women in the garden is like rule number one of raking."

"Shite, I haven't gotten to *Debrett's* Rules of Raking, yet," Tav said, and she laughed into his chest. He cleared his throat in preparation for the fairly important thing he was about to say. Maybe if he didn't make a big deal out of it, she wouldn't. "I didn't bring you to the gardens to ravish you. I lured you out here to ask you to stay."

She went tense in his embrace again, and then her head snapped up, hitting him in the chin. Okay, playing it cool hadn't worked.

"Sorry," she winced. "What do you mean, though?"

"I mean that I don't want you to leave after the apprenticeship is over. I know everything is all mixed up right now, but I want you to stay and to see if maybe we can try dating. Or something?"

She blinked at him, then blinked again. "You want me to stay here, in a foreign country, just to date you?"

"Well, when you put it like that it sounds pretty selfish, actually."

"Didn't you just tell me I should go work for my parents? Now you're asking me to stay? What if I say yes and then tomorrow you change your mind again?"

Tav took a deep breath, trying to find the right words. "I thought you *wanted* to go

work for your parents. You seemed determined and, yeah, I didn't think I could ask
you to stay here on the possibility of more.
I wasn't sure I had the right to ask that. But
I'm doing it now."

She took a deep breath. "I promised my
parents I would take a bigger role in the
family company," she said. "They were
depending on me and I can't —"

"Fuck this up," he said at the same time
as her. "If you want to go that's one thing,
but if you're just going back to make your
parents happy, maybe don't."

"I should stay here to make you happy
instead?" She slid out from under his arms,
and he could feel her pulling away entirely.
"And that's not what I was going to say. I
was going to say I can't use them as an
excuse anymore because they hired someone
else. They decided to go with someone more
useful, and I can't say they made the wrong
choice."

"I know what I want, Portia," Tav said
gently.

"Do you? Or do you just want to make
sure you still have a secretary?"

There was panic building in her voice, and
Tav realized too late that he'd bungled
everything. He'd moved from point A to
point B too fast, when Portia had explicitly

told him she wasn't sure she could make it to point B, or even wanted to. Her actions had said otherwise though, hadn't they?

Like asking you for boundaries?

"I know that I don't want to lose you."

"How exactly do you think that this will play out?" she asked quietly. "I stay, and do what exactly? I don't know anyone here but you and your family. I don't even have any skills. What kind of work would I do?"

Tavish was extremely confused.

"You've done literally everything for the armory, lass."

"And I think that's the problem," she said, ignoring his point. "You probably realize it will be easier to just keep me around instead of getting a new assistant."

"Well, no, I am getting a new assistant. I've said that already."

"Well then, why would you need me?" she asked, in a flat tone that left Tav confused. Depending on what word was emphasized by her emotions, that question could have several different meanings with different answers.

The raw vulnerability in her eyes made him want to gather her close again. But he couldn't just shag her in a hedge bush and assume she understood that meant he cared for her. He'd have to use his words.

"Do you think your only value to me is as an assistant? An apprentice?" He shook his head. "You started out as my apprentice, then you became my indispensable squire, and now you're my . . . my liege lady."

"Your what?" She seemed both annoyed and confused.

Tav struggled to find a way to put it into words without revealing everything but it was too late. Portia would do an internet search on the term anyway. He sighed. "You're my liege. You're the person I'm fighting for."

Her mouth trembled but her expression was incredulous.

"You don't even know me," she said. "I stopped drinking because I was running from myself and trying to find it at the bottom of any handy cocktail glass. I slept around. I disappointed people. I'm almost thirty and I've never even had a stable career!"

Tav chuckled ruefully. "Is that your offensive? You think I'll hate you now and never want to see you again because you're a human being?" He stepped closer to her and slid his hand behind her neck, rubbing soothingly up and down.

"Stop trying to make me feel better," she said.

"Okay, I'll make you feel worse. You're a horrible person who deserves to be trapped forever walking a road covered in discarded Legos, without shoes. Nothing but sharp Lego corners ripping at your soles for eternity."

She didn't say anything.

"Did you catch the pun there? Soles and soul."

"Tavish." She sighed and her eyes finally met his, full of caution. "You really are a wanker."

He dropped a kiss on her forehead.

"I can think of loads of reasons for why I would need you, and no not just for sex, before you go there. For example — you're bloody magnificent. You're smart as fuck, and you can do literally anything you put your mind to."

She hiccupped a sob and wrapped her arms around him.

"I could try to convince you all night, but this is actually your decision. Do you want to explore this thing between us in a non 'itch scratching' manner? If so, do you reckon it would be to your benefit or detriment? Give it a think. Because if anyone should be worrying about not being good enough, it's me. I'm a bloody Bodotria geezer who makes swords and has a shite attitude. Christ, what are you even doing standing this close to me? Are you mad?"

Her next sob turned into choked laughter, and she looked up at him with a sliver of pleasure in her eyes. "Bodotria Geezer is your new supervillain name."

Hope warmed Tav from the inside out.

"Just think about it. If you don't want to stay then maybe we can figure something else out. I don't know you as well as I could. I don't have any right to make demands. But, Christ, I don't want to lose you."

That was the gist of it. He could no longer imagine life without her and he didn't want to. Maybe they'd give it a try and it'd all go to shit. Maybe she wouldn't want to even give them a chance to get to that point. But he'd had to think hard about what he wanted in this new life, and a chance with Portia was high on that list.

"Let's go back inside," she said quietly. "The meal is going to start soon."

She hadn't answered his question. She hadn't said how she felt about him. Tav had gotten two huge life changes he hadn't asked for. He could only hope that this one thing that made sense in his world could be his, too.

CHAPTER 27

Portia's head was pounding. No, not only pounding, it was also *vibrating.* She pried her eyes open and squinted through the morning sunlight streaming into the room. *Morning.*

She and Tavish had spoken the night before. He'd asked her to stay with him. She hadn't answered, but her heart had been filled with possibility when they'd returned to the ball. She remembered schmoozing and sitting down for dinner. Haggis had actually been better than she'd expected — she'd shared that on social media along with some clips of the Highland dancing. The last thing she remembered was getting tossed this way and that during some traditional Scottish reels. Tavish holding her hand so tightly each time they were partnered. Johan bringing her another glass of punch . . .

What is happening?

The vibration echoed in her skull again, and again, and she reached under the pillow and grabbed her phone. She saw that the screen was covered by notification messages just before the battery died and the screen went black. She always carried at least one travel charger that was ready to go and plugged her phone in before bed as religiously as some people said their prayers. She couldn't remember the last time it had died.

When you were drinking. That's when.

She crawled out of bed to find she was still in her frilly, if now flattened, dress. Someone had done her the courtesy of unzipping the bodice so she could breathe while sleeping. Her mouth tasted gross, and from more than a single night of forgetting to brush.

Panic began to set in as she ran her tongue over her teeth. Waking up bleary had once been common for her, but there was no reason she should feel like she'd been hit by a truck heading to Margaritaville with a rush delivery. Not now. She was New Portia and . . .

She pulled her bedroom door open and jogged to the kitchen, where she heard voices echoing down the hall.

"Look, she said flat out she had a drinking problem, bruv. I guess now you can see why she stayed off the sauce," Jamie said, then sighed. "I hope she's okay. She couldn't even walk."

They can't mean — I didn't —

"Oh, how awful. These pictures are obviously taken from strange angles," Cheryl said. "To make it look like . . ."

"The one of us isn't," Tavish said. His voice was subdued, but she felt the anger in it. Was he mad at her? How had this happened? "Fuck's sake, this is a disaster. And I don't even care if she snogged every bastard there, but . . . this is a right disaster."

Portia stepped into the kitchen, the rustle of her disheveled dress drawing everyone's gaze to her.

She'd expected them to be talking over breakfast, but Cheryl was already busy prepping for lunch at Doctor Hu's. Jamie was in his sweaty workout clothes, meaning the morning class was over. Tav was dressed in his usual worn-in jeans and T-shirt, but they all wore similar apprehensive looks on their faces.

"What happened?" she asked. "What — I don't remember anything."

True panic took over then. She'd been truly wasted in her past, but she'd always had some baseline memory, or scraps of

482

them. There hadn't been a total void during which anything could have happened.

"Tavish?"

He pushed himself away from the counter where he'd been leaning. "Looks like we made the papers again."

He shoved her the copy of the *Looking Glass Daily.*

THE DUKE'S DRUNKEN DUCHESS TO BE?

"What? No. I didn't drink anything." Portia didn't understand this. She hadn't had anything but punch. She placed a hand to her chest and tried to pull in a deep breath.

I tried so hard and still somehow I managed to ruin everything.

Tav sighed. "After the dancing. I went to the loo and got stopped by about fifty geezers on my way back. I have no idea how long it took. You'd been fine, but when I found you, you were yelling at Washburn about the results of some cooking competition. Johan was trying to play along and act like this was all normal, but then you keeled over."

His expression was drawn, like he could barely bring himself to remember it.

483

She glanced at the paper again and caught the subhead of the article.

DUKE'S GOOD TIME GIRL FRIDAY MAKES THE ROUNDS OF THE PEERAGE, AND SETS HER SIGHTS ON A PRINCE

She skimmed the text, words like *sordid past* and *promiscuous* and *bully-brained socialite* stood out. There were photos of her that painted a terrible picture. One in which she leaned suggestively toward David, her body pressed against his as he sported a shocked expression. One of her and Johan with locked eyes as they danced. And of course, one of Tavish holding her in the gardens.

"That was when I kicked David in the balls, that's when Johan was telling me an intense story about an overflowing toilet in the royal pool house, and that's . . ." She looked up at Tavish. He knew when that was. It was when he'd asked her to stay. Not to be his apprentice or squire or any combination of the two — he'd asked her to stay for her. For them.

But the warmth that had been in his eyes the night before had banked, like a forge gone cold.

The next picture showed him carrying her over his shoulder toward their carriage and Johan elbowing a paparazzo out of the way.

Tavish's debut. His entry into society. She'd ruined everything.

You knew you would.

She flipped the page and sank down, either chance or reflexes landing her ass in one of the wooden chairs. There, in bullet point format, was an accounting of her scandalous past. Former hookups gleefully discussing their brief times together, happy to cash in on fifteen seconds of fame. Pictures stolen from her social media — or more likely offered up by acquaintances.

"This doesn't make sense," she said.

"We all know the *Looking Glass* is full of lies," Cheryl said comfortingly as she chopped, but her smile was tight. "No one believes this tripe and if they do they'll forget soon enough, aye?"

Portia shook her head and winced at the brief flash of pain. "Some of it is true-ish. Sensationalized, but true. But the stuff about last night — no. I wasn't flirting with anyone! Well, Tavish, maybe, but I'm not some scheming social climber. I'm rich, why would I need to aim for some dusty old Scottish aristocrat with nothing to his name but a crumbling property? They would be coming after me!"

"Portia." Tav's voice was low and there was an undertone to it that she didn't like.

"Tav —"

"I think we should move up the end date for your apprenticeship," he said.

The kitchen spun and she didn't think it was the hangover. She gripped the edge of the table.

"But —"

"Look, you said yourself that this situation was too much for you, and I think last night showed it. Your face is splashed everywhere, everyone is crawling through your past looking for garbage. Because you're here, associated with me."

His nostrils flared.

"Maybe it would be better for you to go back to New York," he said with a firmness that left no room to imagine the *maybe* was anything other than a nicety.

"Come on, Tav," Cheryl said. "Take a minute to think about this."

"To think about what? The fact that the tabloids will leap on everything and everyone related to me and drag them through the mud? I have a responsibility to my family, and to the armory, and . . . and to this title. So I think it's best you go like you planned, get back to your regular life and

486

friends and family."

Portia said the first thing that came to mind. "But who's going to help you?"

Tavish ran his hands through his hair in frustration. "You need to worry about helping yourself right now, Portia. People around the world are reading about your sexual exploits. Have you checked your phone? There are already stories circulating that Johan and I are sharing you, which would be fine if any of us were into that, but that's not the healthy setup being spread around. Aren't you always thinking about optics? What are the optics of constant headlines about you being some kind of —"

He stopped short, but Portia knew what he was going to say. What he had thought. About her.

"I'll book my flight. You already have access to all of the social media accounts and emails on the phone I got you. I'll send you the link to all the important info and files online," she said calmly. She tried to keep her breathing controlled because all it would take was one deep breath to lead to a gasp, to lead to a sob, to lead to showing everyone how Tavish had just ripped her heart out.

"Cheryl, I have all the ideas for the restaurant promotions and menu mock-ups, and

Jamie, the expansion plans for your classes at other gyms. I'll email them."

With that she turned and walked out, as quickly as her hangover allowed.

Portia didn't charge her phone as she gathered her belongings. She knew what awaited her: hot takes on social media, a plethora of dudes who had or would lie about being past lovers. Conjecture about her and Tav, hate from Johan's obsessive fans, disappointment from her parents. She didn't want to know what Reggie would think. Reggie who had let Portia become part of her site and would now have to deal with the blowback.

She packed haphazardly, expecting Tavish to come through the door any minute, to tell her there had been some misunderstanding. That he hadn't really sent her away. Even a mere apprentice would have gotten some fanfare about her departure, or a pat on the back. But when the knock at the door came, it was Cheryl and Jamie, both wearing pinched expressions.

"Are you okay, love?" Jamie asked. His curls were sticking every which way, as if he'd tugged at them in frustration.

"I'm fine," she said. "I'm just packing. I'm going to catch the tram and go find a hotel."

"Wait, you're leaving today?" Cheryl asked. She and Jamie looked at each other. "I don't think he wanted you to leave today."

"Well, if he wants me to leave, that's all there is to it. Why put off the inevitable?"

"Portia, I think maybe both of you should take some time and talk this through," Cheryl said. "The past few weeks have been a whirlwind — maybe wait for the dust to settle a bit before making any rash decisions."

Agitation tightened the back of her neck. Moving halfway around the world to learn how to make a sword had been rash. Falling for her bawbag of a boss, that had been rash. Offering to guide Tavish into the aristocracy when she didn't even know what she was doing with her own life? Rash. Going back to New York would be the first rational thing she had done since applying to the apprenticeship.

"If he wanted to talk this through, he'd be here instead of you. This is for the best anyway. He has Leslie, Johan, and any number of other people willing to help him now. What he doesn't need is a scandal."

"Tav doesn't care about that stuff," Jamie said.

Portia remembered his expression of disgust. "Tavish doesn't, but apparently

Your Grace does. I guess I did my job too well."

She packed in silence, with a tearful Cheryl and a somber Jamie hovering and trying to help but mostly getting in the way. She thought about maaaybe connecting her phone to the charger just to peek, but decided not to. Reality was a safe haven because whatever awaited her once she opened the virtual floodgates would be *too* real.

"Can one of you call Kevyn? I'll need a ride."

Jamie went to make the call while Cheryl helped her carry her bags downstairs. When they were done, Portia waited outside. Both desperate to see Tav one last time and dreading the same.

He was nowhere to be seen.

"Portia," Jamie said. "You know, I've never seen Tav like this before. About a woman. I know he's a wanker, but he's a wanker who cares about you."

"Well the damned honey badger needs to tell her that then," Cheryl said with agitation. She brushed a strand of pink from her face. "He's stone, not the sword in this situation."

Jamie nodded gravely, though Portia was too busy holding herself together to work that one out.

A beautiful Mercedes coupe rolled up, but Portia paid it no mind, waiting for Kevyn's beat-up Vauxhall. A female driver dressed all in black got out and opened the back door and a familiar face poked out.

"Why aren't you answering my texts? Or calls? Or social media messages?" Ledi asked angrily as she rushed up the steps and pulled Portia into a hug.

Portia was shocked for a moment and then shook herself out of it and hugged Ledi back. All of the emotion she'd been burying to get through the packing and leaving rushed to the surface and tears spilled down her cheeks, chased by four heaving sobs that she wrangled into submission. "What are you doing here? You're supposed to be in Thesolo."

"What is the point of being a princess if you can't book an emergency flight around the world? And we weren't in Thesolo, we'd made a stop in Spain for legitimate, totally non-churro-related reasons." Ledi looked around. "Where is Tavish?"

More tears spilled from Portia's eyes, and Ledi's expression went hard. "Okay. Your bags are packed and Tavish is nowhere to be found and I might have to call in Theso-

491

loian special forces to take care of him after all."

"Let's just go," she said. "Please."

Ledi released her hold on Portia and motioned to the driver, who came over to help with the bags. Of course, Ledi refused to let the woman take the bigger bag because being a princess hadn't changed the fact that she preferred her own hard work and was stubborn as hell.

Portia hugged Jamie and Cheryl. "This isn't goodbye," Jamie said. "*Hasta luego,* more like."

Portia didn't feel like lying so she simply kissed his cheek, and then Cheryl's.

"I hope Jamie is right," Cheryl said. "I mean this is totally a Hermione and Ron situation and we all know how that worked out."

Portia had no idea, but she smiled and nodded anyway. It was the polite thing to do.

CHAPTER 28

"Nya wants to know if you're feeling okay," Ledi said, looking up from her phone, the same concern in her eyes that Portia had seen a million times over the years, made slightly more comical by the facial sheet mask Ledi wore. The concern bothered her, though; Ledi had swooped in to make things right for Portia so many times. With Project: New Portia, she thought all of that had changed, but here she was, pampering herself to distract from the fact that not only was she a fuck-up, but the whole world knew about her questionable choices in hookup partners and thought she had a thing for old Scottish men.

She'd snapped an "I'm cool guys" photo to post on social media, and taken a hiatus. From the internet, from her phone, from the reality that she'd allowed herself to think that someone would ask her to stay and mean it. Not checking calls meant avoiding who had called — and who hadn't.

"Tell her I'm okay," she said, trying to smile.

"She's not okay," Ledi spoke aloud as she typed. "But she will be."

Naledi Moshoeshoe nee Smith, actually nee Ajoua, was suddenly an optimist, it seemed. Portia almost laughed, but she felt a painful pulse of envy radiate through her, because she knew what caused that optimism.

"I'm jealous," Portia admitted. One thing she wouldn't fuck up about Project: New Portia was the tenet "Thou shalt not lie to thine bestie."

"Of . . .?" Ledi looked confused and Portia did laugh this time. Ledi was finishing her master's in a field that was actually useful to the world, had found the man of her dreams, and was a goddamned princess. Of course she would be confused as to what exactly was causing Portia's jealousy.

"Of your surety. That you know someone loves you, and that changed you. You were so scared before . . ." Portia trailed off. "I used to think I was protecting you from being hurt when I chased away fuckboys, but I can't even protect myself."

Ledi put down the phone. "You think I'm sure? Of anything? You're lucky I love you or I would be mad that I fooled even you."

A timer pinged on her phone and they both peeled off their masks in unison. Now that the smiling sloth printed on Ledi's mask was gone, Portia could see that her friend was frowning.

"I'm not sure of anything. I wake up every day wondering if this will be the day Thabiso decides he made the wrong decision, the day my in-laws decide they were right about their first impression, or the day my people decide I am not worthy to guide them. Thabiso's love didn't make me sure of anything. I'm scared shitless every day. It was so much easier living behind the barriers I'd put up."

"Then why did you tear them down?" Portia asked.

"Because I'm brave," Ledi said without a hint of self-consciousness. "And I think you were letting yourself be brave too, and that's why this hurts so much."

"I wasn't brave. I was foolish. I let Tav storm my castle."

Ledi shook her head. "Don't you see? That *is* the brave part. Seeing an enemy at the gate, an enemy who could rip you to shreds, and then taking that deep breath, lowering the drawbridge, and inviting them in. You'd been defending your castle for years. Lowering the bridge must have been so hard."

Portia sniffled, felt the heat of tears in her eyes. "No. It was easy. So damned easy."

Ledi came and wrapped an arm around her and let her cry, and then Portia heard her friend sniffling, too.

"Why are *you* crying?" Portia asked.

"Because I'm proud of you," she said. "Because letting down your drawbridge means that somewhere in this thick skull of yours, you've absorbed what I've been trying to tell you all these years."

"Stop drinking so much?"

"Well, no, given what happened. That you are worth so much more than you were giving yourself credit for. Even if Tav isn't the one, even if you decide you don't want to be with anyone long-term ever, it's not because you're unworthy."

Portia didn't ask any more questions. She just hugged her friend and allowed herself to bask in the honest truth, to let itself be engraved on her heart: even if things didn't work out with Tavish, someone had *always* thought she was worth it, had always stuck by her side, and seemingly always would.

"You're pretty great," Portia said, finally reaching for a box of tissues from the hotel bedside table. "Except now I'm going to have puffy eyes, negating the anti-inflammatory sheet mask."

"Oh, I brought this cream from Thesolo that works wonders —"

The phone ringing in the room abruptly silenced Ledi. Their eyes met and Portia knew what both of them were thinking. This is the part where Prince Charming arrives with the glass slipper. This is where the dragon gets slain. Or this is where the hotel double-checks the wakeup call for her flight the next day.

She grabbed the phone off of the receiver. "Hello?"

"Why haven't you answered my fucking texts?" Reggie's slow cadence didn't mask her anger. "You know I hate the phone. Mom and Dad and I were worried sick."

"I'm sorry," Portia said automatically. "I haven't turned it on for a couple of days."

"Well, I get that, but the internet has been going wild."

"Umm, that's what I was avoiding."

"Typical. Stick your head in the sand and everything will just take care of itself, right?"

Portia was instantly submerged in a sea of guilt, and the desire to hang up, to ignore Reggie's reminder of her ultimate fuck-up: pulling away from her twin sister. But this time she didn't. She stood with the portable phone and carried it with her into the bathroom of the suite.

"About that. There's something I have to talk to you about."

"Are you pregnant?" Reggie asked, a little less angry. "Because oh. Em. Gee. Everyone is so invested in this, that would blow their minds."

"No!" Portia said, confused.

"Well, good. I'm too young to be an aunt."

"Reggie! Look. Do you remember when you got sick?"

"Kind of hard. My brain was swelling and pressing against my skull. Not optimal for remembering things." She said it so blandly that Portia might have thought she didn't care.

"Well, I do remember. I'm sorry I didn't come see you enough. I was selfish and cowardly and I ruined everything. I was a terrible sister, and everyone knew it, especially Mom and Dad."

"What are you talking about? You were there all the time. Even when I couldn't talk or move much, I'd open my eyes, and you'd be there."

"I . . . ." Portia's throat closed up. She'd thought she was cried out, but some previously unknown well of tears had been tapped.

She remembered the *Hot Mess Helper*

video about being too hard on yourself. *If there's one thing we're good at, it's feeling bad. Hell, sometimes we'll take a tiny inconsequential thing and turn it into DRAMA for no damn reason. We're so used to being wrong that we invent shit to be wrong about! ADHD is a trip.*

"I don't remember things that way," she said.

"Yeah." Reggie was silent for a bit. "Honestly, it was after I started my recovery that you stopped showing up. *That* really sucked, if you want to apologize."

"I'm sorry."

"Wait, why were you telling me this like it was a confession . . . ooooh fuck. Are you kidding me? Is that what all of this has been about? Guilt?" Reggie was incensed now. "You dumb motherfucker."

"I thought you didn't want me around," Portia said.

"Well, I thought you were ashamed of me!"

Portia had never heard her sister cry — not during the physical therapy. Not when the temporary wheelchair became permanent. She'd always been cool, collected, and ready for all challenges. But she was gasping through a sob on the other end of the line now.

"Reggie, how could I be ashamed of you?" Portia asked. "You've always been this perfect golden child. You always go after what you want and get it no matter what. Everyone knows you're amazing."

"Why would I think that? Hm, maybe never wanting to spend time with me after I started using a wheelchair? Does that ring a bell?"

"That wasn't why," Portia said.

"You're telling me all these years were wasted because you were too fucking stubborn to apologize for something I wasn't even mad about?"

"I wasn't stubborn! I was scared you would hate me even more."

"What the fuck, Portia. More? What does that even mean, more?"

"Yes, more! Because everyone knows it should have been me who got sick instead of you!" She almost dropped the phone but somehow managed to avoid it, even as a wave of nausea rolled through her stomach. There it was, the thing everyone had always avoided saying — but never shied away from implying.

"God, I knew you were selfish, but I had no idea." Reggie took a slow breath. "I'm happy with my life and I don't want or need your pity. You of all people should know that. And guess what? *I* never thought it should have been you. Did you ever think of that? I was always glad it was me and not you. I wouldn't have been able to stand it if something happened to you because I love you, you asshole! I mean, how would I have coped with thaa . . . and oh, I guess maybe I would have spent half a lifetime being a jerk, too."

She laughed in frustration, but Portia was silent. She couldn't talk. She'd already said too much.

"Portia."

"Yeah?"

"I never hated you. Like, why? I obviously got all the good genes. You didn't even know what a tardigrade was."

Portia hiccupped out a laugh, and a little of the pain and fear that was all blocked up in her chest escaped with it.

Reggie sighed heavily. "Jesus. And I thought *I* was a masochist, trying to get your attention all these years. You've been carrying this half our lives."

"I'm sorry," Portia said. "I thought I was protecting you."

"By pushing me away?"

"I didn't say it made sense!" Portia dropped a hand onto her hip.

"You know, I should be mad. But I've

done some nonsensical things myself lately. Speaking of which, the reason I've been blowing up your phone."

Portia was unsurprised by Reggie's pivot. Cool, calm snark was her general setting and she was sure the outbreak of emotion had thrown her off as much as it had Portia.

"My friend saw that pic of you being carried out of that party like a bag of potatoes and he noticed something."

"Friend?"

"Yeah. The guy you found for me? It's a long story. Anywho, he's pretty good about detail stuff. And he noticed something up with your nail polish color. It's pink in the earlier photos and black when you're getting carried out."

Portia's brow crinkled. Ledi had treated her to a manicure when they arrived at the hotel, and she'd been too numb and disappointed with herself to pay attention as her polish was removed.

"That's weird."

"Well, maybe this is nothing, but we've promoted this safety polish on our site a few times. For college students. It changes color if you're drugged."

"Wait." Cheryl had grabbed the polish from the kit they'd received from a company that wanted to provide products for the self-defense courses Portia had talked Cheryl into teaching . . .

"Oh my god." Her face went hot with anger as she realized someone had drugged her and worse — had made her doubt herself. She'd believed that she drank until she passed out, even though it made no damn sense. The world believed it, too. Her past had been dragged out for judgment, and no one had been a harsher judge than Portia. But, as it turned out, Portia was pretty shit when it came to judging herself.

"Was it that prince? That guy is kind of creepy," Reggie said, blunt as usual.

"No, Johan is my friend," Portia said. "But I know who isn't."

"Oh man. Who do we have to kill?"

Portia opened the door to find Ledi pretending she hadn't been listening. "We might just have to shank an ex-duke."

CHAPTER 29

Tavish pulled up the internet browser window on his new smartphone and clicked through the four open tabs — one for each of Portia's social media accounts. There had only been one recent message on each, all posted the day she left. A photo of her staring straight at the camera, a mischievous smirk on her face, wearing a shirt emblazoned with the words *I solemnly swear I am up to no good.* And the caption "Gone fishing."

He'd seen that shirt before. Cheryl had one, too. He was sure Portia had no idea what it really meant either, and that simple thought — one way they were alike in a way that made them somewhat different, and how much he wanted to learn just how different and alike they were — bowled into him, rocking him like a physical blow. He wouldn't have that now; couldn't have that and be fair to her.

Tav had no fucking idea what he was doing. No, that wasn't true — he was certain that he was completely screwing up anything that might have been between him and Portia. But that's what was for the best. He'd crossed the line by asking her to stay anyway, and it was only when he'd seen the tabloids descend upon her like piranhas that he'd realized exactly how he'd messed up.

He didn't care that she'd gotten stumbling drunk at the ball, outside of the fact that he knew she'd be angry with herself about it. He didn't care about what the newspapers had insinuated about her past — loads of people hacked their way into adulthood through the field grown from all the wild oats they'd sown. Some people's fields were smaller, some larger, and Tav didn't think it particularly mattered as long as people reached a mutual agreement about whether their farming days were over, on hiatus, or some kind of special schedule.

What he did care about was exposing Portia to situations that would cause her pain, and whether she was his apprentice, his squire, or something more, her proximity to him would cause her pain. She found any hint of her own unworthiness entirely too credible, and the *Looking Glass Daily* loved nothing more than pointing out

505

perceived flaws and creating ones where they found none. He already had to figure out how to protect Jamie and Cheryl, but he wasn't sure how to protect Portia without drawing her deeper into the very world that would hurt her — and eventually destroy any possibility of love they had.

"Your Grace?" Leslie's voice pulled him out of his daze. He sat across from her in that receiving room where he and Portia had first met with David. Where he'd first decided that he would become a duke if it gave him even the smallest chance of changing things for the better.

David had gone to ground since Tav had replaced him. Leslie said he'd retired to a country estate to formulate his next move. Tav hated him but he imagined it must have been a difficult change for a man so invested in the title.

"Perhaps we should go over the preparations for the garden party one more time," Leslie said in that voice that was both wishy-washy and strident. It wasn't her real voice, simply something she put on for work, like a smart pair of trousers. Tavish had almost requested that she be less formal, but changed his mind. She was his assistant, not his friend.

Boundaries.

"I get dressed up. I present the Queen with some jewels. I stand next to her while people mill about in the garden making inane chatter." He sighed. "I disappoint my students."

I miss Portia like a bloody fool.

"Your Grace, we still haven't settled on the entertainment —"

Tavish's phone rang and he whipped it out of his pocket, hope expanding in his chest and then deflating to a tempered happiness when he saw the word *Mum* flashing on the screen.

"I have to take this," he said, and Leslie nodded and left. She was good at doing what she was told, at scurrying this way and that. Just once, Tav wished she would call him a wanker instead of giving him a treacly smile.

"Hey, Mum."

"I have to say, Tavish, I really like this new 'answering the phone' habit you've picked up. Who knew all it would take was a title?"

That wasn't the real reason he suddenly cared about incoming calls.

"Well, every job requires some sacrifice. Everything okay?"

"Oh, *sí*. The paparazzi here have moved on to other stories, in part because your father went after them with a machete and they don't want to risk their precious cameras over me. Plus, one of them said people were more interested in your Portia anyway."

Hearing the name unexpectedly sucked a bit of the wind from him. "Why? It makes no sense. She is no longer a part of the armory or my life and —"

Tav didn't know why he stopped talking. The words left him like the heat from hot metal dipped into ice water.

"M'hijo." His mum's voice had taken on that round, loving tone that instantly made him feel like a child aching for a hug. "Do you remember what I asked you all those years ago?"

"Why did I have all those page three girl photos in that box under the bathroom sink?" he asked, just to get a rise out of her.

She laughed, indulgent and warm. "You sound miserable. You look miserable in the pictures on these sites. Jamie and Cheryl are worried about you. I meant this question — what are you willing to do?"

"What do you mean? I've turned my life upside down, I'm driving myself mad learning how to properly talk to the Queen, and how to properly be ignored by her. I haven't made a sword in weeks. I miss my students. I'm willing to do whatever it takes to be a good duke."

The laughter on the other end of the phone wasn't warm this time. "Oh you are so much like him. *Pobrecito.* What are you willing to do *to keep her by your side?*"

Tav didn't say anything for a long moment. He was remembering all those years ago: Greer's ultimatums, his stubbornness, their mutual love and pain and how, in the end, he had done . . . nothing. Because he hadn't been able to think of a single goddamn thing. The path of their love that had once seemed to wind forever into the horizon had been overrun by the vines and weeds of reality. There had been no way forward, together, even with a sword in his hand. Especially with a sword in his hand.

But Tavish was at no loss of ideas of what he would do for Portia. He spent every night imagining scenarios, every day being pulled out of reveries. None of them were good enough. None of them were *right.* And none should be acted out because he owed her too much already, and a life lived for herself and not hounded by the press or teaching him manners was the least he could give her.

"She deserves better than me, Mum. A man playing at the peerage who needs his hand held for the simplest thing."

"What the bloody hell, Tavish?" his father suddenly cut in. "What do you think people fall in love for, if not the hand holding? Do you think marriage is two people walking side by side, never touching lest one of them pull the other down?"

He could imagine his father: mustache bristling in annoyance that his son had missed out on this lesson somehow.

"Am I on speakerphone?"

"Sorry, your father wanted to eavesdrop."

"But Mum, you left my fa— the duke. You decided it was better for me to live a life away from all of that."

"You were a child, Tavish. And things were different then. And still, I should have let you decide. Do you really think Portia can't decide on her own what she wants? If you think your judgment is so much better than hers, maybe you *should* leave things as they are."

Tavish remembered the pain in Portia's eyes that morning in the kitchen. How her usually expressive face had gone blank before she slipped into business mode. He'd turned her out on her ear, in front of Jamie and Cheryl, after telling her he wanted more.

"My god, I just might be the thickest bawbag alive."

"Not gonna dispute that, my boy," his father said.

"You've given him some serious competition in your time, love," his mother said sweetly. "Don't get forgetful, now."

His father chuckled, but Tav couldn't join in the mirth of their conversation. He'd messed up in grand fashion. He'd have to apologize in even grander style.

"I might have more than some scraped knees after this grovel, Mum."

"I'll be here to clean the wounds whatever they are — unless Portia decides to do that for you. With alcohol and maybe some salt solution for good measure."

"Mum."

"Oh my, the call is breaking up," his mother said.

"Bye, son! Good luck!" His father's words made it in just before the call disconnected. Luck. He was going to need it.

Leslie entered the room after a few moments of silence. "I have the list of entertainment from the previous years if you'd like. I printed them, since you prefer paper."

"Actually, I won't be needing that." Tavish was known for his offensive abilities during a tourney. He went in hard, attacked relentlessly, and didn't give up without a hell of a fight. If he couldn't apply the same ferociousness toward Portia, he didn't deserve her, or the dukedom she'd helped him claim.

"What do you mean?" Leslie asked.

"I mean, this year we're changing things up."

CHAPTER 30

Portia had grown used to navigating the crack of dawn while stone-cold sober. She'd grown used to navigating the world without the idea of "liquid courage" or "something to take the edge off." But as she figured out how to sneak into a royal garden party, she was tightrope walking along that edge, and her well of courage was dry as the Dust Bowl.

But she remembered she had people behind her. Ledi and Thabiso. Reggie and her mystery assistant. Nya. Even her parents were there — they had their attorneys lined up to intercede on her behalf. And maybe she had someone in front of her, too. She couldn't focus on that too much as she walked in through the service entrance wearing the tuxedo shirt and black pants Ledi had told her to pick up to blend in with the waitstaff. She would have to talk to Tavish about his security management.

The party sounded livelier than she'd imagined. When she'd researched, it had seemed a very staid affair, but she heard shouts and cheers echoing over Holyrood's gardens. Familiar shouts and cheers.

She passed through the crowd, which had gathered in clumps around the garden.

"Run him through!" a distinguished-looking older man shouted, eyes bright, and that was when Portia realized what was going on. Tavish had turned the garden party into an exhibition. He'd been so worried about letting the kids down and he'd found a solution to his problem. She was sure Syed or Emma or Jake were fencing or jousting in one of the clusters of people.

She peeked through a space in another crowd and saw Cheryl and Jamie demonstrating grappling. Tav's students and instructors and family of all shades and ethnic origins were here at this most Scottish of events, staking a claim to their homeland. A sheen of tears welled in Portia's eyes. She was still angry with him, but this was Tav's first official act as a duke, and she couldn't be prouder.

She hoped his second official act would be handing David his ass after she presented him with all the facts, but that remained to be seen.

First, she had to find him.

She pulled out her phone and went to the "find my phone" function. She knew it was some billionaire stalker shit, but his newest smartphone had been registered in her name and it was the fastest and most discreet way to find him. She'd apologize later — and have him register the phone in his own name. Him or whoever his new assistant was. That wasn't her job anymore, and with some space she could see why, no matter what happened, it was good that it wasn't.

A red dot appeared on the phone's screen — he was fifty feet away. Forty-five . . . forty. Anxiety began to roil in her stomach, but she kept marching forward. She was brave. She was worthy. Most importantly — Tavish had appointed her his squire, and a squire watched their knight's back no matter what.

"My name is Portia Hobbs, and I'm bloody magnificent," she murmured to herself. "I can do literally anything I put my mind to."

She reminded herself that loving and being loved both fell under the umbrella of *anything*.

She didn't need to follow the dot anymore once she reached a small cluster of reporters and paparazzi. She moved behind a large shrub landscaped into the shape of a corgi, and peeked from behind the tail.

There was Tav, dressed in his tourney uniform instead of the new formal kilt he'd ordered before she left. She closed her eyes in disbelief for one second. She'd believed him when he said he knew Scottish formal, and then he went and wore this to meet the Queen.

She moved a bit to get a better view of him. He looked down and said something and Portia saw a perfectly coiffed nest of white hair . . . sporting a crown. Tav was standing with the Queen, because of course he was.

"You said you wanted to make an announcement?" one of the reporters shouted.

"Yes," Tav said, and his voice stopped her in her tracks. She had forgotten the feeling it inspired in her, the want and the need and the swell of something encompassing both of those things and more. "I actually need you lot to do me a favor, which is owed after you've been stuck to my arse like a boil."

Portia cringed as "New Duke Says 'Arse' In Presence of the Queen" headlines popped up in her mind.

"I would have gone with wart, but yes,

quite," the Queen said pleasantly.

"Oh god," Portia whispered as shocked laughter rippled through the crowd.

"That works, too," Tav said. "But either way, you all have video cameras and thus you are useful to me. You might want to start recording now. Anyone with a smartphone who can livestream this?"

Several phones were pulled out as the words slowly penetrated Portia's brain. Tavish. Who hated "being videoed" was requesting as many people as possible record him. He was likely about to do something he'd deeply regret.

She began pushing her way through the crowd.

"Portia Hobbs," he said, and both her name and the reverence with which he said it stopped her again. "Portia Hobbs first came into my life as my apprentice at the Bodotria Armory. She then became an aide as I took on a new chapter in my life — becoming a duke. Despite being treated poorly by a great many of the supposed reporters before me, Portia is competent, intelligent, kind, and beautiful, but above all that, she is the woman I love."

"Oh shit," Portia said, and the reporter beside her glanced her way. Her phone was vibrating incessantly in her hand, but she

517

couldn't tear her eyes away from Tavish.

"What are you doing, mate?" a reporter asked. "I mean, Your Grace?"

"I'm publicly declaring my love for someone who was hurt because of me and by me."

"He's groveling," the Queen said with just the right amount of royal contempt, then turned a kinder gaze onto Tav. "Go on."

"Right. Portia, I would like to say, for posterity, that *I* was the fuck-up here. I thought I could protect you —"

Portia remembered her talk with Reggie and cringed, but something also loosened in her chest. He had wanted to protect her. Because he loved her, and sometimes or maybe all of the time, what people did for love was pretty damned illogical. She began pushing her way through the crowd of reporters, who were jostling to capture a member of the peerage engaging in dramatics that would make everyone forget Johan's asscheeks had ever graced the front page of the papers.

"— I did what I did because I thought to protect you, but I didn't bother to ask if you wanted to be protected, or how. So. That's about it, Freckles.

"I don't expect her to take me back, but everyone should know that nothing a paper says, nothing about her past, could change the fact that I love Portia Hobbs. Right. Um, you can stop videoing now. Thank you."

He crossed his arms over his chest and stood awkwardly, but his hands dropped to his side as he caught sight of Portia pushing past the reporters.

"Bloody hell. You're here?"

"This is much more entertaining than the previous garden parties," the Queen said. Portia forgot what *Debrett's* recommended, but curtsied because she certainly wasn't going to shake the Queen's hand.

"Pardon me," Tav said, and once the Queen nodded her assent he turned to Portia. "You were supposed to watch the video on your tablet and then decide what you wanted to do."

"My tablet is at the hotel. Should I . . . go watch it and come back?" she asked. "It was pretty good in person, but I can do that if you want."

Tav shifted from foot to foot, his face suffused with pink. He looked like he could break a man in half but he stood there blushing as the Queen patted his arm in support.

Portia loved him. But she had something else to deal with first.

"I didn't get drunk that night," she said.

"It doesn't matter," Tav said. "We can —"

"It does matter. It means I didn't mess up. It means someone drugged my drink." Chatter burst from the reporters as Tav stepped down from the dais and approached her.

"What do you mean?"

"Remember when Cheryl painted my nails? It was special polish that changes color if you've been drugged at a bar or by your date. And someone noticed my nails were a different color when you carried me out."

Tav's face was still flushed, but with rage this time. He looked furious, but when he reached out to cup her face, his touch was gentle.

"Who?" His gaze bored into hers. "Who am I going to kill?"

"I can't say for sure and it is very clear that you're joking about killing anyone." She glanced at the reporters in her peripheral vision. British libel laws were no joke. "But I will say that, unrelated, I found out some stuff about David Dudgeon. Like, how he's into real estate, using a shell company to buy up property in Bodotria and artificially jack up the rental rates. The same company that was going after Mary's bookshop."

Understanding dawned in his eyes. "And the same company that was trying to buy the armory."

Portia nodded. "He knew who you were all this time. He was hoping to buy the armory before *you* knew who you were. He also had control over several of your father's companies that had been buying from the armory, and bad reviews of the products were traced back to his IP address . . ."

"Oh dear." Leslie's voice was almost lost in the commotion of the reporters. "I told him to just honor the duke's will and let you know. To let you decide whether you wanted it or not. But he said he'd been waiting all his life. I didn't think he would hurt anyone, though." She glanced at Portia. "He said he'd looked you up and that if he got a drink in your hand maybe you'd be out of his hair."

Portia glared at Leslie, but her anger with the woman for not warning her was a discussion for another time.

"Is he here?" Tavish asked.

"I would also like to have a word with Mr. Dudgeon," the Queen said, cutting in. "And I believe Scotland Yard would be of the same opinion."

She looked at Tavish and Portia for a moment, and then shook her head. "I do believe it's time for tea. But perhaps later we can discuss what happened."

"Yes," Tavish said, bowing deeply. "Whatever you desire of me."

"That was an exquisite bow," Portia said after the Queen was on her way.

"I had a great instructor," he said. "You weren't so bad either."

His hands went to her hips, pulled her close.

"At least half of the British media is watching," she said. That didn't stop her from bringing her hand up to his face, tracing the curve of his jaw and the shell of his ear, and smoothing back those salt-and-pepper strands.

"I know. It kind of puts you on the spot, which is why I wanted you to watch the video somewhere else. Pressure leads to bad decisions, like telling the woman you love she should leave. Christ, what kind of sense did that make?"

"I work best under pressure, actually," Portia replied.

"Is that so?" Tav asked.

"Aye," she replied, happiness bursting through her when he grinned. "We still have a lot to talk about you know."

"I am here for any and all Dr. Phil shite, except I'd prefer it from an actually licensed therapist," Tav said. "We'll talk. We'll figure this out, my liege."

Portia kissed him then, and because she knew it would make the front page, she put everything she had into it. She could be called many things, but she had never been one to half-ass the things she truly cared about, and she certainly wouldn't start with Tavish. He had a reputation to uphold, after all.

ABOUT THE AUTHOR

Alyssa Cole is a science editor and romance junkie who lives in the Caribbean. She founded the Jefferson Market Library Romance Book Club and has contributed romance-related articles to publications including RT Book Reviews, Heroes and Heartbreakers, Romance at Random, and The Toast.